yawn

yawn

a thriller

collin piprell

ASIA BOOKS

Published and Distributed by
Asia Books Co. Ltd.,
5 Sukhumvit Road Soi 61,
PO Box 40,
Bangkok 10110,
Thailand.
Tel: (662) 714 0740-2 ext. 221-223
Fax: (662) 381 1621, 391 2277
E-mail: customer_serv@asiabooks.co.th
Web site: www.asiasonline.com

© Collin Piprell, 2000.

All rights reserved. No part of this publication may be reprinted or reproduced, stored in a retrieval system, or transmitted in any form or by any means, mechanical, electronic, photocopying, recording, or otherwise, without prior permission in writing from the publisher.

The characters in this book are fictional,
as are the bars, nightclubs, diveshops, and meditation centers.
Phra Chan and Phra Chan Noi islands are also fictional,
although some readers will recognize
Phra Chan Island's resemblance to Koh Pha Ngan,
site of massive full moon parties that regularly attract
thousands of young revelers to Southern Thailand.

Typeset by COMSET Limited Partnership
Printed by Darnsutha Press Ltd.

ISBN 974-8303-43-8

Thanks to my late brother Craig who,
in making this book more difficult, made it better.

And thanks to Matt Hedrick for a
berth aboard *Pelagian*—the best diveboat
in Southeast Asia—when it was sorely needed.

Sometimes accidents happen in life from which we have need of a little madness to extricate ourselves successfully.
La Rochefoucauld,
Maxims (1665), tr. Kenneth Pratt

yawn, n. & v. expression of fatigue or boredom; voiding of stale air—a reflexive reaction, contagious; to gape, to present a gulf

1 the great escape

One's real life is so often the life that one does not lead.

Oscar Wilde

It was raining the day Spunky hanged himself. The same day that Chloe decided she might have to leave Waylon. Of course it was always raining in Vancouver, and Chloe could have left Waylon on those grounds alone. But now Spunky had hanged himself and Waylon was carrying on as though they had lost the only child they ever had, even though they didn't have a goddamned child.

Waylon had taken Spunky for a wash and trim, and then gone away to find a part for the garburettor. Meredith, Chloe's sister, had this habit of putting spoons and things in the wrong side of the sink, and sometimes, quite often, they would slip down into the drain, so when you turned on the garburettor you got this grinding clatter and Waylon would get into a snit. Waylon hated spoons in the garburettor. And he had been right. You did this thing often enough, and the machine would break down. Not to mention all the screwed-up spoons you had to deal with.

Yawn

Waylon was always dealing with things. Or at least worrying about having to deal with them. Chloe, on the other hand, could have cared less.

Anyway, Waylon went away to get this part for the garburettor and left Spunky to the tender mercies of the Trixie II Kennels and Doggie Spa. When he got back, Spunky was up on a tall stool waiting to be combed out. It was funny, Waylon told Chloe, but right away he thought the dog looked like somebody awaiting execution, what with the chain from his collar attached to a swinging gibbet overhead and all. Then, as the groomer turned to greet Waylon, Spunky launched himself towards his master in an excess of doggy affection, only to be brought up short and plunge to the end of his chain. Spunky might still have been okay, according to Waylon's version of events, but then the attendant had made a dive for him, falling over herself in the process and grabbing Spunky on the way down. Executioners sometimes used to do the same thing—jumping on to the condemned man's back and swinging with him from the gibbet. No sense letting the poor guy suffer.

Chloe had never cared much for that dog anyway, truth be told. She hated the way it would dance on its hind legs in the kitchen—tongue hanging out, eyes all rheumy and slyly importunate—begging for toast and peanut butter. "Look, Chloe. Isn't that cute?" Waylon would say, as Spunky gagged on the peanut butter. "Ack-ack-ack." He'd imitate Spunky's desperate attempts to swallow as the dog writhed about in masochistic ecstasy. Both Waylon and Meredith used to chide Chloe for refusing to share her own toast and peanut butter with the mutt. So one time Chloe smeared a thick layer of the stuff on half a slice of unbuttered toast and gave it to Spunky. "Ack-ack-ack," she had said as the dog's eyes rolled about wildly in their sockets, though it hadn't actually died that time.

"You shouldn't give him that much peanut butter all at once," Waylon had told her.

"Really?" She'd just missed killing the horrible little beggar with kindness. The perfect crime.

THE GREAT ESCAPE

Vancouverites liked to talk about how their city had eclipsed Montreal as the Crime Capital of Canada—talking about it with equal measures of pride and dismay. But the city was pure vanilla, no matter what they thought. Vanilla with mountains and sea and public transport that functioned with obsessive-compulsive efficiency, while everybody everywhere in the shops and in the supermarkets and on the buses and even in the goddamned jails, Chloe was willing to bet, said please and thank you and excuse me until you wanted to tell them to wise up.

"Chloe? Meredith?" The way Waylon shut the cupboard door told them he wasn't happy. "Sorry, but who put the can of three-in-one oil on the condiments turntable?"

Chloe said they should have sued them, the Trixie II Kennels and Doggie Spa. The people at the kennel apologized, of course. They were Canadians, so they apologized and apologized till Chloe thought about threatening to sue them only if they didn't shut up about it. The stupid dog was dead, after all.

Always saying they were sorry. Please and thank you every second sentence. Appending "eh?" to everything they said, craving perpetual consensus or reassurance or something. Chloe didn't know what.

His courtesy was part of what had drawn Chloe to Waylon in the first place. He was a nice guy, as even she would admit. But she wished he would loosen up. Here he was cleaning the kitchen, when they were supposed to be straightening out this question of their trip to the Far East. Or whether they were going to get a divorce, though she hadn't spelled this out for Waylon as yet.

"Doesn't anybody ever put things back where they found them?"

It didn't help that Waylon was going through some sort of mid-life crisis, never mind he was only thirty-two years old. Trust him to suffer a premature attack of the middle-aged heebie jeebies. My God. Chloe was two years older than he was. And now Waylon was right out of control. He had talked himself into male menopause, and you could see him falling apart day by day. He had broken the same toe twice in a month, stumbling around in terror of whatever existence might have in store for him next. And he bought that big

Harley-Davidson over his own arguments that, not only was it absurdly expensive, it was statistically suicide besides. And sure enough, now that he had it, he was afraid to ride it.

Not only that, for a week in July he went around with his hair parted in the middle. And Chloe was pretty sure he'd been bonking his secretary, Miss Whatsis.

Chloe didn't care for the expression "bonking." Where had that term come from anyway? People didn't used to bonk. Everybody used to ball. Or screw. Though what Chloe liked best was to fuck. Any encounter between a cock and a cunt was, properly speaking, a fuck. Any satisfactory encounter, a good fuck. Around the time Waylon had been parting his hair in the middle, he managed to come up with a couple of pretty good fucks for them, which only reinforced Chloe's suspicions regarding Ms. Whatsis. Surprisingly enough, Chloe actually wanted to think Waylon had it in him—that he had had it in Ms. Whatsis, that is—but in truth that would have been out of character; and she feared he'd only thought about it. And now Waylon had hanged the dog.

"Waylon. Why don't you sit down? We have to discuss things."

Waylon was cleaning the kitchen. He was scrubbing and polishing and putting away and reorganizing and puttering and generally driving Chloe into a paroxysm of frustration. His progress was punctuated by sighs intended to communicate despair at her ever doing her share to keep up the house. Chloe's exasperation had lately bordered on rage. This trip to Asia was their last chance. She wanted him to *see*. If he couldn't see it on his own, then she would leave. She'd have to.

Waylon was stripping cans with masterful rakes of his thumbnail. The municipality insisted that tin cans have their labels removed before they were put out for collection. Chloe watched her sister Merry watch Waylon as he stood by the sink and ripped the labels away with tangible satisfaction. But Waylon didn't have the spunk to cheat.

Chloe herself had had an affair or two, these past months. Two, actually. And possibly three, if you wanted to count that debacle in the shrubs with Cameron. Which she didn't. But Chloe didn't see it as cheating. It was more like therapy. Unsuccessful therapy at that, and she couldn't bring herself to feel guilty. It was the boredom. The vague frustration, a feeling that somehow she *had* to. It wasn't that she really wanted to. Especially with that dweeb Roy Schuter, him with his gold chain and Vic Tanny pectorals. Bronzed skin by Fabutan, personality by Dale Carnegie.

"We have to get our tetanus shots." Waylon had cut a finger on the lid of a tuna can, and he was bleeding prodigiously under the tap. "And the rest—the cholera and typhoid. Where's the disinfectant, dear?"

"I have no idea. Just suck on it."

"Saliva is all you need," Meredith offered. "That's why animals lick their wounds."

"And yellow fever," Waylon added.

"Yellow fever's for Africa," Chloe replied.

"Here. Take your malaria pills."

"I'm not taking malaria pills, Waylon. I told you I wasn't going to take them."

"Take your pills, dear."

Asia. A seething hot continent of lush greens and warm flesh tones, fecund with mystery and adventure. In Waylon's mind, it was a festering swamp of tropical disease and opportunities for getting robbed.

Chloe had also taken to resenting Meredith. Her little sister. It was Meredith's fault that Chloe married Waylon in the first place. Meredith had been visiting Chloe in Montreal, and she bought a ticket to a dance at a ski resort up north. But then Merry came down with the 'flu, and Chloe used the ticket instead. And who should she wind up meeting? That first night, after dinner and a movie, she went back to Waylon's place, where she sat beside him on the sofa while he kept asking her if she'd like more drinks, apologizing for the quality of his whiskey and wondering if she'd like to watch a video, although, sorry, he didn't have any very good ones. Flushed with drink and lust by the third highball, Chloe said no, thank you. Why don't we go in the bedroom and fuck instead?

And now Chloe was married to Waylon and living in Vancouver, and Meredith was living with them.

Chloe was a feature writer. One of her specialties was New Age, everything reported straight up with cynical regard for the intelligence of her readers. And Meredith was an invaluable sounding board for anything new, a gauge of its general appeal. "What do you think of this, Merry?" Chloe would ask, for example. "Some people say it's bad to wear rubber-soled shoes because it insulates you from the planetary energy flow."

"That's right," Meredith would answer. "Feet are very important. Just look how many acupressure points there are in the soles of our feet. Each one of us is like an acupuncture needle in the Earth, in fact, and the energy flows up through our feet and out our heads. The Earth depends on us for her health just as much as we need her for ours."

"Say all that again," Chloe would tell her, scribbling furiously.

"Jesus, eh?" The violence of Waylon's splutter was always another litmus test. Any new idea that annoyed him or struck him as ridiculous was prime material for publication.

Meredith smiled a lot, when she wasn't meditating or crying. She described what she did for a living as psychoneuroimmunology, and she was herself a great source of ideas for Chloe's writing. Merry's mission was to teach people how to achieve health through positive attitudes and proper nutrition. Just as illness was so often psychosomatic in origin, health was largely a matter of smiling and being happy. Or something like that.

Meredith also kept telling Chloe and Waylon not to eat certain foods together with other foods, for this upset the natural balance of their bodies and led to mental stress. Fats and proteins, for example, were okay together but you shouldn't eat them with carbohydrates. And fruit was good for you but not till at least three hours after you'd eaten the other stuff. Whatever. Chloe had managed to get three articles out of it.

Meredith's lectures on nutrition often inspired a big appetite for pizza and beer in both Chloe and Waylon.

Meredith had a mantra, as well. She was prone to meditating in the middle of the day, sometimes just after the Sunday afternoon pizza delivery, her sitting exercises accompanied by long-suffering sighs that sometimes bordered on a whine. And she was a great one for herbal teas. "Chloe," she'd say, "you should really try this new tea. It'll help you relax."

For chrissakes loosen up, Chloe would tell her. She didn't need to relax. She didn't want to relax. "If things get any more relaxed around this boring hell-hole," she would say, "we'll all be clinically dead."

And sometimes Meredith would burst into tears. In fact she was doing that quite a lot, these days. Especially for someone who devoted such a large part of her waking life to getting relaxed. Of course Chloe knew that her sister was also doing Prozac, and sometimes Xanax. She wasn't supposed to know this, but twice she found the tell-tale foil shells in the wastebasket in the upstairs bathroom. Chloe was worried. She had read that anti-depressants and tranquillizers could have serious side-effects.

"Meredith," said Waylon. "How long do these birds have to stay in the freezer? Jesus Christ, eh?"

Meredith had a little hawk and an owl of some sort frozen away, feathers and all. She had been planning to render them in water-colors. For about two months, she had been planning this. They looked like roadkill, no matter Meredith had cooed about how pretty they were; and wasn't it a shame they were dead, but no sense in wasting them now that they were.

"These things could have diseases." Waylon put on a pair of rubber gloves and deposited the dead birds in a plastic bag, carefully tying it up with one of the wire twists he kept from the bread loaves.

"I was going to paint them," Meredith said. But she said this in a way that let you know even she didn't believe it anymore.

Waylon sometimes reminded Chloe of her father. In fact, her dad would have approved of this earnest big klutz of a bear waltzing about the kitchen being dutiful, scrubbing and putting away and organizing in the heroic attempt to keep the forces of chaos at bay. It was funny. Chloe had hated living with her father—she'd only learned to admire him after she left home—yet she had gone off to Canada and married his spitting image.

Waylon had cried after Spunky checked out. This big-framed guy with his thick tousle of dark hair and square jaw. His lip had started to quiver and she'd seen tears in his eyes as he turned away. Probably he hadn't heard that today's man wasn't ashamed to cry. (Meredith had also cried, but that was no big deal, since she'd taken to crying for any and all reasons anyway.) Yeah, Spunky had danced at the end of his leash just like a regular outlaw. The dog had resembled a fat black sheep with a spaniel's mournfully stupid head tacked on to one end. He was so fat he could have as easily snapped his neck without any help from the attendant. And Waylon treated the thing like the child they'd decided not to have. Chloe couldn't imagine the child they didn't have without imagining it looking much the same as the dog—a fat miniature Waylon going around looking apologetic and saying "eh? eh?"

Chloe had cried too, but she'd done her weeping in private; and she wasn't sure what it was she'd been crying about. "It was only a dog, Waylon. For chrissakes, eh?" She shuddered, hearing herself append the great Canadian query of existence. She had lived on the West Coast for seven years, of course, five of them married to Waylon.

Then she had said: "Waylon, I want to get out of here. I want to go away."

"What are you talking about? You want to *leave*? What are you talking about, eh?"

"I want to go on a holiday. Someplace far away and different. I want to go now. As soon as we can."

Over all his reasoned objections, his measured resistance to the idea of upsetting the careful structure of their suburban existence, Waylon had finally agreed to a month in Thailand.

2 the yawn

*A yawn is nothing but nature's way of letting
a married man open his friggin' mouth once in a while.*

Leary

Waylon awoke with the dawn. Mightily he yawned. He yawned and yawned, the weariness welling up to vent itself in a great, prolonged animal groan.

"For God's sake, Waylon!" Chloe thrashed in annoyance and pulled the bedclothes over her head.

Not to be deterred from this, his finest yawn in memory, Waylon gave voice again, an amazing leonine roar that began deep in his chest and rose to issue a full-throated challenge to the morning. The soughing of the breeze in the palms, the gentle purling of the surf on the sand not fifty yards from their bungalow, even the querulous binding of his wife under the covers was as nothing beside this yawn. And then his jaw locked.

This surprised him considerably. It also hurt like hell, but astonishment was mostly what he felt. A casual bystander might

YAWN

have found it pretty funny, him standing there agape, but there was no one to see. Chloe was burrowed deep in search of more sleep. He had warned her about drinking all those fancy cocktails the night before. Just because they came served in pineapples with little umbrellas and cherries all over them didn't mean they wouldn't give you a hangover. And when Waylon went to her bed to shake her by the shoulder, she told him to bugger off.

"Bugger off," she said. "Let me sleep, can't you? What on earth's wrong with you this morning?"

He couldn't talk—couldn't utter a word, only make grunts like abortive yawns—so he gave one especially hard poke through the blanket and took to pacing furiously.

"Waylon, if you don't want to sleep, why don't you go out and have a swim?" Chloe's voice dripped with a dangerous sweetness.

Waylon went over to the sink, to the mirror. He carefully hooked a thumb behind his upper teeth, grabbed his lower incisors with the fingers of his other hand, and tried pulling his jaws even farther apart, thinking this might unlock the joints. It didn't, but it did cause knives of pain to shoot through his head.

He stared at himself in the mirror. Tears had started to his eyes, tears of pain and frustration. There was no one to see—Chloe wouldn't see—but he was embarrassed for himself.

He'd never heard of anything like this before. It was ridiculous. Is this what they meant by lockjaw, for God's sake? You could die from that; he seemed to remember as a child his mother seeing to it that he got tetanus shots every time he cut himself or got a sliver. But this couldn't be lockjaw. He'd been yawning, and the hinges of his jaw had slipped out of joint, that was all.

He tried waggling his jaws from side to side, but that hurt even more than pulling them apart. What was he going to do? Maybe he'd have to find a doctor. But how could he go outside like this? How was he going to explain it to anyone? They'd think he was some kind of bedlamite. He'd have to write it out. That's right—get a pencil and some paper.

"Waylon." Chloe's even voice issued forth with no trace of sweetness, dangerous or otherwise. "Get out of here."

About a year before, for no reason he could think of, Waylon's lower lip had rebelled. He was addressing a meeting of the Toastmasters Club when his lower lip involuntarily pursed and started to quiver. Quite violently. For one awful moment he'd felt his eyes moisten and ache in sympathy. Then he brought his address to a premature close with a joke that had no relation to what he'd been saying, and sat down. Apparently, no one noticed a thing—neither quivering lip nor truncated speech. But the quivering didn't go away.

He affected a number of devices, new quirks to cover up his infirmity. He would draw his lips taut, for example, and narrow his eyes in a speculative or sometimes challenging manner, depending upon the situation and his mood. At other times he'd chew on the mutinous lower lip in a way designed to appear reflective. This is what he usually did when he just wanted to rest, to think about nothing at all, but didn't want casual onlookers staring at his lip and waiting for him to start blubbering. Chloe had noticed it, of course. She liked to kid him about keeping a stiff lower lip.

Waylon still couldn't understand why his lip wanted to do this thing, to embarrass him in this way. And it wasn't the kind of thing you could ask your doctor about. The lip was trying to quiver now, he could tell, but that was pretty well impossible the way his mouth was stretched wide open.

He should rip the blankets off Chloe and confront her with his plight. Gape at her till she thought of something. But she would probably just laugh and make comments. So he decided he had better go see Meredith.

"And stay out; I want to sleep," Chloe called after him as he stepped from the air-conditioned bungalow into the soft warm morning light, the sparkle of sea through the palms.

Meredith was staying in the bungalow next door. She was fast becoming an old maid, and Chloe had told her to come along to

Thailand and meet some nice men. "Come on, Merry; it's about time you found a mate. You couldn't do worse than old Waylon, here, if that's what's been worrying you." So they'd found her a bathing suit that showed a lot of back, at the same time contriving to thrust up her bosom to reveal an interesting cleavage. And it was funny—when Waylon married Chloe, Meredith had been the older sister. But the years of Chloe's marriage had somehow left Meredith the younger of the two. He wondered if she'd be awake yet.

A couple of people were walking by, and he held a hand up to his face as though he were still yawning. Meredith was asleep when he knocked.

"Waylon. What is it? *What. . . ?* She had the grace not to laugh. "Where's Chloe? What happened? Oh, my goodness."

All Waylon wanted her to do was find a doctor. That's all. He made furious writing motions, trying to indicate he needed a pen, but she pulled him over to the bed and told him to lie down. "Now you just relax, do you hear me, Waylon? How did this happen; did Chloe do this?"

He rolled his head from side to side, no, and tried to say "Goddammit!" only what he really said was, "Ah, ah, ahhh, *ih*!"

Meredith was wearing a terrycloth beachrobe and nothing underneath, as Waylon could now see. Her full, ripe breasts swung enticingly where the robe fell away, and the musk of woman's body and sleep distracted him from his problem. She was stroking his temples and telling him to relax, and he found he *was* almost relaxing. He wanted to give in—to let himself go. He wanted her to keep on stroking him like this forever, with her soft warm haunch pressed up against him and her breasts swinging there smelling good. He wanted to let himself go altogether. He felt a burn of tears at the back of his eyes and he surrendered himself to Meredith's ministrations. He could get a doctor later. Besides, it didn't hurt as much anymore. Meredith kept stroking him and telling him it would be all right, and then she put one of her large pear-shaped breasts into his mouth, as much of it as would go, anyway, and all at once he felt he was smothering. In his panic, there was a sickening, grinding snap and suddenly he found he could close his jaws again. He pushed her away while he chomped and waggled his jaw back and forth experimentally. It hurt, but everything seemed to work okay.

Meredith put her other breast in his mouth and said, "There, there. Merry'll look after oo-ums." And he sucked and licked and thanked God he didn't have to go to hospital looking like an idiot.

"Does this hurt?" Meredith asked, a little later, and she wasn't referring to his jaw. She was grinding down on him, riding him with a savage passion that made Waylon uneasy. It was unseemly in this woman he'd always associated with walnut pickle and flower print cotton dresses. And it *did* hurt; she was doing her best to wear him down to a stub with her heavings and grindings. But he didn't say anything. He was just grateful he could close his mouth again.

Finally it was over and she let him get up. "Why can't you call me 'Merry'?" she asked him.

Chloe feigned sleep when Waylon got back to the bungalow; she merely rolled over when he crawled into the bed beside her. She was gone when he got up.

He examined himself in the mirror and was impressed at how healthy he looked, all in all and everything considered. He let out a series of little yawns, careful, making a funny face so his mouth didn't open too wide, all the while wishing he could roar.

3 busman's holiday

In shadowy silent distance grew the Iceberg too . . .
No mortal eye could see
The intimate welding of their later history

Thomas Hardy

"Lock-key! Lock-key! Lock-key!" The four women seated at the table between the boxing ring and Waylon were chanting, cheering the shorter of the two fighters, the little bull in the blue trunks. And it looked as though he was going to win. Rock solid, an implacable machine, Locky never backed up, never gave an inch. Methodically, impassively, he kept advancing, fists chopping and jabbing, thick muscular legs lashing out like pistons, elbows and knees employed with devastating effect.

The Gorgon Bar in Pattaya was a colossal establishment with a colossal program. Besides *muay thai* boxing, lurid posters advertised snake shows and go-go dancing. A Rambo film was going full-tilt on a movie screen way down in the back, although the soundtrack was almost drowned out by the eerie clamor and discord of the *muay thai* music and the shouts of the crowd surrounding the boxing ring. There were tables for hundreds of customers, tourists like Waylon, Chloe and Meredith, and single male Westerners with their bargirl companions. And there was the happy gang of four Bangkok bargirls celebrating at the ringside table in front of Waylon.

He figured they were from Bangkok because two of them were wearing oversized T-shirts that read BANGED IN BANGKOK—BOLO'S GO GO BAR. They were the happiest customers in sight, with a large bottle of booze sitting on their table together with a bucket of ice and several bottles of Coke. The ladies were also enjoying an assortment of snacks. Waylon watched, fascinated, as the loudest and most exuberant of the four, a neatly stacked girl with long black hair, threw her head back and dropped something with tentacles right down the hatch, chewing with gusto and washing it back with a big hit of whiskey and Coke. "Yahhh!" she yelled at the fighters, throwing another bit of the squid, if that's what it was, up at the guy wearing the red shorts, the guy that was getting so methodically demolished by Locky the Bull. She added a comment in Thai, some *bon mot* much appreciated and elaborated upon by her three associates and some part of the crowd. Judging by the gestures that accompanied her remarks, these proceedings all had a somewhat bawdy thrust to them.

"Hookers," said Chloe. "Will you look at them. And there's Waylon, goggling away. Go on, Waylon. Why don't you go over and say hello?"

Meredith winked at Waylon and he focused on the ring with new concentration, chewing furiously at his lower lip.

Despite himself, he was taken up in the excitement. He didn't like boxing, normally. But this was different. The music, strange as it was, stirred the blood. The match had begun with the music, the boxers appearing in the ring and going through elaborate bowing and stretching and dancing rituals. They wore funny headbands with sticks jutting out behind, and the taller of the two, the one in red trunks, was covered in blue tattoos—abstract designs, lizards, dragons, some kind of writing. Something Waylon had read, the inflight magazine, had said these tattoos were supposed to be magic, a means of protection from illness and injury. If that was the case, then this guy had been ripped off. He would have been better advised to wear a motorcycle helmet.

"God. Look at the muscles on them. They must be in fantastic condition. Not an ounce of fat. You can see every tendon, every muscle. Beautiful skin." Chloe was showing more enthusiasm than she had even for the ballet, back that time she'd insisted they go see Nureyev perform, although Waylon didn't want to, especially, and though they never had gone to the ballet before. "Of course I like the ballet, Waylon," she'd said, grinning and pouting her gorgeous lower lip at him. "So I've never gone with you. My life didn't start when I met you, you know. I've done lots of things you don't know about."

From the first round, the taller one had been getting murdered. Locky pounded through his opponent's defenses again and again, shrugging off all incoming blows, unleashing devastating bombs to rock Red Shorts back, staggering him, spit and sweat flying. But always the taller one would dance away to collect himself, returning to the fray almost as though nothing had happened. At first the crowd snarled and called for his blood, wanting immediate gratification. But now it was round four, and Red Shorts was still in there, fighting. The crowd roared at his heart, roared at the spectacle of this madman who wouldn't die, who kept taking punishment that should have crippled him. The crowd knew that it would still have its victim, but it howled with delight at being so tantalized, so finely entertained.

At the table where the Bangkok bargirls partied, the ringleader was beside herself, squeezing at her breasts through the T-shirt and mouthing sweet nothings at her champion. She stood, head thrown back and lips parted, moaning in Thai. One of her companions, a cute kid still in her teens by the look of it, grabbed a handful of ice from the bucket and shoved it down her friend's back. The exuberant bawd thereupon left off moaning and took to shrieking instead. She yanked her shirt up, waggling her bottom frantically and letting the world know she wasn't keen on having ice cubes down her back. The boxers took no notice, sticking doggedly to the business of trying to mash one another.

"High times," said Chloe.

"They're having fun," Meredith offered doubtfully.

Indeed they were, thought Waylon. There was something refreshing about this foursome. He liked their zest for life. Not to mention their slender bodies, their fine skin and long black hair. Their tonic spontaneity, their uninhibited appreciation of the animal pleasures, their lusty enthusiasm for whiskey, food, and muscled young fighters.

It all mocked at his own indiscretion with Meredith, this anxious and unfulfilling mockery of an affair of the heart. The closest to passion he could get was alarm, premonition of more to come and complications that didn't even bear thinking about. Even in the middle of the act itself—the very moment at which he betrayed his marriage vows and better sense—Waylon had been thinking of his jaw, and how happy he was it wasn't jammed open anymore, and how it would be nice when Meredith was finished and he could go out and stroll on the tropical beach by himself and think about being in Thailand, the first time he'd ever been away from North America. And the scent of adventure everywhere. Would he have gone to their table if he'd been single? The girls from Bolo's Bar? Waylon wanted to think so. It would have been fun. But he wasn't single. He had Chloe with him. His wife. And his lover, he supposed he had to say now. Meredith. Jesus Christ.

The shorter combatant, the one in the blue shorts, threw a roundhouse punch that connected with the skinny guy's jaw, following through with an acrobatic roundhouse kick right in the face. The taller one stumbled, shook his head, and then danced away, bobbing and sparring. The tattoos weren't doing him a lot of good. His sharp-boned face was swollen, puffy around the eyes; blood streamed from his nose and a cut over his eye. Waylon had winced at the solid whap-swack of fist and bare foot connecting.

Yawn

He tested his own jaw, opening wide to discover only a slight achiness now.

Chloe was breathing heavily, her mouth ajar, curiously intent upon the ring. Her lower lip, characteristically in full pout, still had the power in itself to arouse Waylon. There was color in her face, and she gave avid little nods every time Locky hit his opponent. She grunted, once, when a kick connected with Red Shorts' head. Waylon was surprised to realize he had heard that grunt before: she did that sometimes when she was having a good time. When she was "screwing." (She didn't like to say "making love": it sounded too phony, too refined, as she'd told Waylon a long time ago. She liked to screw or, even better, to fuck.)

Meredith was tut-tutting and generally carrying on like a woman who made walnut pickle, and the casual onlooker would never have been the wiser, not knowing what Waylon knew, not having been ground down to a stub by this vortex of sexual energy in disguise. She held Chloe's arm, and appealed to Waylon with her eyes for some sign of their shared secret.

Waylon wondered at the lugubrious boxer in the red trunks who was getting the shit beaten out of him. As often as the little bull would explode fists and elbows and knees and feet up against his lanky opponent, Red Shorts would reel away, collect his wits, and come back for more. Waylon couldn't understand what kept the man going. Why didn't he just lie down and forget it? What did he have to prove? Why didn't he just bow out while at least some part of his brain wasn't yet turned to soup? There couldn't be much money involved. Who cared who won?

Abruptly Waylon found himself half out of his seat, fist raised, saying, "Yeah! *Yeah*." Red Shorts had taken what should have been a killing kick to the head, a kick that had spun him right around. On the spin, however, drawing on resources that might have been supernatural after all, he suddenly spun even harder, under control, and came out of it with a kick of his own that utterly surprised Locky, catching him squarely in the middle of the face and stunning him long enough for Red Shorts to get in for a fierce flurry of punches that dropped his erstwhile tormentor to the canvas. As one, the whole of the bar rose to its feet and roared.

Waylon looked around, feeling silly at his outburst, although in truth his cry had been no more than a harsh whisper and no one had noticed. Except for Meredith, who was currently into noticing things about Waylon. She was smiling fondly at him, understanding, forgiving him his burst of manly passion, however understated it had been. Chloe, meanwhile, was panting, face swollen with passion and alcohol, blouse stuck to her body with sweat. She loosened her bra away from her breasts. "Order more drinks, Waylon," she instructed him, not looking away from the gladiators for even a moment.

The little bull had gotten to his feet again, and now he and Red Shorts were staggering around on opposite sides of the ring, each apparently at the limits of his stamina. They resembled two men who had lost their contact lenses and couldn't see a thing without them. Then, as they got their bearings and started to close once more, the bell sounded to mark the end of the round and a great sigh went up from the spectators. The combatants had to be led back to their corners by their handlers. If anything, Locky now looked the worse of the two for wear, though neither was what you'd call spruce.

"Let me have the camera, Merry." Chloe took Meredith's automatic Nikon and went to ringside, pushing past the table full of Thai ladies to aim right up at Red Shorts, who was collapsed on a stool, back to the camera, sucking hard at a water bottle. His trainer said something to him and he looked around. Seeing a Western lady ogling him through the lens seemed to revive him more than any amount of splashing with water and sniffing at smelling salts ever had. He drew himself up out of his sprawl into an insolent slouch, grinning rakishly at Chloe. He gave her the thumbs-up, and she gave it right back, shaking her clenched fist and saying something that got a smiling reaction from the boxer and more grins from his trainers. Waylon was bemused at this creature who in many ways resembled his wife. She had only had a couple of gin and tonics. Chloe threw her silk scarf to Red Shorts, the one she'd insisted Waylon buy her, back in Bangkok, even though Waylon knew the shopkeeper was ripping them off. Red Shorts inhaled deeply of the material and, to appreciative whistles and whoops from the crowd, slipped it into the waistband of his trunks.

The bell went again, and the music picked up as the pugilists advanced to center ring. Red Shorts hadn't left off smiling since he'd first set eyes on Chloe, and he looked totally besotted as he re-entered the lists. Visions of big brunettes clouding his judgment. In fact, Waylon offered to bet Chloe twenty bucks Red Shorts wouldn't last the round.

"Sure, Waylon," she said. "I'll bet you. You don't know the first thing about boxing."

The little bull was doing a funky shuffle, describing slow arcs with his fists, his head ducking and bobbing from side to side in time to the wheezing, whining discords of the music, thigh muscles twitching with false starts, trying to fake Red Shorts into misjudging the next kick. Red Shorts wasn't paying attention, however, as even Waylon could see, as ignorant of boxing as he was. No, Red Shorts was putting on his own display, doing his own little dance, rolling his shoulder muscles, looking back to see how Chloe liked his moves. She loved them, it was evident to anyone who cared to look. But Waylon wasn't really looking. He was wondering if the ladies in the Bolo's Bar T-shirts really were hookers. The Happy Hookers, as he thought of them. He was wondering this, and he was wondering if one of the chief Happy Hooker's friends was even sixteen yet, when he was startled by an unprecedented outburst from the crowd. Waylon looked up to see Red Shorts hit the deck, poleaxed, and bounce a bit. He came to rest with his head lolling over the edge of the ring, gazing upside-down and even more stupefiedly than before in Chloe's general direction. Then his eyes rolled up in his skull and he signed off for the nonce.

"Pay," said Waylon.

"That dummy took a dive," Chloe replied.

"A bet is a bet," Meredith told her, smiling at Waylon and doing the little thing with her eyebrows that he'd already come to recognize as their own special sign. His lip began to quiver and he flushed hot under his sunburn. (He couldn't believe he had neglected to put on sunblock after his swim.)

Dragged unceremoniously by his handlers to his corner, propped on the stool, and drenched with water, Red Shorts came around to the extent that his eyes rolled back from their inspection of the inside of his skull; they wandered this way and that in their sockets, perhaps seeking a new hold on consciousness, though evidently not finding one in Chloe's person. Of course she wasn't too wild about him anymore, either. Her champion had walked grinning into a flurry of sucker punches and now she had to pay Waylon twenty dollars, that klutz.

Chloe decided it was time to move on. Boxing bored her. "Come on; let's go eat. I want seafood."

But Waylon didn't want to go. He wanted to see the snake show. He wanted to drink with the Happy Hookers. An undertow of sheer exuberance dragged at him. He wanted to laugh from deep in his belly; he wanted to put ice cubes down girls' backs. He wanted to run rampant. Just for this night, he wanted to howl, careless of the morrow, independent of responsibility to anything but impulse. This feeling took him by surprise. He was ambushed by delight. His whole soul surged with longing. He wanted to *play*. And he wanted to learn what those girls looked like with no clothes on. He wanted to taste that liquor, some kind of Thai whiskey; there was still half a bottle of it on the table. He wanted to laugh and drink and yell at the boxers and hug a bunch of bargirls. He didn't want to eat seafood with Chloe and Meredith, and he didn't want to go sightseeing. Nor did he want to go to Vancouver in a month's time. He didn't want to address the Toastmasters' Club next month, and he didn't even want to think about insurance. He wanted to learn to windsurf. To his astonishment, he realized he wanted to watch more boxing.

"I'm not going," is what he said.

"Come on, Waylon."

"I want another beer."

"You've already had three beers, Waylon. You always complain in the morning if you have more than three beers."

"This is strong beer," added Meredith. "Lots stronger than Molson's, I'll bet."

"You need some food in your stomach, Waylon," said Chloe. "You're tipsy."

Tipsy! His very soul howled for release, spirit set to soar towards mad adventure, and his wife tells him he's *tipsy*. "You go along and have dinner," Waylon heard himself say. "Go on. I'll see you later. At the hotel. I want to stay and watch the boxing. And I'm going to have another beer."

"Oh, c'mon, Waylon."

"We can't leave you here alone," Meredith said.

Waylon sat there while Chloe paid the bill, and then he got up and left with them. He fancied he saw one of the Happy Hookers, the nicer one of the two in Bolo Bar T-shirts, look at him as they went out. And she was smiling.

"I'm deducting that bill from the twenty dollars I owe you," said Chloe.

Waylon felt cheated. It wasn't the money. It was just the principle of the thing. And everything.

4 pedal arpeggios

In Canada, even the female impersonators are women.

Lenny Bruce

They went to a waterfront restaurant and sat outside on a deck overlooking the sea. The sumptuous repast was ash on Waylon's tongue, lead in his stomach. Cleavage yawning, Meredith leaned across to squeeze Waylon's hand. "Thank you for bringing me. This is so wonderful."

"Waylon just couldn't wait to play on the beach this morning," Chloe said. "He was up before the sun. Weren't you, sweetie?"

Waylon didn't answer. He chewed at his lower lip and tried not to look at Meredith. Or at Chloe. Or at much of anything. He needed to think.

Pattaya Bay was calm, the jolly wooden tour boats rocking gently at anchor on a light swell against a sky the color of dying embers, some of the vessels already showing lights. Other lights were twinkling to life along the sweep of the bay. The serenity of the scene mocked at Waylon as this most catastrophic of days drew to a close. But maybe it wasn't that bad, he told himself. Although he knew it was. Meredith, who was sitting on the other side of the table, had kicked off a shoe and was fiddling her bare toes in Waylon's crotch. Waylon rubbed at his jaw, which was sore, and willed his lip to be still. His leg was jumping to a silent spastic beat.

"Look at that, Merry." Chloe pointed to a hulking Westerner sitting at another table with a Thai girl, patently a hooker. "They're sitting there, they can't even talk to each other."

"Yeah, you'd almost think they were married," suggested Waylon, despite himself, and he pretended to ignore the look Chloe gave him. Meredith giggled. Her toes had taken to walking up and down his erect member, performing interesting pedal arpeggios on his organ. Waylon's gaze, meanwhile, surreptitiously caressed the Thai girl with the liquid eyes and porcelain skin who was smoking and ignoring her date, who was ignoring her in favor of the enormous lobster on the platter in front of him. How old was she? Seventeen? Eighteen, maybe? Smooth-skinned, fine-boned. Her skirt barely covered her panties.

"Have another prawn, Waylon, dear." Meredith was calling him "dear" right there in public—right in front of his wife, for Christ's sake, her sister—although Chloe didn't notice as far as he could see. "Have you ever seen prawns so *big*?" She put one into her mouth and slowly pulled it out again through her lips, sucking off the piquant sauce and looking directly into Waylon's eyes.

His lip was raw and quivering, stinging with the sauce from the seafood that he didn't want. He chewed the lip thoughtfully and then took another sip from his glass of lime juice. Which he also hadn't wanted. And he hadn't wanted to leave that bar. Though at the same time he had the feeling he'd taken a step back from a precipice. A kind of vertigo, a lemming impulse had almost dragged him spinning, euphoric, over the edge. But a walk through town with Chloe and Meredith and no more beer and some food had saved him from himself. Of course now he was looking at another precipice, only in this case the prospect inspired a notable lack of euphoria. A relentless tow of retribution was bearing him he didn't want to know where, as the morning's peccadillo with Meredith inexorably ramified itself.

"Open wide." Meredith poked a shrimp at him, leaning across so that her cleavage gaped at him. "Wider. Merry'll give you something nice to chew on. That's a good boy." The sauce burned on his lip. His face flushed. His whole person burned hot with sunburn and chagrin.

He rubbed at his jaw. What a damnfool thing to have happen.

He'd walked for hours along the beach, after he left Meredith's bungalow that morning, stopping now and then to wade or to sprawl in the sun. It had been hot, but the heat was benign, somehow therapeutic. It felt good. It felt *right*.

Walking on the beach was tiring, and he tried to stay on the wet sand at the water's edge, where it was denser and held his weight better. He had to keep detouring around the people who were playing in the surf. Many of these people were Thai girls, and many of these girls smiled at him, sunny smiles of uncomplicated joy and friendliness. Or so it seemed to Waylon. Some of them spoke to him, laughing, but he couldn't understand the Thai; and when they spoke English it was accented, and he didn't pick up on much of it.

"Handsome man!" one of them said to him, and he blushed and muttered "Oh, well; no, I don't think so. You're kidding" and stumbled on because he didn't know what to say to her. She and her companion, another girl of about sixteen or seventeen, were both wearing string bikinis—one of them fluorescent orange and the other lime green, both vivid against flawless honey and cinnamon skin. They looked at him with a directness he didn't know how to interpret. It seemed innocent, but who could tell? He didn't know how things were done in these parts. They were almost naked. He had inhaled the aroma of the coconut oil that glistened, sun-simmered on lithe young bodies.

Out on the water a few windsurfers had glided slowly this way and that. There wasn't much wind, and it looked easy to Waylon. He wanted to try it. And he would, he told himself, tomorrow, first thing. He'd get somebody to show him how. But not today. He had to watch the sun. It had been years since he'd had a suntan and he would burn in a minute if he weren't careful. Anyway, enough had already happened for one day.

"Merry." Jesus Christ. And Chloe. And now he'd done it with Meredith and things could never be the same. What had been only tacit, only potential—a what-if, never-neverland notion—was now a fact. He'd yawned and his jaw had locked and he'd run gaping straight out into a steaming, heaving iceberg named Meredith, only one-tenth of the enormity of that collision yet apparent, the rest still lurking beneath the surface of events, waiting to wreak its havoc. Sisters-in-law were not ships that had a habit of passing in the night. Walnut pickle and needlepoint mottoes at Christmas and Easter. And now this. You just never knew. He thought about going for a swim. He could swim till he was tired.

That morning a sudden shadow had made him look up as he ducked in reflex alarm. No giant bird of prey, a brilliantly colored parasail was passing overhead, passenger suspended ahead of it on the long rope to the powerboat, swinging in the harness, waving to friends on the beach below. Waylon would also try that, he decided, tomorrow or the next day. But look at the way the boat plowed along just beyond the swimmers. That wasn't safe. And that rope; what would happen if it broke? That would be quite a fall. Maybe it would be okay over the water, but that guy had passed right over the beach. Didn't they have to have insurance? Who would be liable if someone were hurt? If there were no insurance?

But there was no insurance to cover what was threatening him right now, and all his direst premonitions were coming true. It was a relief when they left the restaurant and got out on the street again, amid the throngs of people and the traffic. Waylon felt less under scrutiny.

South Pattaya was one long seaside strip of open beer bars, nightclubs, tailors, T-shirt shops, jewelry shops, restaurants, photo shops, and souvenir stands. Street vendors jostled for space along the road, while meats and unidentifiable bits of things were grilling and steaming and giving off enticing aromas. Sidewalk stands were piled high with unfamiliar fruits. Clothing stalls sold T-shirts with USS MIDWAY, PATTAYA BEACH, and FUCK THE COMMIES on them. A hydrocephalic child sat in a shop doorway beside a tin bowl, goggling in gentle amazement at passers-by. Next door a tiny girl, maybe three years old, sat next to a set of bathroom scales; weigh yourself for one baht. People crowded the sidewalks and the pavement: swarthy Arabs in dishdashas, tanned Aussies in bush hats and tanktops, Russians in polyester. Pickup taxis, jeeps, and motorcycles pushed through the crowds. Big bikes cruised by, each with its aging James Dean clone and a barelegged bargirl riding pillion.

And Waylon saw Western men reeling along half-pissed and happy, bargirls on their arms. Touts tried to pull them into restaurants, beds of ice out in front with fresh shrimp as big as lobsters, exotic multicolored lobsters with no claws, crabs, red snappers, oysters, mussels, cockles. Music blared from nightclub entrances under neon signs: Caligula Club, Go Orgy Go, Baby a Gogo III. The girls outside Baby a Gogo looked about fourteen years old.

"Hel-lo, handsome man." A hand plucked at Waylon's arm. "Where you *go*?" The individual attached to his arm was a shapely item in a tight black leather miniskirt and scarlet silk halter top. A skimpy halter top that revealed the promise of an entirely fetching bosom. The voice, however, was that of a truck-driver. A burly truck-driver.

"A transvestite!" Chloe screeched this information at Meredith. "A town full of gorgeous hookers and Studly, here, manages to come up with a *transvestite* first thing, without even trying. I don't believe it!"

Waylon had nothing in particular against homosexuals, though he couldn't say he was comfortable with being picked up by one. Nevertheless, he might have shrugged off the encounter with a smile and some surprise. But Chloe's reaction short-circuited that. The individual in question was not pleased with Chloe's characterization of her, or him, or whatever.

YAWN

"Huhng!" this deceptively feminine item grunted at Chloe, tossing his head and swiveling off in a manner that belied the deception still.

"Relax, Waylon," said Chloe. "I was only kidding. Loosen up, for God sakes. C'mon, smile. This is a holiday."

A bit farther down the road a tout came up to them and thrust a little cardboard menu under Waylon's nose. "Live show? You want live show?" The tout's voice oiled and insinuated and made Waylon want to curse and push past. The tout turned to Meredith. "You want see fucky-fuck? Lookie-lookie; no have to stay. Lookie-lookie only. See?" he continued, shoving the card up under her nose. "Rubber lesbian fuck. Ping-pong girl. Man-woman fucking show. Is *good*!"

"Let's see that." Chloe grabbed the card away from the young Thai man and proceeded to scrutinize it, scowling in confusion. "You," she demanded. "What's a rubber lesbian fuck?"

"Is live show. *Good*!"

"Waylon, I want to see this. Meredith?"

"I don't know, Chloe." Meredith looked to Waylon for guidance. "I don't think it's a very good idea."

"Is good! Is good!" The tout begged to differ. A second youth joined the little assembly to wave another card and confirm the goodness of the whole prospect.

Waylon felt the last thing in the world he wanted to see just then was a rubber lesbian fuck, even if he didn't know what it was. Not in the company of his wife and the other, anyway. Not sober.

Now that they'd left the restaurant he was hungry, and what he would have really liked to do was go find a gang of happy bargirls and eat street food and drink with them till he was sailing off that pinnacle he had sensed earlier, back in the Gorgon Bar. When he thought about it, he wasn't sure that was what he wanted, exactly, but it was something like that. He felt a great restlessness, a nonspecific longing that sounded echoes of his youth and made him think of Saturday night cruises in his pal Juke's old Buick convertible. A poignant ache of loin and throat reminded him of summer vacations and Esther Shaw with the honey-straw-colored hair who smelled like flowers and soap on the school bus when she sat beside him sometimes. It was hard to say how he felt, actually, though he knew he hadn't enjoyed dinner, and he was pissed off that he hadn't been allowed to stay at the Gorgon Bar. And he didn't want to see any rubber lesbian fuck with Meredith and Chloe. That was for sure.

"Massage? You want massage?" Another entrepreneur, walking backward just in front of them and smiling smarmily, expelled booze and garlic and bonhomie right into Waylon's face.

"Go away," Waylon said. "Please."

"What kind of massage?" asked Chloe.

"Good massage. Body massage. Lady can go too." He leered at Chloe. "Go together. Thai body massage."

"Waylon, I want to see this. I've heard about these massages."

"Chloe!" said Meredith.

"Okay, Waylon. You do what you want. I'm going."

5 merry

For there is no friend like a sister.

Christina Rossetti

Meredith didn't like the way her sister abused Waylon. Poor, sweet Waylon.

And wasn't he all flustered now? Trying to pretend nothing had happened. Oh, yes. Look at the darling man. She loved the way he chewed on his lip that way. Like a little boy. So sweet. And to think of such a thing! His jaw had locked, he'd told her. She had to laugh, him standing there looking so funny and nice. He couldn't close his mouth. Who had ever heard of such a thing? It was probably something psychosomatic, living with that woman the way he had to. When he was always so quiet and nice and polite.

And now. . . . The very idea. To have to sit with Waylon and *Chloe*, of all people, through something called a "rubber lesbian . . . ," a "rubber. . . ."

That foul-mouthed cunt. The words sprang unbidden to Meredith's mind, for a moment trembling there on the verge of articulation. She squeezed her eyes shut hard against the lash of shame that writhed through her body. She shuddered. *That bitch.*

"What's wrong?" Chloe asked. "Is the food disagreeing with you already?"

6 shaking heaven

Things fall apart; the centre cannot hold;
Mere anarchy is loosed upon the world.

W. B. Yeats

The big orange and pink neon sign identified the place as the Shaking Heaven Physical Massage. It was an enormous four-story building which, according to its sign, incorporated bowling, snooker, and a massage parlor. As they cruised into the parking lot, Waylon noticed a sprawl of beer bars off to one side—an amazing hive of little open-air bars, all built to a pattern, each with its coterie of girls behind a square bar lined on four sides by barstools. Every bar had its own selection of music blasting away. The cacaphony assaulted them even where they stood in the lot outside the Shaking Heaven. The whole complex was all but deserted of customers.

Inside, the Shaking Heaven resembled a hotel, nicely carpeted, with plaster statuary holding torches and posing bare-titted with classically Greek expressions of lofty reflection. An escalator led upstairs, and upon this conveyance they were placed with much smiling and nodding by their friendly tout, who then indicated he had business elsewhere. This wasn't what Waylon had imagined, when he had bothered to imagine seedy sex joints in Thailand. Escalators and Greek statuary.

At the top of the escalator they were greeted by a dapper Thai in a tuxedo and tennis shoes who said "Good evening. You want massage?" and gestured expansively towards a gigantic picture window that didn't look outside, but instead afforded a view of a large, brightly lit room with bleachers.

"Oh!" said Meredith.

"This is unbelievable," agreed Chloe.

Waylon didn't know what to think.

Off to one side, across from the glassed-in room, a couple of middle-aged men sat at a small bar, backs to the counter, glasses in hand, watching. A few more men stood right up at the glass, how-much-is-that-doggie-in-the-window fashion. Seated on the bleachers behind the glass were forty or fifty women. Women of various shapes, sizes, and ages, mostly very young. Very friendly looking women. Girls dressed in party dresses, a multi-hued covey of bright tropical birds smiling big smiles of welcome. Birds in an aviary, in a pet shop. Or in a supermarket, at the butcher's counter where the cutlets, the nice plump pullets with frilly garters all smiled and beckoned and said, "Me! Eat *me*. I'm so nice." Where the meat might have had price stickers affixed, these ladies had big badges with numbers pinned to their bosoms. Waylon didn't know where to look.

"Look at them! Aren't they pretty, Waylon?" Chloe was affecting delight. "Not as nice as your friend in the leather miniskirt, maybe. Are you sorry you let him get away?"

The girls behind the glass were smiling and beckoning and Waylon wanted to shout through the window at them, "No, no. It's a mistake. I'm looking for the bowling alley." He couldn't bear the thought that anyone might think he was so crass as to come to this human meat market. Not on purpose. God. Some of the girls were spectacular.

"Take your time," the maitre d' was telling them. "Lookie-lookie."

Chloe moved right up to the glass, dragging Meredith in tow, and Waylon realized then that the glass was actually one-way, except for a narrow band of two-way glass at head level. That way the girls could see the customers' faces when they got up close. Otherwise, all their smiling and posturing was so much blind fishing, and all that warmth was directed at anybody who happened to be out there.

"How much do you charge?" Waylon asked their host, for lack of anything else to talk about.

"Hand massage, five hundred baht; body massage one thousand baht. Tip what you want. Talk with girl."

Five hundred baht. That was only about fifteen dollars. "How long does this massage take?"

"Depend. One and half hour. Everything."

"Everything?" Waylon wondered what the difference was between a body massage and a hand massage.

"Waylon, let's have a body massage."

"You're the one, as I recall," replied Waylon, "who suggested you'd rip my balls off if I ever gave you AIDS. Or herpes."

"We don't have to do anything. Just have a massage. You don't get AIDS from massages. For God's sake loosen up a little," she said again. "We're on *holiday*."

Chloe chose Number 86, and she paid the man in the tux a thousand baht. "It's the body massage that's famous. Mary Lou Wallace at the Club, she told me about them. She and Raymond were in Bangkok last year."

Their man spoke into a microphone, and Number 86 got up from her bench, smiling even harder at the two-way strip in the window, and then left her colleagues through a door at the back.

Meredith had been making a variety of tutting noises, and generally carrying on like someone who was distressed. Now she told Chloe and Waylon that she felt she should be getting back to the bungalows. It was late and she still had jetlag, and tomorrow was going to be another big day. Then she left, saying she could get a taxi herself and bursting into tears as she got on the down escalator.

"I can't imagine what gets into Meredith, sometimes," said Chloe. "She's been acting funny all day. It's time she found herself a man and got married."

Waylon went after her, downstairs and out to the parking lot, where he got a taxi for her.

"You're not going to . . . to *do* it with one of those girls, are you, dearest?" Meredith sniffled in what Waylon saw was meant to be a fetching manner.

Now it was "dearest." And Chloe figured Meredith had been acting funny all day. Disaster lurked; he could feel it in the pit of his stomach. He knew this whole matter had to be straightened out, and soon, but he couldn't seem to get started. And Meredith wasn't saying anything. She evidently reckoned they were having an affair, whereas he preferred to think that if they merely ignored that morning's unfortunate incident, eventually it would be just as though it had never happened. If only his jaw hadn't locked that way. If only he had yawned more carefully.

"I'd come with one of those girls if you wanted me to, Waylon. But not with Chloe there."

"I understand," Waylon replied, even though he didn't. At least he didn't want to understand. "You sleep tight, now," he told her, and then he went back upstairs.

Number 86 was a charming and breathtakingly well-formed girl who told them she was twenty-one years old, and she'd been working in Pattaya for only a month. She left Bangkok because the traffic there was so bad, and the air was so dirty. She took Chloe and Waylon up to the fourth floor in an elevator, accompanied by a plain girl with spots who was carrying fresh towels and who said nothing. She led them down a carpeted hallway and let them into a two-room suite.

"Drink?" Number 86 sent the maid to get Waylon's beer and a marguerita for Chloe. Number 86 said she'd have a cola, when Waylon asked.

Yawn

"What's your name, darling?" Chloe amazed Waylon with her matter-of-fact approach to the whole situation. She had kicked off her shoes and was massaging her feet.

"My name Toy," the girl answered. "It mean 'small.'"

Toy had moved to a bathtub which, oddly to Waylon's mind, was situated right in the center of the room. All in all, it was a strange room. Aside from the centerpiece tub, there was nothing in it but a shelf of toiletries and a black rubber air-mattress leaning against the wall. Waylon walked through to the next room. This one was more elaborately furnished. There was a large bed covered in what looked like black rubber. Two walls and the entire ceiling were mirrored. On an end table sat a video machine. Everything was gilt-trimmed and the carpet was red. There were no chairs. A white plaster cupid with his bow broken off perched on a shelf in the corner. The drinks came, and the waiter set them down on the bedside table. Waylon paid him and took a long pull on his beer. Strong and hoppy, it made his regular brew back in Canada insipid by comparison. He laid back on the bed and studied himself in the mirror on the ceiling. The wallpaper, where there were no mirrors, was a pattern of tiny teddy bears having picnics. He could hear running water and laughter from the next room. He got up to investigate.

Waylon was a big happy swollen blob of protoplasm, lazing in a delirium of lust and surrender to whatever this delightful girl might come up with next. Warm, sweet, slithery surprises. Firm soapy flesh sliding, insinuating, trailing, delicately intruding into all his private places. It was doing wonders for his sunburn, as well. He had been given a bath, possibly the most thorough bath he'd had since he was a babe in arms, with Toy finally climbing into the tub with him for the finishing touches. Chloe had watched for a while, and then gone into the other room to look at a porno movie, which she reported loudly back to him, a blow-by-blow commentary.

After the bath, the rest of the furniture was explained to him, and Chloe out of preference to the video returned to watch the action. Under him lay the rubber air-mattress, voluptuous and slick with soap. On top of him, also slick with soap and easily twice as voluptuous, was Toy the Masseuse.

She had gone over his flip side already, punctilious in the application of each of her erogenous zones to the task at hand. Now she was sliding down his body from his chest to his knees, her erect nipples twin trails of concentrated sensation. Now she was coming back on her bottom, an otter at play, solid globes of oiled flesh humping along, squirming artfully at all the right places. Now she was rubbing her sodden, silken pussy slowly back and forth across his chest and tummy, swabbing by tantalizing degrees ever lower. Not since adolescence had his throat clogged this way with lust, not in years had he felt this cell-by-cell erection of his entire being, this delicious sense of imminent explosion, the promise of release into a drugged languor of huge appetite sated. Suddenly, fingernails raked at his scrotum, wrenching him wide-eyed out of his blissful transport.

"Sweetie! Are you having impure thoughts?" Chloe laughed.

"Please let go of my balls, Chloe. It hurts."

His wife unhanded him, and Toy slid down to straddle his cock. "You want sex?" she asked, in tones of sudden inspiration.

"Um," Waylon replied. With a mind of its own, well lubricated the way it was, and without conscious volition or effort on Waylon's part, his member had already found its way up her. It was difficult to say he didn't want sex. "Actually, I don't think this is a very good idea," is what he did say. He didn't want VD. And he didn't much want to do anything anyway, not with his wife right there, that is. After all.

"Oh, go ahead, Waylon. After all, we're on holiday. And it's not like you're cheating with me right here, now is it? Come on. Let's go to the bedroom.

"Have you got any rubbers?" Chloe asked Toy, who was busy toweling Waylon off. "You know—condoms?"

"Have."

Waylon sat on the edge of the bed and covered himself in latex, wondering if the rubber was a good one, whether it might break.

"Randy Raincoat" was not a brand-name he was familiar with. With this ugly green sheath on his dick it looked like he already had some kind of VD. Mold, probably.

When Waylon turned, suited up in his little raincoat, it was to find his wife of five years and the treasurer of the Greater Vancouver Literary Appreciation Society fondling Number 86's breasts, twiddling the nipples with a distant expression on her face, curiously vacant, tuning in to ethereal delights on some hard-to-find wavelength. She pulled and twisted at them, remarking on their length and firmness. She giggled, then, when Toy took one of *Chloe's* nipples between her lips and teased at it. Chloe had a good body. Not as good as Number 86, but pretty good; she liked to stay fit with aerobics and tennis. And squash, these days. She always said her height and reach gave her a real advantage at racquet sports. She had taken off all her clothes as well, no doubt just to make everyone feel comfortable. She kissed Toy lightly on the lips. This behavior was surprising to Waylon.

"I'm getting her ready for you, Waylon. All you have to do is hop on and ride. Just fuck away."

Sitting there on the edge of the bed with his green dick, Waylon smoldered in dull resentment. He never had cared for condoms of any description. He didn't like to "fuck," he liked to make love. And this visit to Thailand had filled him with a mysterious complex of longings and diffuse expectation now largely nullified by Chloe's presence. On top of all that, what if the rubber broke? What were the statistical probabilities of contracting AIDS from one encounter with one masseuse from the Shaking Heaven? How many customers did Toy consort with in a week; and how many partners did each of those customers on average have sex with? All that had to happen was this Randy Raincoat sprang a leak, and he would effectively have had sex with, he didn't know, probably hundreds of people, men and women both. It was a foolhardy act, no question, this thing circumstances were conspiring to force upon him. Most imprudent.

But Toy was sweet. She soon had him in the saddle, and in tactile terms she was a real treat, with or without soap. Engorged with desire, he was prepared to suspend caution for the moment and to hell with the consequences. He was on automatic pilot and damn the flak. Then Chloe took over the controls.

"Higher, sweetie," she badgered. "Don't you want her to enjoy it too?"

One thing about all his paradises of the senses, the steaming fantasies of his adolescence, was that there had never been a coxswain at any of them. Against his better inclinations, Waylon raised himself higher on his elbows, leaning up towards the head of the bed, rubbing the shaft of his dick hard against what Chloe would have described as Toy's "clit." That was another word he didn't like; it conveyed none of the interest and affection he liked a pussy to inspire in him. And this hard rubbing made it all the more likely that the rubber would break. He raised himself on his hands and looked down between them. It was still there, still green. Toy gave a loud groan and heaved from side to side, maybe figuring his move was meant to be some fancy sexual maneuver.

"Come on, sweetie. Harder. You can't be tired already?" Chloe chortled. "Come on!" She slapped him on the ass.

Waylon was thrown into a total confusion of sensations, a snarl of conflicting impulses. Then a surge of exasperation caused him to withdraw from Toy as though he had been ejected, leaving her thrashing about and moaning all on her own. Was she really sincere? he wondered in passing. At the same time he wondered this, he noted that he was coming. Sort of coming, anyway—the pathetic, convulsive little spurts, this post-coitus interruptus drip was an embarrassing and saddening letdown. It was coming awake with a start in church and bursting into song only to realize the singing of the hymn had just finished. "Hey, listen," he said to Chloe. "You know all about how to do it; why don't you do it yourself? Jesus Christ, eh?"

"Hey, don't blame it on me. I told you you were drinking too much beer."

Toy was sitting up now and covering herself with a towel, worried that this was all somehow her fault. Waylon was hopping about on one foot, hopping mad, trying to get the other into its trouser leg.

"Where are you going, Waylon? I don't want to go yet."

"So stay."

"I'm serious. I feel like trying a massage, too. Don't you want to stay and watch my massage?"

"I'm leaving."

"You owe this girl some money, Waylon. It's not her fault you didn't have a good time."

Waylon threw two thousand-baht notes on the bed.

"I'll need some for my massage, too. I didn't bring much with me."

Waylon threw another thousand baht at her, and then another when she said that wouldn't be enough. She'd need a taxi, later; and maybe something to eat.

"You go right back to the bungalow, sweetie. You need some sleep."

Waylon got lost trying to find the elevator, and a maid had to lead him out. Downstairs, he imagined the maitre d' leered when he told him his wife was going to stay. Waylon looked at the girls in the fishtank and thought about taking another one and going upstairs again, to another room where they could be alone. There was a tall, slim beauty waving and smiling in his general direction, and from what he could see she was everything he had ever dreamed of in terms of physical perfection. Did he have enough money left?

"Waylon."

It was Meredith. She sat at the bar, tottering on a stool with a glass in hand.

"Way-*lon*! I'm *drunk*."

"Meredith, what are you doing here?"

"Did you do it with her? That whore?"

"Let me get you a taxi."

"I don't want a taxi. Did you do it? Where's Chloe? That whore." Waving her glass wildly towards the elevator, she spilled the drink all over her blouse, and her bra-less breasts revealed themselves through the thin cotton, icy nipples pointing accusingly at her wayward brother-in-law lover. Meredith had taken to shouting, now, and the few customers in the place were ostentatiously not listening. The smile on the tuxedoed goon's face had grown even uglier and more intimate. Waylon tried giving him a hard stare, which had the effect of bringing him over to join them.

"You want live show?" he asked.

"You mean another one?" asked Waylon. "What the hell do you call *this*?"

"Lookie-lookie only. Not like, not pay."

"Piss off." Waylon had never in all his adult years told a perfect stranger to piss off. But now that he had, he felt a pleasant sense of release. Something inside him seemed to let go, maybe a delayed relaxation of tension, some delayed effect of the massage. "Just piss off," he added.

"I want you," hollered Meredith with as little discretion as possible. The iceberg had shot to the surface, all ten-tenths of it, revealing its implacable mission, the exaction of its due, which was the maximum inconvenience not to mention embarrassment of Waylon Hazard. "I'm going to tell Chloe everything, Waylon. Dearest. It's the only way."

Waylon had a feeling he should try to reason with Meredith, get her away somewhere and talk sense. "Meredith, I think . . ."

"Waaah! You don't care about me."

"Piss off," said Waylon quietly but firmly, surprising himself again, his voice belying some considerable psychic ferment.

"What? What did you say?" He had gotten Meredith's attention, and for the moment she was sounding almost rational. The goon in the tux stood there and looked from one to the other of them with bright intelligence, happy to learn more about life from these interesting folk.

"Piss off," Waylon reiterated, nodding for emphasis, indicating this suggestion was meant to embrace both Meredith and the maitre d'. "Just piss right off." Then Waylon left. He got on the escalator and descended to the parking-lot level. He didn't know where he was going. He didn't want to go back to the bungalows. What he needed was a long walk. Even though he got no farther than the complex of beer bars next door.

"Handsome man! Hey! Where you go? Handsome man?" The girls manning the front line of bars were waving enthusiastically and screaming nice things at him, so he went to have a drink with them. Why not? Only he didn't drink with the ones in front. He managed to penetrate farther into the hive, out of sight of the road and any wives or lovers that happened to be on it.

The girls were nice, though they didn't speak much English, and conversation was limited. He drank and he bought drinks for them. He had beer, while they drank colas and orange juice but were none the less merry for that. He was in possession of a considerable fan club before long, buying drinks the way he was for all and sundry, smiling and laughing a good deal for any reason and none. Of course, he thought, he shouldn't let this new-found popularity go to his head. After all, there wasn't much competition. Despite the general bedlam—the carnival atmosphere of lights and music, a cacophony blaring at top volume from dozens of bars, shrieks of laughter out of all proportion to what was really happening, which was nothing much—there were very few customers. So Waylon had girls hanging on him from both sides and behind, and more behind the bar hanging on his every word and action, wiping at him with cold towels, massaging his hands and shoulders, kissing him, and doing all they could to convince him he was hot stuff.

It was hot, and the girls kept asking him if he wanted another drink, and he kept saying sure, he had nowhere he wanted to go anyway. At one point he noticed it was late, and at another point he had almost agreed to take a charming girl named Pong to a hotel. Somewhere along the line, however, he fell asleep at the bar instead.

When he resurfaced it was late and he felt like hell. Worse. He didn't normally drink much, and he'd never felt quite like this. Not sick, exactly. He was still drunk, he suspected. He was pleased to find that he still had his wallet, anyway. Even though it was almost empty.

There wasn't another customer in the place and most of the girls were asleep, collapsed here and there around the bars. The music and lights still flashed and pounded away, but to even less effect than they had earlier. Pong roused herself to ask if he'd like another beer, and, when he asked her to, was kind enough to put together a cup of coffee instead. She was looking pretty tired herself, and all thoughts of going to a hotel with him seemed to have fled for the time being. Waylon thought he should see about getting back to the bungalows. Although he didn't want to go.

When had things started going wrong? The yawn had precipitated it all. But the signs were there before that. Little things going wrong. He had stubbed his toe, a few months before. His little toe. He'd stubbed toes lots of times in his life, but this was the only toe he'd ever broken. Rushing through their rec' room he kicked the edge of the door. Chloe laughed and he swore foully; and the doctor said sure enough, it was broken. It took weeks to heal, his foot swollen and his shoe hurting him, too tight. Then, striding through his reception area at the office he kicked the sandbox where the rubber tree stood, and he broke his toe again. His secretary had laughed, too late seeing that this wasn't the right response. That was nothing, you might say; what's a broken toe or two? But he'd sensed it was part of something larger. His life had hitherto been a model of measure and calm. He'd devoted himself to establishing a sphere of predictable order within which he could move with maximum invulnerability to the accidents of unreason, the slings and arrows of outrageous fortune as they appeared to smite the unwary, the unprepared.

So Waylon sat, and he noticed the time was nearly two in the morning. He felt himself torn by the discordant music and the lights and the pathos of those girls who had to attend this party without end and without guests. He thought about broken toes and quivering lips. He thought about green rubbers and soapy bodies and unrequited fantasies. He wondered if you could get AIDS from kissing a masseuse, or from slipping up her without a rubber for just a second or two. He also thought about Chloe. She could still surprise him, this wife creature with her militant concern for the rights of women, especially her rights, twiddling a prostitute's nipples. Meanwhile, who knew how much a loose cannon named Merry had accomplished while he drank and slept and grinned at bargirls. Waylon was a complex of vague and not-so-vague alarms and anxieties. He felt himself pushed this way and that way, and none of those ways did he want to travel.

Sitting in that anonymous bar concealed amid a universe of bars, a bar without a name, he felt without name. He was slipping away from himself, an anonymous ego who knew he was because he was worried, but who didn't know why or who or even where he was. The night yawned at him, a void without scope or substance, and he sucked in a deep breath hissing past his upper teeth, which were set deeply into his rebellious lower lip, that harbinger of the general revolt of existence that only in these past twenty hours or so had made itself manifest to him.

It was time to take stock, Waylon decided. Time to get back on the rails. Tomorrow, as soon as he had slept off the booze, he was going to talk to Meredith, tell her this whole affair was no affair at all, in fact. It was just a silly mistake, an accident; and they were going to pretend it had never happened. And he was going to talk to Chloe, and they were going to . . .

Just at that moment the Happy Hookers appeared out of the night, waving a bottle of Thai whiskey and some greasy bags fashioned from newspaper.

"Yahhh!" yelled the nice one, heading straight for Waylon.

7 forgotten memories

One tequila, two tequila, three tequila, floor.

Anon.

Waylon's brain was in a delicate state of balance. A single injudicious move, he feared, might topple it over into madness, maybe even total extinction. He had a funny feeling this was a hangover, though it also occurred to him he might have been hit by a train.

He was wrecked. He came to consciousness by degrees, figuring out first that his name was Waylon Hazard and he was an insurance man from Vancouver. Looming large in this scheme of things was a woman named Chloe, whom he suspected he had reason not to want to talk to just now. Waylon hadn't had a real hangover in years. But he was coming to recognize this as a real hangover. And he had an uneasy feeling the final damage assessment might be more extensive than that. He really didn't want to open his eyes. Although he supposed he had to. Chloe. He had left Chloe in the massage parlor. And Meredith. My God. Meredith. Waylon really didn't want to open his eyes.

"You awake?"

Waylon opened his eyes.

"Daeng go work now."

Daeng. That was her name.

The Happy Hooker, a.k.a. Daeng, dressed in nothing but bikini panties, was brushing out her long hair. A cigarette hung from one corner of her mouth, a couple of bobbie pins from the other. There was a glass on the dresser in front of her, and a half-bottle of whiskey. She squinted against the smoke and said, "You pay."

"Pay? Pay what?"

"Pay money. One thousand baht. No, two thousand."

"Two thousand? *Why*?"

Daeng merely looked at him with disgust. She took a sip from her glass and gagged. Waylon thought she didn't look well. She snapped her bra together around her tummy, tugged it to where the buckle was behind her, and then worked it up over her breasts. She presented his wallet for his approval, and he nodded, incapable of doing anything else. So she removed some money, two thousand baht, maybe, and stuffed it in her bra. She stepped into a skirt, the same one she'd worn the day before, walked over to the window and yanked open the curtains. "I go work now," she said, and left the room. Kind of perfunctory, Waylon reckoned, for someone who'd just made eighty bucks for nothing. At least he hoped it was for nothing. He couldn't remember, exactly.

Waylon closed his eyes against the light and pulled the sheet up over his head. As a rule, he never got drunk. Half the fatal accidents in the home and half of all road fatalities in America involved drink. And the damage you could do to your liver and kidneys didn't bear thinking about. Not to mention your brain. A good bender could kill a million brain cells, he'd read. Never mind. You had ten billion to start with, although it was hard to believe, the way people carried on sometimes. This affair with Meredith, for example.

Hold it. There was no affair with Meredith. If only everybody behaved as though nothing had happened, then for all practical purposes nothing *had* ever happened. Waylon chewed his lower lip and groaned. "Call me Merry," she'd said. He shut his eyes tighter and tried to burrow deeper into the pillow.

"Wail-On."

He peeked out of his cocoon to find another Happy Hooker in the room. Oi was her name—he still had a couple of brain cells left—and *oi* meant "sugar cane."

"Wail-On, I close curtain, *na*? Me lady of the night; sun no good." Oi's laugh turned into a broken sob. "Oh, my God, Wail-On; I think I dying. Drink too mutt. No good." She picked up the glass the first Happy Hooker had left on the dresser and drained it, shuddering.

Waylon wanted to pee, but he was too shy to get out from under the sheet, shy even to ask where the toilet was. He couldn't see his trousers. Then the door opened and yet another one of the gang appeared. She was naked except for a towel around her waist. A face towel, it looked like. A scrap of memory came back—this was the one who had fed him grilled squid tentacles and told him not to drink too much. Out of the lot of them, she won the resilience stakes hands down. Oo—for that was her name—had said she was eighteen years old but, even in the aftermath, she looked no more than sixteen. She radiated good health and high spirits.

"Good time?" Oo inquired. "Maybe good time too mutt last night."

On the one hand, Waylon was worried he had bonked the Happy Hooker. On the other hand, he was kind of worried that he hadn't. Of course, given one thing and another, he was suffering a spell of generalized anxiety that extended to everything from AIDS to the possibility of life after death.

Oi came over to stand by the bed. "I go work now," she said, just as though they'd been playing house for years. Then, her sudden giggle complicated by a cigarette cough, she whipped his sheet off. She looked back as she left the room to say, "Tonight you take me, okay?"

"This morning, why you give money Daeng?" asked Oo, who was now sitting on the edge of the bed in a companionable sort of way. She laughed, oblivious to his blushes, staring unabashedly at where he clutched his privates. "Not do anything last night; only sleep. I not sleep with you, you give me only five hundred baht, okay?"

Waylon was looking for a diplomatic way of telling her that, not only was she too young, he didn't like this idea of paying women for the use of their bodies. And could he have his sheet back? Then she was beside him, and on top of him, and she was showing him a condom with one hand while she was finding something to put it on with the other. And that was that, more or less. She was sweet, and it went on and on, and his hangover felt better. "Uh, thanks," he said when they were done. He supposed he was expected to give her something, now. On his way out to the toilet, which Oo told him was in the hall, he looked in his wallet. It was empty.

This didn't surprise him. In fact, when he thought about it, what did surprise him was where the two thousand baht for Daeng had come from. He'd been nearly broke already when the Happy Hookers had appeared out of the night.

"Oo, I don't have any money. Sorry, eh? I have to . . ."

"No worry," said Oo. "No need. Last night we make money too mutt."

"What?"

"You remember, *na*? We go '*sing*. My *f'en*, Thai boy, number-one *nak 'sing*."

Sing? '*Sing*. Ray-*sing*. Her friend. Racing. Jesus Christ, the motorcycle races.

Oo told him that they'd won five thousand baht between them betting on her boyfriend that very morning. Now she could pay her rent and everything.

Waylon had vague memories of a screaming blitzkrieg, furious light and motion and noise, a racketing storm of bikes erupting from a cloud of exhaust fumes. There had been hundreds of them. On a public road. Incredible.

It was coming back to him now. The night had exploded with a furious, screaming hurricane of motorcycles, mufflers disabled, a hellish chorus of defiance and joy, a slalom course with the five o'clock in the morning traffic as moving markers. All styles of rider. A couple of boys, teenagers, lying flat out on their stomachs, legs trailing in the slipstream, heads cocked back so they could see. Nobody wearing goggles, only a few with helmets. "Jesus Christ," he had yelled at Oo. "Jesus, Jesus Christ. These guys are nuts. They're suicidal. *They're not thinking straight.*"

Sounds and images came back to him like dream fragments. Then a single memory held. The motorcyclist lay mangled on the road. He was wearing his jacket backwards, a precaution designed not so much to enhance his aerodynamic properties as to keep his shirt clean in the thick pollution. He hadn't been wearing a helmet, however, and his brains had done to the road surface what the exhaust fumes would have done to his shirt front, if he hadn't been careful. His head had exploded on impact with the pavement, and then a truck, swerving to miss another bike, had finished the job. The face, a cartoon, was still identifiably human, a circumstance that caused Waylon to start puking. Just the recollection caused him to feel like puking again, and he stumbled out into the hallway looking for the toilet.

There had been a police raid. Everybody had scattered. He remembered somebody, he guessed it was Oo, thrusting some money at him, and she was off on the back of her boyfriend's bike. Everybody was going every which way. Policemen were clubbing people and trashing bikes. Waylon, the only foreigner, stood there as though in a charmed circle. Strangely enough, he had felt somewhat slighted. But more relieved than slighted. He still had only the dimmest recollection of coming back to this hotel, or whatever it was.

When Waylon got back to the room, Oo was gone. Drawing back the curtains, he recoiled from the light. Then he looked again. The street below was a swarm of cars and those funny little three-wheeled vehicles they'd seen in Bangkok. *Tuk-tuks*. Chloe had insisted they ride in one even though, as Waylon told her, they wouldn't have allowed them on the road in Canada.

Yawn

The sidewalks were alive with vendors and pedestrians and, here and there, motorcycles. The street itself had more motorcycles than you'd believe, all of them much smaller than his 1200cc machine back in Vancouver. This was the "idyllic seaside resort" their travel agent had sold them on?

It was time for some damage control. The first thing was to plot a rational course of action. He had to talk to Chloe. And to Meredith. He had to get things back on track before it was too late. He locked the room behind him, and made his way down three dark flights of stairs to where he found a closed door.

8 shanghaied

The richness of life lies in memories we have forgotten.

Cesare Pavese

Waylon opened the door to an explosion of flashing lights and country music. Then all else was drowned in a bellow of laughter erupting from a crowd of two men down by the cashier. Daeng, the Happy Hooker-in-chief, was climbing up into a little cage, where she started to shuffle around to the Jimmy Buffet song blaring from speakers mounted high on the walls.

He had no recollection of this place; it must have been after closing time when they had got in the night before. Daeng looked over and grimaced at Waylon, though it could have been a smile. Oi sat at a cash register behind the bar at the far end. Neither of the two other men were paying any attention to Daeng's terpsichorean efforts. One of them had a beer and a shot glass in front of him. The other, a barrel-chested Southerner with a laugh to match, was drinking coffee. He gave Waylon a nod. "Hey," he bellowed. "You get a good sleep? Gosh. You young lads."

Waylon looked at his watch. It was two-thirty in the afternoon. What was he going to tell Chloe? What, God help him, had Meredith already told Chloe? He knew they shouldn't have come to Thailand. He had argued against it.

"Oi, here, tells me you're a holy terror, my friend." The guy with the laugh laughed again, and Waylon winced. "She says you took care of the whole friggin' Gang of Four and, if that's true, then, gosh, you're a better man than me." He laughed once more, just enough to rattle the bottles behind the bar, and Daeng yelled down at him: "Leary! It too early to laugh. Please not laugh now, okay?"

Waylon was watching Daeng inspect herself in the big mirror behind the go-go cage, turning this way and that and sucking in her gut, when the door to the toilet slammed open. "Haven't you got any god-damned *music*?" The critic was a giant—a six-foot-six-inch thirtysomething with a long black ponytail, earrings, and lots of tattooed muscles popping out of a Singha Beer tanktop. Waylon slumped at the end of the bar away from the action. Between the guy with the laugh and slamming toilet doors and Jimmy Buffet, he could see that he'd have to make a move pretty soon. Only he couldn't face the thought of exposing himself to the light of day. Not to mention trying to figure out where he was and what was what, and everything. But he had to take care of things.

"Call me Merry" she had said. Meredith wasn't about to let it drop. She wasn't going to share in this nice fiction, this idea that it never really happened at all. If only everybody behaved as though nothing happened, then for all practical purposes it never happened. But evidently she didn't want it not to have happened. "Call me Merry." Jesus Christ. Waylon could feel his lip quivering.

"Drinks for everybody," yelled the giant. Going by his manner, you might have thought this was Saturday night and people were lined up outside waiting to get in.

Waylon waved weakly from his end of the bar and said, "No thanks. I guess I had enough last night." Then he had to shout it all over again so anybody could hear him. He was never going to drink again.

"You're not gonna drink with me?" The giant asshole was amazed and indignant. "My booze isn't good enough for you? I been one solid month on the rig, and I'm gonna have me a time. Got no time for party-poopers. You hear me? *Have a drink.*"

"It's kind of early for me." Waylon had had one or two hangovers before, but never anything like this. He chewed on his lip reflectively and his leg was jumping. He had to get out of there and find Chloe.

"C'mon, stranger. It looks to me like you might actually need a darned drink," bellowed the guy with the laugh. Leary, Daeng had called him. "Anyway, you can always just sit back and admire it. Gosh. Nobody says you got to drink it. And I'll have another coffee," he told Oi.

"Nobody drinks coffee on my round."

"So you say. But I'm afraid I friggin' well do, son." There was gentle surprise and reproach in Leary's rejoinder, and for a long moment they held each other's gaze.

"A coffee for the old guy, here," the giant finally told Oi. "And put some bourbon in it. Jack Daniels Black."

Oi looked at Leary, who shook his head. "Wail-On!" she called. "What you drink?"

Waylon was meditating on the mirror behind the go-go cage. It was smeared with colored lights and smudged with sweat from where go-go dancers had dragged their tired bottoms across it, the way Daeng was doing now. There were handprints higher up, as though the dancers occasionally had to assume the position—though there wasn't much to frisk, there being no obvious place to hide anything in that costume. Waylon didn't want to drink anything. He wanted to sleep. To sleep and wake up and discover that this had all been a dream, and everything was okay and Chloe was in the next room and Meredith was lost in darkest Africa or maybe married and living on the East Coast.

Oi put a shot glass full of a clear liquor on a saucer in front of him. There was a pile of salt and a wedge of lime on the side.

53

"What's this?" he asked, though already it was coming back to him. He leaned over to sniff at the glass. Then he staggered to his feet and headed for the toilet.

"Last night," Oi called after him. "Last night you say te-qui-*la* best drink. Make from natural cactus only, so no prob-lem."

When Waylon re-emerged, he found everybody with their drinks, the girls too, only now there was another member of the Happy Hookers, or Gang of Four, or whatever they were, and she and Daeng and Oi were all halfway down the bar clustered around the giant, whose name, Waylon heard, was Rafe.

"I no smoke, Rafe, dah-ling," said Daeng, something Waylon knew to be patently untrue. In fact, she was in the process of expelling a huge cloud of smoke even as she made this claim.

"You come upstairs and you smoke me," Rafe replied. "Hey. That's your job. My job is working on the rigs; your job is making me happy when I get my leave. Come on. I'll take both of you." Rafe held up double handfuls of folding money. "Let's have us a party."

Oo appeared in a sudden stream of sunshine from the street. She came right over to Waylon. "Wail-On!" she observed. "You drink te-qui-*la*? Drink too mutt no good. Eat this." She thrust a greasy little bag fashioned from newspaper at him, and he found it full of large greasy insects with their legs sticking out. Fried grasshoppers had a cloyingly sweet aroma. "Good!" Oo informed him. "Good to eat when drink."

As Waylon made his way back to the toilet, Oo drank his tequila for him. It was the least she could do, under the circumstances. Upon re-entering society this time, Waylon found Oo had joined Rafe's circle of admirers. Rafe was ostentatiously chewing a grasshopper, his great blue-bearded jaws working away almost as though this were a real treat. A grasshopper leg protruded from between his lips. He pushed that in as well, using his little finger with some delicacy, and washed it down with a swig of beer. "That tastes like plain shit, I'll tell you; but I did it, so the least *you* can do now, my sweet little Oo-*wee*, is smoke me. Hey, you can all smoke me; there's plenty to go around. Let's do it. Upstairs. Let's go." But it was plain that none of the girls were keen.

"What the fuck's wrong with you people? Nobody wants to drink my liquor. None of you slanty-eyed bitches want to smoke my dick. Where the fuck am I? Salt Lake City?" Rafe didn't seem to be drunk. But he was on some kind of real adrenaline high, and the next thing he'd thrown his empty glass across the bar at the mirror behind the go-go cage. There was no one in the cage, and the glass only shattered all over the place, not even cracking the mirror. But it was a pretty aggressive thing to be doing, Waylon had to think.

The girls were all crowded together down behind Leary and the gray-haired guy with Leary. And it seemed clear that Rafe had not much advanced his cause in that quarter.

"I'd smoke you," offered Leary's friend. "I'd use a 12-gauge, both barrels."

"What's that?" Now that Rafe didn't have a glass in his hands, it seemed that he was at loose ends about what to do with them. "What'd you say?"

"Nothing."

Leary was all smiles. "Now, we know you want to have a good time. Gosh. It's a long time on the rig. But the day's still young; darn it, the night ain't even begun. Don't you think you could settle down a bit, I mean, and just friggin' enjoy things? And talk more polite to these ladies?"

"Them whores?"

"Hey, now. That's not very polite." Waylon was overcome by amazement the moment he heard these words, apparently issuing from his own mouth, surely the after-effects of all the tequila and beer. "Who the hell do you think you're talking to, eh?" Or maybe there was a ventriloquist in the crowd, one with a sick sense of humor. And a quaver in his voice, Waylon had to note. "Um," he added, experiencing the fleetingest flashback to the motorcyclist lying there with his head flattened.

Yawn

At first Rafe was almost as nonplused as Waylon. This guy who wouldn't even drink his tequila, talking like a gunslinger. Then he started towards Waylon.

"*Son.*" A voice like Moses' intervened. "I don't think you're welcome here anymore. Darn it. It's best you leave. Now."

Leary had gotten Rafe's attention. The guy wheeled away from Waylon and went straight at Leary, who was no doubt a more entertaining prospect for mammoth psychopaths. Waylon wasn't too sure what happened at that point. One minute Rafe the Giant was looming in front of Leary, hands on hips and chest stuck way out, muscles bulging everywhere, and the next he was doubled over gasping and making funny squeaking noises. Leary had been leaning in a relaxed sort of way against the bar. Then there was a blur of movement and a whack like somebody hitting a wrestling mat with a large mallet. Next thing Leary had the back of Rafe's neck in one gnarled paw and was bent over talking in Rafe's ear.

The music had stopped, mercifully enough. You could hear traffic noises from outside and Leary's quiet words. Rafe, who was having some problem with his breathing, let Leary have the floor. "Now, we're sorry you ain't in such a good mood and all, but, darn it, maybe it's best if you go, okay?"

As soon as Rafe had his breath back, he left.

"It's a long time on the rig," Leary said, "and a month can seem like three. But you work a month on and a month off. And that month off can be pretty darned sweet. It's kind of a sweet and sour life, and the sweet wouldn't be so sweet without the sour. That young feller just lost track, I guess, of which was which."

"Wail-On. This for you. Free, okay?" Oo had brought a glass of tequila over to Waylon. What she'd really said was "*Flee*, okay?" which he thought was good advice, but he chugged it back in one anyway. It didn't taste so bad after all. The salt and lime helped. He asked for a glass of water to chase it. And then another. Oo gave him a cold towel to hold against his face for a while, and it felt great. Oi asked him if he wanted another tequila, and he said no. "No, thanks. Jesus Christ, eh?" His lip had stopped quivering.

Leary introduced him to the gray-haired man, who turned out to be the manager of Bolo's Go Go Bar. "Sorry about the trouble," said the manager. "That guy was set to spend a bundle, but no amount of money covers aggravation like that. Have another drink on the house."

"Thanks. But I've got to get back to my hotel. I've got a little problem." Waylon didn't think it was fitting to mention Chloe, given what these fellows knew about him. Or at least what he thought they knew about him.

"What's your hotel?" asked Leary.

"The Jomtien Jungalows."

"Gosh. That's in Pattaya. You're in luck, my boy. I'm headed down that way myself. Got my truck outside. But, darn it, we got to go now, or it'll take us the rest of our friggin' lives, what with rush-hour traffic."

Just when he thought the disorientation was clearing up, Waylon found himself more confused than ever.

"It's going to take a good three hours. Gosh, it'll take us an hour just to get out of the city, all this friggin' traffic. I don't know how anybody can live in Bangkok anymore."

"Bangkok?"

Leary gave him a look. "Son," he said. "You had a bit to drink last night, didn't you?" Leary finished his coffee and paid the bill.

Bangkok. He was in Bangkok. How was he going to explain any of this to Chloe?

Leary's truck was a little Toyota pickup with a mashed front fender and DOWN DOWN DIVING CENTER—THE COMPLETE DIVE EXPERIENCE emblazoned on the door panels. They moved out into a snarling river of traffic running through urban canyons, high-rise office buildings soaring either side, streets and sidewalks aswarm with vehicles and pedestrians and vendors. Every time a traffic light turned green, Waylon got to see something that looked a lot like the races from the previous night, massed motorcycles storming away in a dense cloud of exhaust. He was horrified. He saw women pillion passengers riding side-saddle, whole families on little motorcycles, tuk-tuks careening through any momentary opening in traffic, no lane discipline, lurching great buses belching black smoke, jaywalkers with as much contempt for the hurtling vehicles as the drivers had for these mere flesh-and-blood boogies in their path.

"Leary," Waylon said. "This is crazy. It isn't *safe*. How can anybody live here?" Waylon's leg was jumping and he had chewed his lip till it was raw.

"You need to relax, my boy. Gosh. What you need is a scuba-diving course." Leary suddenly put on this expression, like he had only now got this really good idea. "That's right. And it just happens I got the best dive shop in Pattaya. Not only that—are you in gosh-darned luck or what?—I got a woman who's dying to do a dive course herself. She's kind of pretty, as well, at least for a friggin' Western gal, and she needs a buddy. We don't like to teach one person at a time."

"Leary," Waylon replied. "I've got some stuff I've got to look after when we get back. It's pretty important stuff, to tell the truth. I don't think I've got time for a dive course."

"Gosh, it's only four days. That's for the basic open water course. Then you got your certification for the rest of your life. Take my word, you won't regret it." And he explained again how this other customer was a nice woman. Kind of attractive, if you liked that kind of thing.

Now they were out on the highway to Pattaya, still negotiating long lines of traffic, but with fewer motorcycles and no *tuk-tuk*s. Instead, life was made interesting by big trucks and tour buses that charged through on the principle that might means right of way. Waylon noticed the burnt-out hulks of a couple of these items down in the ditch on the side of the road. Leary was clutching the steering wheel in a classic ten o'clock-two o'clock grip. It was easy to see that his hands and arms, all sinew and veins and scar tissue, had seen a lot of hard use in one way and another. And there were fresh abrasions on the knuckles of the hand closest to Waylon. Leary was sweating. "Gosh-darned air-conditioning. Never did work right." There he was, Waylon thought, flying down the highway, probably towards his doom, feeling good. And that made him nervous. But it was nice to be alive, he decided, never mind tequila hangovers and sisters-in-law. It was nice, for one thing, that he hadn't been pounded to pulp by an enormous oilrig worker. Chloe would never believe all this. Although if Waylon had his way, she'd never even hear about most of it.

Leary was droning on about dive courses, talking about breathing control and how it was better than drugs or yoga if you wanted to relax, and the sun shone hot through the window, and Waylon alternately dozed and thought about the old days with Chloe. He'd first met her at a ski resort north of Montreal. They were both at university. She was from Oregon, and was used to better skiing. Waylon was wearing his ski jacket of many colors. Normally, in fact, it was a nice conservative blue, but it was reversible, and this one night he was high enough to wear it wild side out. That's what first attracted Chloe to him. That, she later told him, together with the fact that his shoes, the soles of which were worn through, were leaking soggy bits of newspaper all over the dance floor. He was a grad student at the time, not too rich, and he'd stuffed the business section in there as insulation, trying to keep his feet dry. Chloe had a car, inherited from her dad, who'd recently passed away, and she drove Waylon back into the city, a mad tear through the night. She actually clipped a toll gate on the expressway. The toll booths were closed and dark, the gates wide open. Still, it had to make you think. Waylon slid down with the wine bottle to where he couldn't see anything but the dashboard. The speedometer was registering ninety miles an hour when he heard the quick scrape and felt the car shudder. She drove him all the way to his apartment, and then she had come in.

So how had they got from there to here? To the way they were now, and to this little situation they found themselves in on this holiday gone completely haywire before it even got started. Jesus Christ. What was he going to say to her when he got back?

"Gosh, Waylon," Leary assured him. "You're going to love this lady. Your new dive buddy, I mean. Her name's Jessie."

9 free-fall

*Lovers of air travel find it exhilarating to hang
poised between the illusion of immortality
and the fact of death.*

Alexander Chase

The cloud of vomit hung there in front of her. In mid-air. Weightless. Just as though it had been especially presented for Chloe's bemusement. What a surprise. Only a moment before, she'd been fighting the urge to scream. Several people were in fact shrieking their heads off, which had been making it all the more difficult not to give in to terror. The little twin-engine plane lurched and slewed. Then it dropped again—another air pocket. Free-fall forever and ever. Strapped in tight to her seat, guts clogging her throat, Chloe sat frozen with fear and amazement.

At the very instant they'd plummeted the first time, the kid in the seat in front of her had left off wailing to spew vomit. And now, utterly improbable, the cloud of puke hung right there in front of her. It hung for a long moment before it hit the ceiling with a splat. And then it dripped.

Chloe blamed Meredith for all this. Chloe could have taken a train, for God's sake, if she hadn't been so worried. But here she was on this tiny airplane, she had forgotten that planes had propellers, and there was puke everywhere and unpleasant sounds of people in terror. She wanted to be on the ground. She really wanted to be on the ground.

"I don't much care for kids," said the woman sitting next to Chloe.

"What?" Chloe asked, a little wildly. "What did you say?" She turned to look at her seatmate, whose manner registered satisfaction at the fact that the puke cloud had settled back mostly on the child, who was crying again, and on its mother.

"I don't really like kids. Do you think that's terrible?"

The plane staggered through another, gentler patch of turbulence.

"Some kids are better than others," Chloe suggested, disoriented by this particular conversational gambit but glad of the distraction. "I don't have any, myself."

"I could tell," answered her seatmate, a fit-looking, fortyish blonde with a wry twist to her mouth. "What sign are you, anyway?"

"Aries."

"Somehow I knew that. I'm a Libra. My name's Prue."

"Chloe."

"What a lovely name."

Everybody had gone crazy. It was kind of interesting—just one surprise after another.

Travel was meant to expand the mind. Or so it was written. Meredith's mind seemed to have already expanded out of control—much like a festering boil on the verge of bursting. Chloe's little sister. "Don't worry," the note had said. "I can look after myself."

A claim, in Chloe's opinion, that was patently untrue. And Waylon had disappeared, just vanished into the night. Chloe hadn't the faintest idea where he was. That bonehead. Why did he have to take things so seriously? Anyway, he was going to have to look after himself, for now. It was Meredith that Chloe was worried about. Meredith had gotten herself to a monastery, which admittedly was better than a nunnery. But still.

What kind of a holiday was this? She'd spent most of the day before yesterday sitting around the bungalow waiting for Waylon to show up. Waylon, wherever he was, had left everything in the bungalow. Chloe asked the desk to check the local police station and hospitals, and then spent the afternoon touring the bar strip in South Pattaya. The next morning, there was a message from Waylon at the hotel:

Chloe, if you get this message, please leave me one in return. I'm okay, and I hope you're well. It's hard to explain what happened. But I'm okay. I'm sorry if I've seemed to kind of disappear. It was an accident. Really. Now I need a little time to get myself together. If you really want to contact me, tell me. I'll explain everything when we meet. Anyway, it's not you; it's me.

When Chloe called their answering machine at home in Vancouver, she found almost exactly the same message there, except that it was riddled with "*eh?*"s. So she left a reply for Waylon on the machine, and another version with the hotel desk when she checked out:

Waylon? I got your message. I don't understand you, Waylon. And Meredith is very upset. Have you got any idea why? She's run off somewhere and I have to go find her. I'll talk to you when I talk to you. And we need to have a talk. I have to believe you when you say you're okay. I also need some time to be with myself. Maybe it's better if we each make our own way back home. I'll look after Meredith. Your tickets, your passport, and one of the credit cards are with the desk. Whatever it is you're doing, I hope you enjoy yourself. I guess I'll see you in Vancouver.

Chloe also left a note with the American Embassy in Bangkok, just in case. To tell the truth, she'd been in a state of high pique. She was pissed off at Waylon, worried about Meredith, and just plain anxious to get on with having a proper holiday.

After Waylon left the massage parlor, Chloe actually wept. Whether from sorrow or anger, it was hard to tell. Both, probably. In part, she was pissed off at the tears themselves. But basically she was pissed off at Waylon. She'd wanted to do something different. Together with Waylon. Something really different. Maybe it would help to blast them out of the horrid suburban trenches into which they'd sunk over the past years. She supposed she loved Waylon, whatever that meant. She knew she did. But she was coming to hate their marriage. And herself. What she was in danger of becoming. Couldn't Waylon see that? Toy the Masseuse had held her and stroked her and said, "Never mind, never mind" over and over till the tears had stopped. Then Chloe dressed, paid Toy for her time, and left. Without her massage.

All the fun gone out of the evening, she had drinks in a series of open bars on the strip, talking to bargirls, fending off all the touts and the occasional male customer who wanted to change his luck. She got so high she decided to take a hotel room in Pattaya for the night, sleeping alone and hurt and drunk enough to wake up with a hangover.

Waylon wasn't there when she got back to their bungalow on Jomtien the next day. He hadn't been back.

And Meredith was gone. She'd checked out, taking her things and leaving a message that she needed to get away by herself. She was headed for a meditation temple in the south of Thailand. Just like that. Where on earth had this idea come from? On a hunch, Chloe looked in their Thailand travel guide, turning to "meditation" in the index. Sure enough, there were a few meditation centers listed, including two with penciled tick-marks in the margin. One place—a famous Buddhist temple, according to the guidebook—conducted strict *vipassana* retreats for foreigners in English. The writer warned that "strict" meant something like eleven hours of scheduled meditation a day, no talking except to the instructors, no smoking, no drinking, no fraternizing with the opposite sex, no phone calls, no letters or writing of any sort, no books, no religious talismans of any kind, two vegetarian meals a day, getting up at four o'clock in the morning, and going to bed at sundown. Meredith had underlined this passage.

"I'll tell you the truth," Chloe said. "I'm not too happy with this little airplane. I'm not usually afraid of flying, but I was terrified back there, when we went through the turbulence."

Mother and child had returned from the toilet, and the mother was applying a bunch of damp paper towels to their seats. Red-faced, hair slicked back, the kid stood in the aisle staring at Prue, who smiled in a maternal way and offered him her barf bag. Chloe rummaged in her bag to find a chocolate bar and passed it to the boy.

"I dreamed I was on a plane just a couple of nights ago," said Prue. "I'm practicing lucid dream control therapy. You can learn to control your own dreams. The idea is, you're supposed to recognize your own worst fears and then confront them in your dreams, where you know it's safe. If you hate snakes, you dream up a bunch of them in your sleeping bag. If you're climbing a mountain, and you're afraid of heights, you jump. You know you're dreaming, so you know you're not going to die. But your *body* knows it's going to die and responds accordingly. If you dream you're in an airplane, for example, and you're afraid of flying, you make the plane crash."

Chloe felt a stab of anxiety as she considered the idea of plane crashes. "And what happened? In your dream, I mean."

"I didn't crash," replied Prue. "My problem isn't fear of flying; I'm claustrophobic. So I trapped myself in the toilet. That should have been good enough, but some part of my psyche also had this guy Al Dente from the 4H Club stuck in there with me. There was no room to breathe and he was trying to show me a bunch of photos he'd taken. What a nightmare. That one got out of control."

"The '4H Club'?"

"The Holistic Herbal Garden and Institute of Holographic Healing. The 4H Club."

"You're kidding," said Chloe. The New Umbilicus travel guide had had a short entry on the Holistic Herbal Garden and Institute of Holographic Healing right after the section on Wat Nai Fun. "I'm on my way to visit a meditation temple right next door."

"Wat Nai Fun? Forget it. Their courses start on the first of every month, and you've just missed it. They're quite strict about that. In fact, they're incredibly strict about everything. Do you know anything about their program?"

"Just what I got from the guidebook."

"Forget it. Unless you're a red-hot meditator already. My God. If you don't quit out of boredom, you're liable to go crazy. And they don't let just anybody in. You've got to have an interview with the abbot. Anyway, now you'd have to wait till the beginning of next month."

Chloe explained that she only wanted to talk to her sister, and Prue told her that she wouldn't even be able to visit Meredith until her course was finished or she quit.

"Look, I can recommend a good guesthouse in the village, not too far from the temple. Better still—why don't you stay at the 4H Club? I can introduce you to the meditation master this afternoon. It's not expensive, and they're doing some interesting things. It's much more relaxed than Wat Nai Fun. You can keep tabs on your sister from there."

"Okay," said Chloe, thinking again that Waylon was just going to have to look after himself.

10 buddies

*If a man stands in a forest speaking and there's
no woman around to hear him, is he still wrong?*

Stephen Wright

Waylon homed in on Jessica's crotch, on the quiver and wobble of thigh. The underwater visibility didn't extend more than fifteen feet, and, apart from the view directly ahead, Waylon's world was a featureless void. Pubic hairs darkened the white crescents where the swimsuit had pulled up and away from her suntan. Her fins kicked erratically only inches from his facemask. They weren't really that close, though. Just a day or two ago, Waylon had learned all about the twenty-five-percent magnification effect underwater. So her thighs probably weren't that big either.

Breathe deeply. Breathe out slowly, slowly. Make sure all the air has been expelled from your respiratory passages. Good. Breathe in. . . . Breathe out.

Waylon breathed as slowly and regularly as he could, trying to expel whole lungfuls before inhaling again, maximizing his air supply. It was also calming. Good breathing control relaxed you, making you less susceptible to panic. It improved buoyancy control, which was important; and it extended your bottom time, since relaxed divers burned air more slowly.

He had been learning a lot, this past couple of days. For example, the first rule was "Keep breathing." If you held your breath with a lungful of pressurized air while ascending even a few feet, you ruptured your lungs. Another thing he learned was that you shouldn't take any medication at all before diving. The effects of various medicines under pressure were uncertain. And you should never drink alcohol before diving; nor should you dive with a hangover. What you should do is always go diving with a "buddy." This was maybe the second cardinal rule of safe sport diving—always dive with a buddy, and always know where your buddy is at any given moment. You were responsible for each other's life.

So here he was under thirty feet of water, breathing assiduously and diving with a junkie for a buddy. "Call me Jessie," she told him the night they met. She offered him a shot of vodka, poured herself a hefty dollop—neat, no ice—and then washed down a handful of Valium. "You can buy this stuff over the counter in Thailand," she said. "By the kilo, if you want." That was the night before they started the dive course.

She dropped a couple more Valiums before the pool practice session on that first day. "I hate putting my head under water," she told Waylon. "I'm really phobic about it."

Waylon had finally got back from Bangkok to the bungalows on Jomtien Beach two days late.

Leary's truck had broken down out in the middle of nowhere. Eventually they found a tow service, but then had to wait till morning for repairs. Making the best of a bad situation, Leary prescribed a "little hair of the friggn' dog," and they wound up camped at a rundown roadside hotel with a coffee shop downstairs. Thai-style coffee shops, as it turned out, bore no resemblance to those back home. For one thing, they didn't involve any coffee that Waylon could find. It was probably a coincidence that Leary knew the lady who managed the joint and half the singers as well. Waylon called the bungalows several times, but got no response. They'd got moving about noon the following day, and Waylon hadn't felt notably better than he had the day before. Worse, in fact, whenever he stopped to think about Chloe, which was often. And Meredith.

Chloe was gone. She'd left a message at the desk of the hotel in Pattaya, together with a package including one of their credit cards and half the traveler's checks. So he had money again. But he didn't have the faintest idea where Chloe was. He was amazed and alarmed that she hadn't waited. The desk told him she'd left the evening before. All they knew was that she'd asked for a taxi to take her all the way up to Bangkok Airport. Meredith had left a couple of hours before that. No, they didn't know where she had gone. Waylon had a bad feeling about all this; he should have never left Meredith in the shape she'd been in. He left new messages on their answering machine at home in Vancouver, at the American Express office in Bangkok, at the hotel in Bangkok, and at their former hotel in Pattaya. Then he moved into a cheaper place—a modest bungalow recommended by Leary, just up a side lane from the beach road and within an easy walk of the Down Down Diving Center.

"I don't know how you men do it." Jessica looked up from her dive tables. She'd been calculating how much surface interval she would need after spending forty minutes under water at a maximum depth of sixty feet. They had a test the next morning. "I don't know how you can live with yourselves."

"What are you talking about?" asked Waylon.

"You come here from Australia, from Europe, from all over. Fat middle-aged roués. And you buy these girls. It's revolting."

"I guess it is at that. You're right." Then he thought it over. He wasn't fat. He wasn't even really middle-aged. He could still get life insurance on favorable terms. Actuarially he was still okay. What the hell was she talking about? He felt he had to amend his earlier attitude. "Oh, piss off," he said. Then he repeated it, rolling the phrase around on his palate, savoring every robust nuance. "Just piss off."

"I won't sleep with you, you know."

"No? Well, I guess that's okay. I understand."

"Do you? I don't think you do."

"I do. You've only known me for two days. And we've never gone further than checking each other's weight belts. After all, eh? Anyway, I'm a married man."

"I don't want AIDS."

"I don't have AIDS," said Waylon, thinking he didn't want to sleep with her in any case. Really, it was enough just to swim behind her watching her thighs and stuff. She was kind of cute, with her lucent gray eyes and the fetching sprinkle of freckles across her nose. But what he wanted to do was finish their homework so he could get some sleep and be ready for the next day's diving.

"If you go around sleeping with prostitutes, you're going to have AIDS. I don't want it."

"I don't go around sleeping with prostitutes." And that was true, Waylon told himself. He wasn't the type who went around buying sex.

"How many girls have you slept with since you got here?"

"Why don't we finish these exercises? We've got a test tomorrow, you know. And I'm kind of tired; it must be all the sun." Waylon chewed at his lip and gazed sternly off into some distance full of significant things he had to think about.

"Waylon, how am I supposed to study with you shaking the floor that way?" Waylon's knee was jumping, frenetic, to some internal drum that telegraphed total alarm at the way things were going.

Jessica finally left and Waylon went to bed. Eventually he found himself drifting in a luxurious state where coral fish and brown-skinned girls floated through a boudoir full of silk and incense and soft fragrances. Suddenly, Meredith appeared and the sea was coming in the windows; he was struggling to keep his head above water, panicking. He awoke to a tapping on the door and a low voice.

"Waylon?"

"Jessie?"

"Let me in, Waylon. They're trying to break in."

"Who are?"

"The burglars."

"What burglars?"

"The burglars who are outside my bungalow. Are you *awake*? They were at the windows. After they tried the door. I'm scared, Waylon. Can I stay here tonight? I won't bother you."

"Okay. Sure."

"I'll be okay on the floor. You can have the bed."

"Thanks."

"But I'm just going to sit up for a couple of minutes. The burglars upset me." Jessica had a bottle of vodka with her, and she proceeded to pour a whack of it into one of the glasses on Waylon's dresser. "Do you want a drink, Waylon?"

He didn't. He watched as she popped a couple of Valiums and then shot the vodka back, gagging.

"Can I lie beside you, Waylon? Promise not to try anything, though. We're dive buddies, okay? But that's as far as it goes."

"Okay," Waylon replied, turning to the wall and wondering if he would ever get to sleep now.

He was in fact just drifting off, although he'd lost the boudoir full of fish and girls forever, when he became conscious of a leg draping itself across his hip. This development was soon followed by a hand that ran along his upper arm and across his neck, tickling him. Fingers tousled his hair.

"I was scared," Jessica whispered.

"That's okay."

There was a certain amount of fumbling about, in the course of which Waylon became disentangled from the bedclothes. Jessie removed his shorts and then swung aboard to straddle him.

"Jessie," he said.

"Oh, Waylon."

"Jessie, shouldn't we be using a condom?"

"I trust you, Waylon."

Waylon wanted to use a condom. He didn't want AIDS.

"Oh, Waylon," she reiterated, while he reflected on the fact that he had had sex with his sister-in-law and two or three virtual strangers in just the past five or six days. On at least two occasions—this one and with Meredith—he'd worn no condom. On another, in the massage parlor, he'd briefly slipped in bareback. Then, during that night with the Happy Hooker, he really had no idea what had transpired. And there was the kid, in the morning. Jesus Christ. And now Jessica.

"Are you going to wear that Walkman to bed, Jessie?"

"I always sleep with my tape. Here, listen to this."

Waylon held the phones to his ears. A gentle surf was breaking on a beach; leaves rustled in the wind. Gulls cried in the distance.

"Keep listening."

A whining, repetitive sort of chanting gradually impinged. It swelled and swelled till it drowned out the natural sound effects. "I made a copy of my mother's relaxation tape before I left Cincinnati. She had cancer. This was part of the therapy." Jessica took the headphones back and flicked the rewind switch. "She died ten months ago."

"I'm sorry."

"No problem. Waylon? There really were men outside my bungalow."

"Maybe they were just kids."

"Maybe."

Jessica donned her sleeping mask and plugged herself back into the Walkman.

Waylon lay there reviewing his situation. Hardly a week into the holiday, and he had cheated on Chloe with three and possibly four different women. That wasn't counting Toy the Masseuse, since nobody could have called that cheating. Troubled by the sense that things would never be the same again, Waylon was a long time getting back to sleep.

11 interlude

"Somebody's boring me," he said. "I think it's me."

Dylan Thomas

Chloe had no sooner dropped her bags in the women's dorm, the first day, when this guy appeared, long black hair and beard, olive skin, piercing blue eyes with black smudges beneath them, testament to soulfulness. "Hi," he told her. "My name's Allen. I'm a photographer." Just like that; and he dropped something on her pallet. "Here's my portfolio." She was looking for some way to tell him to bugger off, but he'd already performed a graceful descent to sit beside her. Look, Ma—no hands. His legs had simply caved in and there he was, sitting in a half-lotus opening a photo album.

"This was my trip to Cambodia," he said. And from there he proceeded to show her snapshots from trips all over Asia. Everywhere he'd gone, he'd captured lots of street vendors with half their heads cropped off and street children with their fingers up their noses.

"Oh, yes," Chloe enthused. "Well, well."

Eventually there were no more photos, and Al Dente started in on the story of his life. Al Dente hadn't gone to the full moon party with the others from the 4H Club because there was this guy, see, who had a girlfriend, yeah? And the month before, at the last full moon party, she came on to Al Dente in the biggest way, so what could you do? So now it was best if he laid low for a month or so. No problem. And there was some other woman he was anxious to avoid, but Chloe didn't listen to the details. He was from the Midwest, as she might have guessed, no matter how much he resembled a blue-eyed yet otherwise realistically Semitic version of the Christian Messiah come back to Earth. He was from Greenfield, Ohio. And no, Chloe had never been there, she told him, failing to hide the gratitude in her voice.

"So, Al. What brings you out this way?"

"My name is Allen," he replied. Al Dente's real name was Allen Pesci, and he insisted upon being called Allen. Al Dente had been in ashrams and monasteries all over Asia and the Pacific Northwest. He had even been in the Thai monkhood for six months, he claimed, but he'd left. He couldn't do without his dope and his women.

"Sure, I've slept with him," Prue had told Chloe that morning before breakfast. "Who hasn't? But I didn't enjoy it. He only gets half a hard-on at the best of times, never mind he's always talking about how big it is and how many women want a piece of it. I call him Al Dente, which is maybe just right for spaghetti, but it leaves a little to be desired in the sack. I ask you—premature ejaculation *and* only half a hard-on. Give me a break. Bibi likes him, though. Don't tell her you slept with him." Bibi was one of the members who were away at the full moon party. Chloe made a mental note to tread cautiously.

"Thai women find me too big," Al Dente had told Chloe. "They like me, okay? But I'm just too big. They say it hurts."

Chloe lifted his limp member. Exhibit A. It looked pretty ordinary to her, so far as limp dicks went. "The monster," she said.

Oblivious to sarcasm, it began to stiffen again. The first time, he had ejaculated as Chloe was fitting the condom. It occurred to her to wonder what the hell she was doing here in bed with this guy. She'd caved in without even really trying to say no. In part, it was the massage.

The 4H Club provided men's and women's dorms as well as a couple of separate bungalows for those who wanted some time alone together. But it was all "short-time action," in Al Dente's words; everyone had to return to the segregated dorms by lights out. "Come on," he'd told her. "Lie down. You'll enjoy this, It's traditional Thai massage. This isn't like Western massage. It focuses on acupressure points, realigns the energy channels. Balances the yin and the yang."

New Age blither had infected the whole world, Chloe reflected. This wasn't much different from being in Vancouver. And Al Dente wasn't much different from any Vancouver suburbanite, with his hands up under her towel and everything.

Before the massage, there had been the herbal tea and the herbal steam bath. An hour of alternating steam baths and cool showers till they were both relaxed unto floppiness. Still, she'd given in only reluctantly and only because she was so relaxed by the herbal junk and the massage and so stupefied by the man's amazing capacity to bore that any diversion was welcome. Anyway, this was a holiday. And Waylon had gone off and left her. She had enjoyed watching him with that massage girl. If only he hadn't been so uptight about it all. But old Waylon had to get into a snit and storm off. He looked ridiculous, swearing and hopping about on one leg, only half into his pants. Jesus Christ, Waylon.

Al Dente was reaching between her legs. Despite herself, she was fascinated by the man. She loved his spare body, honed by vegetarianism and yoga and, if you could believe him, by sex. They had only just met, yet he had already referred to several other women he'd fucked. He insisted on using that word, and Chloe loved it. She loved his eyes, blue anomalies in that swarthy, aquiline face. The scraggly black beard and long hair, with the eyes, made her think of a desert warrior, a prophet, a Messiah. His hair was parted in the middle and hung on his head like a ragged tent. Chloe asked why he didn't tie it back in a ponytail like everybody else. It looked as though he'd cut it himself. He had cut it himself, he told her; he couldn't trust Thai barbers to get it right. She was fascinated by his self-preoccupation, his amazing conceit.

Waylon's was bigger, if anything. And he wielded it with more consideration. "Whoa," said Chloe. "What's the rush? We hardly know each other." But Al Dente had worked his way in, and now he rose up, stiff-armed and arch-backed, to ride it in to the hilt.

"Ow," Chloe said. "I wasn't ready."

"Am I too big?"

"No, no. Yeah, sure. Just go ahead. Don't talk." Now that Chloe was ready it was already over. She had barely started to ride the swell when Al Dente groaned and rolled off to collapse spread-eagled beside her, panting with something, Chloe didn't know what. Certainly not exertion. "That's it?" she asked. She lay there, eyes closed, disappointed, trying to husband the sweet tension in her throat and belly. She reached down to caress herself.

"Ackk!" said Al Dente. "Ahhh!"

Chloe opened her eyes. Al Dente was staring at his blood-stained hand in horror. Both hands in the air, as though he were being held at gunpoint. He next contemplated his dick, which, as it turned out, was also covered with blood. "Ahhh! Ackk!" he said again.

"I guess my period's early," said Chloe with some surprise, inspecting her own hand, which was similarly bloody. As were the sheets.

"Help me! Wash it off."

"Wash it off yourself. Anyway, you're wearing a condom, you dork."

"You do it. Please take it off for me."

Later, drawing himself erect, his feet meticulously folded atop his thighs, his spine rigid with outrage or maybe only *kundalini*, he had told her: "You don't like me."

"I like you, Al. Allen. But this is all a mistake. I'm sorry, but I'm a married woman. It was great. Now let's just pretend it never happened. Okay?"

12 the 4h club

*Nowhere can man find a quieter or more
untroubled retreat than in his own soul.*

Marcus Aurelius

*H*earing. . . .
 Chloe heard a bark—one sharp, excited exclamation from Pup. *Hearing.* . . .
 The sound came from across the yard. At the same time it came from within her, from within the center of all things, which was somehow the same; and for one moment it brought everything together—a casual declaration that this was the way things were, and that was only as it should be. Even as she reflected on this perception, it began to slip away.
 The golden afternoon smeared in the heat and sun. Chloe herself began to smear. Her *chakra* centers—whatever—her tummy was turning to butter, to warm honey. She attended to her breathing. *Rising.* . . . *Falling.* . . . Breathe longer on the exhalation. Rising. . . . Falling. . . . *Feeling.* . . . Feeling breath against nostrils. *Rising.* . . . The

Yawn

sun was warm on her shoulder, on her breast. Feeling the sun. *Feeling.* . . . Must keep eyes open. *Thinking.* . . . Eyes open. *Thinking.* . . . Mustn't sleep. Warm. Feeling warm sun. . . .

Chloe was on a boat, a gently rocking boat on a pond. Then it was a huge river and the boat was much larger, and there were some young hunks in suntans and shorts and tank-tops with big numbers on them. This was a dream, she realized. At the same time it felt real. She felt a furry burst of lust. This was *her* dream, it occurred to her, and she should be able to do whatever she liked with it. So experiment, already. She willed the tall rower with the blonde crew-cut and the charming smile to stand up and take off his shorts. What the hell, why not have them *all* take off their shorts. This was only a dream, after all. Chloe flushed with pleasure at the thought of having her way with this fine collection of six-foot Ken dolls. Check them out for anatomical correctness, that was the first thing. Yeah. Only the scene had shifted, and now she found herself in a waiting room with potted plants and four or five men in business suits. This wasn't so interesting a proposition. Another be-suited fellow, an older man, was beckoning her through a doorway and she went, thinking that this wasn't working out the way it was supposed to.

Her dreamworld, complex and intractable, remained annoyingly similar to the mundane version of events. For a while, it might have been an eternity or it might have been only a few seconds, Chloe lost herself, and forgot she was dreaming. By means many and obscure, she eventually wound up in bed making love—slow, passionate love—with somebody who turned out to be Waylon. "This is the way it's supposed to be," he told her, and Chloe awoke to herself where she sat in a patch of sunlight.

Al Dente sat in half-profile just ahead of her and to the side. He could have been the cover shot for a how-to book on yoga. Since that little episode, he'd been pretending nothing ever happened between them. Thank God.

Gorgi, smiling a hint of his sly smile through a scraggly black goatee, sat at the front of the hall facing his acolytes in a lotus-position puddle of white robes. He snorted a breath and then let it out slowly with an eerie, high-pitched mewling. There was an answering snort from Ruthie's vicinity and a stifled giggle from Prue. The Rev, meanwhile, just kept panting like a big floppy dog trying to cool off in the heat. A florid, portly individual of about thirty-five years with prematurely silver sideburns and a salt-and-pepper beard, the Rev favored black trousers and a white shirt buttoned to the collar, which gave him an ecclesiastical air. Sometimes he wore a black shirt with black trousers. And lace-up black Oxfords, out of doors; black socks even in the meditation hall. The *sala*. No matter he had even less tolerance for the heat than Chloe did, although he'd been in Thailand more than a year.

Chloe concentrated on her breathing. Her feet and ankles had gone numb and she wished her knees would as well.

The meditation sala was big enough for twenty times the six meditators poised there in a range of approximations to the lotus position. There was lots of room for expansion, which probably explained Gorgi's sly smile—the image of the saint who'd swallowed the canary. There was space for lots more suckers where these came from. But Chloe tended towards cynicism, as she was the first to admit. He had probably noticed that she'd nodded off, and was only savoring the thought of her penalty.

The 4H Club included traditional wooden Thai buildings thatched with palm in a walled compound, the whole of it set amid flowers, coconut palms, and a wild diversity of shrubs and trees. The yard was clean, freshly swept sand. Altogether, Chloe imagined, it had the atmosphere of a small rural temple.

The sala—a raised platform with a high-pitched tiled roof in the Thai style and a floor of enormous polished teak planks—was open to the breeze on four sides. The meditationists, a lazy little archipelago of windows on consciousness, were spaced as far apart as possible, maybe to minimize the gravitational effects of individuated egos.

Chloe suppressed a giggle of her own. But she wasn't supposed to be thinking. She was supposed to be attending to the experience of being. Or something. Together with all her fellow explorers.

Yawn

Ruthie, a smoldering volcano of blessedness on the boil, sat up front, closest to Gorgi and half-turned towards the others. She sat so erect, so correct you could have hung a plumbline from nose-tip to crotch. Steel-rimmed glasses with blue-tinted lenses perched askew halfway down her nose.

Ruthie was a living reproach to the Rev, who slumped more than sat, his legs tucked back and to the side, body propped on one thick arm. He was panting and sighing and shifting from one arm to the other, every shift requiring the redisposition of his legs. Chloe thought she could hear sweat dripping on the polished floor. The Rev's meditation practice had a desperate quality to it, as though he meant to achieve enlightenment before his arm buckled and he fell over on his head.

"This is kid's stuff," Ruthie had told Chloe the previous afternoon, following the interview with Gorgi. "You want to try a real vipassana retreat."

The fact was, her whole manner proclaimed, Ruthie was a heavyweight. She was karmically pumped up to the point she could only scoff at someone like Chloe, the spiritual equivalent of a dilettante on an exercise bicycle. Ruthie had already spent eight months at the 4H Club, interspersed with retreats at "more serious" centers. She had just come away from a strict vipassana session at Wat Nai Fun and she was "incredibly sensitized."

Yeah, she knew Meredith—that was if Chloe's sister was the woman who had entered just a few days ago. Ruthie remembered her as the newcomer who'd been scolded by an instructor for whining during meditation practice. Ruthie had planned to stay for a second consecutive tour of duty. But after the first couple of days of the course now in progress, she said, the abbot asked her to leave. He had determined that she was at a critical stage in her practice, one that meant she had to go back out into the world for a while. Ruthie was returning just as soon as the time was right. She wanted to do three months, minimum. But the abbot told her that it would probably be a while before the time was right.

In the meantime, she'd elected herself Gorgi's lieutenant, the 4H Club's correctness monitor and chief of protocol, and Gorgi seemed to be tolerating it.

The Holistic Herbal Garden and Institute of Holographic Healing imposed fines for various infractions. Sleeping during meditation practice, for instance, cost the equivalent of a dollar and a half. Smoking set you back a hundred baht. Prue reckoned that was her single biggest expense, these days. "But no problem," she told Chloe. "My third husband left me some insurance money. I do okay." Taking any sort of intoxicants, including tobacco or alcohol, sleeping overnight in one of the conjugal "villas"—these things were forbidden. If you wanted more than two meals a day it cost extra, and all meals were vegetarian.

Gorgi had no trouble justifying his policy of penalizing disciplinary lapses: "They're budget travelers, no? *Atcha.*" He had wobbled at Chloe in the East Indian manner, almost as though shaking the head no, but meaning yes. His speech patterns also seemed Indian, from time to time. (Prue said he wasn't from India, but at the same time wasn't sure where he was really from.) "Then what is more important than money to them while they are on the road? Why do they walk half the day to get to a place that serves the cheapest hamburgers in Thailand if they are not being obsessed with money?

"So." Gorgi wound some wisps of beard around a forefinger and tugged. Chloe noted that he had black on his fingers, like ink. Or shoe-polish. "My system of little fines is designed to keep them mindful of their goal."

"It's for their own good," Ruthie elaborated.

She stood behind Gorgi during Chloe's interview, alternately massaging the Master's shoulders and dabbing at his face with a towel that she dipped in a silver bucket of ice water with creamy white flower buds floating on top. Chloe caught a faint scent of jasmine. A boxy air-conditioner stuck out of a hole in the wall at the far end of the room, wheezing and rattling and keeping things cooler, at least, than they were outside, which was hotter than the hubs of hell, or in the dorm, which had only a couple of tired old fans.

Gorgi's office was an eclectic mix of East and West, of secular and religious, of the sublime and the ridiculous. During Chloe's audience, he sat cross-legged on cushions atop a richly carved wooden dais in the center of the room. On the floor beside him, aside from the ice bucket, stood a spittoon and a high-legged table with a teapot, cups, and a toilet roll. An enormous desk finished in simulated mahogany and complete with swivel chair was parked against one wall.

On the desk sat a computer with a large screen. Prue had told Chloe that Gorgi liked to smoke dope and watch screensavers till he was pretty well as enlightened as he was ever going to get. Although how she knew that she refused to say.

Against the opposite wall, a Buddhist shrine ascended in stages from the floor. Red- and gold-painted wooden tables held a crowd of images of various sizes as well as offerings of flower garlands, joss-sticks, and candles. Bowls of water and plates of food sat on a mat in front. An intricately designed Tibetan *tanka*, a mandala, hung on the same wall. A big bronze Ganesh stood in one corner, next to a huge Chinese vase and a battered old putter. Another wall held framed diplomas.

Among other things, Gorgi's qualifications included a certificate attesting to his having completed a three-month retreat at an ashram in Kerala, India; a license issued in Bangkok to practice Tantric Soul Control; a diploma in traditional Thai massage from a school in Chiang Mai; and a certificate from Bombay permitting him to teach English as a Foreign Language.

There was also a big print of the Challenger space shuttle and a faded poster depicting penises from the animal kingdom and their relative sizes. (The whale dick was impressive.) Bookcases held everything from histories of Buddhism to meditation guides to something by Shirley MacLaine to vegetarian cookbooks to several volumes on the management of small businesses, two Tom Clancy novels, *The Joy of Sex*, and a tattered volume on the benefits of colonic irrigation.

There was more, most of it New Age in flavor, but Chloe's investigations were cut short by Gorgi, who had esconsced himself on his dais and accepted a cup of herbal tea from Ruthie. Chloe was invited to come forward and pour her own, an honor she declined.

"So, then. Good. You have made your way here to the Holistic Herbal Garden and Institute of Holographic Healing," Gorgi said. "Why?"

"I want to experience something different," suggested Chloe. "Beaches bore me. Also I'm looking for my sister. I believe she's staying at the temple down the road."

"*Atcha*. Good. If you stay with us, you will find something more valuable than your sister. You will find yourself. And you will experience something different. You'll learn to see experience for what it is. Every experience you have ever had or ever will have will be transformed." Gorgi stopped smiling, briefly, and tried to look profound, but only succeeded in appearing devious. He brandished a finger in warning: "You will change. Your world will change."

"Okay. I'm interested." And that was true, Chloe realized, with a sudden lift of excitement. It was so nice to be doing something *different*. And the compound outside was full of banana plants, palm trees, and arbors smothered with impossibly vivid bougainvillea. A papaya tree stood just outside the sala, like an anorexic palm, gigantic fruit growing straight from the skinny trunk. A gorgeous great tree with fern-like foliage and red flowers shaded the center of the yard. A jacaranda, an amethyst and green mist, somehow evoked coolness in Chloe, though it was hotter than summer could ever have been in Canada or Oregon. The previous night, palm fronds silhouetted against the full moon had really convinced her she was in the tropics.

"We are a real community, here," Gorgi said. "We understand what the whole person is, and we cater for the whole person and the whole group. This is a place of personal healing and development."

Holographic healing, as Gorgi explained, took a holistic approach to the reintegration of the person—mind, body, and spirit. "Do you know what a hologram is? Yes? Good. Well, the universe is a hologram. Every bit of the universe contains within it every other bit of the universe, and every action, no matter how small, no matter how apparently insignificant, affects every other action in the universe. When you know this—*know* this, you understand—nothing can ever be the same again. Good. You are a writer. Yes. But at the same time you are a book. While you are here, you must not write; you must learn to *read.*"

Unaccountably, to Chloe's mind, Gorgi chortled. Ruthie had got up to be behind him again, and she dabbed and dabbed, cooling him off. "You will learn to read the book that is your self. And you will come to read that book of which you are only an aspect, the book we call Existence itself. If you dedicate yourself to your practice, and if you are lucky, you may even glimpse what lies behind Existence. The Truth of Being."

In truth, all Chloe wanted was the savor of existence, at least for the time being. But what she said was, "Wow. And how much will all that cost me?"

"The bottom line, no?" Gorgi chortled and did the head-wobble. "*Atcha.* We are requiring only a modest donation. Only what you can afford." At that point they were interrupted by the ringing of Gorgi's cellphone. "Tomorrow we will talk more," he said by way of dismissal. "Remain mindful. Think of holograms."

The interview, although it lasted half an hour, had been only *pro forma*—more a means test than a serious inquiry into any spiritual motivation. He was especially interested in what she did for a living. "So you are writing for popular magazines? In America. You are not a newspaper writer?" From the moment he tumbled to the fact she wasn't a standard backpack traveler, her candidacy suddenly started to look like a sure bet.

Basically, she reckoned, this was a profit-oriented establishment and they would have admitted Jack the Ripper, if it had looked as though he might stick around and spend some money. It was odd, though; there didn't seem to be very many customers for such a lavishly appointed establishment.

"You don't suppose the 4H Club could be a front for a bookie joint?" Chloe had asked Prue, only joking.

"Nothing would surprise me around here. There's more to this place than meets the eye."

Chloe breathed in on the count of one . . . *rising* . . . letting her belly swell. She expelled the air slowly on the count of two . . . *falling* . . . trying to feel the air against her nasal membranes.

Rising. . . . Falling. . . . Rising. . . .

Feeling. . . .

She could feel an insect crawling on her arm. She focused on the sensations, just as Gorgi had instructed her to do. *Feeling. . . .*

Feeling irritation at that . . . that *irritating* man. *Thinking. . . .* This was probably the most interesting thing Waylon had done in years and she didn't even know what it was he was doing. Some holiday. God. Renew the relationship. Right. Less than a week into the trip and she'd mislaid her husband. Her sister was probably going to need deprogramming. You had to laugh. Chloe hadn't even gotten to meet any Thais, aside from a few touts, pimps, and hookers. Except for the sun and the coconut palms, she might have still been in Vancouver, sitting here with this bunch of New Age seekers after truth. Then, as if to make a liar of her, a big lizard scuttled up the papaya tree, distracting her from her meditation. Vancouver didn't have lizards, overlooking the lounge variety. Roy Schuter, for example.

Chloe had met most of the denizens of the 4H Club. The others were away at a full moon party on an island somewhere off the coast, not too far away. Tomorrow or the next day, Prue had told her, she'd probably get to meet them as well. Chloe was looking forward to it. In the meantime, aside from Gorgi, Ruthie, the Rev, and herself, there were just Prue and Al Dente. Prue hadn't gone to the beach party. "Most of these kids," she said, "they're from another world. They're so young, all covered with tattoos and rings and things, listening to shitty music. They make me depressed.

"It's not that bad," she then confided in Chloe. "It's really just the PMS. I feel like hell." Prue expelled twin streams of smoke through her nose. Then she went on, articulating little smoke puffs together with her words: "My God, you know. Basically it's all the same shit."

Now, in the meditation sala, Prue was parked across from Chloe, sitting in her own eccentric posture, left leg folded under and right leg stuck straight out in front, the sole of her foot pointed right at Gorgi and his chief fan. It was funny, but after just a couple of days Chloe felt that she'd known Prue for years. She knew, for example, why Prue limped and why she had to sit the way she did. It had happened one night many years ago. After a single introductory karate lesson, full of enthusiasm and maybe a drink or two, she had demonstrated a roundhouse kick to a boyfriend, managing to dislocate her knee and then fall, screaming in pain, off a balcony. "Only the second floor," Prue said. "But still." The leg had never worked right again.

The late afternoon sun slanted through palms and banana plants to dapple the floor of the sala. One luscious shaft of sunlight held Chloe transfixed. She judged by the angle of the sun that it must be about four o'clock, but she wasn't sure. The shadow of the papaya tree stretched all the way to Gorgi. This close to the equator, she'd discovered, nightfall was astonishingly abrupt. They weren't allowed to wear watches. Timepieces, along with weapons and mind-bending substances of any description, had to be checked at the gate. They had let her keep her notebooks and pens, although they'd tried to get her to check those as well.

But it had to be just about time to knock off. My God. They'd been up since four that morning. The klonging of the big bronze bell had been totally unnecessary, given the boisterous gang of cocks out in the yard, that strident chorus of insomniacal roosters who'd never heard they were supposed to wait till dawn before punching in.

Steady breathing, longer on the out-breath than on the in-breath. Attend to the tidal passage of air. Mindfulness. *Rising . . . falling . . . rising. . . .* Gorgi didn't believe in counting breaths. Some practitioners counted odd numbers on the inhalations and even numbers on the exhalations. Gorgi said that got in the way of No-mind, so he prescribed mindful attention to the physical sensations unmediated by such abstractions from experience as numbers. Or so Chloe understood him to say. It even made a certain sense. Before long, Gorgi told her, she wouldn't need even the rising-falling prop; it would fall away to leave her achieving a state that would bring her closer to a pure apprehension of being. Right.

Chloe was amazed that her sister had committed herself to a discipline as strict as that at Wat Nai Fun. She'd assumed Meredith had a stash of Xanax or something. But Prue told her the meditationists practically had to undergo a strip search, and there was nowhere in the dorms to hide anything. All your personal possessions were kept for you until you left. The Rev had news of her sister. In fact, he told Chloe, he might be falling in love with her. This was surprising news, under the circumstances. "I know you were both in the same place for days," Chloe said, "and I can see neither of you are the type to rush into things, but how did you manage to fall in love in a meditation temple that doesn't permit contact between the sexes?"

There had been no privacy, communal dorms segregated by sex, one change of light cotton shift and pantaloon—nowhere to hide anything. But no problem, as it turned out. The Rev had a tobacco habit and he had a connection at Wat Nai Fun. For a modest retainer, every day one of the groundskeepers would bring the Rev his pipe and tobacco at a pre-arranged time, and place them in a remote corner of the temple grounds. But the Rev reeked of tobacco and, finally, after repeated warnings, he was expelled from the monastery. This had been only a couple of days before Meredith arrived in town. He ran into her at a noodle shop and, upon learning of her plan, gave her two days of counseling. Meredith had admitted she was dependent on tranquillizers and antidepressants, and told the Rev she was terrified of the no-drugs rule. He kindly arranged to supply her through his contact, passing Xanax, Prozac, and little notes of encouragement every day. The plan was to cut her fix gradually back to half a milligram of Xanax per day; he said Meredith felt confident that soon she'd kick her habit altogether. The Rev agreed that he would pass messages from Chloe as well.

Chloe slipped away from thoughts of Meredith to thoughts of calming drugs and then back to her breathing exercises. Suddenly, she felt as though she were soaring. Benumbed legs aside, she was lifted with a joyous sense of freedom and anticipation. She was glad that Waylon had gone missing. She was sure he was okay. And Meredith was safely stashed away in a Buddhist monastery. What could happen to her there? Except that she might go nuts, and she was nuts anyway. Chloe tried attending to this welcome sense of joy. *Rising . . . falling. . . .* Hearing. Pup was barking again, but this time it was a whole chorus of yapping, joined in by Sweet Mama's deeper, more deferential bark. Hearing.

"Fuck the fuckin' fuck! Ow, *fuck*, man. *Ow.*"

Hearing. . . .

"I'll kill that son of a bitch," Ruthie remarked with an intensity and certainty that could only have come from months of self-reflection and insight into one's own innermost needs and desires.

The meditation session was over.

13 world processors

Much madness is divinest sense
To a discerning eye;
Much sense the starkest madness.

Emily Dickenson

"**O**w. *Shit*. Get away! Go on—*fuck off*, man."

Snarling and shaking his head, Pup had set his teeth into Freddie's leg-warmer. Freddie lifted his leg and kicked. Pup, a daschhundy sort of specimen, kept his jaws locked as his skinny little body snapped back and forth. There had probably been a wee bulldog in Sweet Mama's woodpile. Sweet Mama herself was flopping about just out of range, barking in her deferential yet insistent manner, to all appearances enjoying proceedings enormously.

"This is the universe, yeah? But it's only one universe among many, man. And this one is on its way out, okay?" Freddie was filling Chloe in on a few things. He was dressed in a tatty, skin-tight pink-and-yellow Lycra jumpsuit and one leg-warmer. "You can call me Fast Freddie, man. This Lycra shit, it cuts down the drag, you know?" A superhero out of bedlam, he also wore a shimmering cape of magnetic tape unwound from music cassettes. He wasn't wearing underwear, Chloe had to notice. Grinning rakishly, the sculptor reached down to rearrange his parts, remodeling them against the clinging Lycra.

Freddie was putting the finishing touches to the elaborate structure he referred to as an "organization." This construction emerged in strangely organic elements upon seven crooked brushwood legs, skinny ends set into Pepsi bottles. Incorporating bits of cardboard, packaging salvaged from the garbage, burnt-out fluorescent lighting tubes, bamboo, and deadfall coconuts, it crouched, bouncing gently on its spindly extremities, alive. Rough balls of wire hung like crazy Christmas tree ornaments. It was so high, at this point, that Freddie had to stand on a wooden bench to reach the apex of his creation, from which he was suspending a noose.

The late afternoon sun was casting long shadows and a fine golden light over the whole scene. Al Dente was catching a few late rays, stripped to the waist and doing a complicated calisthenics routine with an iron bar. He was wearing black Chinese pajama bottoms and aviator sunglasses, and studiously ignoring Chloe. Prue sat on a bench under the big tree in the center of the compound; she was doing leg-lifts while smoking a cigarette.

Ruthie was quick to note the transgression. "That'll cost you a hundred baht," she said, straightening her glasses.

"Cheap at the price." Prue shrugged and expelled a stream of smoke in Ruthie's direction.

Ruthie was practicing her walking meditation in the shade of the tree. Heel to toe—slowly, slowly, with great and obvious mindfulness—she performed her precise circumambulations with only a brief orbital eccentricity to evade Prue's smoke attack. So recently back from her karmic filling station, Wat Nai Fun, Ruthie moved as though brimming with some precious essence that might spill over and run away. She was fasting. She was almost finished a seven-day fast complete with two herbal colonic irrigations per day and, according to Freddie, she was still full of shit.

Prue had been telling Chloe about her own spiritual Odyssey. By now, she reckoned, she'd seen everything, done everything and, Chloe understood, mistrusted everything. "I've tried it all. My God. You name it—ESSEN, acid, Zen Buddhism. The works. Alpha Mind Control."

"It's all about control, man. Control. Yeah, I don't need that shit. I do my own thing, here." Freddie wanted them to know why he didn't join the communal meditation sessions. "It's control out there, man; it's control in here. It's control everywhere. But I know what I'm doing. *Ow, ow*, man. Shit!" Pup had latched on to Freddie's ankle again.

"Shut the fuck up, can't you?" Ruthie yelled, taking a recess from her quest for spiritual perfection.

Sweet Mama scampered away to disappear under the sala. Pup left off exercising Freddie and went over to Al Dente, trying to jump high enough to snatch his iron bar. Prue took a long pull on her cigarette, sucking the smoke down to her inner being. "Basically it's all the same schtick." But before she could expand on this insight, Freddie spat out the bit of drinking straw he'd been chewing on and said, "Give me a cigarette, man." Prue gave him a cigarette, lighting it and another for herself off the butt of the first one. "I thought you quit, Freddie."

"In a good cause, man. All in a good cause. Whatever pisses off the Screw, okay?" said Freddie, using his pet name for Ruthie. "Ah, shit." He threw the cigarette away after one puff.

Although he'd given up cigarettes, according to Prue he was prepared to ingest anything else in the world that might alter his consciousness. In fact, she claimed, his ganja intake alone was enough to set off sniffer dogs at a range of five hundred yards. In polite society, however, he had mainly taken to sucking on waxed paper straws cut up into thirds. Whenever he got agitated—any time he had anything to say—he'd take a couple of quick tokes off his straw and then, holding it between thumb and forefinger, flick at it with his ring finger, obsessively keeping the tip clean of ashes that weren't there. And now the Rev, a volcano, was lighting his pipe, his entire head lost in great billows of smoke, flashes of fire from within as he sucked at the lighter.

"You filthy son of a bitch," Ruthie said. "You stink of tobacco. No wonder they threw you out of the temple. If I had my way, we'd throw you out of here as well. You say you're an ordained minister? You're a selfish, suicidal son of a bitch. Do you never think how you're polluting the planet for the rest of us?"

"So don't breathe," replied the Rev, expelling a smokescreen that obscured his entire person. "Anyway, plants like carbon dioxide. It's good for them. I'm feeding the tree, okay?"

"You're all fined." Ruthie strode off towards Gorgi's quarters.

Prue slowly released a thick rope of tobacco smoke from her mouth, drawing it up through her nostrils—what Chloe's crowd called "frenching," back when they used to smoke in the girls' toilets at school. Then she sucked it back deep into her lungs and blew it out hard in the direction Ruthie had gone. "Poor woman," she said, without much sympathy.

"Fascist fuck," said Freddie. "The Screw strikes again. Goodie two-shoes fascist fuck." Shrugging her off, he turned back to his project. "The store down the road, man. They got no goddamned Coca Cola." Freddie was indignant. "Never have Coca Cola. Only this Pepsi shit." Freddie, Prue had already explained, used sticks shoved into Pepsi bottles for the base of his organizations. And he always put some gasoline in the bottom of each. There were no soft drinks of any kind at the 4H Club, so he had to go down the road to the noodle shop to get them. On the way back, he'd stop at the gas pump in front of the motorcycle shop and have a bottle or two filled with Unleaded Super. According to Prue, he generally smelled of Mekhong whiskey upon his return; and Chloe thought she could smell it on him today, although, what with the pervasive reek of gasoline, it was hard to tell. He had fused each Pepsi bottle with a twist of paper.

Freddie had a television tube, God knows where he'd found it, and he set about suspending it from the noose.

"Back in the sixties, you know, the CIA was getting everybody to do acid. They wanted us all to watch TV all the time. Instead, man, instead everybody was throwing the TVs out the windows. TVs and everything, you know? Now there's this band back in the States, the percussionist uses old TVs and videos and shit. Lead pipes for drumsticks, man."

Every time he said "man," Freddie's head ducked forward like a turkey's and his eyes rolled up so that, just for a moment, nothing showed but the whites. Maybe he was inspecting the inside of his head, just checking to see that everything was still okay on the psychical front.

"They got everybody sucking on the glass tit, man. You get these good, good alpha waves pumping along and everything is just fine, you know? This technological-instrumental shit, man. And brain waves."

Freddie moved the bench back and then stood back himself to get his creation in perspective.

"And fuckin' computers, man. Word processors. You know?" Fast Freddie proceeded to light the fuses with Prue's disposable plastic lighter. First, he lit a series of little containers of fuel that sat higher in the assembly. Then he circumnavigated the organization in a frantic attempt to light all the Pepsi bottles before he went up in smoke himself. He lit one, considered for a moment, and then dashed around to light another on the other side. And another. Then back the other way to do another. Though how it could make any difference which way he did it, given this Rube Goldberg model of chaos, Chloe could not see.

"Word processors. Yeah. No. I mean, *world* processors is what we've really got here. Virtual realities, man. That's all we ever had anyway, you know?—realities created by the Powers That Be, man. The status fuckin' quo. And you know who I'm talking about here. But the world processors, now, they're just another easy fix. Nice, safe little realities designed to take the pressure off, man. They don't want you looking for *real* alternatives, you know what I mean? The Pope, man. Fuckin' A. And Coca Cola. Big Oil. You *know* what I mean."

The Pepsi bottles were going off like a succession of fiery geysers, and the flames climbed quickly. The crowns of the coconut palms across the yard shimmered through the heat. A brushwood leg snapped, and the organization listed to one side, the TV tube swinging, its screen blackening in the smoke from some tar paper. One of the lighting tubes shattered, and then another. A second leg collapsed. The whole structure rotated through several degrees but, amazingly, settled again so the main structure remained upright. Freddie, meanwhile, capered around his creation chortling and muttering and making the dogs nervous. "Burn, baby. Burn. Oh, yes. Look at it burn. See that? The Pepsi Generation. Yeah."

The dogs had gone crazy, Sweet Mama back out from under cover, and they were dancing around with Freddie, snapping at his heels and his cape. "Will you *stop* with that goddammed stuff?" Ruthie also reappeared, dressed in a white robe that was too big for her. "*Jesus*. How's anybody supposed to concentrate around here with you burning everything down? You're polluting the whole place."

"*Pollution*? I'll give you pollution. Shit. Let's talk about spiritual pollution, man." Freddie's eyes rolled back in his skull far enough to catch sight of the lower brain stem. "Shit. You know what we got now? We got no more Gypsy caravans in Albania. You know that? *Did you know that*? Not since the mid-sixties. We got wine coolers. Hey. We got yuppie motherfuckers drinking mescal out of brandy snifters in Manhattan. Fuck that, man."

Ruthie started yelling at him again, saying that nobody could meditate with this kind of shit going on; why didn't he go on back to the guesthouse, or Denver, or wherever he came from? Couldn't he just get the hell out?

"Man, you know, you fuckin' ballbreaker. . . . You *screw*, man." Flicking away on his straw, Freddie lapsed into incoherent splutters, and his eyeballs rolled up in his head as though he were experiencing some sort of seizure. "Fuckin' bull dyke, man."

It wasn't a fair shot, Chloe reckoned. Fred's eyes rolled back on the "man," and Ruthie hit him while he was still inspecting the inside of his head. "You asshole," she yelled, and caught him full-swing with an open hand right across the face. "You fucking druggie *asshole.*"

None of this was really funny, but Prue got laughing so hard her cough started up, and she was laughing and choking and Chloe was pounding her on the back while the Rev was anxiously realigning his paraphernalia, which had already been arranged all around him where he sat on the sala. Sweet Mama was hiding under the platform again, but Pup had yet to learn fear and he was right up at ringside barking at anybody and everybody, probably taking them *all* for assholes. Freddie was so surprised and pissed off that he could have been speaking in tongues, for all Chloe could make of it, and he kept jabbing both forefingers in Ruthie's general direction as she stalked off towards the dorm.

"It's her time of month," Prue suggested. "And maybe she's been working out too hard on the spiritual front."

Freddie spat out the bit of drinking straw he'd held on to right through Ruthie's assault and said, "Give me a cigarette, man."

"No, Freddie," said Prue.

"Skinniness is next to godliness, yeah? That's right. And the more she can lose the curves, man, all the softness, the more she can be just like Daddy. Fucked-up role models, man."

The organization was collapsing. Soon there was nothing but a smoking, reeking pile of blackened members and ash, the remains of some giant extraterrestrial insect crashed to Earth. Chloe, Prue, Al Dente, and the Rev sat around under the tree coming down from all the excitement, entering a comfortable kind of funk that could maybe have been described as meditative, but really wasn't. Chloe jumped at a sudden loud bang from the smoldering debris. "No problem," said Prue. "That's just a coconut going off. Or it could be a bamboo section. It only happens when he gets a really good fire going, a really hot one." Another sharp explosion showered bright sparks everywhere, making Pup jump this time. They watched Freddie collect the ashes and bits of unburnt material and rake the sand clean.

"He always finishes that way," said Prue. "Hey. I had another airplane dream last night. This time the plane was crashing; but I didn't have anything to do with it, at least not consciously. It was just happening. So I tried the locked-in-the-toilet bit again. But this time I find the little barfer from the other day and his mother locked in there with me. Inner circle of hell."

"Plane crash, come soon, eh?"

"As it turned out, no. Maybe some people really can take control in their dreams, but I still have problems. About the time I recognized the full horror of my situation, the mother disappeared and the kid had changed into a big blonde jock in shorts and a tanktop. My God. It was great. He initiated me into the Mile-High Club, never mind we were supposed to be in the middle of a plane crash."

"Prue. This jock of yours—he didn't have a crewcut, did he?"

"Yeah! And his shirt had a big number eight on it. Like he was a runner, or something. He was sweet—reminded me of my first husband, only taller and with muscles. And I guess the dream therapy worked out anyway because I forgot the claustrophobia. Yeah. All I have to do, next time I get stuck in an elevator, is make sure I've got a giant stud with me. No problem."

Chloe told Prue about her Ken-doll dream gone wrong during that afternoon's meditation session, and Prue said she'd known from the outset they were karmic sisters.

Prue had a message for everybody, she said. Somebody had been into her stash of dope. "If you want some, just tell me, okay? I'll give it to you." At least she was pretty sure somebody had been taking her grass. "To tell the truth," she confided in Chloe, "maybe it was me. Last night we had a dope-smoking contest. Freddie, Al Dente, and me. My God. Everybody lost." Prue was trying a new abdominal exercise, one where she had to lie flat on her back, spread her legs, lock her hands behind her head, and rise part way up from the waist, twisting to one side and then the other, repeating these in sets of three a side before resting a moment. "My lower back just kills me, sometimes. It's this leg that does it. But Olga knows what to do. Wait till you meet her. She's amazing. She could be part of my retinue any day. God, if only I had a retinue."

Eventually, all the others wandered off to look after their chores. Chloe sat scratching Sweet Mama behind the ears and watching Pup torment Freddie. Sweet Mama cringed if you looked at her; she'd never outgrown some terror imprinted back in her days as a stray. She seemed especially afraid of Ruthie. For whatever reason, she was almost relaxed with Freddie. And she liked Chloe.

Chloe asked Freddie if he was okay. She reached to touch his cheek where it still flamed from Ruthie's roundhouse.

"Yeah. No problem. You want to fuck?" he asked, in a casual sort of way.

"*No*," Chloe replied.

"Oh. That's okay, you know. I was just asking, man. No problem." Freddie reached to rearrange his private parts and lifted one leg for a moment, like a dog about to pee. "I was just thinking, you know?"

To her surprise, Chloe was moved. "No, thanks, Freddie. I'm married. And things have already gotten too complicated around here. But thanks, okay?"

Freddie, an aging gamin, showed her a missing incisor in a big grin. "I got something for you," he said. "Some information, man." His eyes rolled up and his whole manner suggested he'd found something totally amazing way back inside there somewhere.

14 creatures of habit

No man is a hypocrite in his pleasures.

Samuel Johnson

After the burning of the organization, Freddie led Chloe out to a clearing in the woods about twenty minutes' walk from the 4H Club compound. "I got something to fuckin' show you, man," he told her.

They climbed a big tree, where the criss-crossing grip of a strangler fig offered a ladder to the first branches, and they perched there waiting. Chloe found a chewed-up third of a paper drinking straw stuck in the crotch of a branch. Freddie's spoor. Freddie whispered to her that they shouldn't talk, and they should wait till the shadow of the big dead tree stump reached the far edge of the clearing. At almost exactly that time, Chloe became aware of a rustle of leaves and snap of twigs from the direction they'd come earlier.

Then Ruthie appeared. She crossed to a rocky outcrop almost directly below their vantage point, and looked all around before removing a bit of deadfall. Reaching under an overhang, she produced a big tin cookie container and sat on a rock to open it. Before long she'd rolled a big spliff and lit up. She smoked half before pinching it out and returning it to a bag. Then she fished something else out of the tin.

"Fuckin' Twinkie, man," Freddie whispered. "She's got Twinkies."

It looked to Chloe more like some local cake. Whatever. Ruthie disposed of it in two bites.

It was dusk by the time Ruthie left. "Okay, man," Freddie told Chloe. "Let's go. The fuckin' ants are eating me. Ow! Shit. That's the mistake, man. Creatures of habit. That's how they get you. They're always watching; they can figure out every move you make." He sounded pleased with himself. Then, as though it were an afterthought: "Hey, you see over there, on the other side? That big dead tree?" It was already so dark Chloe couldn't see much of anything, but it was the same tree Freddie had used for a timepiece. "It's hollow, man. And that's where Prue and Bibi used to keep their stuff. Guess whose shit the Screw is smoking. Fuckin' A."

15 safety first

There are two kinds of adventurers: those who go truly hoping to find adventure and those who go secretly hoping they won't.

William Least Heat-Moon

"**A**ck!" said Jessica. And well she might have, because she'd just blown up like a pufferfish, arms akimbo, eyes goggling away right in character. Then she waddled in a circle, fins flapping, eyes wide with horror, going "ack, ack" and trying to figure out how existence had turned on her this time. Oscar, the bigger and dumber of Leary's two dive instructors, was reeling around and laughing so hard he almost fell over the side. Eddie, the other instructor, was also impressed with Jessica's performance. That was the first time he'd ever seen anybody panic while still on deck. Waylon finally grabbed her, making reassuring noises while Eddie pulled the exhaust cord on the flotation jacket and told her to hug herself to expel the air.

Wanting to deflate a bit before entering the water, she had yanked what she thought was the air release on her jacket. Instead, she popped the CO_2 cartridge—the one intended, in dire emergency, to deliver the diver express to the surface. "You've got to remember which cord is which," Eddie told Jessica. "If you'd done that under water, you'd have shot to the surface like a cork. A great way to get bent." Eddie decided not to replace the CO_2 cartridge.

"What a stupid design," Jessica said, glaring at Oscar as though he'd invented the device himself, just to piss her off.

"You okay?" Eddie asked her. "Okay to dive?"

"Of course I am," she replied. She breathed slowly and deeply till she was what would have to pass for calm. Then she and Waylon checked each other's gear, the way they'd been taught. They inflated their jackets just a little, and then, regulators in place and holding masks against faces, they performed a "giant stride" entry off the side.

On surface, a scuba diver looked like a pile of orbital debris crashed to earth. You staggered around in your fins like a drunken duck, strutted about like an alien captain of industry, hoses and gauges and straps flapping, the tank threatening to swing you off balance. Until you hit the water. Consigning yourself to the depths, you deflated your flotation jacket and sank or swam to whatever depth you wanted before squeezing a few squirts of air off your inflator hose to establish a nicely neutral buoyancy. Then you were free. Free to fly. To swoop, to hover. The first dive of the morning had started with a controlled descent down a buoyed line. Buoyancy control was one of the most important skills a new diver could acquire. And Eddie had reminded them before they went down that this was just another aspect of breathing control. Fill your lungs a bit more and you rose; breathe out a little and you descended. Get it just right and you hovered, weightless.

They did a quick review of flooding and clearing masks before going to the bottom and doing the remove-and-replace-mask drills. In the third of their open-water dives, they practiced taking their masks off at fifteen feet and then putting them back on under water. Then they did it with all of their gear, first at the surface, and then on the bottom. They'd already done this in the pool, but it was different in the sea. Oscar had been patient, working with Jessica from water shallow enough to stand in, gradually going deeper and deeper till she could ignore the fact that she had all that water over her head.

Underwater, Oscar assumed another persona. He dropped his rude rectilinearity in a world of round holes to gain new grace and balance as a creature of the sea. He perched on the line, mugging for them, then toppled backwards to hang from his legs for a while. Grabbing his fins in a crouch and rolling over to hover upside down, he peered at Jessica through her face-plate. She punched him.

Next they did a simple exercise in compass navigation before coming up for lunch on the tiny forward deck.

Their boat hadn't inspired confidence in Waylon, the first time he saw it, weathered timbers covered with untold layers of blistered and peeling paint revealed by time and the elements, so many bits of faded yellow and blue and red and orange and white, laminae of gaily painted days past, that it wasn't clear what the most recent colors were meant to be. But it was beautiful. The exfoliation had produced a scaly pastel quality like a butterfly's wing. The superstructure included a stacked flying bridge resembling a high-rise shantytown tenement. "That's because all the fish are disappearing," Leary told them. They're fishing the Gulf of Thailand right out. Darn it. So they build their bridges higher and higher so they can see farther and farther. One of these days, they'll build them up so high they'll fall over, but that won't matter because the fish stocks will be friggin' finished anyway."

Leary normally rented the same boat, which belonged to a wiry Thai fishermen friend of indeterminate age from the village of Samae San, about an hour's drive from Pattaya. Captain Ot's face was almost as seamed and weathered as the timbers of his hull, though not as colorful. His trousers and shirt were patched and faded to the point you didn't know what the original plan had been. He had a permanent list, as though he'd grown up on a steep hill, and he appeared to maintain his balance with the flask of whiskey he always held in his right hand, even when at the wheel. "Never mind, never mind," was his stock response to any remark or query in English directed his way. Leary told Waylon not to worry about the whiskey—Captain Ot made a great skipper, so long as he kept himself topped up. You'd never want him driving without the whiskey.

Lunch was fresh Thai-style squid salad, which Jessica wouldn't eat, tuna salad sandwiches, and lemonade. "Waylon," she told him. "I'm going inside for a nap. I'll see you later, okay?"

Soon everybody was looking for a place to crash. The boat's minuscule decks were already covered with people and gear, so Waylon climbed up on top of the wheelhouse by the radio antennae, looking for a place to lie down and relax and think about things. He hoisted himself up on top to find Jessica there already, sitting with her back to him.

"George," she was saying. "Listen to me. Everything's going fine. No, no. No problem. . . . What? For God's sake, Terdsak isn't going to do anything now. Don't worry about it."

Waylon coughed and scrabbled on the ladder as though he'd just arrived. "Jessie," he said.

She ran her phone antennae down and turned.

"Hi," said Waylon. "Who were you talking to?"

"When?"

"On the phone just now."

"Oh, on my *mobile*. Yeah. I thought I might get better reception up here. I was talking to my bank. Up in Bangkok."

"Who's George?"

"My banker."

Waylon didn't ask what a bank would be doing talking to her on a public holiday. Earlier, Leary had been telling Waylon about how many public holidays there were in Thailand. Every time a government feared their popularity was sagging, he said, they doled out surplus rice to the poor and declared another national holiday. Leary had needed to check on a transfer to Singapore. "Nance is just about finished her business down there, I reckon. She'll be on her way back up here to Pattaya before long."

They went back down on deck to find Oscar and Eddie swapping stories of professional conquests. Something about Japanese office girls who came on five-day tours where they had to dive, sail, shop, and make it with a foreign lover, all of it on rails because they had to get back to work.

"You don't make a lot of money," Eddie said, "but the fringe benefits are great."

"That's right." Oscar leered at Jessica. "How many jobs do you get where you meet the public and they're, like, almost naked? Mostly young, in good shape. Dressed in bikinis and everything? Oh, yeah."

"I don't believe this." Jessica shot a look at Waylon, who was probably smiling too much. "You've got to be kidding. People's *lives* depend on your doing a professional job. And to you it's nothing but a candy store full of free pussy."

Oscar, who knew no fear, was grinning and nodding enthusiastically.

"No, no," Eddie said. "It's a teacher-student relationship, like a psychiatrist-patient type of thing. You're right. They really depend on you."

"Yeah. We call it 'clubbing baby seals.'" Oscar wanted Jessica to understand. "It's like, the first time they put their head underwater you get these big doe eyes looking out at you from the mask; and there you are. *Bonk*. Clubbed another baby seal, great big trusting eyes and all. Bonkety-bonk-bonk."

"You're an asshole," Jessica said. "You're all assholes." Waylon could see he was included in this to-his-mind-unfair generalization.

"Snake!" shouted Oscar, dropping a clapped-out regulator hose on Jessica's shoulder.

"*Asshole*." She restated the assessment with some force.

Now they were going to be diving again, and Waylon was looking forward to it in a way he hadn't looked forward to things for a long time. He practiced his breathing control even though he

Safety First

wasn't underwater, sucking in big lungfuls of air and then slowly blowing them out all the way till he was empty. It felt good. Glancing over at Jessica, he saw her slip something into her mouth under cover of pretending to cough. She made a face at him. Waylon then watched as she slammed a vodka chaser. "Whatever it takes, Waylon," she told him, returning the flask to her bag, a large leather item with straps that meant business. Where she went, she'd early explained, The Bag went.

That morning they had practiced recovering their regulators and clearing them. During the break, Oscar talked about how to clear puke, should you decide you had to toss breakfast in the middle of a dive. He described in some detail what it was like to have bits of breakfast stuck in the regulator mouthpiece. "Here's another rule of safe and pleasant diving," Eddie added. "Never eat diced carrots before entering the water; they clog up the mouthpiece." Anyway, should you ever feel the need, Oscar continued, which to tell the truth he himself did that very morning—it was probably some bad tequila the night before—then relax, go ahead and do it. Just hold the regulator just off to one side of your mouth and press the purge valve as you blow. In between times, you can snatch a bit of air. But don't ever dive in the condition he was in. "Remember: drinking and diving don't mix. Ditto for drugs."

"Yeah," said Eddie, mouthing a big smoke ring and then blowing a smaller one right through it. "And don't smoke."

Back in the water, they practiced flooding and clearing masks again. Jessica was still having problems, but she managed it, with Eddie right there staring into her mask and holding her. Then they breathed from each other's octopuses—their spare regulator mouthpieces. They went down to sixty feet, the maximum safe depth during the course; and, on their last dive of the day, they did a straight out and straight back compass navigation.

At the end of it all, they took an underwater pleasure cruise.

They'd been diving on shallow marine deserts, well suited to diving instruction, but boring. Waylon was anxious to see some real tropical reefs. So far they'd encountered little more than sand, some chunks of dead coral, sea urchins with long black spines, and the occasional fish. "Don't you worry," Oscar told them during a break. "Soon we're going to see lots of fish, and coral too. Maybe some *sharks*." As though that were a special treat. Anyway, it wasn't the prospect of sharks that was Jessica's problem. That afternoon they had encountered sea cucumbers. These were about the liveliest things they'd found, and all they did was loll around. Fat black giant worms with warts, was how Jessica described them. And Jessica had a phobia when it came to worms. So when Oscar picked one up and thrust it towards her, she wasn't impressed. As Oscar explained after they had returned to surface, these animals weren't really dangerous. But you should wear gloves if you picked one up. "Or you could get a rash. See?" Oscar's gloves had holes in them, and there was a rash on two of his fingers. "Itches like hell," he told them, and Jessica said she was glad. "If you touch one," Oscar added, "don't rub your eyes afterward, okay?"

"Okay," Jessica told him, furthermore suggesting that he must be even dumber than he looked if he thought she was going to go around cuddling sea cucumbers.

The best thing that had happened that day was the mass spawning of the sea cucumbers they'd witnessed on the second dive of the afternoon. They noticed one of the fat worms rearing up and expelling clouds of what looked like cum. And that's what it turned out to be. Before long they realized that several more sea cucumbers in the vicinity were similarly rampant. Jessica, once out of phobia range, was intrigued. Back on the boat, she wanted to know what had inspired this submarine circle jerk. Oscar said it was the sight of Jessica in her new bikini. But Eddie thought it must be the moon. On Australia's Great Barrier Reef, the full moon triggered mass orgies where you got dozens of species of corals for hundreds of miles up and down the reef all spawning at the same time, although Eddie seemed to recall it usually happened four days before the actual full moon.

Maybe it was the full moon that had sent him spinning off on this series of bizarre interludes, Waylon thought, when all he was supposed to be doing was having a vacation. And what was the moon doing to Chloe, meanwhile? Her recklessness had attracted Waylon, especially at the beginning. Over the years, however, he'd found himself becoming more staid, moving in reaction towards the uptight pole of existence. There had been a couple of times—at parties, after she'd been drinking—when he'd sensed something was amiss, seriously amiss, but he'd chosen not to think about these things too much. Anyway, he couldn't believe she was interested in a dork like Roy Schuter.

They were going to finish the basic open water course the next day. Among other things, they were going to practice buddy breathing.

On the last dive of the last day they saw a jellyfish, big as a dinner plate and magnified by the twenty-five percent factor to the size of a platter. Waylon was mesmerized by the creature, its lacy bell slowly pulsing, yard-long tentacles trailing as it made its mysterious way through the sea like a silvery starship in miniature.

This one was probably harmless. In fact, as he and Jessica had been taught, there was nothing really dangerous to divers in these waters—not so long as you took the trouble to learn something about the natural history of the local marine life and took a few basic precautions. The most basic of these: Don't touch anything with which you are not familiar and which you don't know to be harmless; and don't stick hands or other parts of your anatomy into unexamined holes or crevices.

Waylon had already fucked up on both these counts with the most dangerous creature he had so far encountered underwater.

Waylon's dive buddy at that moment seemed to have Oscar in some kind of death grip. It was buddy breathing time. Even before the pool practice, a couple of days before, Oscar had promoted this prospect as something only slightly less exciting than one's first experience with sex.

"Buddy breathing," he had said, licking his lips. "*Buddy* breathing."

Yawn

Chances were, Oscar was finding things pretty exciting right then, given the fact Jessica was doing her best to drown him.

"Remember," Eddie had said, "don't bogarde the regulator. The donor takes two big hits off it and then passes it to the buddy. Then you alternate breaths till you reach surface. But the donor never lets go of either the regulator or your buddy. In a real emergency, this is an encounter of the closest kind."

"True togetherness," Oscar had added.

Eddie, in the meantime, was giving Waylon the thumbs-up, asking for an affirmative response. Waylon left his tank and flotation jacket on the bottom and went to surface sharing Eddie's regulator.

They'd successfully done the drills where they took turns breathing off each other's octopus during an ascent from thirty feet. But even in the pool practice Jessica didn't want to relinquish the regulator, once she had her hands on it. Here in thirty feet of water, she was less keen still. It was okay as long as they both had their tanks on and their extra regulators right at hand. Waylon and Jessica, paired with Eddie and Oscar respectively, managed this successfully; and then they did it together. The trouble came when they told Jessica to drop her gear on the bottom and then share Waylon's primary regulator. Waylon barely had time to get his initial two breaths in before she'd grabbed his regulator and refused to give it back.

Waylon looked at Jessica through her mask. She didn't seem panicked, exactly. But her features were set like stone and her grip on the mouthpiece was like steel. All she meant to tell him was, "This is mine, all mine, and you're not going to have it. Period." It was simple, really. Of course, all Waylon had to do was reach down for his octopus, but he wanted to do this right. He wasn't worried, he was pleased to note. For one thing, there was the octopus, and Oscar was somewhere right at hand. And it wasn't far to surface. He'd been well primed for the controled ascent, where you went all the way to surface on a single lungful of air, not holding your breath, not deliberately expelling air, but simply keeping your mouth open, allowing the pressurized air to escape gradually. So he went all the way on the last breath from his own regulator. So much for buddy breathing.

Back at his bungalow that night, after they'd finished their homework and their showers, and Jessica had had her vodka and pills and donned her Walkman, she told Waylon to lie down and relax. She was sorry she'd failed to give up the regulator. "I panicked," she said softly. "Let me make it up to you, Waylon." She told him she wanted to do something special for him. She worked his shorts down and off over his feet. Then she aroused him with her hand between his legs and her lips on his nipples, ever so gentle and then biting, tiny nips, first one and then the other, alternating the biting and the licking. "Do you like that?" she asked, pulling the headphones away from one ear so she could hear his response.

"Yes," he replied. "Don't stop."

Jessica swapped mouth and fingers and Waylon also liked that. After a while she said, "Fuck me," and he did, and Waylon thought it was the best it had been with her. She told him she had come, but she sounded kind of matter-of-fact about it. Jessica had another vodka and then, about the time he was nodding off, she said, "Waylon. Will you do something special for me?"

Vague alarms sounding in his mind, Waylon asked, "What's that, Jessie?"

By way of an answer, she put her glass on the night table and began nuzzling in intimate places till Waylon wasn't too sleepy anymore. "I want you to help me, Waylon." She rolled over and then back again with a plastic bag she'd picked up from beside the bed. "Make love to me," she said. After a while, as she started making the noises that signaled her coming, she reached back and pulled the bag over her head, gathering it under her chin. FOODLAND, the bag said, and there was some Thai writing on it as well. It was opaque, so Waylon couldn't see her face, and he felt a surge of lust at the sudden anonymity. Then Jessica tore the bag away from her head, gasping, eyes wide and frightened, although it had been only a few seconds. *"Don't stop,"* she told him. *"Don't stop."* Her breathing gentled, grew deeper and more regular, and then quickened again as she gathered the storm in her loins once more. She pulled the bag over her head again, holding it tight. Waylon rose back on outstretched arms to watch, saw the plastic where it gathered at her mouth as she sucked in, trying to get air. She held out for six or seven seconds this time, and recovered more quickly. Then she pushed Waylon off so she could turn over and offer herself on hands and knees. "This time you do it, Waylon. When I tell you. And hold the bag longer. I want to come with the bag on my head."

Some time later she said, "Now, Waylon," and arched her head back for the bag, which he pulled tight. He came as she began thrashing back and forth and clawing at the plastic that muffled her groans and, finally, her screams.

"Shit, Waylon. I've broken a nail." As though it were his fault. And, a while later: "You know the way I feel when I have that bag over my head?"

Waylon didn't.

"It's like when I'm underwater. But I trust you. My trusty dive buddy."

And this was his dive buddy. Jesus Christ. Waylon sat on the side of the bed with his leg jumping till Jessica told him to knock it off and go to sleep. "We've got our final tests tomorrow."

She said she was going out on the porch for a minute to get a breath of air. When Waylon went out to join her, he found her putting her cellphone back in her bag. The Bag. "I'm going to bed now, Waylon. You stay up if you want to." When he asked, she told him she'd been talking to her brother in New Haven. No, she said, his name wasn't George. Her gray eyes went steely and the freckles gathered tighter 'round her nose.

"Don't worry," she told Waylon later, just before he slipped away into sleep. "I'll be there when you need me."

16 hot licks

In skating over thin ice, our safety is in our speed.

Ralph Waldo Emerson

"Hey, you!" The shrill refrain assaulted Waylon from out front of Hot Licks. "Hey, you!"

The Hummingbird was a tiny, fine-boned creature, strung tight and, as Oscar put it, built for speed. Her features were at once hard-edged and doll-like. "Hey, you!" she called. Hey, you!" Her eyes were unfocused—there was no one in sight, aside from Waylon. Then the Hummingbird recognized him and did focus, more or less: "Hey, you! Wail-On! Where Jes-*see*?"

Waylon had dubbed her "The Hummingbird," and that was before he learned that her Thai nickname was Nok, which meant "bird." Nok hovered outside the Hot Licks Beer Bar, right next to the Down Down Diving Center. Even all the long afternoon and early evening before happy hour, while the other girls lounged around inside in various attitudes of boredom and lethargy, the Hummingbird flew, eager and shrill. While her colleagues painted toenails and watched TV game shows, she hustled: "Hello! Welcome inside, please." She did this even when there was no one out there, at least no one that Waylon could see.

"Hey, you! Welcome inside." The Hummingbird was staring somewhere out beyond, vibrating, jumping in time to an inner riff all her own. Inside, happy hour was now in full swing, with three customers counting Leary. Everybody congratulated Waylon on his new status as a qualified Open Water Diver.

Merle Haggard was lamenting lost love on the CD player, and Boom was behind the bar watching silent TV. Big Toy was doing something with an accounts ledger. Dinky Toy, Big Toy's partner, chief lieutenant, and oldest friend, sat at the far end of the bar, bad side to the wall. Her reluctance to look full on at anyone might have passed for demureness, the scar tissue out of sight but still there in her attitude. You could see from her good side that she had once been pretty. She looked great in short skirts and she was sweet.

Leary was sitting at the end of the bar closest to the door. "Fosdick," he called. "Darn it. Come on over here and have a drink. I hear tell you're just about ready to show Cousteau a thing or two."

Leary had dubbed him Fosdick—"Fearless Friggin' Fosdick," rarely missing a chance to add alliterative spice to an observation. His name was Waylon, Waylon had replied. "What's a name?" said Leary. "Your mama called you Waylon, I don't know why. But I'm gonna call you Fosdick. 'Fearless Friggin' Fosdick' is just too darned long. Gosh."

According to Eddie, Leary hadn't always been so moderate in tone. Anything but, and what could you expect from a man who'd spent his life working on offshore oil rigs, aside from a spell as a civilian contractor to the American military on the Mekong River? But he'd lived with a Singaporean Chinese woman for years, had even married her. And Nancy had removed some of the rough edges. So now "gosh" was salt and "darn" was pepper. "Friggin'" was reserved for special emphasis, and completed the range of linguistic condiments. And Waylon was Fearless Friggin' Fosdick because Leary, for one thing, was impressed with anybody who had the nerve to dive with Jessica. "Anybody who can not only run with the gosh-darned Gang of Four but dive with Jessie here as well, they got my respect." Waylon hadn't even told him about the vodka and Valium.

"Fosdick, do hangovers make you horny? Gosh. They make me horny. Boom! I'm *horny.*"

"Only sicko cock, *tilac*. Too early." Boom was the barmaid.

"'Only six o'clock, darlin'.' That's the trouble with these Thai ladies, Fosdick. They're too darned conventional. Don't get me wrong, now. It's nice they're so polite and all. But sometimes it gets downright boring. They're too well adjusted. I said it long ago and I'll say it again: what you need is somebody—some Frankenstein, maybe—who can drop a friggin' Western brain into one of these here Thai chassis. The thing is, we need our women to be just a little neurotic, you know what I mean? Not too much, mind. Just enough to keep things interesting."

Keeow, the newest girl on the staff, was keeping things interesting for a third of the crowd, at least—a U.S. naval rating on shore leave—even without any help from Dr. Frankenstein. She was quite flushed with her social success and, who knows, maybe some Mekhong whiskey in her cola as well, although generally Big Toy didn't like the girls drinking. It was okay for Big Toy to have a shot of tequila now and then, mind you, since she had this kind of nervous condition. Anyway, she was the boss. And of course Dinky Toy had every right to drink any time she wanted.

Waylon watched Dinky Toy examine herself in the mirror behind the bar. She looked at her face in half-profile for a time, turning the unburned side this way and that, as though trying to decide which angle to display in future. The left side of her face was all shiny and puckered. Her mouth was permanently hooked in an ironic smirk, and the eye, barren of lashes, was half closed. The fingers of her left hand were talons. Dinky Toy always sat at the far end of the bar, close to the wall, unless a customer had already taken the stool. If someone was sitting there, she'd generally stand behind him and massage his neck and back, maybe whisper sweet nothings over his left shoulder.

Once, Leary had told Waylon, when Dinky Toy was still working at Boon Doc's, up in Bangkok, they'd had a party to celebrate her upcoming marriage to a toolpusher from Australia. They even decorated the joint with streamers and balloons. The balloons, it turned out, were filled with hydrogen because when Dinky Toy, full of high spirits and tequila shooters, popped one of them with a cigarette, it exploded, setting off several more and leaving third-degree burns on her face and one hand. Her hair grew back, most of it, but her fiancé faded away long before the physical pain of her burns had gone. The new-model Dinky Toy probably offended his aesthetic sensibilities.

"Now, Jessie—there's a woman who ain't gonna bore you. Though she might kill you in some other way." Leary's laugh brought the Hummingbird to the door claiming it was scaring customers away. "You making it with her, Fosdick?"

"Leary, I've got a problem."

"We've all got our problems, Fosdick." Leary was rubbing a whiskey glass back and forth across his forehead. Then he banged it down on the bar. "Boom!" he hollered. "Bring me a friggin' towel and a bucket of ice. Gosh. I been out this way for going on twenty years and I still can't get used to the darned heat. But you sit down, my boy, and tell us all about it."

"Leary, I came out here for a holiday. My wife and I were going to straighten out a few things. Get our lives back on track, eh? But suddenly everything started to go haywire." Waylon turned away from Leary to chew at his lip. "It's crazy. I feel like I've skated way out on to black ice. You know what I mean? You look down and you can see right through to the deep water underneath. You're afraid to go any farther, at the same time you're afraid to go back."

"Steady there, Fosdick. Where's all this darned thin ice? You're in a tropical seaside resort, you got a girlfriend, you're gonna take a nice dive ticket away as a souvenir. Gosh, you already got a suntan fit to turn all the folks back home green. I seen lots worse thin ice than that. Only meta-friggin'-phorically speaking, of course. Got no frozen lakes where I come from."

"I've got a home and a business back in Vancouver. I've got a wife, Leary. I had one, anyway. I don't even know where she is. Jesus Christ. I'm an insurance man. My job is securing people against risk. I'm the one who's supposed to know the dangers. Jesus Christ, eh? All I did was yawn. Next thing I know, I've slept with my sister-in-law. First day of a tropical holiday with my wife and I bonk her sister."

"Gosh-darn it, you never told me that."

"She may be a mental case, right on the edge of collapse. And she's going to take me with her."

"Boom. You bring this boy a beer. Darn it, give him a tequila shooter on the side. Put it on my bill. Gosh. Pour yourself a co-la while you're at it. And I'll have another whiskey and a fresh bucket of ice."

"I don't know what Chloe—that's my wife—I don't know what she's going to do. I've slept with two, maybe three bargirls. I got so drunk I woke up in Bangkok thinking it was Pattaya. I didn't even remember the motorcycle race till Oo reminded me. Unbelievable. There I was, *betting* on them. Brains all over the road. Now I'm diving with Jessie. Jesus Christ, Leary. And she wants me to do the advanced open water course with her."

"That's frig-all, Fosdick. Anyhow, you don't have to do it."

"Maybe. But I feel like I do have to. What's the matter with me? Eh?"

"Gosh. If you feel like you gotta do it, then do it. Darn it, my boy. You're Fearless Friggin' Fosdick."

Boom brought the fresh drinks, and Leary settled back to instruct Waylon on this business of getting along in life. "Go on and calculate all the terrible things that can happen. Before long you won't go outside in case you get hit by a car. And next thing you know the roof falls on your head. That's right. You listen to me. Life is just this beer in front of you. And maybe the next one. Life is this darned night, here, and that darned barmaid who better stop smiling at me like that. You hear me, Boom? What was I saying? Darn it. It's all well and good to have your life insurance policies and your savings accounts. But mind this: that money is banked up for other times and other people. You're not the same darned person now, not necessarily, that you're going to be in ten years' time. You might not be here at all, Heaven friggin' forbid and all. But still. You see that ant?" Leary had seen Waylon watching an ant carry a bit of potato chip along the edge of the bar. "That ant has got it all figured out. Gotta get this food stored up. . . ."

At that moment, her hand no doubt directed by some design in the cosmic scheme of things, Boom reached over to eliminate ant and chip with a swipe of her damp rag.

"See there?" said Leary. "There's no such thing as security. Gosh. You figure it. People give up on Santa Claus early in life. Most of us, though, we're still looking for security when we're lying there on our death beds. But it's a myth. A superstition. There's no such thing, Fosdick; that's pure and simple fact."

Right on cue, Jessica showed up. She sat at the bar a couple of stools down, next to Dinky Toy, and rummaged in her bag. With the insouciant air of a master conjurer, she proceeded to build a pile on the bar, beginning with a key chained to a wooden board— the key to her bungalow, although why she carried it with her Waylon didn't know, since she'd slept in his bed every night since the course began. Next appeared a gray and black silk scarf, a black bathing suit bottom, a plastic dive wheel for calculating bottom times, a little plastic drugstore bag, a couple of hairy red-green rambutans, which she looked at with surprise and some distaste, and a cassette music tape—a collection of sacred music from around the world. "Dinky Toy," she said. "Can we play this tape for a change?"

"Hey, Jessica," Oscar called from the table where he sat with Nok and Keeow. "You got any rabbits in there? I need a rabbit." Waylon wouldn't have been that surprised to see Jessica produce a rabbit, but she only told Oscar to fuck off.

"Yeah, and can you turn that gosh-darned music down? A man can't hear himself think around here." Leary explained to Waylon the Thai love of loud music and its equation with good times. "The invention of the electronic amplifier and the giant speaker was a blessing straight from the friggin' gods. Next thing you knew all the gosh-darned disc jockeys in the country started going deaf. Darn it. So they had to keep turning the music up so they could hear it, and pretty soon everybody else started going deaf too. So now the record-player companies, they got to keep coming up with more powerful systems or nobody's going to know whether they're having a good time or not. Before long, the whole country'll be stone deaf and nobody'll ever have a party again."

Leary hadn't finished with the theme of security. "You take a look at these ladies here, now, Fosdick." Jessica had by now removed an assortment of pharmaceuticals from her bag. She and the Hummingbird, who'd come in to take a break from her touting, were rooting through them, maybe looking for the ultimate fix. "Here you got Nok. Her mummy and daddy sold her to a brothel in Roi Et. They saw a chance to buy a TV set, and that's something that don't come along every day. Gosh. There was nothing for her to do in her village, anyway. Not even plant rice. There was no work, what with the drought, and all the young men had gone to Bangkok to drive *tuk-tuks*. And her folks couldn't afford to friggin' feed her; there wasn't any food.

"Since then, Nok's gone freelance. She came down here to live by the sea and all. And she's been in love more times than you might believe. And now she's with Oscar. You talk about security. But what's the difference between her and Jessie, here? Jessie's got her good looks, her education, money to travel. But she's just as hot to dope herself up as Nok is. She's just as scared of what's going to happen next."

Whatever it was they had in common, Jessica and the Hummingbird were getting along so well Oscar looked jealous. The next thing, Waylon reckoned, they'd be swapping uppers and downers and talking about taking an apartment together. Meanwhile, Jessica's music was droning away making everybody else uncomfortable, maybe giving them the idea they were drinking in a temple instead of a bar, no matter how things looked otherwise.

"Do you think Nok *enjoys* being with you?" Waylon overheard Jessica ask Oscar this in the same kind of tones she might have asked him if he thought somebody enjoyed being trapped in an elevator with a skunk.

"Yeah." Oscar was indignant. "Sure she does."

"No, she doesn't." Jessica set him straight while the Hummingbird hummed and vibrated and stared off somewhere else. "Right now she's strung out on speed, just so she can keep on keeping on. And tonight she'll do sleeping pills so she can forget it all and go to sleep."

For the Hummingbird, drugs were an occupational thing, something she needed to keep on going, and Captagon and Rohypnol were her main uppers and downers. Jessica, on the other hand, used drugs to engineer life writ large.

But Oscar didn't know about that, and all he said was, "Nok likes me." Then he gave Jessica a big grin and added, "She's a woman, isn't she?"

A few customers had come in, and Nok, who paid no attention to the whole exchange, had to go tend to her social obligations. Big Toy slipped the Merle Haggard CD back into the player and the room loosened up again.

The Chinese-looking fellow with the pencil mustache and the unpleasant manner was back. My Bottle, as they had dubbed him, was sitting by himself in the far corner and nursing a whiskey Coke, probably still "waiting for his friend." The evening before, Jessica had asked, "Leary, that guy over there, the one in the corner, the Chinese-looking guy. Do you know who he is?"

"Nope. Though now that you mention it, I have seen him around, this past week or two."

"There's something funny about him. He's just sitting there with that glass in front of him, all alone, not talking to any of the girls. Only drinking a drink or two. And smoking those fucking cigars."

"Gosh. I guess Big Toy won't like that either. The guy sounds like a friggin' liability. You go over there, Jessie, and you tell him he's gotta stand, if he ain't gonna drink more than a darned drink or two. We have to keep the tables for our big drinkers. Yessir. You go ahead and tell him that."

"Well, I don't like it." So Jessica asked Big Toy about the guy, and Big Toy asked Boom, who said Nok had talked to him the other day, and he said he was waiting for a friend. But Big Toy could relax because he'd bought a whole bottle of Black Label whiskey for himself and had them stash it behind the bar. When Jessica asked Boom to check the sticker on the bottle and tell her what it said, Boom told her "My Bottle." That's what he'd told her to write on it. And there was still way more than half the bottle left, never mind it had been behind the bar for a week now.

So they decided to call the guy My Bottle, and Waylon got talking to Boom about the Internet, while Leary went back to check the toilet because Eddie was complaining that the flush wasn't working again. Jessie told Waylon she had to go out to the drugstore for a minute, and he saw that My Bottle was watching Jessica as she went out, blowing a stream of cigar smoke after her in a reflective kind of way.

Waylon wouldn't have thought any more about it—Jessica did have a nice way of walking—but, a minute later, he happened to notice My Bottle get up and stroll over to the window, elaborately casual, and look out before returning to his table. On his way to the toilet, Waylon also looked out through the hole in the frosted glass front window and saw Jessica standing down the street a bit, just inside the alleyway between the Russian restaurant and the Sikh tailor. She had her cellphone up to her ear and she was engaged in animated conversation. At one point, she slapped the flat of her hand against the shop wall and then turned deeper into the alley, huddled over the phone.

When Waylon came out again, My Bottle was gone. Another guy was sitting there with a beer and he was already in trouble.

He had bought Dinky Toy a drink and was getting obnoxious because she told him she didn't want to go away with him. Leary was over there standing beside their table being affable and formidable all at the same time. "You see, this lady here don't have to do nothing she don't want to. Darn it, boy. She's a person just like you and me."

"Who are you calling 'boy,' *old*-timer?"

"So, gosh. It's the same thing. How you going to feel if I tell you you're not wanted in this bar, never mind you figure you want to stay?"

The guy was almost drunk enough to argue the point. At the same time, he was sufficiently sober to look at Leary's eyes and his hands and general deportment, and to revise his earlier assessment of the situation. "I was only kidding with her," he said.

"Well, that's okay then. Why don't you finish up your darned drink, my boy? Let's all enjoy ourselves, you hear me now?"

Leary joined Waylon at the bar. "Some guys," he said. "They want to have a good time, but they just got no gosh-darned idea how to go about it. Where's Jessie?"

"She's outside making a phone call."

At that moment Jessica came back in.

"Who were you talking to, Jessie?" Waylon asked.

"Nobody, Waylon. I just went for a walk. Down to the drugstore."

"Didn't you make a phone call?"

"No. . . . Oh, you mean on my *mobile*. Yeah. I was talking to a friend. Waylon. Look at that."

"What?"

Keeow's sailor had gone. Now a new guy, a roundish individual of some thirty years, was sitting with her. He wore an electric acid DayGlo sports shirt, Bermuda shorts, and a pathetically earnest expression. He was doing something weird with both hands right up in Keeow's face. Fingers like tentacles, the mating ritual of two epileptic sea anemones, moved in a dance so fast and complex there seemed to be more than ten of them.

"You wouldn't want to wake up in that shirt the morning after a night out," said Oscar. "Scare the shit out of you."

"I'll bet you he's an English teacher," Eddie told them. Actually, he yelled it right in their ears. The music had gotten so loud again you almost had to use sign language. "I used to teach English for a while, up in Bangkok, and what he's doing is finger correction. You see there? Each finger is a word. Now he's shaking his ring finger with his other hand, yeah? And now he's twisting it around to where it could pass as a forefinger? That's finger correction. She's getting the order of her words wrong."

Maybe. But the guy's fingers writhed and waggled about even when he was the only one talking. He'd probably been hanging around with second-language users so long he had to remind himself how to put a sentence together. Keeow's eyes, never mind a double helping of Captagon, were glazed over, mesmerized by lust-crazed anemones.

"How can you do it, Waylon?"

"Do what, Jessie?" It was exhausting, trying to carry on a conversation under the circumstances. "Do *what?*"

"You men, sleeping with these girls and you can't even talk to them. This guy with all the fingers, for example. What kind of relationship do you have if you can't even *communicate?*"

"I don't know, Jessie. Jesus Christ, eh? *I can't hear you.*"

Communication. What a laugh. Waylon had to wonder if men and women ever really communicated, no matter what language they did or didn't have in common. What did he know about Jessica, when it came down to it? What did she really know about him? What did anybody know about anybody else, come to that; and where the hell had Chloe gotten to? Waylon had checked their answering machine in Vancouver and found a message from his mother:

> I got your card. But I don't understand your message, Waylon. What do you mean? How long are you going to be gone? And what about your business? You be careful, now. You know how sensitive your skin is. You take care of him, Chloe. I don't know if this scuba diving is a good idea.

And Chloe had a message from Roy Schuter. Waylon didn't like the guy, but he was a good client. He'd taken life insurance policies for himself and his wife, as well as insurance on their cars, their house, and his business. There was also just the start of a message from Chloe: "What is your mother talking about. . . ?" Then the tape ran to the end. When he tried to rewind it by remote, nothing happened. He asked Leary where he could get access to e-mail.

"Don't need it, myself," Leary replied. "Haven't gotten used to the friggin' fax yet. But you talk to Boom. Chances are she can help."

Boom, whose big heart was maybe too capacious by somewhat, according to Leary, had set up a worldwide social security system entailing many late nights and more glasses of co-la than are good for a person, and now she maintained a multinational string of five likely young gentlemen, all of whom were wired to the Internet and none of whom suspected the existence of the others.

"But three of them are coming here on holiday at the same time next month," said Leary. "Gosh. And Boom, here, has a little problem on the planning and scheduling side of things. Now ain't that right, Boom my beauty?"

"Always problem too mutt," she replied, with the world-weary air of any business person confronted with the vicissitudes of an inconsiderate fortune.

But she had let Waylon use her account to send a message home to Vancouver. All he said was:

Everything fine. Looking forward to seeing you again. Where are you now, and what are you doing? How is Meredith?

17 full house

*If a man does not keep pace with his companions,
perhaps it is because he hears a different drummer.*

Henry David Thoreau

The others were back from Phra Chan Island and the full moon party, and the number of meditators had swelled by three.

Tippawan sat in the full lotus position more naturally than anyone else there. The only Thai at the 4H Club, she was thin to the point of emaciation, self-effacing to the point of invisibility. Her head had been shaved bald in the manner of Thai nuns, although it was growing out again and she wasn't wearing the white robes any longer. "Call me Tip," she had said. Physically, Chloe towered over her. Yet she felt somehow at a disadvantage. However retiring Tip might appear, her manner bespoke strength and complete self-possession.

Ruthie, as always, sat up close to Gorgi. Dangerously near but apparently unperturbed by the intensity of Ruthie's personal aura, Bibi Bulambowitz was disposed in a loose half-lotus, head back as though in search of divine revelation. Chloe had only spoken to Bibi briefly—long enough to be diagnosed as a Virgo even though she was an Aries.

Bibi was sweet. She had lovely big green eyes, odd in an otherwise rather Asian face. Chloe had the eerie sensation of looking into Bibi's eyes and right out through the back of her skull into a happy sunlit world of butterflies and teddy bears and candies growing on bushes. Bibi was Jewish and South African. She had left South Africa with the coming of the Nelson Mandela millennium, no longer feeling that it would be cowardly to do so. Now she had a niggling sense that it was irresponsible, nevertheless, and she was traveling the earth in search of something that would make it okay. Chances were, Al Dente would do the trick.

In defiance of both her cultural and national backgrounds, Chloe had to think, Bibi was naïvely exuberant about everything, relentlessly upbeat. "Oh, my GOD!" "*FABULOUS!*" "Oh, NO!" "That's totally *AWESOME*!" "That's IN*CRED*IBLE!" I don't BE*LIEVE* it!" She spoke in all-caps. The most mundane iota of experience was rendered in bold italics, while anything else merited two-inch headlines. It made Chloe tired.

Right now, Bibi was gulping air. Chloe found this distracting, and she could hear Ruthie snort impatiently. Gorgi smiled some more, no doubt calculating the appropriate fines. It sounded as though Bibi were hyperventilating.

Olga the Russian, the third full moon party veteran, was a big blonde goddess of a woman with skin like peaches and cream. She sat as in a calisthenics class, rolling her shoulders from time to time and arching forward from the small of her back. She uttered an occasional grunt, the sort of thing you might hear in a gym. Or a porno movie.

And Bibi was gulping air again. How were you supposed to focus on your own breathing when you had to listen to someone else's? Chloe tried switching to the *hearing . . . hearing . . .* drill. But she found herself torn between Bibi's gulping, the Rev's panting, Olga's grunts and Ruthie's snorts of disgust at it all. Occasionally

Gorgi would mewl as well, probably excited at the thought of the accumulating fines. Except for Al Dente, who could have been carved from stone, and Tip, who you had to look hard at to be sure she was there, it was a total zoo.

Hearing.... At that moment the beep of a cellphone intruded on the scene. Chloe looked around to see who was going to be fined. But Gorgi himself produced a mobile from a fold in his robes. He pulled the antenna, listened intently for a moment, said something, and then rose. After a solicitous glance at his disciples—as much as to say he had to answer a message from some higher dimension—he walked down and away towards the tree to continue his conversation. As he went down the steps, Chloe could hear: "It has to be *soon*.... Yes, yes, Jessica. Wait. I can't talk here."

Ruthie's head turned—forget the meditation—radar locked on and all systems armed in face of this "Jessica," whoever she was.

Chloe breathed in on the count of one, letting her belly swell ... *rising* ... and expelled the air slowly on the count of two ... *falling* ... trying to feel the air against her nasal passages. *Hearing....* All the way from the tree, Chloe heard Gorgi say, "I do not care!" He sounded more upset than your standard guru ought to. The rest of it was largely unintelligible. Except Chloe thought she heard something about the "Blue Buddha." The Blue Buddha? But Chloe wasn't supposed to be thinking. The trick was to hear but not listen. Or something like that. *Seeing*—trying not to *watch*—as Gorgi left the tree and proceeded towards his quarters.

Chloe felt an insect crawling on her arm.... *Feeling, feeling, feeling....* She focused on the sensations, just as Gorgi had instructed her to do. Feeling.... *Thinking.* Unbidden, thoughts of Waylon came to her. They were supposed to be working things out, and she didn't even know where he was. Almost as alarming, it occurred to her, she wasn't nearly as distraught as she should be. If anything, she was more excited than distraught. Chloe had walked to the shop down the road and paid twice too much to call Vancouver and check the answering machine again. There were a few messages from editors. One of them wondered whether Chloe might be interested in doing a story on the connection between brain tumors and creativity. Another had heard that grapefruit diets were potentially lethal, and thought Chloe would want to follow up on it. There had been a short message from Waylon, only saying everything was fine, for now, and why didn't she tell him where she was (at the same time failing to say where he was). He sounded different. Younger, somehow. More positive than he had in a long time.

Feeling. . . . Chloe's attention shifted from the swell of her belly to the soft warm spread of horniness in her groin. *Thinking.* . . . Waylon with the green sheath on his dick. It was no good. There was no reining in her mind. *Remembering.* . . . Early in their relationship, Chloe and Waylon had discovered how good it was eating peanut butter and toast together with boiled eggs. That had been back in the days before Spunky. Here she had come halfway around the world to find some excitement. And now look at her. Not only that, she had wanted to give things another chance with Waylon. But she didn't even know where he was.

It had been so hard to get Waylon out of the house, the past year or two. "I've had a hard day, Chloe," he'd tell her. "I've had a hard week," on the weekends. And then he'd spend another hard day or weekend at home doing housework, balancing books, or lecturing her and Meredith on the fine art of being orderly. Waylon still had a good body from all the skiing and hiking in the old days, but he'd be going to flab soon, body and spirit, if he weren't careful. He refused to play tennis at the Club. He didn't even ride his motorcycle much.

And so Chloe traveled out of herself through recollection of things past to exploration of possible futures, and from there to worlds that were in no way possible. Eventually she found herself in a state much like sleep, judging by the snores she heard coming from herself, drifting in and out of dreams. Then she woke up. Her breathing deep and controlled, as natural as the tides, her mind utterly focused, in balance, and alert to no more than its own pure awareness. Or so Chloe was to write in her journal. She also described how the experience was interrupted.

"Who took my fucking prunes?" Ruthie sounded furious. "I can't leave anything around here. Those were my own *personal* prunes. Shit."

18 fuckin' fatties

The abstinent run away from what they desire
But carry their desires with them.

Bhagavad-Gita

"I hate fat," said Ruthie.

Al Dente leaned towards Ruthie, the flame of his intensity merging with hers. "Me too!" he said.

"Fat people are compulsives." Ruthie pawed through a bowl of vegetables to come up with a tomato. She ingested it in two bites, a bit of juice like blood running down her chin. "They just can't help themselves. It's disgusting."

"I know exactly what you mean," Al Dente answered, adding lime juice to his salad. He refused to use oil unless it was olive oil, and there wasn't any olive oil left. "It really is disgusting. I don't know why they do it to themselves. It doesn't look good. And it isn't healthy. But they just can't help themselves. Eating all the time."

"And eating the wrong kind of food. Junk food. Pizzas. Fried chicken. Fried everything."

"American national dish, man. Hot fried greasy fuckin' salt." Freddie chewed frantically on a section of straw. Being on the same wavelength as Ruthie confused him. "And Coca Cola."

"Ice cream," Ruthie, ignoring Freddie, continued her litany. "Hot apple pie and ice cream. Chocolate cake. But it's more than that, you know. The way things are going, there won't be enough food for everybody, the way people are making babies and everybody's wasting everything. Before you know it, we'll have used up the whole world's resources."

"That's right." Al Dente pulled back his hair to peer from his little tent. "And there's the ozone hole and everything." Then he shook his head and the hair fell forward to half obscure his face.

"That's right," Ruthie said, although she looked uncertain for a moment.

"Do you know how many years you lose off your life for every extra pound you carry around?" asked Al Dente.

"How many?"

"I don't remember; but you're killing yourself."

"That's right. And it's only ignorance. If they only knew, how could they do it? Really. And they smell; I swear. You can smell the fat. Like grease."

"Yeah, I notice that sometimes. It's awful."

"And half the time there's no room on the subway, fat people everywhere."

"They should pay extra."

"They should pay more taxes, too."

"They should put them in jail till they lose some weight. For their own good." Al Dente emerged from his tent to fix Ruthie, again, with the intensity of his gaze. "Fucking fatties."

"Oh, NO. *SERIOUSLY*. SOME fat people are really *NICE*," suggested Bibi Bulambowitz, enthralled by proceedings, especially as they proceeded from the lips of Al Dente, but clearly worried the Rev would be wounded.

"I hate fat," Ruthie reiterated, shining with virtue.

"God, I wish I had a pizza," said Chloe.

"Me, too." Prue was doing leg lifts and, with not much enthusiasm, using carrot sticks to scoop yogurt dip.

"I think the best thing I ever ate was this lamb and yogurt dish in a Greek restaurant in Houston, one time." The Rev looked wistful and took to scraping his pipe.

"Pass the cabbage," Ruthie instructed Chloe.

Chloe sent the cabbage, half a head straight up, by way of the Rev. She didn't want to get too close for fear that, in her nice new orange-red sundress, she'd be mistaken for a tomato. Ruthie was slavering. She had a piece of pumpkin stuck to her chin; her eyes burned and a sheen of sweat had broken out across her brow. Ruthie resembled a starved wolf, if you could imagine a vegetarian wolf with steel-rimmed spectacles—a starved wolf with the munchies.

Between mouthfuls of cabbage, Ruthie swigged at some muddy slop from a big blender jar. "Papaya, watermelon, pineapple, bean sprouts, wheat germ, and yoghurt." She itemized the ingredients as though they were pharmaceuticals. Chloe had already watched Ruthie devour a green salad, two tomatoes, three mangoes—only small ones—and two bowls of vegetable stew. She had hardly stopped to chew.

"That's INCREDIBLE," remarked Bibi for the fourth or fifth time. "I still can't BELIEVE it! It's *AWESOME*."

Ruthie had just done a seven-day fast, the second in as many months. Her stated ambition was to follow this *tour de force* of hugely self-affirming self-denial with two ten-day fasts end-to-end, allowing herself one-day fueling stops between. The Twinkies probably didn't count. After that, she said, her goal was forty days: four ten-day sessions with half-day recesses. On the whole, however, for someone out to show Mahatma Gandhi a few tricks on the fasting front, Ruthie seemed strangely preoccupied with food.

"You're doing too much fasting," Prue told her. "Look at your legs. You're losing muscle tissue."

"Yes," said Tip. "Too much of anything is bad. The middle way is always best." Given her exquisite bone structure, Tip was herself more slender than Ruthie could ever hope to be without actually starving to death. And Tip wore her dimensions more comfortably. Even when she wasn't meditating, she suggested lightness and lean energy securely contained, under control and focused.

"'Forty days and forty nights,'" intoned the Rev. "'I did neither eat bread nor drink water, because of all your sins which ye sinned.' Deuteronomy: chapter nine, verse eighteen." When he grinned, which was often—never mind his grin sometimes resembled a grimace—he had the manner of a distinguished if somewhat nervous disciple of Bacchus. In fact, the Rev was an ordained Methodist minister. He had come as a missionary to bring the good word to Thailand, and had himself been half converted to some sort of agnosticism-cum-Buddhism.

Chloe liked the Rev. He reminded her of Waylon, just a little. She watched as he brought order to his cosmos. He extracted a pipe from his cotton Shan shoulder bag, carefully unwrapped the bent-stem Italian briar from a blue-checked cotton Khmer scarf and arranged it on the table directly in front of him. His pipe-cleaning implement emerged next, and found its place twelve inches to the right of the pipe. He deployed a soft leather tobacco pouch, stained with sweat and age, at arm's length out past the pipe. This was Waylon's fuss-budget side magnified and ramified into an elaborate canon of little habits designed to hold the universe together.

To the accompaniment of nasty gurglings from the bowels of his pipe, the Rev ran his lighter around the rim of the bowl, again and again, puffing mightily. A shower of burning dottle settled to add a new constellation of little burns to his shirtfront. A voice emerged from the great cloud of blue smoke: "'Abstainer—a weak person who yields to the temptation of denying himself a pleasure.' Or herself, as the case may be. Ambrose Bierce, *The Devil's Dictionary*."

"Ah!" Gorgi appeared from behind the tree. "So much smoke! A double fine for you." He had stopped by—not to join them for dinner, since he normally dined alone in his house—but just to say hello and see that his flock were abiding by the rules.

YAWN

The Rev was one of Gorgi's favorites, according to Prue, even though he smoked all the time and, what with his constant sweating, had ruined the finish on his patch of the meditation sala floor. Gorgi thought the Rev should dye his hair. "You see," said Gorgi, tittering with delight, "I dye my beard. *Atcha.* And I lose twenty years."

The loyal members of the 4H Club pretended not to look where his skin showed dark blotches through the straggly whiskers.

The Rev sighed mightily. "If I lost twenty years," he replied, "I'd be too young to drink." He removed his thick, black-plastic-framed glasses and smeared them with his sweat-dampened cotton scarf.

"You are still vigorous." Gorgi pursued his case. "You are still a good-looking man. But the girls, they see white hair, especially in this part of the world, and you are an old man. That is not fair, you understand. All the world is illusion. If circumstance turns your hair white before it is time, then you take control. You give the color back to your life. You must learn to see behind the illusion of reality, but part of the discipline is learning how to shape the illusions with mindfulness. *Atcha.* You fashion the reality, you understand, that suits *you.*"

"I LIKE the way his hair is NOW," said Bibi. "I think it's DISTINGUISHED."

The Rev had a hard time blushing and looking pontifical at the same time, but he tried. "This stew is delicious," he said. "All these vegetables and herbs. It's great. You don't even miss the meat."

"Thanks," said Al Dente. You could see he also thought his stew was pretty hot stuff. Cook for the day, he'd distinguished himself at breakfast by serving Thai-style rice porridge with garlic, shallots, fresh ginger, and a raw egg stirred in. For lunch, now—the main meal of the day—they were eating an aromatic stew seasoned with no more than fresh herbs and black pepper. Ruthie, so far as Chloe could see, had moved on from the stew in a determined effort to assimilate the entire week's provisions.

"FAN*TAS*TIC," said Bibi, and she looked in the pot to see if there was any more.

"Though it's hard to beat stewed lamb." The Rev wasn't finished. "You know—after several hours, when the meat gets really tender and starts to shred? If you add just a little red wine, and not too much olive oil. A hint of rosemary. . . ."

"Will you shut up?" suggested Chloe. "Now I'm hungry again."

"I read that red wine is an antidote to the cholesterol in red meat," Prue said. "If only they'd tell me that cigarettes are good for you, I'd believe in God."

"Tobacco covers your lungs with a layer of tar that protects you from air pollution." The Rev scraped at his cold pipe, caressed the bowl.

"Shit," said Ruthie, pushing her glasses up on her nose. Some vegetable matter clung to one lens. "Do you have to bring that filthy thing to the table?"

"That Greek dish I was talking about? They cooked the meat and fresh yoghurt together in a clay pot. Then they served it with hot bread and fresh spring onions."

Ruthie had eaten the entire half-head of cabbage, only a small one, and now she looked at the Rev in a way that should have made him glad there was no clay pot and yogurt at hand.

"I lived on a commune in Vermont, once," Prue said. "We spent half our time talking about all the food we wished we had. We practically lived on chicken and rice."

"Hey, man." Freddie pulled a fresh section of straw from a jumpsuit pocket and flicked it furiously in Prue and Chloe's direction. "I lived in a fuckin' commune, man. This bitch Jennie who half ran the place, she made us all eat vegetarian shit, man; it made you puke. She was feeding us her righteousness. 'I eat worse than this,' it's like she's telling us, 'and now you're going to eat worse too, just so you know.' Fuck. She gave us this brown fucking rice, one day, it wasn't even cooked; it was like eating gravel. I couldn't believe it. So I told her she was a bitch and couldn't cook shit, and she dumped the whole fuckin' pot of rice on my head. It wasn't cooked, like I say, but it was *hot*, man. I left that commune right away. That was, like, enough. You know? Uncooked brown fucking rice. Fascist bitch, man." His eyes rolled back with every utterance of "man" until it looked as though he might be having a fit.

Ruthie got up to stack her dishes, running a finger around the inside of the stew bowl and licking it. Freddie was scraping leftover rice and vegetables into a bowl for Sweet Mama, and Pup was lapping the plates as fast as Freddie put them down, maybe wanting to help Chloe, whose turn it was to wash up. Then Pup yelped and shied away. Sweet Mama hid under a bench. "I've told you before," Ruthie snapped. "I'm not going to eat from the same dishes as those animals. What's wrong with you, anyway?"

"How can you hurt a poor little puppy?" To this point Tip had been so retiring as to be invisible. In her own quiet way, she was upset enough that her English suffered. "If you behave like that, you hurt yourself more. Next time, before you do such a thing, ask yourself why you want to do like this." You could tell these were strong words, by Tip's standards, and Ruthie looked chastened, if you caught her in just the right light.

Freddie added a dash or two of fermented fish sauce to the leftovers, the way Sweet Mama liked it, and tried to tempt her back out from under cover. "Go on. Beat it," he said to Pup, who was back already. "Get out of here; your mama's hungry, man."

"That's my salad bowl, you bastard."

"Fuck off."

"Come here, Sweet Mama," Tip called softly. "Come." And she came, on her belly and looking nervously in Ruthie's direction, but she came back out to eat.

Chloe took out her notebook and doodled a few notes on the day's events. All sorts of things were finding their way into her meditation diary, most of them having little to do with meditation and everything to do with a writing vocation that had been drifting away from her, these past years working in Vancouver as a hack. Just now she found herself instead trying to capture Freddie's speech patterns, the flavor of his views on life.

Aside from Sweet Mama, Freddie didn't seem to have any friends, though Prue said she liked him. And Tip obviously warmed to him, although she was nice to everybody. He kept to himself, shunning the collective meditation sessions and living by himself somewhere in the woods outside the compound. Chloe asked him where he came from, and what he did for a living, but she was none the wiser for her efforts. "It's like holograms, man. You know what I mean? 'Jeweled Net of Indra' and shit. Everything there is reflected in everything there is. Cool. You take any part of it, and you've got every part of it. It's all the same thing, man. So I'm anybody I want to be. And everybody. I'm here, I'm there, I'm every fuckin' where. I'm *Chicken Man.*" Freddie adopted a sly look and rubbed thumb and forefinger together. "No, no. Only joking. Ha, ha. Give me five baht." It was amazing. Freddie had turned into Gorgi, right before Chloe's eyes. Then he reverted to type. "I'm everywhere and I'm nowhere, man." Eyes rolled back and paper straw flicking almost faster than the eye could follow, Freddie shimmied from side to side, leg-warmer crumpled down around one ankle. "I'm anybody and I'm nobody."

"You said it, you asshole," said Ruthie, but in a friendly sort of way, maybe mellowed out on all the food.

"Come on, Freddie." Chloe really did want to know. "What were you doing before you came to Thailand?"

"Forget it, man. I don't do anything. That's what I do, okay? No-thing. And I'm from no-where. I'm from any place I want to be. And that's the only way I can stay one step ahead of them, man. And you *know* who I mean." Freddie broke off, suddenly spell-bound. "Hey, look," he said. Pup was crouching down on his front legs again and staring, also spellbound, at a big warty toad. Every time the toad flopped along, Pup hopped after it. "Pup's teaching the toad to hop."

Ruthie had taken to chewing gum according to a complicated rhythm that bespoke with-it-ness. The muscles in her jaws bunched and flexed impressively, a slight sheen of perspiration on her face. "I really have to get back to the temple. To Wat Nai Fun. I have to get back to more intensive work." She took off her glasses and, just for a moment as she blinked and gazed around myopically, she looked quite vulnerable. Then she put them back on and went all hard edged again. "What's that you're doing?" She turned to Chloe with some of the ferocity she'd earlier unleashed on the cabbage. "What are you writing?"

"She's probably a reporter," said Freddie. "No, wait. No, no. She's one of Them. She's filing a fuckin' report, man. Look at that. Yeah. That's a steno pad, man. She's a fuckin' agent for that whole fuckin' bunch. Big Oil, man. And the Pope. All of them are in it together. Coca Cola and shit."

"Shut up, Freddie," said Prue. "God, sometimes you give me a pain in the ass."

"*Atcha*," Freddie replied, with a look of splendid cunning. "Only joking. Chill, man."

"It's a meditation diary," Chloe told them.

"In Wat Nai Fun, you aren't allowed to write anything. You can't have a pencil or pen or paper. You can't even talk. Not unless you've got a special problem you have to discuss with the meditation master. Language just gets in the way. They're serious over there. Not like this bullshit."

"You must keep your eyes open," Gorgi intoned. "You are not here to sleep."

"I *have* to close my eyes," snapped Chloe. "The sweat gets into them and it burns. Why don't you have fans?" They had been meditating for hours already and there was an evening session still to come. Just as Prue had warned, Chloe had gone through the phases of irritation to crashing boredom and restlessness to utter rage, earlier in the afternoon when the heat of the day had blinded her with sweat and sapped her will even to live, much less spiritually excel.

"*Atcha*," Gorgi told her. "You are to remain alert to yourself in your interaction with the world. In this way, if you persist, you will come to see that you are not really you. And the world is not really the world." There was more, most of it on the level of simple practicalities. For example, Chloe informed him that, if she had to try sitting in this goddamned lotus position for one more minute, she was leaving. She couldn't even approximate the lotus position. Her fitness trainer back in Vancouver left some bits of her anatomy out of the limbering program. She was afraid she was already half crippled. No, she couldn't use a chair, Gorgi said, tittering away at this outré notion, a fine joke. But he did allow her to adopt the kneeling-position-with-cushion posture instead. So she was kneeling on a flat, firm little cushion to take some of the strain off her sinews as, sitting back on her heels, she sought both physical and spiritual poise. And now, as the day died and the breeze came up, it was cooler and Chloe suspected she was actually getting somewhere with all this.

She liked to think she'd made progress. Already she could sit for minutes at a time and not think. Sometimes, anyway. Her knees didn't hurt so much. And things were happening. She wasn't sure exactly *what* was going on, but she sensed changes in herself. Tip had just that morning cautioned Chloe that she should expect both advances and reverses, and that she had to learn to accept the setbacks with equanimity. Keep on with her practice. Try to remain mindful during her everyday life and she would progress, slowly but surely. She shouldn't be impatient.

In the meantime she was enjoying things, for the most part. What a gang of characters, this amazing collection of human driftwood in this strange little tropical backwater.

But she was sensing anomalies in the local scene. The 4H Club was like one of those laminated pictures that appeared to be the Messiah, in one light, and Satan in another. One moment the place seemed fairly idyllic, on the whole, if a bit silly. The next it was shot through with veins of something darker. Perhaps much darker. And so Chloe mused while she should have been meditating.

Then the Rev fell over sideways with an oath and a thud.

"Fuck!" said Ruthie, adding an observation of her own.

"Now, now, my children," Gorgi said. And then he mewled, no doubt deciding the Rev's collapse was sufficient circumstantial evidence he'd gone to sleep.

19 keeping sharp

It's possible to keep your mind so open your brain falls out.

Anon.

A shaft of sun leaked from the apex of the pyramid, shining down on Chloe where she was sitting back on her heels in the precise center of the steam room. Swarms of minute droplets, oily with healing essences, danced in the golden rays.

Chloe sought a more comfortable position, trying to adopt a meditative attitude. *Feeling.* . . . She could feel the sarong shift on her nipples. *Feeling.* . . . And the itchy-sexy feeling in her crotch was either randiness or something Al Dente had given her, God forbid. But he'd worn a rubber, so it was probably just horniness. Roy Schuter didn't like to use condoms, although Chloe insisted. With his usual flair for the inappropriate, he said it was like sucking a nipple through a nightgown, which is what Chloe's father used to say about filtered cigarettes.

Chloe let these things drift to surface and fall away again. Tip's advice was to relax and let it all come, to examine each thought, each feeling, and see it for what it was. *Rising . . . falling. . . . Rising. . . .* Chloe tried to open herself to whatever floated up.

"Existence is holographic," Gorgi had told her the day before. "You are a hologram. Every node in existence is reflected in every other node. Everything that is, is in you, if only you learn how to see it and understand it. *Atcha.* In the same way, you are in everything in this universe and all others. Yes. Think about it."

Having already been briefed by Prue, Chloe saw which way that conversation was going. What with her in everything and everything in her, why shouldn't this clown also get a piece of the action? After all. Cosmically speaking he was already in her anyway, right? The next move would be an invitation to see his secret manuscripts or something. "What do you know about tantric yoga?" he had asked her, smiling slyly and mewling only a little.

Rising . . . falling. . . .

Gorgi promised her that this particular herbal mixture would tone all her major organs, including the skin—"The skin is the biggest organ in the body, yes?"—while reducing her appetite, something that had been tormenting her these past couple of days. He also recommended colonic irrigations twice a day, with four gallons of herbal tea each time—the same tea she'd been enjoying in the afternoons after lunch and before the evening snack. The infusion was the pale yellow of chamomile and tasted of something sweet, together with a touch of something else astringent. Taro wood and lemongrass were two of the ingredients, Prue had told her.

"Coffee irrigations are also good," Gorgi informed her, unnecessarily, for then he added, "*Atcha.* But we do not permit coffee here. No. Ha, ha."

By now, Chloe would take her coffee almost any way she could get it. What a buzz, the day before, when Prue had taken her out to her stash in the woods, bringing along a thermos of hot water, and they'd made instant coffee. Prue even had condensed milk and sugar, and Chloe drank two cups, three spoons of sugar, and lots of milk in each. They all had their stashes in the woods, except for

139

Gorgi, who didn't need one. Prue had her goodies, including a cellphone. The Rev had his supply of tobacco and malt whiskey, Tip her notebooks and camera, and Ruthie her dope, including the junk food, although nobody was supposed to know about that. Freddie, of course, had established his entire home and atelier out there.

The colonic irrigations, Gorgi had said, worked best if you also fasted at least seven days at a time. He prepared herbal pills that kept you nourished all the while, and little balls of roughage to fool your gut into thinking it had eaten. Chloe told him she wasn't ready for either fasting or irrigations. Not yet. Gorgi had this fascinating collection of things in bottles—some of them resembled twisted and fossilized bean pods. Large ones. He claimed they'd been hosed from the guts of fasting members. And these were just the more visible manifestations of a body's toxification. But Chloe suspected her own fossilized horrors were more likely psychic ones, and she wondered how much meditation it would take to flush them out.

Someone, probably Gorgi, had turned up the steam and added fresh herbs. She really did feel her pores and her breathing passages, even maybe her heart and mind, opening up to the cleansing vapors, dispelling the staleness of the past months.

Seduced by sun and heat and, who knew, maybe the herbs as well, Chloe was drifting. She forced herself to open her eyes and, at the same time, to unfocus, to sharpen her apprehension of being, while not *thinking* about any particular thing that impinged. Letting it be and being with it, without analysis, without judgment. She could hear herself snoring. Not very loudly. Shreds of dream episodes, subconscious channel-surfing. . . . She knew she was dreaming—half-dreaming, half asleep—but she couldn't do anything with these fleeting, poorly tuned emanations.

"Later," Gorgi had told her, "as you become more focused, more in tune with yourself, we will introduce you to dream control therapy. We can teach you to control your own dreams. You will learn to know when you are dreaming—this is while you sleep, you understand—and then to direct proceedings. *Atcha.* You need to recognize your worst fears—your *worst* fears, you understand—and then confront them. If in your dream you are climbing a mountain, and you fear heights, you jump. On one level you know you are dreaming, so you understand you are not going to die. But your body *knows* it is going to die, and it responds. Eventually, you learn to recognize other fears—not so obvious ones, yes? And, if you confront them often enough, you begin to lose your fears.

"Of course, all this is only practice. As you become better at piloting your karmic vehicle, you need to lose your *metaphysical* fear of flying. In forcing your low self to come to terms with its fears, your high self frees itself for the greatest transaction of all—the encounter with Nothingness. When No-mind encounters Nothingness, then all becomes clear. You understand?"

"Sure."

"*Atcha.* Good. That will be five hundred baht. Ha, ha. No! Only kidding."

But he hadn't been kidding when he told her, the first day, that a stay in the Institute would run two hundred dollars per week. This was not just for room and board, she had to understand, nor was it merely for the exceptional standard of instruction. Part of her "donation"—no, she must choose to donate at least that amount, or else she could not stay—part of her donation was to go towards establishing sister Institutes around Thailand, first, and then the rest of Asia. The members of the 4H Club, as Chloe understood it, were to be only the vanguard of a vast army of seekers after rejuvenation, spiritual alertness, metaphysical truth, and better sex. Eventually, moreover, Gorgi meant to cater to every taste and budget.

Freddie, for example, ate at the 4H Club, what little he did eat; but he slept in his own camp—nothing but a scrap timber and corrugated metal lean-to with a rough stone hearth in the woods outside the compound. He didn't have enough money for the full-on five-star Holistic Herbal Garden and Institute of Holographic Healing treatment. Anyway, he said, he didn't like to subject himself to any kind of official control. But Freddie was given access to most of the facilities. And, no matter he kept complaining how difficult it was to keep a joint lit in the place, Freddie was a big advocate of the pyramidal steam room. "The power of the pyramid, yeah? It sharpens the fuckin' focus. And razor blades, too, they tell me, though I don't believe that shit, man." In fact, Freddie spent so much time in there that people were complaining to Gorgi that no one else could use it. Sometimes Bibi would join him in there, although to get the full effect—of the pyramid, not the dope—there was only room for one at the focus.

Prue claimed she got a distinct buzz off one of the mixes—the low-energy treatment Gorgi prepared for her—even without any dope. And Bibi often saw things while meditating. One regular feature was a luminescent blue ball that coalesced right in front of her face. For lack of a better description, she described this as "my MIND," and it appeared most predictably when she was in the pyramid with the steam remedy for stiff joints; she didn't know why. Bibi also claimed that something in her own special herbal mix, together with sustained meditation, took her back to previous lives, including one, she was sure, where she lived in Egypt by the Nile. "A BIG river, anyway. With old BOATS made of PAPYRUS or something. And I'm WASHING *CLOTHES*." A circumstance that seemed to excite her more than it did anyone else.

Chloe, herself, in the middle of her meditation exercises one afternoon—in the pyramid, for whatever that was worth—discovered a juicy big hot-dog smothered in mustard and onions hanging there in mid-air, right beneath her nose, just where Bibi always saw her mind form. And right in front of her lips, which were wet with desire. Which was no wonder, what with nothing but vegetarian food at the 4H Club. If they wanted more than the two meals a day, they were charged extra at the same time Ruthie tried to make them feel like gluttons. Never mind they had to do their own cooking and washing up.

Gorgi used the same rationale McDonald's did, trying to browbeat customers into being their own waiters: "This is why we can keep everything so cheap, you understand?" Although he had thought of another reason. "*Atcha*. And it is good to have basic daily routines that you learn to do with mindfulness, to help you stay in touch with your self."

Chloe could hear Pup whining outside, which suggested that in his mind, at least, her time in the pyramid was up. Gorgi recommended twenty-five minutes in the steam room, although without a watch it was hard to say how long you'd been in there. You sat dead center, if you wanted the full pyramid effect. This should be followed by a shower—a traditional Thai dip shower from a big rain jar—before moving to the open sala for a ninety-minute massage. "The combination of massage, the power of the pyramid, and the ancient Thai secret mixture of healing herbs," said Gorgi, a huckster on a roll, "leaves you relaxed and full of vitality. The pyramid joins the earth and the sun, you see? So when we sit in the middle of the pyramid, we gain energy in the body." His steam room, he said, was good for the brain, the heart, the lungs, and the stomach, and it would cure colds, fever, anxiety, and insomnia.

"Insomnia?" Chloe said. "God. Just put me in a room alone with those roosters. I'll show you a cure for insomnia."

"*Atcha*. It is not the same."

Gorgi had given her a grand tour of the 4H Club, that first week, introducing her to some of the plants he cultivated. The grounds contained a vast pharmacopoeia. Gorgi collected all his own ingredients, either there, within the compound, or else wild from some land back in the hills. He showed her everything from things to make your skin soft to hangover cures to the Seven Buffalo Tree: "If you mix this with whiskey and pour it into the mouth of a woman who has died in childbirth, it is said, she will revive in five minutes ."

"Why 'Seven Buffalo Tree'?"

"That is because the price of this plant used to be seven buffalo chained together. Of course that was a long time ago, more than one hundred years." Gorgi laughed. "Atcha. Maybe today it is the One Hundred Buffalo Tree."

Could be, thought Chloe. But Freddie had already advised her against smoking it, which is something she would never have thought of doing anyway. He claimed it didn't do a thing for you. Of course, this left in question the hundreds of other medicinal plants around the place, all of which, Ruthie insisted, Freddie had tried eating, smoking, or infusing since he'd appeared on the scene.

Meredith would just love this stuff, Chloe thought.

"And this one," he said, clapping his hands at another, "dances with the sound." The leaves, to Chloe's amazement, reacted rhythmically to the sound. "It is good for fever."

Gorgi picked a leaf from a nondescript herb and told Chloe to smell the fragrance. It was the same plant that Bibi had seen Pup eating, a couple of days before, and she claimed it had to be good for something. "Well, *SURE*. Animals just *KNOW* about these things. It's AMAZING." Maybe, thought Chloe, but Pup seemed prepared to eat just about anything from Al Dente's iron exercise bars to the Rev's tobacco pouch, so what did this young dog really know about life? Having eaten Ruthie's prunes, for example, Pup had suffered the double indignity of getting a boot from Ruthie and a bad case of the trots. Prue said she'd had to clean up the incriminating evidence in the meditation sala.

Gorgi told Chloe he had studied with a master of the traditional lore: "This man, he learned from his father, who learned from his." Gorgi had also done a course in Thai herbal medicine at a university in Bangkok.

No one at the 4H Club knew much about Gorgi's background, beyond what he told them and what you could read off the diplomas in his office. Ruthie claimed to know, she didn't say how, that he'd been a famous guru in India, but had been forced to flee because of professional jealousies. Prue had heard vague rumors that Gorgi, involved in various dark dealings, had lived other lives under other names. Be that as it may, he resembled a diminutive South Asian Santa Claus with shoe polish in his beard. And maybe Chloe only imagined the occasional glimpses of someone considerably less jolly lurking beneath all the wry sweetness and light.

Chloe finally gave in to Pup's importunings, stepping out of the steamroom into the golden afternoon. She practiced her walking meditation across the yard to the shade of the cookhouse, Pup dancing attendance all the way, nipping at her ankles and generally testing her powers of concentration. The water from the big earthenware rain jar was delightfully cooling, and she washed twice in Gorgi's all-natural herbal shampoo, which left her hair smelling luscious.

Olga had told Chloe to come to the meditation sala for a massage, when she was finished. The big Russian girl was everybody's favorite masseuse, and she spent a good portion of her free hours giving people her own special combination of a Russian sports massage and the traditional Thai variety. For Chloe, the most acute pleasure came when the pain stopped, after Olga tried to turn her major muscle groups into hamburger with her elbows.

Now Chloe was lying on her stomach on a mat, enjoying the breeze and the attention. She was also thinking about all the things that Gorgi had shown her that day. He had saved the herbal whiskies for the last, and was insistent that she try a few of them. It was probably part of his concept of tantric yoga. "You try this," he told her, uncorking a big clear glass bottle of a murky liquid labeled "Sexy Superwoman" and passing her a shot-glassful.

"Not now," she'd said, responding with a sly smile of her own. "I'm meditating this afternoon."

"Herbal tea is good," he told her. "Yes. But maybe this is better." The shelves in the back room to his office sagged under the weight of Sexy Superwoman, Superman, Old Man Jump the Wall, Stand Up Straight, Singapore Skyscraper, and a few unlabelled bottles with things floating in them—dried tiger's penis, as he explained, a six-inch centipede, and a coiled snake. "Thai men, and Chinese—they believe these things give them power." Cases of whiskey stood stacked against the far wall.

Chloe didn't know what to make of him. The meditation master of the 4H Club could seem almost wise, in one breath, and come across as a complete charlatan in the next. "I thought this was a health spa," Chloe had told him. "And here you're selling umpteen varieties of bootleg booze."

"Anything is harming you, if you take too much," Gorgi assured her. "And many harmful things, if you take only a little bit, can be good for you. It is the same with my medicinal plants. They can soothe the nerves or they can destroy them." Gorgi flashed her a disarming smile. "You can do many things with the ancient knowledge. Yes. Some plants can kill. They can kill slow or they can kill fast, and no one will know why. You can heal and you can harm."

For a moment, Gorgi's smile had turned anything but disarming, but maybe it was only her imagination.

Whoa! The snap had probably only been a tendon. It wasn't painful enough to have been a bone. Not quite. Once again, Olga pushed the heel of Chloe's left foot back till it came in contact with the corresponding buttock.

Sessions with Olga began with a gentle exploration of the energy lines in the back. "Do you feel pain?" she would ask before getting down to the more serious business, applying the straight-armed weight of her body through thumbs, heel of hand, and elbow, seeking acupressure points in the ankles and feet. Then she would dig her fists into the torso, alternating with twisting, two-handed pressures and radical stretchings of the limbs. All these pummelings and contortions elicited funny little releases, sudden sensations of ease. That morning, for example, Chloe had discovered an ache around her hamstrings—something to do with her sitting back on her heels for hours every day. Without a word from her patient, Olga had sensed the problem, responding perhaps to the tenor of Chloe's sighs and groans, working at knots of tension around the tendons until all pain and traces of fatigue had gone. Before Olga moved back up to the legs, Chloe was treated to a version of "This Little Piggy Went to Market," with Olga coaxing gentle pops from the toe joints, releasing still more tension Chloe hadn't till then been aware of.

Soon the massage fell back into a strong, steady rhythm, and Chloe slipped once again into a state of contented awareness, hovering between wakefulness and sleep. Except for the rustle of palm fronds and the birdsong, the sala was still. Chloe felt as at one with the world as she had in some time, and that world was in better shape than usual. Never mind missing husbands and sisters, not to mention early mornings and vegetarian food. She felt great.

It was in part the massage, but during the evening meditation session she was feeling more energized, calmer, despite everything that was going on around her. Maybe it was also the vegetarian food and no booze. Perhaps the meditation even had something to do with it. Just the change—being away from Vancouver and Waylon and Meredith and the rest of it—that alone was enough to fill her with a sense of new horizons.

Listening. . . .

Bibi was gulping air again. Chloe discovered a peculiar dissonance in trying to focus on her own respiration while in fact attending to someone else's breathing. So she changed tack.

Feeling. . . .

She noted a funny kind of hollow aching—an emptiness, a hunger for something unspecified. It was like nostalgia, only future oriented. A tropism. In recent months she had mistaken it for lust, but brief affairs with a couple of the local studs had disabused her of that notion. Here at the 4H Club it was still there, but complicated by an excitement that nibbled and gnawed away in her belly. Chloe returned to her breathing exercises. *Rising . . . falling. . . . Rising . . . falling. . . . Rising. . . .*

Rising . . . rising . . . risingrisingrising. The rising wouldn't stop. It had shifted from her belly to high in her chest. "You can do many things with the ancient knowledge," Gorgi had said. Who *was* this guy, really? And Ruthie. . . . *Risingrisingrising.* . . .

Something appeared on the periphery of her perception, something vaguely cellular slowly exploding to fill the space of the sala. A corresponding anxiety swelled in her breast. Chloe held desperately to her breathing. *Rising . . . falling, rising, falling, risingfallingrisingfallingrising.*

She fought the urge to hyperventilate, slowing her breathing, trying to focus on the touch of air in her nasal passages. She was suddenly conscious of Bibi, beside her, who had begun gulping air again, as though in sympathy with Chloe's panic. Then the soft explosion of dread slowed and halted. *Risingfallingrising, falling, rising . . . falling . . . rising . . . falling. . . .*

Now it was receding; and the existential foam that had threatened to smother her was changing. She didn't, wouldn't look directly at it—it remained on the periphery—but now it suggested a mass of blue bubbles, blues of all shades shot through with pink. It was beautiful and somehow restful.

It swirled away as she went to sleep.

20 compensation

I had an aunt in Yucatan
Who bought a python from a man
And kept it for a pet.
She died, because she never knew
These simple little rules and few;—
The snake is living yet.

Hilaire Belloc

The Gorgon Bar was packed. The boxing hadn't excited Waylon as much this time. The most impressive part of the fights, for him, had been the match between the big American sailor and the *muay thai* boxer. The swab had looked entirely confident, as well he might have, since he weighed easily twice as much as his opponent and had biceps the size of the other guy's thigh. His shipmates had cheered and offered to bet on their man with all and sundry.

In a remarkably short time, the Thai had worn Goliath down to a shambling wreck on the verge of tears. The professional boxer had bobbed and weaved and danced just out of range, eluding the barrage of big punches and, when one did connect, sustaining the blow with little sign of distress. As the larger man tired, the smaller moved in to land more and more kicks to ribs and head till finally the swab caved in, dropping to the mat like so much dead meat. The matter of settling outstanding bets led to a couple more fights among the spectators.

"Boys will be boys." Jessica had evinced only boredom at the whole performance. The Hummingbird, on the other hand, had vibrated and darted and dipped in time to the action in the ring, wincing and saying no, no, every time anybody got hit, it didn't matter who. Oscar lost two hundred baht. "What did you expect?" he said. "The Thai guy's a trained fighter. And he's lucky the big guy was so clumsy."

Waylon had been looking forward to the snake show. As the MC was announcing it, a skinny guy clambered up on stage. He was dressed in a sarong tied up between his legs and an aged FUCK THE COMMIES T-shirt. The posters billed him as the Fearless Suthisak. As he mounted the platform, he slipped and banged his knee. Never mind, he seemed to say. He limped to center stage and gravely *wai*-ed the audience in four directions. A couple of young assistants, meanwhile, had placed two tightly woven wicker baskets beside him, one of them shaped in the classic snake-charmer style, the other one bigger, more like a steamer trunk.

The Hummingbird was already squirming and making noises like she wanted to leave. "Not like snake," she said.

"Hey, no problem, little honey," Oscar told her. "It's okay. I'll look after you."

"Not like."

The Fearless Suthisak's arms were covered in intricate blue tattoos, and Waylon thought he might have used one or two more, if protection was what he was after. The assistants backed well away while, in time to the whining, clashing discords of the same music that had accompanied the boxing, the snake man did an elaborate, high-stepping routine all around the baskets, which sat there looking sinister and making Nok nervous. At one point, he stepped on the heel of his own rubber flip-flop, almost falling on the largest basket. As he pushed himself erect again, you could hear something *big* move inside the basket. But it was the smaller container that featured first. Suthisak pushed the top ajar, and one of his helpers passed him a recorder, upon which he began to play a pretty good facsimile of Paul McCartney's "Yesterday." Within seconds a scaly great head emerged, a Beatles fan from hell as far as Nok was concerned—an eight-foot king cobra with hood flared.

Gradually, Suthisak enticed the entire length of the snake from its basket and they entered into an extended sparring match. The snake would strike with lazy speed and grace, never losing its poise, while the man ducked and weaved and stumbled and defied all the odds against remaining unbitten.

After he'd used a big stick to get the snake back under cover, Suthisak took a bow and Oscar hollered at him to come down and join them for a drink.

"No problem. Snake bite me many time." Suthisak giggled and fingered a cluster of Buddha amulets on chains around his neck. "Before I get sick, but now no problem."

He had just a small beer before getting back on stage for the second part of his show. The python was even more beautifully colored and patterned than the cobra, and at least twice as big. But the show was less exciting. All the snake did was wrap itself around its handler and the assistants, most notably the shapely female assistant. Oscar, for one, quickly tired of it all, and waved the guy and his snake over to the edge of the stage.

"C'mon. It won't hurt you." Oscar wanted the Hummingbird to put the snake around her shoulders.

"Not like. *Mai ow, mai ow.* No!" Nok's waist was about the same diameter as the snake's.

"Do you have to be a total asshole?" Jessica asked Oscar. "Leave her alone; she's afraid of snakes."

"Yeah? That's funny. She never seems too scared of the old one-eyed trouser snake. In fact, she's kind of partial to it, aren't you, honey?"

151

"All that talk. It's just compensation."

"*Compensation?*" Judging by Oscar's expression, this was a new word.

"Underneath it all, *you*'re scared of snakes. Just like all your talk of dicks and the fact you can't get sex unless you pay for it. I'll bet you can't even get it up half the time."

"You!" Oscar told the snake handler. "Bring that snake over here."

Nok shied away, hiding behind Waylon and grabbing his belt with both hands.

"Be careful," said the Fearless Suthisak. "Snake in bad mood."

"Ah, I can fix that. C'mon," Oscar said, addressing the snake. "Give us a kiss, darlin'."

Oscar was explaining how safe it was and how it was all a matter of confidence—you couldn't show fear—when the snake bit his face.

A python has quite a bite, necessarily so, since it is in the habit of swallowing whole goats and things. And this particular python managed to cover Oscar's entire face with a giant yawn, setting its numerous teeth into Oscar's scalp and jaw. Pythons have large teeth that point back towards their throats, a feature, as Oscar was discovering, that prevents their meals from thrashing free. Oscar was trying to tell them something, but it was hard to understand what it was, what with this snake on his face. And Waylon could see that snakes and worms were two entirely different kettles of fish, since Jessica was stroking the snake with no sign of fear whatsoever and telling it, "There, there. Don't be frightened. The nasty man won't hurt you."

Suthisak, with some effort and much sweet talk, wrestled the snake's jaws open and pried the animal off Oscar. Eddie had to take the victim to the hospital, since blood was running into his eyes and everyone agreed it wouldn't be safe for him to drive his motorbike. Waylon bought the Fearless Suthisak a drink and Jessica bought him two. This time he went for Mekhong sodas.

Later, back at Hot Licks, everybody was in a fine mood, which probably had nothing to do with the snakebite story. The Hummingbird and Jessica were sitting at the bar, handbags half emptied all over the countertop, chatting away and comparing pharmaceuticals. Oscar came in with an interesting pattern of iodine and tiny round plasters all over his face, looking something like a Maori warrior but even more like the horse's ass Jessica claimed he really was. Nok's concern also seemed kind of *pro forma*.

Waylon knew he was a little drunk, but he felt great. He laughed till his guts ached.

"Boom!" said Leary. "You give Oscar here a double bourbon on ice. Tell him it's for snakebite. Drink it or pour it on the wounds, it's up to him."

"Leary, maybe better you send drink over for snake." That was Big Toy's contribution to the general concern over Oscar's welfare.

Leary said he was thinking of awarding Oscar a new certification. "Yep. The Diving Straight into the Jaws of Death Specialty. Gosh-darn it, Oscar. Next time you try to French kiss a twenty-foot python, I recommend you strap a plank to your butt just to make sure you don't go all the friggin' way. Can't leave that boy without a chaperone."

Towards the end of the evening the Fearless Suthisak showed up—to some acclaim and to Nok's relief, since he hadn't brought his snakes with him. He was already sloshed, and he proudly displayed two fresh puncture marks on his arm, spaced about two and a half inches apart. "Never mind," he said with a giggle. "No problem." And then he looked over at Oscar, who'd been quieter than his wont all night, and said again, with a big grin, "Never mind. No problem," winning no friends in that quarter.

About the time Waylon decided it was late enough and he'd had enough to drink, except maybe for one more whiskey, Jessica came back over and said, "Waylon. Let's go."

"I'm not ready yet, Jessie."

"We've got to talk, Waylon. I've got something important to tell you." Then, under cover of her bag and the music, she put a hand between his legs. "And I've got something special for you tonight, Waylon."

Yawn

After they got back to his place and undressed for a bath, Jessica explained that they would have to do some extra diving before the advanced course.

"What advanced course?" said Waylon.

"Waylon. We have to do the advanced course."

"Okay," he said, only a little surprised to hear himself agree. Aghast at his own behavior over the past week, he had nevertheless achieved a more distanced aghastness, one that involved less real alarm. Anyway, he told himself, whatever else happened, he was now a full-fledged open water diver.

"Waylon. What do you like best?" Jessica asked him later, when they were in bed. "Sex, I mean. What do you want me to do for you? Don't be shy. Anything you want, okay?"

He chewed at his lip and willed his leg to be still. Where was Chloe, anyway? The last time he'd called the house in Vancouver the message machine still wasn't working, and, when he used Big Toy's computer to check their e-mail account, there had been nothing there either. Just a bunch of business messages, some junk mail and about three megabytes of jokes from an old university friend who was the Sorcerer's Apprentice of Internet correspondents.

He felt things slipping away from him, out of control. And now it was the advanced course. With Jessica. Just what did he think he was doing, anyway? *Eh?*

Jessica had had something else to tell him that night. She reported someone had been inside her bungalow and gone through all her things. Never mind, Waylon reflected, most of her things were by now in his bungalow anyway.

The next morning, Leary expressed concern. "Fosdick. You had any trouble at your place?"

"Not so far as I can see." Not aside from Jessica's invasion, Waylon wanted to say.

"Well, we've never had a problem before. But I'll put a word in the local gendarmes' ear, not that it'll do any good. And I'll ask the security company I pay to check the shop, here, to keep a bit of an eye on things.

"Gosh, Fosdick. Maybe it's not my place to say, but I reckon that woman is about as deep as that darned bag she carries around, and it could be that some of the friggin' baggage she carries around in her head turns out to be just as surprising. You watch our Jessie, you hear me? She's your dive buddy and all, and you got to look after her. That's right. But you watch your own friggin' butt at the same time. You hear me?"

"I hear you." Waylon was reassured by a touch of the old familiar alarm.

21 bump in the night

*Lighten our darkness . . . and . . . defend us
from all perils and dangers of this night.*

Book of Common Prayer

The inky darkness came alive, revealing a whole other dimension to the underwater world.

What a light show. Eerie ribbons and streaks and points of purplish light appeared everywhere. That pulsating ball of ghostly white fire was probably a jellyfish. The abrupt streaks of light were squid or fish. Tiny winking points indicated zooplankton, while other, sometimes strange and unidentifiable patterns might simply have been light-emitting bacteria in the process of consuming dead fish.

Oscar and Eddie had explained the various phenomena to Jessica and Waylon on the boat before the dive. Waylon swept his arm through the water and watched the sparkle of phosphorescence that followed. He switched on his torch again, just for a moment, to catch the agent of one particularly impressive serpentine trail, and saw nothing. There was no neon snake, no new and wonderful animal. It was merely a fish, already long gone, that had darted past and fired a path of phosphorescent plankton.

Waylon liked night diving. He enjoyed the sense of drifting along in the cocoon of light from his underwater torch. It was like a tour, with vivid marine life impinging on your little world as you moved along. There was more color than you got in the day, except at shallow depths still lit by sun. You didn't have to go very deep—thirty feet or so—before the water began absorbing the longer wavelengths of light, starting with the reds, yellows, and oranges. By ninety feet, most things were rendered in shades of blue and black. At night, however, torches restored the corals and fish to their full glory.

But now, strung along the anchor line towards the end of the night dive, they had switched off their torches and ditched Jessica's chemical lightstick so they could enjoy the bioluminescent spectacle. Eddie had put the lightstick on Jessica's tank and told her that she was the group's anchor. The idea was to give her a sense of function, to offset any anxiety at the thought of diving in the dark.

Waylon looked up to where the waning moon lay shattered on a gentle ripple forty feet above. He was savoring a novel and contradictory sense of profound peace which was at the same time excitement. Then Jessica freaked out. She came rocketing up the anchor line in a storm of bubbles—evidence, at least, that she wasn't holding her breath. On the way past, she punched Waylon right in the balls. So much for foot-a-second ascents. Oscar followed her up to offer reassurances, while Eddie and Waylon spent a few more minutes hanging out on the line. Waylon was distracted from the adventure by the sickness in the pit of his stomach.

Later, when they were all back on the boat, Eddie gave Jessica a lecture. He told her that if she had come up that way from ninety or a hundred feet, instead of only thirty or forty feet, she might well have been bent. Yeah, Oscar added: here it was Jessica who freaked out and shot to the surface, but Waylon was the one who got the bends. A true buddy.

"Have you any idea how much that hurts?" Waylon asked her.

"Just don't get in the way," she replied. Then she smiled to show she was only kidding.

Back on shore, Leary took Waylon aside. "I swear, Fosdick, you watch yourself with her. She just doesn't like the darned water. We can maybe break her of that, if we go slow, but you remember that panic is the number-one cause of diving accidents. You got to remember, you're responsible for your buddy when you're underwater. Darn it. And your buddy's responsible for you. You be careful, now. I don't know what it is about that woman. Sometimes she seems as tough as they come. Other times she's only just holding herself together. And she keeps herself half doped up. I shouldn't let her dive at all." Leary looked hard at Waylon. "You be careful, now."

But, yeah, they could do the rest of the advanced open water course. "Gosh, Fosdick. You take to this like a divin' duck to friggin' water. And Jessie, here, I guess is about as ready as she's ever going to get. So, yeah. I guess you might as well do the darned advanced course. Why not?" But Leary figured they were going to need some extra dives. "You want to do another night dive or two, and a few dives to sixty feet in the daytime. You're doing fine. And Jessie'll come along."

Jessica was improving. She'd eased off on the Valium, Waylon believed. Now it was mostly vodka before bed.

They had a couple of drinks at Hot Licks and then borscht, baked fish, and potatoes with Leary at a Russian restaurant across the way.

When they got back to Waylon's bungalow, they found it had been broken into. The bedroom window, the one behind the house and covered by banana plants and things, had been jimmied. The intruders had left the window open, not caring who knew about it. Nothing was missing, as far as Waylon could make out, but every drawer, every cupboard and cabinet in the place was turned out. The place was a mess. Whoever had done it had even scattered Waylon's and Jessica's course notes all over the floor and the bed. What had happened to all the protection Leary had talked about?

"It must've been kids," Waylon said.

"Probably," agreed Jessica. She took two hits of Valium and vodka before bed.

22 therapies

It amazes me that organs that piss
Can give human beings such perfect bliss.

Irving Layton

His legs! Waylon kicked again, but nothing happened.
 His legs were gone.
 He couldn't swim, and the current was sweeping him away from the others. Stop! Breathe. . . . *Think*. Never act in panic. The first thing was simply to stop. Get your breathing under control. Then think. Decide what the problem was and go about addressing it in the best way possible. Waylon sucked hard on his regulator, breathing deep and *thinking*, thinking a shark couldn't have taken his legs, or he'd feel the pain. Wouldn't he?
 Officious, full of his fast-approaching advanced open water diver status, Waylon had done buddy checks on Eddie and Oscar, whom he saw were about to enter the water without bothering to examine each other's equipment, and then he did one on Jessica. Jessica checked Waylon in return, tugging at his hoses and weight-

belt and sucking bursts of air off his regulator mouthpieces. She squeezed another burst off the low-pressure hose on his flotation jacket, looked at his gauges and goosed him, just for luck, before making her stride entry through the side gate. Waylon followed. Only to discover he'd neglected to put on his fins.

So there he was, drifting away in the current, waiting for the boat to come around to drop his gear off for him. Fortunately, it was a live-boat dive—they'd planned a drift dive with the current, so their boat hadn't anchored. And the current wasn't that bad. The others simply stayed on the surface together and waited till Waylon signaled he was ready, and then they met up on the way down.

Waylon practiced his controlled breathing the whole time, trying to counter the effects of excitement, embarrassment, and the effort of getting his fins on in the water. By the time he eyeballed Oscar through his mask and exchanged reassuring signs so Oscar knew he was okay, Waylon's breathing was fine, and they all descended together.

The drift dive was exhilarating. The ultimate underwater tourists, they soared along over an alien landscape in effortless luxury, weightless. For part of the dive, they were carried through a fantasy garden of fan corals, whip corals, sponges, and branching hard corals like ornamental shrubs. At one point, Oscar grabbed on to a rock. He'd spotted something under a coral head, and he beckoned to Waylon and Jessica. Getting a grip on the outcrop and pulling themselves down to look, they saw a couple of big round eyes staring back at them. Then the creature moved. What Waylon first thought was a fish suddenly transformed itself into the great hook-beaked head of a sea turtle. It wanted to escape, but they were blocking its path. Finally, it decided to break cover. As soon as it got clear, it headed for the hills, its front flippers like wings. Meanwhile, huge schools of tangs and blue-and-yellow fusiliers swam a parallel course just off the reef slope.

Faster than Waylon would have liked—he was having fun—the advanced course was all but over. True, they were skating a few things where Jessica was concerned, and that made him uncomfortable. But these guys were pros; they knew what they were doing. Still, buddy breathing was a non-starter with Jessica. Anyway, Leary had explained that he considered it almost suicide to try buddy breathing in earnest. "But you don't want to tell basic open-water students that. It's not exactly reassuring news, darn it, and a lot of what we're trying to do is build confidence."

Neither was Jessica happy with diving at night. She had gone in after dark three times, now. But she couldn't get comfortable with it. The deep dive qualification had been another problem. Oscar had demonstrated how a ping-pong ball imploded under the pressure at around a hundred feet, and Leary had asked them to do a series of arithmetical problems on the boat, working against the clock, and scored them. Then he took them down to a hundred and ten feet on the anchor line in a raging current. "Now you be careful," he told them. "Pull yourself down the line and don't turn your face to the side, or the current could tear your mask right off."

They hooked themselves on the line with one arm, underwater slate in hand, and, with the other, worked out a series of problems similar to those they'd done on surface. Then they compared scores. The object of this exercise was in part to demonstrate the effects of nitrogen narcosis—the absorption of nitrogen into the bloodstream and brain under pressure—on your mental faculties. Waylon hadn't felt stoned or anything. Just slightly nervous with the current and the limited visibility. Still, he scored noticeably lower than he had on surface. Jessica had got one answer out of ten correct. She had devoted all her faculties to not freaking out, Waylon suspected, although maybe she had been narked as well. In fact, that was a safe bet, given she was kind of narked even at the best of times.

Waylon and Jessica agreed search and salvage had been best. Side by side in thirty feet of water, they had swum a triangle about a hundred feet on a side using underwater compass navigation, shooting bearings off rocks and coral heads, and steering around sea cucumbers until they came back to the aluminum ladder they'd dropped from the boat. Then they tied the ladder and two weight-belts to lift bags, one at each end. Squeezing the purge valves on their regulators, they'd filled the bags a little at a time, keeping the ladder and its load of tanks level, and then ascended together with their booty, adjusting their own buoyancy and that of the load as they went, keeping things steady.

They did the search and recovery part twice, at Jessica's insistence, once before lunch and once after, even though they'd got it right the first time. "This is *fun*, Waylon," she'd said. She'd hardly felt nervous at all, this time. "It makes all the difference when you've got something sensible to do."

She'd been arguing that they should practice it a third time, she would pay for the extra dive if necessary. Then she got stabbed.

One of the reasons buoyancy control was so important was it meant you were less likely to bump into things. In the heat of the second salvage operation, Jessica lost track and brushed against what was described in their natural history notes as a black long-spined sea urchin. As she thrashed around and threatened to panic, Waylon noted, the wounds had bled wisps of muddy green, just the way they were supposed to at depths where water filtered out the red and orange wavelengths. The creature wasn't poisonous, but its spines, which were many and indeed long, could inflict painful wounds on the unwary. The barbed tips of the spines break off, and Jessica came to surface with a messy constellation of black puncture marks on her haunch.

"This hurts," she informed them. "Oscar? What are we going to do about this?"

"Waylon kiss and make better."

"Why don't you kiss my ass, Oscar?" she suggested.

As Oscar said, and as Jessica should have remembered from her course notes, the best treatment was to apply citrus juice, vinegar, or even urine. "*Your*-ein," he said.

"Your *what*?" Jessica said.

"Your piss," replied Eddie.

"Or whoever's." Oscar leered.

Eddie said he'd get a lime and Jessica said don't bother, she had one in her bag. They sliced it and Waylon rubbed it gently over the punctures. "Squeeze the spines," Eddie suggested. "It hurts, but break them up and you absorb them faster."

So Waylon squeezed and Jessica whined. He rubbed lime on the wounds, and she said she was going to order a big pitcher of margueritas when they got back to Hot Licks. She kept the other half of the lime, and periodically rubbed it on herself on the way back to shore.

In Waylon's bungalow that night, full of tequila and pleasure at having finished the advanced course, Jessica turned affectionate. "Waylon," she said. "Let's have a shower together." Waylon had wanted to go to sleep, although now, with Jessica's soapy butt squirming in his crotch, he could see he wasn't that sleepy after all.

"Ow!" said Jessica. "Careful. My sea urchin wounds. Waylon? Do you think Oscar was serious about the urine?"

"What?"

"About the piss, Waylon. Pissing on sea urchin wounds."

"Well, yeah. It's the acid."

"Waylon. Do it for me. Okay? They still hurt."

"Are you serious?"

"Come on, Waylon."

She knelt down in front of him and he pissed on her. Then she wanted to piss on a little patch of coral burn she'd found on his shoulder. She had him sit on the floor of the shower stall, and she showed him a trick using two fingers that allowed her to pee standing up. "See, Waylon? There's nothing you guys can do better than us."

"Jesus Christ, eh?" It felt warm and sort of comforting, Waylon had to concede, and it might have reduced the stinging, which had been minimal anyway. But the whole scene left him feeling like a goof. And it took some doing on Jessica's part, back in the bedroom, to get him in the mood again. Then she wanted to use the bag again, but this time it put him off completely. And he passed on the opportunity to try it himself. "It just isn't my bag, Jessica," he said, but she didn't laugh.

"Waylon. We have to do the wreck diving course."

"*Why?*"

"Come on, Waylon. We've just about got this thing beat."

What "thing"? What was she talking about? Her claustrophobia? His marriage? "Jesus Christ, eh?" he told her again. After all. It was time to get his life back on track. There wasn't a hint of a quiver in his lip.

"Waylon. Would you stop? How am I supposed to relax? It's like an earthquake in here."

"What?"

"Your leg, Waylon. Your *leg*. The whole damned bungalow is shaking. Stop it."

23 golden age

Things are always going to get worse, and we just have to take what friggin' solace we can from that.

Leary

The submerged castle lay indistinct in the murky water, half obscured by seaweed. One fish—it looked a lot like a shark—darted out through a ruined tower directly towards Waylon.

Black with a red tail and about three inches long, it stopped just short of the glass. A goldfish cruised past, one of those Chinese sports with bobbling big eyeballs. It goggled at Waylon in amazement. Standing there having a piss in the single toilet at the back of Hot Licks, Waylon watched several fish going 'round and 'round in a box aquarium mounted at head level on the wall above the throne. What an odd place to put an aquarium. Leary must have installed the thing that very day, Waylon thought, as he pulled the chain flush on the side of the porcelain watercloset. And the fishtank emptied. All the little fish, guppies and things, were left flapping high and dry on a bed of beach pebbles and marbles.

Waylon was standing there agape, dick in hand, and the tank was starting to fill again when the door opened and Boom said, "You okay, Wail-On? Somebody look for you."

Waylon hadn't yet fully come to terms with the new toilet flush when his sensibilities were assaulted again. "Yahhh!" said Daeng, the happy-hooker-in-chief, as she bore down on Waylon. "Wail-On! Wail-*On*." The whole Gang of Four descended on Waylon like a tribe of joyous banshees. "Bar Bangkok all close. No good, Wail-On. We come for another holl-ee-*day*." Oo looked great, Waylon noted in passing.

The graduation party for Jessica and Waylon just happened to coincide with a Bangkok municipal election. And the Happy Hookers were taking a busman's holiday, as Leary put it. Bangkok establishments had been prohibited from serving alcohol for two days because of the election. Pattaya, however, was immune from such afflictions as religious or electoral holidays. This was a no-man's land of all-night bars and sex with anybody of any gender or any age. The town was ruled by the tourist dollar, and if tourists wanted to stay up all night three hundred and sixty five days a year, then welcome. Everything else took second place to the overriding business of extracting money from visiting funseekers.

Waylon tried to explain that the Gang of Four were actually Leary's friends, but Jessica wasn't listening. For one thing, it had just turned six o'clock and the music abruptly swelled to serious good-time levels which, even by Thai standards, promised very good times indeed.

Paper streamers and clusters of balloons festooned the bar. Actually, they were condoms in ugly shades of red and green, but they did the trick all the same. "I guess everybody's using helium, nowadays, eh?" Waylon was still outraged at the story of Dinky Toy's disfigurement.

"Ian who?" replied Big Toy, yelling so she could be heard over the music.

In honor of Waylon's and Jessica's graduation, Hot Licks was all dolled up and every available surface was covered with one kind of food or another. "*Aroi, aroi.*" Delicious, Nok and Boom proclaimed in unison. "*Aroi, phet!*" Sweat, not to mention tears of pain and ecstasy, streamed down their faces. *Somtam phoo*, Laotian-style green papaya salad, was hot enough to set your sideburns on fire. Thai women favored the dish, Leary told Waylon, because it contained fermented black crabs which in turn contained a number of totally fireproof bacteria. "Gosh, this is the Thai *pooying*'s number-one weight control program. You eat some of this darned stuff and you got what they call a 'running stomach' for two days or more."

"That's a 'walking stomach,'" amended Jessica. "*Thong deu-un.*"

"Call it anything you like. My stomach gets up and runs just at the sight of it."

Waylon, wondering how Jessica knew what to call diarrhea in Thai, tried some of the salad and found it good. God knows what kind of germs were in it, but, as he realized with a sense of liberation, he didn't care too much. He washed it down with a Mekhong whiskey soda.

Jessica was getting along on rice, raw vegetables, and vodka. "I'm the same way," said Leary. "I don't believe in eating this oriental food. Never did and never will. Give me good old-fashioned American chow, something that sticks to the ribs and don't fry your friggin' tonsils." Leary helped himself to a second plateful of barbecued chicken and baked potatoes, a bowl of Texas-style chili on the side.

Keeow was brushing a gloss into Dinky Toy's long black hair while Dinky Toy talked to Big Toy, who was scowling at an accounts ledger on the bar. A saucer with a wedge of lime, salt, and a shot glass of tequila lay within easy reach. Waylon had already had more Mekhong sodas than was good for a person, and the evening was still young. So roll on evening. The surge of joy was followed right away by a sickening void that opened deep in his gut, a visceral recognition of doom. Jesus Christ. What was he doing? At what point had he had stepped off the precipice? But the moment passed. "Gosh," said a familiar voice inside him. "That's frig-all. Just relax." And here he was, more exhilarated than terrified, which in itself was worrying. A dream-like quality colored everything that had happened since he arrived in Thailand. Ever since he'd yawned that mighty yawn.

Oo, the kid, grabbed Waylon in a big hug. She smelled of Mekhong and she was crying. Her boyfriend the motorcycle racer was dead.

"Jesus Christ. I'm sorry." Waylon didn't know what to say. "Really sorry, eh?"

It hadn't been a racing accident, Oo reported. No, he had drunk too much Mekhong while eating durian. Or so the story went, Daeng added. They had said the same thing about her uncle Chainat, forget that he'd drunk a large bottle of Mekhong every day for twenty years and you could blame it on the durian if you wanted to. Waylon didn't even know what a durian was.

"Never mind, Wail-On." Oo threw her arms around him and laid a big kiss on his cheek.

"So who's this, Waylon?" Jessica appeared beside them at the bar. "Your chess partner?"

Then Daeng and Oi and the other one had to kiss him as well, and Waylon was thinking he needed a diversion. Just then My Bottle appeared in the bathroom door looking pretty shaken, the sneer trying to regain a grip on his face. It was probably something to do with the novel flush mechanism.

"That toilet," said Jessica. "That's really cruel to the fish."

"Hah," Leary told them. "Just put that sucker in there this morning. First saw one of those one time in a little bar in Indonesia. Gosh-darnedest thing, I thought to myself. Could see I'd have to have one just like it, one day. So now we get to take our pee and do our friggin' philosophizing all at the same time.

"You see, that's just the way things are. Gosh. You do your stuff. You take care of business, thinking you're in control, when somewhere out there you got forces you never even thought of doing *their* things. You work hard all your life and everything's breaking your way, maybe you just won the Nobel Prize and the Braves took the pennant and you come home drunk and your wife don't say a thing. Then, all of a sudden, somebody or something up there takes a pee and you're left high and dry and you don't even know why. Darn it. We're no different from those friggin' fish, when it comes right down to it. That's what they call life, Fosdick. The only thing we can do is get on with living it, in between the times somebody up there has got to take a pee."

Nobody but Leary had a voice loud enough to communicate all that over the music. Jessica had her hand on Waylon's thigh and was trying to tell him something about dive buddies, when a flash, brighter than the disco lights, and a sudden *brraaat-brat-brat*, louder than the music, sent Leary to ground. He was on the floor with the end of the bar between him and where the explosions had come from. By the time Waylon thought of looking for cover it was too late to worry about it, and he could hear screaming.

The ringing in Waylon's ears from the explosions was continuous with a high-pitched mewling from Boom, who was on her back with hands extended above her like claws. The screaming was Keeow. Nok was kneeling beside Boom, wailing and making as though to touch Boom's face, where the hydrogen-filled balloons had burnt her, but not doing it. Leary got up off the floor and took command of things inside a minute. "Turn off that friggin' music," he said. Rather than chance waiting for an ambulance, he wrapped Boom in a tablecloth and carried her out to his car. Then, with Nok and Dinky Toy riding shotgun, he took her straight to a hospital.

Big Toy and Keeow stayed behind to look after things at Hot Licks, with the Happy Hookers and even Jessica pitching in to attend to the needs of My Bottle and the six or seven other male customers who remained. A couple of hours later Leary and the girls—minus Boom, who'd been admitted to the hospital—showed up again to fill everybody in on her condition.

"You know," Leary told Waylon, "I'm getting tired of this town. It's not like it used to be. Gosh. Twenty-five years ago it was a fishing village, though I never did see it then, and this was one of the most beautiful bays in the world. Next thing you knew, it was 'Thailand's premier seaside resort' and, according to some, the biggest friggin' brothel in the world. That was maybe an exaggeration, but before long the bay was full of garbage and turds and the newspapers warned everybody not to swim in it. Sometimes I think it's time for me to clear out. Trouble is, where would I go from here?"

A couple of bourbons-on-ice later, after Big Toy had done an inspired impersonation of Leary demanding the music be turned down, and after Dinky Toy had presented him with a po'-boy sandwich the likes of which he'd never seen before, Leary brightened a little. For one thing, as he said, Boom wasn't hurt as bad as they'd first feared.

In fact, things were never really as bad as they seemed, claimed Leary. Not if you looked at life in just the right light. "Now, here's a gosh-darned natural law," he declared. "As anybody who wants to look around can see, everything turns to shit over time." He held his glass against his forehead for a long moment and then slammed the drink down on the bar. "That's just the way things are. Gosh. Things are always going to get worse, and we have to take what friggin' solace we can from that. What it means, we're always living in a golden age, at least looking back from any time in the future. Think about it."

Nok had a half-cob of roasted corn. She was pulling the kernels off one by one and popping them into her mouth. She was curiously intent, amid all the pounding music and flashing lights. It could have been boredom, but Waylon thought it could also have been hunger because she started popping them faster and faster, and there was a tear in the corner of the eye nearest him.

Back at the bungalow, Jessica wanted to talk about Oo. "Don't tell me you haven't slept with her, Waylon."

He didn't. He merely told her to piss off. But he didn't like what he saw in her eyes.

24 just wanna ride my lunar-cycle

There may always be another reality
To make fiction of the truth we think we've arrived at.

Christopher Fry

"*A*WESOME. I could stay here FOREVER," said Bibi. "This *IS* forever. INCREDIBLE! It's like THIS AFTERNOON will never *END*. Don't you FEEL it?"

"Yeah," said Chloe, wondering how meditation practice could leave anyone so wound up.

"Sure," said Prue, gazing out at the sand and sea and coconut palms with the same cynical regard she pretended to give anything that inspired enthusiasm in the masses. "Bibi's not bad when she's stoned," Prue had told Chloe. "All she does is giggle. Quietly, even. It's quite pleasant." Apparently the grass Bibi was sharing with Al Dente hadn't taken hold yet.

Earlier, Bibi had given Chloe the full scoop on the *full* moon party, all the while sneaking looks at Al Dente, who hid behind his sunglasses. "It's just totally *MEGA*," she said. "You wouldn't

BELIEVE it. THOUSANDS of PEOPLE. THOUSANDS and *THOUSANDS*."

"Have some more." Al Dente passed a joint to Bibi, his blanket-mate.

Bibi was the one who suggested a dark moon party. The full moon was still two weeks away and everybody felt the need to get away from the 4H Club for a while. Prue, for one, was quick to agree: "I've had enough belly-button gazing for now. Let's go have some fun." Ruthie and Tip hadn't come. Tip said she had errands. Ruthie wanted to stay behind to do some things for Gorgi while he was away in Bangkok on business.

So that morning, the seven of them—Chloe, Prue, Bibi, Olga, Freddie, the Rev, and Al Dente—came to Haad Hey, the main party beach, in a rented longtail boat, an open wooden vessel with an upthrust prow and a big truck engine mounted on a pivot and trailing a long propeller shaft—the "tail"—that could be lifted and swung as needed when negotiating shallow water or crowded anchorages.

The upswept wooden prow of their boat was ornamented with offerings to the sea gods, including a garish plastic flower garland. Before setting out, Buk, their boatman, lit jossticks and a string of firecrackers. Chloe jumped at the sharp rattle as they went off in a cloud of pungent smoke and paper fragments. "Scare away bad spirit," explained Buk.

They had had some trouble getting underway, despite the precautions, with the long propeller shaft swinging this way and that, threatening to knock other drivers off their boats where they rocked at anchor, everybody laughing and ducking, except a few who were only ducking and swearing.

"Not like water." His cousin owned this boat, Buk said. "Cousin sick, *na*?" he further explained, looking kind of sick himself. He took a slug from a bottle of Mekhong rice whiskey before passing it to Somsak, his helper, who only looked impassive. You couldn't tell whether he liked water or not. Or anything else, come to that. As far as Chloe gradually understood it, Buk's cousin had actually died and Buk, to his dismay, inherited half of the boat. Somsak, who was another cousin, inherited the other half.

They finally got underway, but Al Dente first had to give them another bottle of Mekhong, not to mention serve as pilot, pointing out which of the islands they should be headed for. Buk and Somsak finished the bottle by the time they got to the beach, and within a minute of arrival were asleep in the shade of a tree back of the beach.

Bibi's brainstorm, as it turned out, was already behind the times—several hundred other people had already had the same good idea. Dark moon parties were all the rage. And Bibi had it wrong. They arrived a day late, just in time to find the beach strewn with a couple of hundred fairly wrecked revelers, human flotsam and jetsam from the night before.

Freddie, at least, was quick to adapt. "Watch this, man," he told a gang of admirers on the beach as he sucked on a snorkel, toking enough good ganja to confuse half a dozen seekers after truth. "It's a *snorkelbong*, man. Far out." Freddie was strutting around in magnetic cape, bikini bathing suit and swim-fins, totally deadpan, flipping sand everywhere and getting attacked by Pup, whom he'd brought along for company. He had a plastic snorkel he'd turned into a bong, and he appeared entirely serious about whatever it was he thought he was doing.

Al Dente was the one who first suggested they move to Koh Phra Chan Noi, or "Little Moon Island," and that, of course, had nothing to do with the young admirer who was paying court to Bibi.

Bibi was explaining some of the finer points of astrology to this Thai guy who'd sold them cotton sarongs to use as beachtowels, formal evening wear, and, in the Asian style, as convenient change houses. Although why anybody would worry about modesty, under the circumstances, was a mystery to Chloe. More than half the ladies present were topless and many more were bottomless as well. But it is ancient wisdom that only hinting at fleshly mysteries can be more erotic than flaunting them. That's the success of striptease. So the young Thai kept nodding just as though he knew what Bibi was talking about, while his primary interest clearly lay in what bobbed and swung in rough unison under her sleeveless blouse. All the bobbing and swinging wasn't entirely unconscious, on Bibi's part. And—in much the same way this guy wasn't looking up Bibi's armhole—Al Dente, who was sitting in the sand not far away behind his aviator sunglasses, was studiously taking no interest in proceedings. "Hey," Al Dente said, eventually seeing his chance to get a word in edgewise. "Why don't we get some food and beers and go over to that other island? Have a private party."

"I'm going to need two hamburgers," said Prue. "With bacon, cheese, and a fried egg on each."

"Hot fried greasy fuckin' salt, man." Chloe had rolled her eyes back in their sockets and did the turkey thing. She still didn't look much like Freddie, she was relieved to hear.

They left Freddie demonstrating his snorkelbong. Olga, who was ministering to the men's national volleyball team from Italy, also decided to stay. Hitting the nearest beachside stand, they bought a bunch of greasy burgers and some french fries, and—as a concession to Al Dente, who was brainwashed—a big bag of tossed salad. Chloe also wolfed two burgers, realizing at the same time that she wasn't enjoying them. In fact she felt vaguely poisoned, as though some sullen weight had descended on her belly. How easily one was corrupted by clean living.

It took them a while to find Buk and Somsak. They weren't into hamburgers, opting instead for fried rice and another bottle of Mekhong. By the time they got to Phra Chan Noi Island, they'd demolished most of the whiskey.

"Not like water," Buk told them just before he ran the bow of the boat up on to the beach, in the process falling off the stern and into the shallows. "Not like boat," he added, after he'd cleared the water from his tubes and got his breath back. "Cannot swim. Not like."

Buk was from a village in the Northeast of Thailand and had been a farmer. "Now no work." Rapacious logging, drought, and ill-advised agricultural policies had destroyed the local economy, as Tip had told Chloe some days before. So the sons and daughters of the Northeast were being just as carelessly expended as the forests and the land had been, worked to death in rice godowns or as tuk-tuk drivers in Bangkok, selling themselves as "service people" to the booming sex trade—whether as waitresses, hostesses, masseuses, go-go dancers, straight-up prostitutes, or sex-show performers. Buk was lucky to have his own business, even if he didn't like it.

The nearer bay on Phra Chan Noi had some fancy buildings, and the headland on one side sprouted what looked like a lighthouse or, maybe, a guard tower. They gave all that a wide berth, and ran into an utterly deserted little cove on the north side of the island.

Prue frowned at her abdominals. She was smoking a cigarette and doing leg lifts. Chloe was also looking down at herself. She flicked sand from a nipple. Her breasts were still full and firm, almost symmetrical. She was thinking about Waylon. This was the sort of holiday they'd imagined they would have together. Chloe felt a pang of something like sorrow—regret laced with irritation. She actually missed Waylon. That twit. Mostly she was numb, though. Numb because of the recent changes in her life, but maybe also because of too many Singha beers in the sun, so who could tell how much numbness was this and how much numbness was that?

Chloe liked Prue. She had a sense of perspective. And she was an individualist. So was Bibi, as it turned out. Earlier that day, she'd been the only lady out of the assortment arranged on the sand at Haad Hey who'd had the gumption to bathe with her top on. On Phra Chan Island, wearing your *bottom* was considered pretty radical; but there she'd been, cool as a cucumber with full bikini top, polka dots and all. Chloe had been impressed. And she liked Bibi's tattoo, a little teddy bear on her tummy just below and to one side of her bellybutton ring.

Half the women on the beaches, and half the men, had tattoos. Chloe had thought about it. Maybe a tasteful little flower or bug somewhere discreet. But the idea would have appealed more if half the world weren't already rushing to get decorated. What would next season's fashion dictate? What about the time when having a tattoo wouldn't be cool anymore? Mostly, however, Chloe realized she just wasn't ready to define herself, to commit herself to one thing or the other right now. More than popular tastes, she was afraid her own predilections would change. No, that was wrong. She was afraid they wouldn't.

The Rev was smoking his pipe. Every once in a while he took a hit off a silver-plated flask of single malt whiskey, a special treat from his rapidly diminishing cache in the woods. He was drinking beer as well, claiming the whiskey was only because it tasted good, while in this climate the cold beer was a basic necessity. He seemed to be enjoying himself. Although how he could be doing this was beyond Chloe. As usual, the Rev was wearing black trousers with creases and a black shirt buttoned to the collar. He had removed his black lace-ups, but he still wore black socks. A collective offering to the god Rahu.

The full moon was a time of lunacy, a time when tidal forces triggered primordial urges and cycles. But the dark moon was the even more mysterious flip-side. In Thailand, Tip had told them, many people believed that an eclipse meant the god Rahu was eating the moon, and some believed the same thing happened with the dark moon. People all over the country made lots of noise, going outside to bang on pots and pans and let off firecrackers. At the same time they offered tribute to Rahu, eight black things— boiled black chicken, black candles, black incense sticks, black coffee, black rice, and whatnot—so he'd go away. This was a dangerous time, what with monsters munching on the moon, a time to keep your head down and not be thinking of new projects and new directions. This particular great black offering, red-faced and panting, drenched in sweat, was enough to give even the gods pause.

Since moving to Phra Chan Noi they'd seen only one other person. A long leisurely lady of vaguely Mediterranean origin, olive-skinned with fine dark hairs on her legs and an enormous pubic bush, had ambled up to them from the other end of the beach, all legs and glossy black hair.

"Good grief, that's not a bathing suit! Look at that. She hasn't got a stitch on!" It was hard to figure the scandalized tone in the Rev's voice; they'd already seen more nude women that day than your average adolescent male dreams of in a week. Haad Hey had been littered with them, and with nude men as well. Prue and Ruthie had had great fun window shopping for ideal types. Bibi had already found hers, of course, while Chloe came down with a mild case of Canadian inhibition. And Olga had no patience for window shopping.

The nymph looked up from her investigation of the shoreline and walked directly over to them. The Rev made a sound like someone trying to gargle and hiccup at the same time.

"Was that a death rattle?" asked Prue. "Or what? Why don't you take off your shirt? And your socks, for God's sake."

"Gas." said the Rev, rubbing his belly. "It's the Thai beer."

Prue made room for their visitor on her sarong. She sat down, one leg sprawled out, hair spilling down in cascades, and cradled the other foot, sole uppermost, in her hands, saying she thought she'd stepped on a sea urchin spine. She wore nothing except a small pouch which hung from a thong between her pomegranate breasts. Al Dente offered to bang on the foot with a rock, recommended first aid for sea urchin stabs. He said it broke up the imbedded tip of the spine so the body could absorb it more quickly. The visitor passed on the first aid, to Al Dente's visible disappointment and Bibi's relief. Although she hid it well. "Oh, NO," she said. "You should let him DO it; he REALLY *KNOWS* about these things."

Neither did the visitor want a beer. She told them she had "magic," which Al Dente and the Rev evidently thought was true, although the lift of the Rev's eyebrow suggested it was a trifle immodest of her to say so. But what she meant was that she had magic mushrooms. Would they like some? She had opened the pouch that hung from her neck.

Prue said sure. And so did Chloe, obeying some unlooked-for impulse. Besides, she was half bombed on beer and sun, and not entirely responsible. She wanted the savor of something new. Ring in the changes; damn the consequences. That's hormones for you. All of a sudden you're young and stupid again. So Chloe ate a mushroom, her first ever. "So I'm a jerk," she told herself, gagging at the acrid taste.

Chloe didn't even like to smoke dope. She'd smoked Thai stick with Prue and Freddie, once, just to be sociable. Which was a laugh, when she thought about it, because smoking always made her asocial. Not anti-social—she liked to be around people when she was stoned. But the dope cut her off. She withdrew into herself. If she got stoned enough she lost the power to understand words, much less articulate them. That could be scary, unless you were with just the right people in just the right situation. What she really liked was to have a few drinks with friends and hang out.

The Rev also ate a mushroom, though Bibi, never mind she was too young to have been a member of the never-trust-anyone-over-thirty generation, tried to dissuade him. To tell the truth Chloe also felt there was something wrong with a thirty-five-year-old man of the cloth, of sorts, doing psychedelics. But Magic Lady smiled sweetly, mysteriously, and fed the Rev a morsel of mushroom, brushing his lips gently with a fingertip, as though sealing them, sealing his fate.

"Aren't you having any yourself?" Chloe asked.

She shook her head and smiled. Having dispensed her magic, she got up and left, strolling the way she'd come, revealing a rear end as enthralling to the gentlemen as her front. She'd said little more than "sea-urchin spines," "enjoy," and "the sky is beautiful" during their whole acquaintanceship. And "My name is Selene."

Chloe and the other three left behind were silent for a while, half-dozing in the late sun.

"I hope they're good mushrooms," Al Dente said.

Personally, Chloe hoped they weren't. She wondered if it was too late to puke them up. Even though she didn't feel anything yet. The sea was smooth, with only the slightest swell making the sky dance. The last soft shell-pink and orange sigh of day was squeezed out in the gentle curved hug of the bay, a serrated silhouette of coconut palms cut out and pasted against the dying afternoon.

"I could use another beer," said the Rev. "This mushroom rubbish isn't doing a thing for me. The stuff isn't having any effect on me at all."

"Look at that." Prue chuckled and gave Chloe a poke. The Rev was leaning forward and staring off across the bay with a peculiar intensity. He was goggling away and shaking his head, saying, "Nothing. No effect at all. Not a thing. I'm going to have another beer." He was silent for a moment. "That's something. Look there. You see the way the sky comes down and meets the sea just that way? Just there. Good Lord. That's really something." The Rev was quietly freaking away, only he hadn't noticed it yet.

But Chloe still didn't feel a thing. Magic mushrooms, eh? She took a swig from her beer and stared off across the bay. She'd been stupid to eat that mushroom, especially after all the beer. But what the hell, it wasn't having any effect anyway.

The Rev was rapping on as though he'd just been sprung from two years in the Hole. In meditation sessions, he said, he kept feeling he was coming closer to God. Though, as he understood it, this wasn't what he was supposed to find, from the Buddhist perspective. "In the Zen tradition, for Pete's sake, if you meet the Buddha in your spiritual wanderings, you're supposed to 'kill' him. If you encounter God, or the Buddha, that's a delusion."

The Rev was teaching English in Bangkok, and was now on a three-month vacation, which he had devoted to Wat Nai Fun and then the 4H Club. He was thinking of getting a job in Saudi Arabia or Japan to save the money he needed to join a contemplative order of monks. "I have to get rich enough to pay my debts. Till then, I'm too poor to qualify for the vow of poverty." But for the time being he'd come down south to practice meditation. He reckoned he was going to need it. Why hadn't he stayed at Wat Nai Fun? He was expelled for repeated infringements of the no-smoking rule. Not to mention he talked too much. He liked to talk—the thought of his entering the Carmelites who, among other things, took vows of silence, struck Chloe as improbable. And, of course, there was this little matter of his professed love for her sister Meredith.

The Rev was ripped out of his tree. Bibi was snuggled up to Al Dente, quiet, not sleeping, only listening to the Rev and nuzzling and sighing with satisfaction like a child being entertained at bedtime. She was also stoned, Chloe thought. So why wasn't this stuff affecting *her*? She felt only preternaturally sharp and at one with things. The muzzying effects of the beer had vanished, leaving the glow of a day's sunbathing and this clear-headed appreciation of things as they were.

After a time, Chloe caught the cruelly poignant scent of night-flowering jasmine. Tip had explained how its flowers only bloomed after dark. It was black night, now. Inky black velvety night, and Chloe listened to a miniature surf crashing quietly up around the grains of sand and fragments of shell at the water's edge. Night falls fast in the tropics. The sky, overcast these past couple of days, was almost clear of clouds. She gazed up at the hard electric ache of the stars, impossibly bright, impossibly many. Hard, brilliant points. Not points. Holes. Conduits between this sphere and a higher one. Five thousand, five billion calls to her psyche, winkling her soul out through every pore of her being.

Chloe forgot to attend to her breathing and, after a while, she realized she'd been away from herself. Away and yet aware. She had felt a wholeness that was not her at all. She was far, far away and yet there, at the center of things. She had slipped away for a moment, but the experience had been a timeless apprehension of something beyond words. It had been an eternity and it had been less than a moment. Reluctantly she came back to herself and found the Rev still talking. He was recalling how, once when he was a kid, they caught fireflies—hundreds of them. Glowworms. And Kenny

Page rubbed them all over his body at a weiner roast on the beach and scared little Millie Johnson. She fell off the end of the dock and drowned before anybody could find her.

"Oh, that's just FANTASTIC. GLOWWORMS. I LOVE GLOWWORMS." Then Bibi reconsidered what the Rev had just told them. "DROWNED? *DROWNED*? But that's so *SAD*." Then she didn't say anything for a long time. Nobody did. Bibi cried and cried into Al Dente's armpit.

A crisp sliver of new moon had appeared in the sky as if by magic. A last cloud must have fled, or maybe it had risen while Chloe had been away on her extra-dimensional travels. It promised renewal, a fresh start. Something more than mere gravity tugged at Chloe, spoke directly to her soul.

They slept overnight on their new sarongs, anointed in insect repellent against mosquitoes and sand fleas, open to the stars and moon. Chloe dreamed of diamonds strewn across a velvet sky. A luminous blue Buddha image rose from a crystal forest, its enigmatic smile becoming an ugly leer. In the morning they had company.

One of the men, the one with the shotgun, was grabbing at his crotch and leering at Chloe, who stood up to wrap herself tightly in her sarong. The other intruder hooked his assault rifle into Bibi's bikini top, which she'd put back on to receive the visitors, and yanked hard. The strap held, but the top came up half over Bibi's face, the muzzle pointing right at her forehead, her arms raised as though in surrender. She struggled the rest of the way out of the swimsuit herself. "DON'T HURT ME!" she pleaded. "*PLEASE*." For once the headlines were merited. Al Dente didn't move.

"See here," the Rev began.

"No talk!" barked Chloe's admirer, his shotgun swinging to point at the Rev's belly. An ugly unease rose deep in Chloe's guts, a dark anxiety bordering on panic.

The men with guns fired a few abrupt questions in Thai at them. Failing to get intelligible answers, they started in on Buk and Somsak.

The boatman and his helper were answering questions with alacrity, but they were kicked and beaten with gunbutts anyway, maybe a rudimentary form of lie-detector test. Bibi was crying, and Al Dente was only looking as though he wished he could. The Rev was sweating buckets even though the sun had hardly risen, and Prue was lighting a second cigarette off the first and coughing, a deep bronchial honk that elicited what for all the world looked like an expression of concern from one of the gunmen.

Then—all of a sudden, from the point of view of those who couldn't speak Thai—they were being hustled towards their boat. Buk fell off the stern once while getting underway and Al Dente and the Rev had to help him back on the boat, since Somsak's arms were hurting too badly from the beating. Buk was bleeding from a couple of cuts on his face, but they were superficial.

One of the gunmen fired a quick burst from his rifle into the water, pop-pop-pop—a parting salute—and then turned to join the others, all of whom disappeared into the trees.

"We go back now, *na*?" said Buk. "Okay?"

Later, terrified at the idea, Buk and Somsak pleaded with them not to report the incident to the police. But Chloe and the others agreed that you couldn't let people go around threatening you with guns, much less beating up your boatmen for no good reason. The police in town, back on the mainland, asked a few perfunctory questions, mostly, it seemed, aimed at establishing why the foreigners had gone to the island in the first place.

"No good," the ranking police officer told them. "No good; better go other island. Koh Phra Chan good for party."

"But they had *GUNS*," Bibi told them. "THEY WERE SHOOTING *GUNS*."

"No problem," the policeman responded, so wound up about it all he looked as though he might fall asleep and slide right off his chair. "We take care."

25 serpent in the garden

A fantasy can be equivalent to a paradise, and if the fantasy passes, better yet, because eternal paradise would be very boring.

Juan Ramon Jimenez

The snake was a good six feet long. Beautifully articulated in form and color, a biological and aesthetic marvel, it made its way through the shade of the big tree and on across the yard, its passage marked by an elegant series of runes in the sand.

Chloe was spellbound. All was quiet but for the slitherswish of the snake, a snatch of fluting birdsong, and a sudden *tuk-kae . . . tuk-kae. . . .* Chloe counted. Tip had told her that, if the tuk-kae lizard called seven times, it meant good luck. Chloe counted only six. For a moment, the sun shone hotter, the trees grew greener and more finely textured, each individual leaf distinct, the whole hard-edged and grainless.

Then Pup barked once, emphatically. The snake froze, a zagged branch innocent in the dust. At the same time, Sweet Mama emerged from under the bench where she'd been snoozing in the

Serpent in the Garden

cool of the tree. Pup took a single tentative step toward the branch. Then he took another and barked again. Reanimated, the snake changed tack, making for the space under the sala. Yapping furiously now, Pup circled to head it off. The snake abruptly reared high and flared its hood. A cobra. Pup backed off just out of range. Sweet Mama, meanwhile, charged in from the flank barking, feinting and dodging, ears flopping. "Snake! Snake!" screamed Ruthie, probably glad of the diversion from her walking meditation. At this point, the snake in question left off threatening Pup and decided to make a break for the crawlspace.

Freddie emerged ready for action in his Lycra jumpsuit and cape of many tapes. He flew towards Pup, made a grab and missed as Pup leapt to one side. The snake turned to rear and flare again. Freddie stumbled backwards to fall on Sweet Mama, who yelped counterpoint to Ruthie's "Snake! Snake!" All in all, Chloe thought, it was quite a merry scene, even though Pup and Freddie were in imminent danger of snakebite and Sweet Mama was going to wind up mashed, the way things were going.

"Don't let it bite the dogs." Gorgi stood over in front of his office holding a putter and looking wise.

"Sweet Ma-ma. Sweet Ma-ma. Pup!" Tip was calling. "Come here. Please come here."

Everybody else was outside the dorm, by this time. The snake had just one escape route open to it now; and it didn't surprise Chloe, somehow, that Al Dente, big stick in hand, should appear at that moment right in its path. Somebody was going to get bitten, that much seemed certain.

And so things stood when four men—three Thais and a Westerner—came out of the office to stand beside Gorgi. One Thai wore a tie and white shirt; the Westerner's white shirt was open necked. The other two Thais—one tall and thin, the other short and round—were dressed in jeans, T-shirts, and light motorcycle jackets. Despite the heat, they all looked cool. Thais just didn't sweat, as far as Chloe could see. The two white collars held a brief consultation; then the open-necked one turned to point across the yard at the snake. At that, their two less formally dressed associates drew pistols from beneath their jackets and blew the snake's head off. Blam, blam, blam, blam. The third and fourth shots were probably redundant. The headless body convulsed briefly and then lay there, lifeless and saddening.

Al Dente was flat on his belly yelling, "Don't shoot! Holy shit. Don't shoot!" And Ruthie had taken to screaming "Gun! He's got a gun!" which was a change from "Snake! Snake!" but served no more useful purpose. Bibi simply stood there, looking from one element of the scene to another and remarking, in much the same tones she would normally say good morning: "MY GOD! *ALLEN*. I DONT BELIEVE IT! OH, MY *GOD*; BE CAREFUL! *GUNS*. THIS IS INCREDIBLE!" Prue was lighting a cigarette off the Rev's pipe and coughing. Ruthie was so wound up she didn't even notice.

The man in the tie said something to Gorgi and then the two of them went back into the office. The armed gentlemen remained outside, where they lit cigarettes and traded hitman stares with Ruthie, who decided not to apply the no-smoking rule in this instance.

Pup had the bloody end of the snake in his teeth, growling and trying, with little success, to crack the whip with the meaty big hose. Chloe had always liked snakes. The summer she was thirteen, she kept a lovely green grass snake in a screened box in the back yard. Of course she brought it into the house, even though her mother told her she mustn't, and it had escaped. Its next appearance, still in the house, inspired the resignation of the only reliable baby-sitter in town, according to Chloe's mother. Chloe's next pet, only grudgingly allowed, was a hamster.

Al Dente carried the dead snake away on his stick and flung it into the long grass. Pup disappeared after it. Sweet Mama retired from the arena for another snooze, and a kind of peace settled over the 4H Club again.

A big Mercedes-Benz was parked just inside the gate. It was steel-gray with gold grill and hood ornament. The metal trim around the windshield was also gold. Probably only gold plated,

Chloe was thinking. She looked all over for Olga, who had promised to give her a massage, but the Russian was nowhere to be found. "Prue," she asked, "have you seen Olga anywhere?"

"She was here a while ago. Before the snake. I haven't seen her since."

It wasn't like Olga to miss all the action.

Chloe went back to the dormitory to make some notes. But it was gone. The case with all her notes. She stood there a moment thinking, "No. It can't be. I've put them somewhere else. I must have." She looked everywhere, which didn't take long, there being almost nowhere to look except under the bed and on top of the wardrobe. She had had the same gut-shot sensation the summer before when her hard drive crashed.

Gorgi appeared in the doorway. "There is someone I want you to meet."

26 ego-tourism

Dream, diversify—and never miss an angle.

Walt Disney

One of the T-shirted gunmen—the tall, thin one—was on the floor in a pushup position, propped on the tips of rigidly outspread fingers, trembling uncontrollably. His body was ramrod straight, tendons popping out on his hands and forearms, sweat burning his eyes and pooling beneath him. He looked desperate. Chloe thought it must be some sort of bet, at first, but everyone else seemed largely uninterested. The Western guy sported an exuberant blond quiff, upswept and sprayed like Fabian in heat. He was leaning back in a chair, entirely relaxed, watching the exercise freak through half-closed eyes. The other gunman, the round one, was sitting on the floor in a corner cleaning an automatic pistol, the stripped-down parts arrayed in front of him on a towel.

You didn't get to see gunmen cleaning their guns every day, where Chloe came from. Is this what the brochures meant by adventure tourism?

Ego-tourism

"Mr. Terdsak is the brains—and the money, ha, ha—behind the Holistic Herbal Garden and Institute of Holographic Healing." Gorgi introduced the man in the white shirt and tie. Some old skin problem had left Terdsak's face a pitted asteroid. Now clear of everything except the scars and an aura of utter complacency, the man nevertheless remained an oily individual, with his shiny black cap of slicked-back hair and air of a community leader with some nasty secret.

"And those are his security men," Gorgi said. "Every successful man has enemies, people who wish him harm. Yes. So you have to protect yourself."

Everybody, especially the one doing the pushup, ignored Gorgi's pass at introducing Chloe to the bodyguards. Terdsak merely looked bored. Neung and Soon were collectively known as "Sip," explained Gorgi. Neung, the skinny exercise freak, was "One," in English, and Soon, the short fat element of the twosome, was "Zero." They were always together, and together they were Sip, or "Ten." Terdsak's security chief, the one with the hair and the air of competence, was a Russian named Igor, or "E-go," as Terdsak would have it. E-go spoke neither Thai nor English, so far as Chloe could make out.

Terdsak didn't visit often, according to Gorgi, but he took an interest in every aspect of the Institute's operation, including its guests. And now he was interested in Chloe. So was Gorgi, come to that.

"Usually I do not have much time for reading." Gorgi waved a notebook at her and smiled. "But I am finding this fascinating. Who is this 'Master' you talk about? The one who is always saying 'atcha'?"

"Where did you get that?"

"We tell our guests that it is better not to write things while they are with us."

"That's my notebook. Give it give it back to me."

"Give notebook." Terdsak was flipping the top of a chunky gold lighter. "So. You write about Institute. Why?"

"Read it," Chloe suggested. "I'm a writer. Writing is what I do. This is a diary—notes, so I can write about my experiences later. It's a meditation diary."

"Words only get in the way," said Gorgi.

"Who is this 'tight-ass' you talk about?" Ruthie asked.

"You." Terdsak directed this at Ruthie as he passed his fingers back and forth, not too close, over the flame from his lighter. "You go."

Ruthie's eyes flashed and she turned to Gorgi for support, but he was looking away.

"You go now," Terdsak reiterated, jabbing a finger first at Ruthie, then at E-go and then at the window. Before E-go could interpret this, Ruthie left of her own accord.

"You are writer," said Terdsak. "What you write?"

A bit of this and a bit of that, Chloe told him, letting him know she was pissed off. Stuff for the women's magazines, mostly.

"Why you not go Wat Nai Fun? Big temple, *na*? Famous too mutt."

"Women are treated like second-class citizens in Thai monasteries. I'm not going to let myself be treated like menial labor. Especially if men are treated differently." Chloe wondered why she had to explain herself to this guy. Never mind he hadn't understood a thing she'd just said.

"Have *other* notebook?"

"Yeah. A couple of others, but there's nothing in them." Chloe wanted to tell him to get stuffed. But she sensed she should go carefully with Terdsak. Even if he was a caricature of a gangster. In fact, she wished she could say she had written more. There was material here for a book. But she had right away fallen into a lazy pattern of meditation, eating, sleeping, and mundane chores. A real lotus eater.

"You are *good* writer? Have good grammar, good spelling, *na*?" Terdsak took a gulp of some vile-looking substance from a water tumbler and shuddered. "Gorgi. Need more special drink. Make more too mutt, *na*? You deliver."

Like his Mercedes-Benz, Terdsak was lavishly ornamented with gold. He took to excavating an ear with a gold pendant on a gold chain, with a little spoon at one end and a toothpick at the other. "Gorgi," he said. "Give the concept. Tell about bisnet."

"*Atcha*. The century of Asia and the Pacific is dawning," pronounced Gorgi in oracular tones. "What Asia has, and what the West is wanting, is wisdom. So, good. We offer something new: we are selling wisdom for everyman."

"What's new?" said Chloe. "The tourist guides are full of meditation centers."

"Meditation temples? Wat Nai Fun? No problem. How many people want to meditate twelve hours a day, day after day? No talking. Little food. No connections with the opposite sex? These places, they are good for our business—they are demanding too much and delivering too little." He giggled. "We get their rejects. Good. *Atcha*. This is the middle way. We target the mainstream market. The drug culture is mostly sink or swim; do your shit and take your chances. Make what you can of it. Buddhist meditation, on the other hand, is too strict. It is too hard. And Wat Nai Fun does not offer any guarantees, does it? No, it does not. Yes. So it is best to take out some insurance. That is what we provide. *Atcha*. We have something for everyone and everything for anyone."

As Gorgi explained it to Chloe, the Rajneeshees had it almost right, but you couldn't go around pissing off the mainstream. And you didn't want the authorities getting all wound up. The next thing you knew, you got the morality police sniffing around and the newspapers stirring up the silent majority, and the whole thing was just totally bad for business. "Drugs, for example, that is bad for us. In a way it is our competition."

"Keep market separate, *na*?" Terdsak elaborated.

"One" had only done the one pushup, but Chloe was impressed—he'd held it for several minutes already. He was starting to sag, however. The guy in the white shirt, E-go, barked at him and he straightened again, but only for a moment. Then he collapsed. Zero looked up briefly before going back to weapons hygiene.

"Teach con-sen-tray-*shon*," Terdsak explained, obviously reciting a lesson well learned. "Do good work; be mindful of job."

He pulled his solid gold ear-cleaner-cum-toothpick on a chain from beneath his shirt and slid it up a nostril. Probing for a moment or two, he then sneezed explosively. "This is basic."

When Chloe asked what the guy had done, Gorgi told her he had taken a couple of shots at the snake without orders. Terdsak had instructed E-go to tell the other guy to do it. Of course, nobody could ever understand what E-go was saying anyway, according to Gorgi. "But you speak good Russian, don't you, E-go?"

"Da, da. Russia good. *Dee, dee maak.*"

"Ignorant no ac-cuse," said Terdsak, somewhat cryptically, wiping at his nose and looking prim, or at least as prim as a Thai gangster could readily look. Ignorance was no excuse. Then he induced another sneeze. He stepped to the door and blew his nose violently against a forefinger, flinging a string of mucus at the ground. "Medicine," he said, coming back into the room. "Mobile, mobile." E-go brought him a phone, while Gorgi poured him another glass from the whiskey bottle. Terdsak shot the drink back, winced, wiped at his nose and his eyes, and punched a number with the thumb of the hand holding the phone. "Hello?" he said. "Hello?" Then he launched into rapid-fire Thai in a voice twice as loud and maybe twenty percent more self-assured, if that were possible, than his normal manner of speaking.

It was some kind of communications storm, for now Gorgi's cellphone started ringing. He listened for a second and then said: "Not now. Call later, okay? No, no. Yes. Not now." He turned back to Chloe. "Another thing. This boy also put a scratch on the side of Terdsak's car this morning, driving through town. He must learn to focus." Gorgi smiled reassuringly. "Anyway, don't worry. One—Neung, here—used to be a Thai boxer. He has strong fingers and Thai boxers must learn to accept pain."

Terdsak raised his empty glass and rattled the ice cubes. His solid gold Rolex slid down to collide with the cuff of his tailored shirt. "E-go," he said. "Medicine."

E-go said something guttural to the recent penitent, underlining his intent with vigorous finger pointings and scowls, and One, hands and arms trembling, moved to serve Terdsak from the herbal whiskey bottle.

Everybody in Southern Thailand was running bungalows, restaurants, boat services—the usual tourist things, Terdsak and Gorgi explained. But the market was glutted. And tourism was changing. What the young tourists wanted was adventure. Green tourism. Eco-tourism. All that stuff. But most of the forests were gone.

"Before, make good money from log, *na*?" Terdsak said, momentarily wistful for a golden past. "Now hard too mutt. Need new bisnet idea."

"New frontiers," suggested Gorgi.

"This is the concept," Terdsak told Chloe. "Can use. Write in notebook."

"Everywhere these travelers are looking for something exotic," Gorgi explained, "but nothing is exotic anymore. Everywhere is the same. Still, the young ones want to travel—they want adventure; they want to expand their minds. And we are ready to help. Adventures in inner space. *Atcha*. Inner space is the new travel frontier and it is virgin territory." They were going after the great majority of seekers, those who fell between drugs' easy promise and the rigors of strict vipassana retreats. "With the spa and meditation center," said Gorgi, "we give them a fountain of youth, a shortcut to renewing body and spirit. And not too far from a good beach. Ha, ha."

"This is the concept," added Terdsak. "Show story."

Gorgi passed her a ring binder full of magazine clippings. All the stories had to do with tropical health spas and meditation centers. Terdsak might have a proposition for Chloe, Gorgi said. The 4H Club needed a professional writer. To begin with, they wanted somebody who could write favorable stories and place them in advantageous markets. The eclectic approach to inner adventures was the wave of the future, and the projected chain of Holistic Herbal Gardens and Institutes of Holographic Healing was the prototype and ideal model. As part of this, it seemed, the writer would also be asked to mount a propaganda campaign directed at competitors. "We must be telling the truth about these things." Gorgi mewled self-righteously. "Now we have this business 'Travels in the Interior, Inc.,' for example, and more will come who are stealing my ideas. But they do not know, yes? No, they do not. *Atcha.* And people must see, so you can tell them this also."

"This is basic, *na*? Enough. Gorgi, give my idea."

As Gorgi explained, diversification was the key to staying ahead in business in these times of rapid change. The Institute provided instruction and guidance in various meditative techniques, massages both Western and Asian, herbal steam baths, and much more. Gorgi showed her around a back room where a whole range of herbal and New Age products were on display, everything from aromatic essences for use in aromatherapy to massage oils, skin creams, medicines, and herbal teas.

One idea they were developing, Gorgi revealed, was natural herbal cosmetics. "Thai women have beautiful skin, yes? One reason is they put cucumber and papaya juice on their face. No, that is two reasons. Ha, ha. But I know many other plants to make you beautiful. Women pay much money for this kind of thing. Some men, too."

"Sell rice cheap," Terdsak told her. "This is basic. But vegetable extra, meat extra. Cost money. Like Bangkok tailor. Sell suit, finit twenty-four hour. Very cheap, no problem. Sell shirt-tie make money too mutt. Get the concept?"

Meditation and massage were the rice, Chloe had to assume. Or the suit.

"This is the modern world," Gorgi added. "The global community. You get people from all over, they know about everything from reflexology to Bach flower therapy and they think they need it. So we are a spiritual emporium. We offer more products. We have the wisdoms; we have the techniques." Eyes shining, Gorgi gazed off into a distant dimension visible only to himself. "Manifold are the paths to enlightenment. *Atcha.* And we are Grand Central Station. We put you on the track to your destination."

EGO-TOURISM

Chloe asked what it was Terdsak was drinking.

"Special Superman," said Terdsak. "Very special, *na*? Only Gorgi know how. Special medicine. Nobody know." Terdsak took a long sip. "Ginseng, you know? This better. Make me strong. Live long."

Special Superman, Gorgi explained, was reserved only for Terdsak. And sometimes for special customers.

"But Zero had a drink of it," said Chloe.

"Zero is the taster. Sometimes it is One."

A long shelf held whiskey bottles, "Superman" among others, labeled in Chinese, Thai, and English.

"*Special* Superman number one," Terdsak told her. "Have many thing. Ginseng, have. Deer horn, rhino horn? Have. Tiger *pee-nut*, have *douay*. Ha, ha. Is good. Keep me young. Keep me strong. Keep me long and strong all night long."

"It's dickheads like you who are killing off half the animals in Asia," thought Chloe. "How many pieces of ass do you get for every dead tiger?" What she said was, "My, my." There were fewer than five thousand tigers worldwide, she had read somewhere. And those were rapidly being hunted to extinction. They would be gone, every one of them, in only a few years. And the rhinos. And jerks like Terdsak would still be getting hard-ons.

Terdsak's shirt was open to the third button, showing a number of gold chains. Aside from his a gold toothpick-cum-ear-cleaner, he had a cluster of gold amulets and a gold phallus the size of a peanut. "Special power," he told Chloe when he saw her looking at them. Judging by what he went on to say, the relative power of each respective amulet was directly related to how much it had cost. "Have more gold." He leered and fingered his chains some more. "*Pooying. Guh* like gold. Want my *special* gold."

But for now Terdsak was clearly impatient to get negotiations wrapped up. "Finit now," he told Gorgi. "Give concept and we go."

Eyes shining, Gorgi elaborated. "Many people are coming to the East to find wisdom. The West is materialistic. The East is spiritual. And we can market that. How can we say it? Spirituality is a hot commodity."

YAWN

The commercialization of spirituality was nothing new, of course, but they were bringing an especially vigorous marketing approach to the enterprise. Eventually, they planned to establish centers around Thailand, and maybe overseas as well. What better headquarters for a multinational chain of New Age centers than a country with a centuries-long tradition of Buddhist meditation? Inevitably, as Gorgi pointed out, there would be copycat competition, so it had to be strike hard and strike fast. Unable to resist the brag, Terdsak let her know that some other centers had had unfortunate experiences with everything from the authorities to accidental fires. Probably it was their bad karma. He did say how she could write some things about some of the other centers in the area, and tell people how they were not as good as the Institute.

Terdsak wanted her to do a little PR on the side, Gorgi explained, placing stories in magazines here and there. She could be as promotional or as uncomplimentary as she liked: "We don't care what they say, so long as they talk about us. *Atcha.* We must be getting our name out there."

"Do good work," added Terdsak. "Make right people happy, keep low profile. This my secret. Is basic. Also give money politician. Help the people. Okay? Write in notebook, *na*? Build temple, *douay*. And home for—how you say?—children not have mama and papa."

Despite herself, Chloe was drawn to Terdsak. There was a kind of sinister innocence in this penny-ante godfather, a rapacious enthusiasm for profit and empire. And she loved Gorgi's mix of mystical claptrap and commercial patter. But, she told them, she was only here on holiday. She was a married woman with a career and a home back in Canada, and she was afraid they'd have to find somebody else.

"We pay."

"I'm sorry. I can't."

Terdsak, ostentatiously unconcerned, fingered the collection of gold *objets* hanging from his neck. Zero uncorked a fresh bottle of Special Superman and poured his boss another shot.

"*Soon,*" Terdsak said. Then he proceeded to berate Zero in rapid-fire Thai before turning to E-go: "This *new* bottle, *na*? Special Superman. E-go, you no look?"

Chloe watched in amazement as Terdsak began winding himself up into a rage.

"Maybe poison. This is the concept? *Na*? Who pay? *Who pay kill me*?"

E-go made reassuring noises. Given his minimal English, he couldn't explain himself to Terdsak and, having almost no Thai, he couldn't help berate Zero. But he knew there was danger and the boss was talking about killing, so he whipped out his pistol just in case it was needed. First, he covered Zero, who reached for the sky, obviously trying to get his hands as far as possible away from his own gun, which he had just finished reassembling. Then E-go swung the gun across at Chloe and Gorgi, no doubt in case he had misunderstood and was supposed to shoot them instead.

Terdsak looked as though he might start foaming at the mouth. "Give me," he screamed, extending a hand in E-go's direction. "Gun. *Give me gun.*"

E-go surrendered his pistol with as much enthusiasm as if he'd been asked to point it at his own head and pull the trigger.

Terdsak started waving the weapon at Zero. "Give whiskey," he said, probably forgetting Zero didn't speak English, and then repeated himself in Thai.

Zero poured a shot into the tumbler, the neck of the bottle tapping a frenzied tinkle against the rim of the glass.

"*Eek, eek.*" Terdsak waggled the gun at the drink.

"More, more," E-go translated, happy to know both the Thai and the English, in this case, and careless of Zero's total lack of English.

Zero kept pouring till the glass was full.

Still using E-go's pistol to focus his attention, Terdsak indicated that Zero should kneel in front of him. He plunged the barrel into the whiskey, the gunsight taking a chip out of the rim of the glass in the process, and then he held it, dripping, in Zero's face, and said something in Thai.

"Eat!" said E-go, delighted to have handled yet another interpretation job with such ease.

So Terdsak dipped the gun a few times and Zero sucked the barrel, so frightened his teeth chattered on the gunmetal, sweat pouring off his face. Finally, Terdsak pulled the barrel out, not breaking any teeth. At Terdsak's command, Zero swigged half the glass, choking on it, tears streaming.

One poured some Special Superman into another glass, sipped at it, and then presented it to Terdsak, who sat back, calmer. With an air of satisfaction, he said, "No problem. To success in this life, must make people see good help you success." Terdsak had recovered his English together with his composure. He played with the gold chains around his neck and smiled winningly at Chloe. The audience was over.

"What's this?" Chloe asked, as she got up to go. She was unnerved by Terdsak's little drama, and the only way she could pretend she hadn't been was by focusing on the trivial. She pointed to where a crystal pendant, a chunky piece of quartz set in a hexagonal metal setting on a silver chain, sat in a presentation box on a shelf.

"This has been blessed by a powerful monk," Gorgi told her. "*Atcha*. It also has a microchip inside."

"A microchip?"

Terdsak liked this. It was hi-tech. "This world change, change too mutt, *na*?" he told Chloe. "Must change *douay*. How you say? Must *adapt*. Or dead."

"Yes, yes," said Gorgi. "It is powered by the sun and the moon and the energy of the crystal. I could tell you more, but it is secret. This amulet amplifies your personal electromagnetic aura. You see? Like a force field protecting from negative vibrations. You must be wearing it all the time. But not in the shower. No, the microchip is not so waterproof. Maybe only the blessing. Ha, ha."

The Institute was planning to deal in electronic amulets, he told her. These items would guard you against such things as microwave radiation from computer monitors and bad vibes from unfortunate personal auras. "If you tell me when you were born—the exact date and time, you understand—and exactly where you were born, so I can find the latitude and longitude, then I can assign you your own personal amulet. It will keep you in tune with your natal lunar cycles and so on, no matter where you are in the world. It is like you are wearing your own guardian angel. Only forty-five dollars American. *Atcha*. For you, since you are already a member and a very nice one at that—ha, ha—I am letting you have one of these unique personal accessories, inscribed with your own name on the back—or your number, whatever you are wanting—for just thirty-three dollars. American. In cash."

Chloe knew her birthdate and birthplace, but she had to make up a time. "Midnight," she told Gorgi. "Hey, I'm a writer. It was a dark and stormy night of the full moon."

"Okay. Enough. You have the concept?" Terdsak asked Chloe.

"McMeditators?" she suggested.

Terdsak frowned, uncomprehending, and looked to Gorgi for help. Gorgi also looked puzzled for a moment; then his eyes narrowed in thought and he smiled. "*Atcha*." And he smiled some more. Chloe could see his lips moving as he savored the word. "Indeed," he replied. "Perhaps."

Terdsak and Co. all seemed to be pals again. E-go had his pistol back. He had wiped it off on Zero's T-shirt, which was wet anyway. Zero was packing his own piece in the belt of his jeans, managing to look like a gunman again. One, newly animated, was chattering away to everyone while Terdsak made a point of tolerating this behavior.

"Think, *na*?" he said to Chloe. "Take story. Read. Maybe you-me we do bisnet." Terdsak and his security team went outside and Zero started the Mercedes-Benz while his boss stood twenty feet away to make sure there was no bomb wired to the ignition. Then everybody climbed in and they drove away into the night.

The boss had many enemies, Gorgi explained again, and he couldn't be too careful. Neither, it seemed, could employees entrusted with his protection be too careful.

Back in the dorm, Chloe was jotting notes in her meditation diary when she noticed that a couple of pages had been ripped from the notebook—notes from more than a week before. From the day she'd first met Tip. And Bibi. The day Ruthie had hit the ground slavering, coming off that seven-day fast. What was missing? At the top of the following page Chloe read this: "Who took my fucking prunes?" Ruthie sounded furious. "I can't leave anything around here. Those were my own *personal* prunes. Shit."

Gone was the bit about awakening to what had been, in Chloe's experience, a completely novel level and focus of awareness. She would never recapture the perceptions as they'd come fresh from her pen that day. And there'd been some stuff about Gorgi and his phone. Gently mocking stuff—him looking so sanctimonious about interrupting the meditation session with his cellphone, and then losing his cool under the tree, talking to someone named Jessica, raving about a blue Buddha or something. Why on earth would anybody have taken these particular passages? It had to have been Gorgi or Ruthie. She couldn't see Terdsak personally reading, much less censoring, the notebook. However futile the effort, Chloe tried to reconstruct on paper the insights of that day. She thought about confronting Gorgi. Who the hell did he think he was, anyway? In the end, she decided to hold her peace. For now.

She had been at the 4H Club almost a month already. Unbelievable.

She still didn't know where Waylon was, and Meredith still hadn't emerged from Wat Nai Fun. The Rev had relayed a second message from her and it was almost identical to the first:

All's well. Signed up for another ten-day program. Don't wait for me. Hope you're enjoying your vacation.

Chloe liked to think that the messages were so terse only as a matter of necessity. Since writing implements were forbidden at Wat Nai Fun, Meredith had scratched her responses, apparently with burnt sticks, on the backs of Chloe's own notes. Chloe herself had been meditating religiously every day and, although she still regarded her fellow meditationists as crackpots for the most part, she had to admit the new routine left her feeling fit and refreshed. Not only that, she'd stumbled on a motherlode of material for her writing career. Supposing she could find a way of ensuring her notes survived. And all sorts of interesting things were floating up to consciousness, in meditation and out of it. Although Chloe wasn't yet ready to fully articulate or analyze most of it. For one thing, a combination of heat and meditation and the general environment was killing her capacity for consecutive thought.

She reflected on the morning's meeting with Guru-in-chief Gorgi. What a character. A jolly rogue, a waggish scoundrel full of pseudo-mystical and ultimately commercial claptrap on truth and meaning and the universe and everything. And he'd told her he wanted to hear all her dreams. As though he were some kind of psychiatrist or something. She was to keep a complete dream diary, recording everything she could remember and relating it to him. Everything. Yeah, right. Not likely.

Gorgi had also offered to show her how the irrigatorium worked. "Some people are shy about using it by themselves. They are requiring a guide. I can show you." Although Chloe didn't need the advice, Prue had warned her in advance about this one, suggesting it might not be a good idea.

Anyway, what was so wrong with this idea of a New Age Grand Central Station? Many are the roads to Zen. Take any one of them, Gorgi and Co. seemed to say. Take them all. Why not? This was what Fast Freddie termed "ego-tourism." The wave of the future: short programs in ego-tourism. Quick explorations of the self. To Freddie, of course, it was all part of a worldwide plot.

And with that thought, Freddie himself appeared beside her. "Shh!" he said. "Shit, man." He motioned Chloe to be silent and to remove her amulet. She took it off and handed it to him. He shook his head and indicated she should put it down and follow him, leading her away from the tree and towards the woods. "You wear that shit, man? You crazy? It's got a microchip inside. Did you know that? You wear those things, they got you, man. They know where you are every minute; they hear everything you say." He lowered his voice and looked all around. "They can even check out what you *think*. Not the fuckin' details, but the general ideas, okay?"

Freddie drew Chloe a little farther into the cool shadows and peace of the woods. "I got something to tell you. Olga, she's staying at my place. And she's fuckin' scared. You know? But don't tell anybody, okay? Where she's staying, I mean. You can't tell any fuckin' body, man. It's, like, a matter of life and death. We got to get her out of here."

27 anger

*I neglect God and his angels for the noise of a fly,
for the rattling of a coach, for the whining of a door.*

John Donne

"Seek the stillness at the center of your being," Gorgi had told Chloe, sensing her agitation. He attributed at least part of her anxiety to Olga's disappearance. Fearing Freddie's paranoia was proving contagious, Chloe didn't reveal she actually knew the Russian's current whereabouts.

Now Chloe was in morning meditation seeking the stillness at the center of her being. Her mind battered around her skull like a trapped bird. And her knees were killing her—she was never going to get used to sitting back on her heels, much less the lotus position.

She hated Gorgi, who wouldn't allow chairs in the sala. He said she was progressing unusually quickly; but the longer she sat there the closer she came to psychic meltdown. What on earth was she doing here with this pack of crazies, sitting in pain for hours trying to think about nothing at all? When her sister was being held incommunicado by a Buddhist monastery and her husband was nowhere to be found. And when, after a month, she was still suffering from a persistent case of thrush, her reward for a single peccadillo with a New Age jerk from Pseud City named Al Dente. (Ruthie was going to ask Gorgi for a herbal cure. Why not?) She couldn't believe she'd slept with the guy. Especially now that she'd known him for a month. He hadn't even told her they were doing it in the "Villa," which was essentially a fuck pad, something you needed if you were going to go with segregated dorms. But they might as well have done it in the middle of the yard. Talk about being discreet. And now Bibi looked at her with hurt in her eyes, as though Chloe should have known.

Chloe wasn't meditating so much as reviewing her situation. She thought she'd been making progress, for a while, but now she was back to square one. Worse. Anyway, what good was all this meditation and whatnot if you were so easily betrayed by your own blood chemistry? Her breasts ached—no matter Gorgi's electronic amulet hung between them, assiduously not keeping the bad vibes at bay—and she felt she had been invaded by a tired, colorless, bitchy facsimile of herself. A classic episode of PMS. Here she was in this fine bedlam full of crackpots under the palm trees, practicing meditation and eating vegetarian food, doing everything right. Yet she felt as though a red-raw rash had inflamed her soul.

There were goddamned roosters everywhere, no respect for sunrises or anything, screeching away any time they felt like it. Just in case you were deaf or dead or something, and you could sleep through cockcrow, there was a big bronze gong at four o'clock in the morning—even though this wasn't a Buddhist temple, only a funny farm for New Age delinquents. This was the hour when you were closest to yourself, Tip told her. Ruthie said three in the morning was even better, and got up earlier than any of them so she could get a head start on enlightenment. Not to mention being the one who got to bang the gong.

To Chloe's right, Tip was disposed in an effortlessly perfect lotus position. Her limbs were like rubber. Earlier, she had shown Chloe how she could bend her fingers back till they touched her wrist. "All Thai girls, they learn this when they are children. It's for Thai dance. Though not every girl learns this now. For people with money, it's all cars and TV and nightclubs and fast-food restaurants. Not Thai food, but American fast food. The children are getting fat. And they aren't learning the old ways anymore. Even the poor children watch TV, now, and all they want is to be like the golden people they see there."

Tip was so nice she wasn't real. So committed and idealistic. For a moment Chloe believed Tip really wasn't genuine. This was immediately followed by shame at the very idea. And then by resentment that Tip should be responsible for this additional discomfort.

Chloe was distracted from her anger by a sudden intake of breath and a long whining, mewling exhalation. There you had the charming Gorgi, shepherd to the 4H flock and toady to gangsters. Spiritually perfected to the point he could have meals prepared separately and served in his own quarters. So adept at self-knowing he could while away an afternoon of golf, turning this to an exercise in mindfulness. He didn't have to deny himself anything anymore. It couldn't harm him anyway, so he might as well enjoy. And the way he talked about "colonic irrigations," as though they were a cross between the universal panacea and a sexual game, perfect for cocktail conversation. As long as you attached "herbal" to something these days, you identified it as being natural, which in turn defined it as unadulterated good shit.

The 4H Club had its own arbiter of what was good shit and what wasn't. Basically, whatever happened at Wat Nai Fun was good and whatever happened at the 4H Club wasn't. Among other things, Ruthie said, at Wat Nai Fun everybody was focused on the same thing. This had a synergistic effect. There was an aura about the whole place, an atmosphere of peace and nurturing. "Not like this nuthouse," she added, chewing sugar-free gum as though it were calisthenics. "And the food rules are too lax here."

Today, this fine collection of characters seemed more like a bunch of nitwits, and Chloe was out of patience. Just as well she couldn't get focused, she thought. If she focused her anger, she might burn a hole right through the teak floor.

God it was hot. But Chloe felt better than she had that morning. Despite the heat. Sort of better, anyway. She had given up on the walking meditation practice. No matter how mindfully, no matter how slowly she proceeded, she poured with sweat, mugged, the afternoon still and humid.

She sat under the tree with the Rev and Tip, ostensibly meditating but really trying to compose notes in her head, trying to fix them till she got to her notebook. But there was so much. That morning, for example, Bibi had noticed Chloe's crystal and tried to explain its efficacy. "Well, *YEAH*. The core of the planet is ONE SINGLE ENORMOUS IRON CRYSTAL, *PERFECTLY* ordered and a THOUSAND MILES ACROSS." Bibi went on to suggest that it was therefore important to find the crystal that was right for you, because then it would resonate in harmony with the heart of the Earth.

It required a mental discipline Chloe lacked just to hold the ideas in mind before they spun out of control. Her thoughts were butterflies that needed pinning, undead butterflies that returned to life to fly from the pin, that transformed themselves into caterpillars and back again to new and ever more fantastic butterflies. She felt herself nodding off, caught a snatch of dream where she was trying to pin a Jello rainbow to the wall.

The Rev was scraping at his pipe and melting and muttering. Suddenly his voice rose in declamation: "'They shall hunger no more, neither thirst any more; neither shall the sun light on them, nor any heat.' Revelations, I don't remember where. '*Nor any heat.*' Nor thirst, nor hunger. Would that this heat kill me soon and send me on my way to Heaven. Lamb chops, good wine. *Air-conditioning.* Chapter seven, I think, maybe verse sixteen."

Today was the Rev's turn to cook. Breakfast had been refried rice with onions and eggs. Chloe liked the burnt bits from the bottom of the pan best. Lunch had been more of the same, cleverly disguised with the addition of baby eggplants and some kind of weedy green vegetable. And he used more oil this time. A lot more oil. The *pièce de résistance*, in his mind, had clearly been the soup, something concocted from herbs out of Gorgi's garden. It tasted so vile that Ruthie claimed it had to be very good for you. Bibi had been sick to her stomach all afternoon, but maybe that was something else. "UNBELIEVABLE," she had informed them. "I *NEVER* get sick to my STOMACH." And they still had dinner to look forward to, those of them desperate enough to want to pay extra for it.

Al Dente, stripped to the waist and wearing black Chinese pajama bottoms, had Bibi up on the sala floor. He was doing something esoteric that involved looking grave and passing his hands slowly back and forth a few inches over Bibi's chest and pubic area.

"*INCREDIBLE*," she said.

Maybe he was trying to exorcise the headline writer in her, thought Chloe. Whatever, it appeared to be having a levitational effect on Bibi's bosom, which heaved ever higher in search of contact with truth.

Prue, despite the heat, was doing abdominal crunches on the far side of the sala. She stopped to cough her racking smoker's cough. "I've always been prone to colds," she said, "though how anybody can catch a cold in this weather is beyond me. My God."

Freddie dropped down on the bench beside Chloe. "You still wearing that amulet, man? Bad idea." For a minute he played with Pup, who was trying to take possession of his leg-warmer. Then he produced a piece of paper straw and chewed at it a moment before asking whether she'd talked to Olga yet. Chloe said she hadn't. Not yet.

Later, alone in the dorm, Chloe was surprised to find she'd been scribbling away for more than an hour. And she was pleased to find herself writing for the sake of the ideas, rather than just because she wanted to serve it up hot and mail her invoice. When had it happened? Somewhere, over the past years, she'd turned into a short-order hack, churning out fast-food copy. That was exactly what the magazines wanted, of course, but it showed no respect for her readers or, ultimately, for herself or her craft.

Eventually she wound down to jotting notes on her fellow meditationists.

Ruthie, for example, treated most of the others with imperious contempt. She criticized Tip for bowing to a sexist society, yet she herself, housekeeper and chief acolyte, was slavishly devoted to Gorgi's every whim. She accused the Rev of being a glutton and a cop-out. Al Dente was a phony and an imbecile, although Prue claimed Ruthie had slept with him back in the early days. ("But, like I say, who hasn't?") Bibi was okay, but it was hard to say anything bad about Bibi, especially on ideological grounds. They all had their respective ways of coping with Ruthie. Al Dente pretended she didn't exist, while Freddie used the Screw to keep his adrenaline glands in top condition. The Rev liked to light his pipe in her general vicinity, while Bibi simply giggled and said "GET REAL."

Ruthie was unhappy and she was indignant that this should be the case. It was clear that somebody was to blame, and someone should pay. Just about anybody from all the men in the world to fat people to heretics who meditated in chairs might be held responsible, depending on her mood and the given circumstances. And Ruthie's enemies of the moment were always castigated in terms of an ideological world-view that brooked no criticism.

Chloe hated the intolerance that comes with buying half-baked dogmas. At the same time she hated this sort of certainty, she also hated the apologetic dithering of people who couldn't *decide*, who couldn't commit to anything and who—like Waylon and the whole Canadian nation, it seemed—went around apologizing for their mere presence on earth. But the dogmatists were the worst.

> *You find a kind of free-floating moral outrage at large, these days. What with the failure of the Western metaphysic and changing times and widespread uncertainty about what's what, the ambient outrage can*

precipitate around almost anything. If you're a woman, and you aren't happy, then this is a moral outrage, and someone is responsible. If you are a black, or a Chicano, or bald or short or stupid, and you aren't happy, this is also an outrage, and somebody's got to do something about it. You get entirely unself-critical, narrow-minded moral warriors appointing themselves good-conduct monitors for a civilization and coming up with plans to reform all of society. Converts to such causes tend to show all the intelligence, courtesy and humor of neo-Nazi football club supporters.

With those of us more prone to cynicism than indignation, it's easy to get caught in the crossfire of moral outrage.

Chloe wrote that in her notebook. It sounded good, but what was she really saying about herself? Cynicism, in the final analysis, wasn't much different from wishy-washiness. It only posed as something tougher and more potent. It was just as much a cop-out, a refusal to commit to anything.

Where was Waylon? She should feel guilty. But she didn't. She'd worried about her responsibility to Waylon and their marriage, and she'd spent the last few years essentially unhappy with her life. She had worried about Meredith; and she'd worried, a little and in some ill-defined way, about Merry and Waylon and herself in their pallid little suburban *ménage à trois*, and she suspected they were all three unhappy with their lives. So what the hell. They had wanted a new perspective on things, and that was what they were getting. She didn't know what Waylon was doing, but, for her part, she wasn't ready to go back to business as usual. Not by a long shot.

Meanwhile, Meredith was squirreled away playing her usual mind games. Once, for a year or two, Meredith had lived with a man. Bob Lohmer had been a mechanic and welder-turned-sculptor, someone to whom nothing was sacred, especially routines and promises to women who lived with him. After a brief euphoria—about three weeks' worth of honeymoon—Meredith never knew if Bob was coming home or not. And he'd blow up if she had the temerity to ask where he'd been. Chloe believed he'd been beating her, but Meredith kept saying the bruises were clumsiness and that he was an artist and he "needed room." That he'd come around if she loved him enough. One night Meredith went so far as to arrange herself at the bottom of the stairs, feigning near-death and awaiting Bob's late return. "He'll be sorry," she thought to herself. He got back long after she'd given up and gone to bed. Shortly after that he was killed in a car accident. He'd been drunk. The woman with him had lived, but she'd been permanently disfigured. Meredith still had one of his sculptures, a greasy scrapyard *objet* that looked as though it had been welded together by the elements.

Chloe suspected Meredith's extended retreat at Wat Nai Fun, at basis, wasn't entirely dissimilar from the sprawled-at-the-foot-of-the-stairs ploy. And it was likely to get just as much sympathy.

And who could say what Waylon was doing. Prue had warned her about what happened to foreign couples out here. "Chloe, have you any idea what the divorce rate is among Western couples in Thailand? It's amazing." She coughed and sucked hard on her cigarette. Then she amended the earlier wisdom. "It's not really so amazing, I guess. You get all these pretty girls, cheap and available, willing to be seen with older Western men—reasonably affluent older Western men, anyway. Suddenly these guys are attractive to all these girls with great skin and great asses, and they don't share a language, so they don't have to explain themselves. Even better, they can interpret what the women feel towards them any way they want. Especially men confronted with the onset of middle age. The poor dear nitwits."

But that just didn't seem like Waylon.

Chloe had found an unctuous message from Dweebilious, Roy Schuter himself, even though she had told him that enough was enough—even more than enough. The nerve of the guy.

> Nothing much. Hi, Waylon. Chloe, I wanted to talk to you about contributing your very considerable editorial skills to our little charity project. You know we don't have a budget for promotions. So how about this? Let me buy you a drink, cloud your judgment a bit, and

try to get you on side. What do you say? Call me when you get back, okay? Hope you're having a great holiday.

And there'd been something from Waylon's mother, something about *scuba* diving, for God's sake. Chloe had tried to leave a message for Waylon, but the tape had run out, and, try as she might, she hadn't been able to wind it back. Scratch one channel of communication.

28 environmental engineering

Do not seek to modify the world,
but change your own responses to it . . .
Properly and sensibly used, it seems to me that
psychoactive drugs can help achieve this goal.

Richard Restak

"Jessie. . . ? *Jessie.*"

Jessica rolled over and pulled an earphone away. "I'm sick," she replied. "Shut up."

"Jessie, look at me."

She pulled her sleeping mask away from one eye. "I'm looking, Waylon. And I don't like what I see."

Everybody had hangovers that morning. But Boom was suffering a great deal more than any of them. They'd gone in to visit her the evening after the graduation party and again this morning, before setting off to Samae San to get the boat. Boom was lucky. There seemed to be no damage to the eyes, and the doctors believed there'd be little permanent scarring. That's what the doctors said, but she was terrified she would wind up like Dinky Toy. "And Dinky Toy have bisnet. What Boom have? Nothing." That wasn't quite true, if you counted her e-mail correspondents, although she was right—they'd disappear fast enough if she lost her looks. Anyway, it would be some weeks, if not months, before she was back to anything like normal.

Dinky Toy and Nok had been taking it in turns to stay in her room twenty-four hours a day. Although Oscar had convinced Nok to come away with him and cook for the diving daytrip.

Leary had had words with Big Toy and Dinky Toy. How the heck, he wanted to know, could any two partners of his have been so stupid as to use balloons filled with hydrogen, especially after what had happened to Dinky Toy? "Not our fault, Leary," they told him, sounding at least as indignant as he did. "We say *hee-lee*-um. They say sure, sure. *Hee-lee*-um. But not."

Everybody came by Hot Licks to hear how Boom was doing, and before long a full-fledged party was underway, a belated continuation of the night before. Even My Bottle showed up again. Paper streamers still decorated the bar, although the balloons were gone. And leftovers from the night before were augmented with satay and peanut sauce and grilled squid kebabs from street vendors.

Only by accident did they discover it was Leary's birthday. His fiftieth birthday, on top of that, and he'd been going to let the half-century mark slide by unremarked.

"The Big Five-O," he told them. "Somehow I never thought I'd live to see the day I'd be telling anybody I was fifty friggin' years old. Gosh. I don't feel any different from when I was twenty-five. Same touch of a hangover, same funny feeling in my pants when I look at a beautiful woman." Leary ogled at Keeow, who came right over, judging from his expression he wanted something, maybe another drink.

So Waylon bought Leary a glass of whiskey, a double bourbon with soda and lots of ice. Leary pressed it up against one temple and then the other, before raising it in response to Waylon's birthday toast. "It's this way, Fosdick. A lot of people figure it's just karma, whatever happens. Everybody's got a stockpile of good and bad karma they've built up over this life and other ones too. And whatever happens is only balancing the credit and debit sides of it all."

Leary rubbed the whiskey glass furiously back and forth across his forehead. Then he slammed the glass down on the bar, and whipped out his hanky to dry his face, dabbing at his eyes in passing. "Gosh. But you'd think it wouldn't hurt their karma if they'd only use their friggin' heads once in a while."

The next morning, no matter how little they all had used their heads the night before, as it turned out, the wreck diving course was to go ahead on schedule. Jessica didn't care how many hangovers they had.

Any speediness from the Maxipheds she'd taken for her cold should have nicely balanced the downers she'd taken to calm her for the wreck dive. It was hard to say what the blue capsules were doing, whatever they were. Or the red tablets, for that matter. For his part, Waylon was starting to think he should accept the Lomotils that Jessica had dredged from the depths of her bag. He had the worst case of diarrhea since arriving in Thailand. Most likely the green papaya salad from the graduation party, Leary had told him. Oscar's informal notes to the official course covered this kind of diving emergency, but Waylon wasn't anxious to test procedures.

Jessica offered Waylon a colorful handful of pills and capsules. "Go ahead, Waylon. It'll help."

"What are these things, Jessie?"

"Vitamins. And other things. Painkillers. Uppers and downers. You know."

"Jessie, do you have any idea what that shit is doing to you? Especially when you take it all together?"

"Okay, Waylon. Have a hangover if you want to."

Waylon chugged a glass of water and groaned mightily. "Hey. The experience isn't complete till you pay your dues." He laughed, sort of, and added, "Just a touch of the old Protestant ethic, there."

Environmental Engineering

"Give me a break, Waylon. If it's cold out, what do you do? You wear more clothes. You go inside. You go to Miami. Whatever. What you don't do is stand around freezing your ass. You modify your environment. Or you take a shot of whiskey and that makes you feel better for a while." Jessie poured herself a shot of vodka and slammed it. Then she poured another and put it on the dresser. "Only now you're fixing your internal environment. Right?"

"Maybe. As long as I was sure it wasn't doing something else to me I didn't want."

"Waylon. Maybe the house is full of radon gas, or dust mites. Maybe you've got asbestos wall insulation and twenty-five years later you die of lung cancer. Christ, Waylon. You wear longjohns and you get crotchrot. You want to get warm, you take your chances."

But what happened, Waylon reflected, in cases where you couldn't decide whether you were hot or cold? Or whether you were actually scared or angry? So you took a bit of this and you took a bit of that, and before long you'd forgotten who you were or what you felt like when you started all this. And now you were taking some drug to make you cooler because some other stuff was making you hot; and you were taking this red capsule to make you happy because this blue pill was making you sad. Waylon tried to say all this to Jessica, but she had her earphones on, lifting one of them occasionally to ask, "What did you say, Waylon?" or, once, to say, "Pass me my drink."

She had explained it to him before: "You change the spaces around you to suit your needs, Waylon. Everybody does it. And the difference between your inner space and the spaces around you isn't always that clear. So you modify your inner spaces *and* your outer spaces. See?"

"Okay, Jessie. You're the expert on outer space."

Now they were out on Captain Ot's little fishing-boat-of-many-colors, anchored on the wreck of a steel-hulled freighter that had gone down forty years before. Leary said he wanted to have a look at things first, and Waylon and Jessica should hang loose for a few minutes. He'd be back. Stocky legs churning against the current, Leary disappeared into the murk. Captain Ot grinned at them, listing away and taking a swig from his whiskey bottle

Oscar, who said he might have had a worse hangover but couldn't remember when, suggested there was no hurry. He took a long look at the skipper's bottle, but then shook his head.

Eddie told them he wanted to go through the briefing one more time before Leary returned. "This will give you your Wreck Diver specialty certification," he intoned. "And you get to practice your underwater navigation skills."

The first dive was just to get them oriented, to get a picture of what the wreck looked like and how it lay. On that dive, they would do some measurements and shoot some compass bearings; when they returned to surface, they could produce a sketch of the site. On the second dive, they would do a penetration with a line, first staging an emergency tank inside.

"I don't need to remind you, but these will be deep dives and it's important you plan your dive profiles carefully, making sure you take enough of a surface interval. We do not want the bends."

You had to govern your ascent rate. Faster than sixty feet a second and you could get into trouble. A rule of thumb was to ascend no faster than your bubbles. But the dive computers most people wore on their wrists beeped at you if you went up too fast. And you should pay attention. Depending on how long you'd been underwater and how deep you'd gone over a number of dives, your blood could start to boil. As you went up and the pressure decreased, the nitrogen that had entered the bloodstream under pressure at depth bubbled out of solution. This interesting and excruciatingly painful phenomenon played havoc with tissues in the joints and vital organs, often leading to permanent disability or death. Depending on the severity of the "bends," Oscar and Eddie had impressed upon them, death could seem a mercy.

Reading off a crib sheet, Eddie reviewed the basic rules of safe wreck diving—things like carrying spare torches and ensuring an extra margin with your air supply. Then he had them parrot the rules back at him. He reminded them that you always dived with a buddy. But on a wreck dive, you never, ever dived alone. The key thing—as with diving in general, but more so with wreck diving— was to keep your head. If you stayed cool, there was little risk. But panic could be deadly.

"Visibility's no heck," Leary reported, a few minutes later. "And we've got some current, I guess. But we're right on the darned wreck, around the middle." He told them to go down the anchor line as quickly as possible and not turn their heads in case the current ripped their masks off.

He also told Waylon he wanted him to look after Jessica, and Waylon thought that might be kind of irresponsible.

"When you get to where we've hooked the wreck," said Leary, "pull yourselves over the side, into the lee of the current, and go down to the bottom and wait. We'll all meet there before we get on with the next part of it. Okay? Make sure you're holding on to something at all times till you're out of the current.

"Jessie, you okay with that? Waylon? Right, then. Let's go."

They hadn't descended far when the wreck began to loom beneath them. They hauled themselves down the anchor line and over the side of the wreck into the lee of the current, gently finishing their descent to rest belly down on the bottom, where they stopped to look around for a moment.

The first thing they noticed, a few yards from where they lay, was a pair of eyes sitting there in the sand ogling in alarm. Waylon and Leary, Jessica in between, moved towards them, inches at a time, till all of a sudden the sand erupted to launch a four-foot stingray. Cover blown, it flapped off out of sight, its panic triggering more explosions, chain-reaction-style, as a couple more rays also decided to make themselves scarce. Waylon was delighted. Jessica was clutching his hand hard enough to hurt. Waylon pointed into his mask, indicating that she should look at his eyes and then signaling that she should breathe slowly and regularly. He also tried to make reassuring faces, not easy when you were peering through a couple of faceplates.

Yawn

The steel-hulled freighter was a casualty of World War II. Either Indonesian or Thai, depending on who you talked to, it had been commandeered by the Japanese and later sunk by the Allied forces sometime between 1942 and 1944. It now rested on its side in ninety feet of water on a sand bottom. Using dive compasses and a knotted line, they got the general dimensions of the wreck and established its orientation. Approximately two hundred feet long, it lay roughly north-south on its starboard side, bow pointing south, hull relatively intact. The superstructure had deteriorated, but its general outlines were still apparent. The remnants of the funnel were resting on the sea floor, with the foremast nearby.

They made a safety decompression stop on the way up and, the way Jessica kept giving everybody the thumbs-up sign, you might have thought they'd just discovered the lost treasure of the Incas.

When they surfaced, they found a Thai coastguard vessel had approached and wanted to know what they were doing. An officer was booming away through a bullhorn, while Captain Ot grinned a lot and hollered back at them through his own bullhorn, mostly saying "*mai pen rai*" several times, which meant "never mind." Eventually, the boat anchored about a hundred yards away and sat there looking official.

They had sandwiches and fruit on the boat, and then everybody found patches of shade and got some sleep.

On the second dive they swam inside the wreck from one end to the other, checking out the engine room, which was exposed to daylight by way of a big square hole cut in the port side, decades earlier, to salvage the engines. The enormous algae- and barnacle-encrusted crankshaft remained in place, and in the forward section they could see the old fire bricks inside the boilers. In the forward hold, with the aid of torches, they could make out the remnants of rusted forty-four-gallon drums buried in silt. Eddie had told them in the briefing that these were said to have contained chemicals, so it was advisable to avoid contact with the surrounding sediment. He also told them to avoid bumping into things—some of the internal beams and deck frames were buckling due to corrosion and age.

The wreck was draped with the tattered nets of fishing trawlers snagged over the years. Standing in for the ghost of a crewman dead these past five decades, Jessica was a shadowy form framed against the dim light from surface in a steel hatchway ragged with corrosion and coral growth. Peering past her, Waylon was treated to a wheeling and turning dance of batfish and Moorish idols. A blue-ringed angelfish swam by, its regal gold and blue raiment splendid in the beam of Waylon's underwater torch. Soft corals and feather stars decorated the encrusted metal plates of the hull. A butterfly fish suddenly emerged from a huge barrel sponge. The wreck was an environmental boon, a huge artificial reef, the substrate for a thriving community of marine life.

Jessica was amazing. She still wasn't too keen about going inside where it was dark, but on the whole she was acquitting herself like a trouper. Never mind she was doped to the gills and stayed so close to Waylon the whole time it made *him* claustrophobic.

They had done the critical coursework, but the day was still young. If they wanted, they had time for another sortie. Jessica had come up from the second dive high on success and adrenaline. So she asked Leary whether they could do some search-and-recovery on the third one.

"Darn it. Good idea. I spotted an anchor hooked on the wreck. Let's see if we can take it up. Give it to Captain Ot, here."

The salvage operation wasn't a deep one, and it didn't take long. Waylon and Jessica applied the lessons they'd learned in the advanced open water course, and were pleased to see that everything worked fine, just the way it was supposed to. They came up together with two bright orange lift bags, which popped to the surface with the anchor hanging beneath them. The coastguard boat was still there, but the officials, all of them sitting on the other side of the bow, hadn't noticed a thing.

"Typical." Leary snorted. "They come up on us, bullhorn blazing, wanting to know what we're doing. Then what? They're sitting there friggin' fishing while we could be salvaging a ton of heroin and a shrink-wrapped Mercedes."

Another boat stood farther off, on the other side of the coastguard vessel.

"Leary," Jessica said. "What's that boat?"

Waylon noticed Jessica dipping into her stash again.

"It's just a tourboat. They're probably taking a lunch break. Maybe wanted company."

"That guy's watching us through binoculars."

"And you're watching him through binoculars. So? Speaking of which, Fosdick, I had an eye on you and Jessica all the time. On all three dives. I was never more than five seconds away. You did a good job. I do believe we'll make a diver out of you yet. You too, Jessie."

Afterwards, they had a picnic on a tiny island just half an hour from port. It was uninhabited except for a few Italian tourists skinny-dipping at the other end of the beach.

"Darn it," observed Leary. "If God had wanted us to run around naked, he wouldn't have had us born with clothes on."

"I'm going to go over and tell that pretty one she's going to give herself skin cancer," said Eddie.

"You do," Oscar replied, "and you're dead meat. You just leave her alone. She knows exactly what she's doing." Then Oscar guzzled four more bottles of beer and crashed out on the sand in full sunlight. The snake-bite wounds on his face were healing, though a clear pattern of marks remained.

"We should wake him up," said Waylon. "He's going to get sunstroke."

"Wreck divers, wrecked divers—we got 'em all. Won't do him no harm to cook his brains a bit," replied Leary. "Darn it. Could be they're a little underdone, as it is."

Waylon called Oscar a couple of times, without response. The thought of actually standing up and going over to shake him awake was too much, no matter whether Oscar was going to fry or not. Nok was asleep, collapsed in the shade of some mangroves back of the beach where Eddie was musing over the parts of a faulty regulator he'd stripped down and spread out on a towel. Nok had her top off, which was no big deal, according to Leary. "She's friggin' flat as a boy, 'cept for those nipples sticking up there like two little joysticks."

Leary had a theory of topless bathing. "You get those full moon parties, over there on Koh Phra Chan? Just about everybody has to take their tops off. And it's mainly peer pressure that leads 'em to it. Gosh. They'll tell you it's healthy and natural, of course, and that's why they do it. But that's not it. Darn it. They friggin' well *have* to do it, or everybody'll think they're uptight or they've got Brewer's Droop, or something."

Chances were Leary meant "Cooper's Droop," but Waylon felt it impertinent to correct a venerable soul of fifty years such as Leary now claimed to be. In fact, beyond Waylon and Jessica's graduation as wreck divers, they were celebrating Leary's fiftieth birthday again that very afternoon, never mind the night before. And, with the license of his age and a bunch of beers guzzled under the hot sun, Leary asked Jessica pointblank why she wasn't going topless, gosh-darn it, given that the rest of her kind—Nok and all the Italian señoritas—had been so obliging as to expose their very fine and natural knockers to the sun, not to mention the admiration of casual passers-by.

"This is a new bathing suit," she told him. "I just bought it yesterday." After all, what good's a new swimsuit if nobody gets to see it? And this specimen was a beauty—hot orange with big yellow polka dots; it looked good against her tan.

Upon hearing Jessica's rationale for lying around almost fully dressed, Leary amended his theory of toplessness. "Tits or tops." He shrugged. "It's all nothing but vanity. Nature, my butt. Gosh. I like that. Maybe I'll put it in my book." Leary, now that he'd reached

221

the half-century mark, had decided he was going to write a book. An adventure novel based on his second fifty years.

The day was fast waning. The Italians had long since left, taking their happy uproar with them. The divers had almost finished the beer they'd brought with them, and Jessica finally took her top off, maybe to prove there was nothing wrong with her breasts.

On the way back in to Pattaya they put out a trolling line and picked up a nice barracuda, close to four feet long. "Gosh, this is going to make a fine dinner," said Leary. "We can give it to Dinky Toy. She'll know just what to do with this honey. Cook it three or four different ways. Make some salad. Enough here to feed the lot of us and the girls too."

Not content with just the barracuda, next Oscar hooked a rubber flip-flop and reeled it in to the boat. This item put up a magnificent battle, thrashing along on surface, diving and jumping up as though trying to throw the hook.

"Plastic bags got more muscle," said Leary, "but for style give me your friggin' flip-flops any day. Real fighters." He told Waylon about the days, not that long ago, when you didn't catch anything but fish and maybe the occasional piece of seaweed.

Waylon asked what the strangest thing was any of them had ever caught. For starters he told them about a bag full of drowned kittens he'd come up with as a kid, bottom-fishing for catfish in Quebec.

"Here's one for you," said Oscar, "A friend of mine was fishing off the Barrier Reef, trolling belly strips for blue marlin. This other guy on the boat, he hooked a floater. A dead guy, all swollen up with gases. What we called a 'whistler,' when I was with the police force."

"A whistler?" asked Waylon.

"Yeah. It's the gas. When you gaff them, they start to whistle." Oscar laughed. "It's disgusting. Enough to make you sick."

"You make me sick, Oscar," said Jessica.

They had sex that evening, back at the bungalow. Jessica seemed strangely distant, but afterwards she wanted to cuddle. Waylon reflected on just how little he knew about his dive buddy. She came from Connecticut, that much he did know; but he had no idea how long she'd been in Thailand, for example.

"Oh, a while, Waylon," she'd told him. "I've been here two or three times."

"Were you married?"

"A couple of times, Waylon. I don't want to talk about it, okay? What about your wife? Are you breaking up? Or what?"

"No!" Waylon was affronted. Jessica had no business asking that kind of question. This affair of theirs was nothing but a peccadillo, something out of the mainstream of his experience; it had no business spilling over into his real life. "No, we're just having a separate holiday."

His leg was jumping, and he told himself to breathe slowly and deeply. *In. . . . Out. . . . In. . . .* He was surprised at the vehemence of his reaction to this novel proposition, this idea that he and Chloe might be breaking up.

"I've given myself to you, Waylon. A married man. You've used my body, and what have you given me in return? Don't you think you owe me something?"

"Hey, I've been a good dive buddy, haven't I?" What Waylon wanted to say was, "Who started all this, anyway? Eh? I would've rather had a sleep, that first time." Who was using whom, here?

"I want you to come with me." Jessica was checking her bag of Valium to see how much she had left. She looked reassured, started to put the bag away again, then reconsidered and popped two more tabs.

"Come where?"

"Waylon."

He recognized the tone—it was exactly like the one she'd used, almost a month before, to ask whether she could spend the night in his bungalow. The tone that said: "This is all very reasonable and you're not going to get fucked."

"Waylon. I want you to come on a dive cruise with me."

"No way. I mean it."

"Waylon. This is important. This is what it's all been about."

"What do you mean? What kind of a dive cruise, Jessica?" His leg was jumping.

"You've come this far, Waylon. Just *trust* me." Her tones soothed, but her eyes flickered and blinked. "I have to go look for something." She leaned towards him, cleavage yawning with promise and danger. "But it has to be a secret between you and me, okay? A dead secret."

"Forget it. You're not even going to tell we what we're doing?"

"Only on a need-to-know basis, Waylon."

Later, in the deep of night, Waylon awoke to find Jessica sitting upright in bed, sleeping mask askew, wire to her earphones hanging off her head. She spoke in portentous tones, an arm extended to point accusingly, just missing Waylon, who stared in amazement and alarm. "Turd. Sack! You-are-ug-ly. *Ug*-ly!" She said more, all of it unintelligible except when, once more, she repeated "turd!" and "sack!" Then she lay down again, and in moments was snoring ever so softly, sleeping the sleep of the righteous. His dive buddy.

Waylon lay awake till just before dawn.

29 high times

The awful daring of a moment's surrender.

T. S. Eliot

Jessica was an ant.

"C'mon, Fosdick!" Eddie, another ant, was calling up to him.

Waylon stood a hundred and seventy feet above the pond, toes out over the edge of the platform, hands locked on to the steel handles either side of the gate. He breathed deeply and slowly, as though he were underwater and taking air off a regulator rather than standing up there on top of the world.

Jessica hadn't been willing to go up on the tower, much less jump. "You go if you have to, Waylon. I don't have to."

It was funny, but he didn't have to. He hadn't even wanted to, but there he was, standing on the edge of the Abyss. "The Complete Dive Experience"—that was the Down Down Diving Center's motto, and the experience included a bungee tower. Leary had set up this part of the enterprise together with a former movie stuntman from the States. The two of them first met when a Hollywood crew was using Leary's offshore rig as a set for a disaster movie. "And, gosh, that movie was a friggin' disaster, let me tell you," Leary liked to say. "Though it wasn't my buddy's fault." His friend had bungee operations all over, from Southeast Asia to Poland to Brazil.

"Gosh, Fosdick," Leary had told him, "you already got your basic and advanced open water tickets, not to mention your deep diver and night diver specialties. You did your wreck diver. And, darn it, I believe I'm gonna award you an honorary Totally Wrecked Diver certificate just for that afternoon you woke up in Bangkok thinking it was Pattaya. So I reckon it's time."

"High dive! High dive!" Oscar started it, with Eddie taking up the chant.

"That's right," added Leary. "It's time for the High Dive specialty."

"Forget it." There was no doubt Jessica meant what she said.

"Forget it," Waylon had said.

"Do you want to go right down into the water, or just touch it with your hands?" Leary asked.

"No way."

And now look. Jesus Christ. Here he was way up on this little platform looking out at the sea and the green hills in the distance, admiring the scenery in the hope it would distract him from his imminent death.

"Don't look down and keep your head back. I'm gonna count down from five. When I get to three, you crouch right down like this. When I hit five you jump, darn it. You jump up and 'way friggin' out there, head back and arms out like you was gonna throw a hug at Big Toy."

They had tied Waylon's legs together, wrapping what looked like a length of indoor-outdoor carpeting around his ankles, then winding the tow-rope for a car around between them and attaching it to the big steel D-ring on the end of the bungee cord. Waylon had a moment of real anxiety, trussed up as he was, ritually prepared for a blackly comic sacrifice to the great God of Goofballs. All the way to the top, he'd practiced his controlled breathing. And he'd talked to Leary and his jumpmaster, a young Thai with an air of utter composure. Soothed by the confident voices and careful procedures, Waylon asked questions about the construction of the tower, the design of the bungee cord, and the safety features. Once on top, the jumpmaster had offered to help him to the gate. Instead, Waylon stood to grab an overhead beam and swung himself over in one smooth motion, twisting to the side as he set himself down at the gate.

For a moment he felt godlike. Looking far out across the bay and the hills to the north, across the town and the fields towards Bangkok, a faint gray pall in the west, Waylon wondered where Chloe was, at this instant, and what she was doing.

"Ready?" asked Leary.

"Ready." Waylon focused on the business at hand.

"*Five. . . . Four. . . . Three. . . .*"

He crouched, self-conscious.

"*Two. . . . One. . . .* Bungee!"

Waylon sprang forth. With all his strength he launched himself into the Void.

30 orgies

For one heat, all know, doth drive out another,
One passion doth expel another still.

George Chapman

Enveloped by the muggy afternoon, half suffocated, Chloe slumped on the bench, the shade of the tree offering little respite.

Prue and Bibi sat beside her, while Sweet Mama cowered under them. Al Dente was across the yard in the steam room, although you had to wonder why; the climate was much the same inside the pyramid or out. The Rev was asleep in the dorm and damn the rules about daytime sleeping. Chloe didn't know where Tip was. She had said earlier she wanted to talk to Chloe about Terdsak, but now she was nowhere to be found. Ever since Chloe's meeting with that amazing man, she hadn't been able to shake an oppressive sense of premonition.

Heat, chronic hunger, and lack of sleep, the droning whine and buzz of insects, some taped chanting that leaked from Gorgi's air-conditioned quarters—all of it was inducing a trance-like state in

Chloe. The golden sand and wooden buildings, the gold-painted fretwork eaves around the teak sala, the gorgeous greens of the foliage, the purple-blue jacaranda smoke and the scarlet flame-tree fire were being forged together in the midday furnace. The golden-green dream mixed intoxicating fragrance of flower and herb with the must of jungle decay and dust.

Despite the heat, Chloe felt a roil of excitement akin to the nostril-quivering tantalization of a city dog on a country walk. A bird broke the silence, its sullen chirp unfamilar to Chloe. In the lane outside the 4H Club, a sing-song refrain in Thai and a clackety-clack of bamboo sticks heralded the passing of the knife-and-scissors sharpener on his bicycle cart. Chloe, prepared to make a pact with Satan if need be, found herself listening for the tinkle of the ice-cream vendor.

Then Prue revealed a treasure. Chocolate. She had a chunky bar of rich dark bittersweet chocolate only somewhat melted in the heat. Chloe, Bibi, and Prue each took a double square and popped it, sucking the sticky sweetness off their fingers and trying not to drool. Chloe ascended to another plane where everything took on a mellow tone of sepia passion.

"They say chocolate triggers some of the same physiological and emotional response as being in love." Chloe slurped as she said this. "I wrote about it once."

"That explains the orgasm," Prue said.

"To DIE for." Ravished by the chocolate rush, Bibi's big green eyes dazzled at the wonderful sin of it all.

The orgiastic idyll was interrupted by a yelp of pain, and then another.

"That's *it*. I'm going to kill you, you filthy little son of a bitch." Ruthie held a broom like a quarterstaff. Pup, a cellophane packet of some foodstuff clamped in his jaws, scrambled and dodged and did his best to avoid being flattened by Ruthie, who came clomping down the steps from Gorgi's quarters in hot pursuit. "God *damn* it," Ruthie yelled, and Chloe felt Sweet Mama cringe against her ankles as she retreated deeper under cover.

Yawn

Pup started for the big tree and friendly territory. Then he recalculated as Ruthie bore down on him, and made for the meditation sala instead, under which he found sanctuary a split second before Ruthie's broom descended with a whack and a cloud of dust.

The Rev abruptly appeared in the doorway to the dorm. "You loud and obnoxious nimcompoop," he roared. "You . . . you intolerant harridan. Be *silent.* You are interrupting a much needed siesta. You're also abusing an innocent puppy."

Amazed at the Rev's unwonted vehemence and admiring of his inspired invective, Chloe led Prue and Bibi in a round of applause.

"That 'innocent puppy' stole my beef jerky," Ruthie proclaimed. Then her voice rose, not quite to a screech: "And who are you calling a harridan?"

"Beef jerky?" said the Rev. "*Beef jerky*? This is a vegetarian establishment, is it not? What, may I ask, are you doing with beef jerky?"

"Don't you talk about rules to me, you fat prick."

The hitherto peaceful afternoon was starting to resemble a July heatwave in Watts.

Gorgi appeared on his porch, rubbing sleep from his eyes and looking less a guru than usual. Al Dente, meanwhile, had joined Chloe and the others under the tree. He seemed prepared to skip the cool shower phase of the steam therapy, seduced by the promise of dramatic action and the foil from the chocolate bar, which he was now licking. Muttering to himself, the Rev abandoned both nap and the field of combat, coming over to join the others in the shade.

Things might have died down at that point, had Tip not emerged from the woods, coming from the direction of Freddie and Olga's hideout. Without further ado, she interposed her slight frame between Ruthie and the others. "How can you talk to a person in that way?" she admonished Ruthie. "To a *nice* person. The Rev is a nice man."

It was hard to say whether the florid complexion of the man in question was due to heat, rage, or modesty. Probably all of the above.

"That 'nice man'. . . ," Ruthie began.

"And you are hurting Pup again."

As though in response, a single yap issued from beneath the sala, followed immediately by the agent of said yap. Pup had either eaten the jerky or stashed it for later. Ruthie's steely gaze almost sent him back under cover, but, maybe smelling chocolate, he elected instead to scamper in a wide detour around Ruthie to join the crowd under the tree. He barked at Ruthie again.

"You must learn to be more accepting." Tip's tone was gentler. "You cannot always put yourself first."

"Let me tell you something, my oh-so-holy little friend." Ruthie pushed her glasses up on her nose, jabbing so hard she might have poked an eye out if she'd missed. "That's your main problem. This 'accepting' everything. Look at women in Thai society today. And you were a 'nun.' Thai Buddhism won't even ordain women as real nuns. You aren't accepted as equals. Nothing more than housekeepers for the monks. Be more accepting. Right. You've just got no idea. Try getting out into the *real* world sometime."

Both Ruthie and Tip stood in full sunlight, Tip still dry, Ruthie dripping sweat. She pushed her glasses up again. "You Thais. And your Buddhism. Especially you Thai women. Anything's better than challenging the status quo. You've got no idea. Every male pig's dream girl. You just go along, not doing anything to change things. What kind of world are your children going to live in? If you ever have any children."

The color had risen in Tip's face and she leaned forward into the storm of Ruthie's anger. "Do not talk about things you do not know. You know nothing about Buddhism or you would not act in this way. And you know nothing about Thai people or about me. So you should shut your mouth."

"Don't you tell me to shut up." The volume of Ruthie's voice suggested this had indeed been counterproductive.

"You. You with all your fasting and your meditating. . . . You're no more than a—how do you say it?—a *dolly bird*. A 'housekeeper' for Gorgi."

Chances were Ruthie didn't even know what a dolly bird was. But she reacted hotly: "Gorgi is my teacher."

"Teacher! What do you know about this man? He has an English-teaching certificate from India. Maybe at least he can teach you polite English."

Gorgi had been standing on his porch the whole time, and Chloe was watching him as Tip said this. Dropping his habitual air of benign venality, he looked harder at Tip. Only for a moment, and then he interrupted. "Come, come, my children. It is too hot to be fighting. Yes. And who is suffering from your anger? Only yourself." Then he withdrew to his air-conditioning. Before he closed the door he turned to consider Tip again, giving her a long and thoughtful look.

"'Let all bitterness and wrath, and anger, and clamour, and evil speaking, be put away from you, with all maliciousness.' Paul, chapter four, verse thirty-one. Good lord, it's hot," the Rev added.

Ruthie took off her glasses and her eyes swam. "You don't understand," she told Tip in tones that asked for understanding. Then she slipped her glasses back on and turned to where Chloe and the others watched from under the tree. "You really just have no idea." Then she stomped away and back up the steps to join Gorgi inside.

"Probably time for her lesson," said Chloe, and Prue chuckled.

"I am sorry I was hot," Tip told them, settling down between Chloe and Prue and reaching to pet Sweet Mama, who emerged for the first time since all the fun started. Pup had found traces of chocolate on the foil, which he was turning into silver confetti.

"Everybody's hot today," said Prue. "Don't worry about it."

"I should not have lost my temper. Gorgi was right—you only hurt yourself."

"Relax," Chloe told her. "There were extenuating circumstances. Anyway, giving Ruthie hell might even be good karma. An exception to the rule, okay?"

"Ruthie does not really mean to hurt anyone," said Tip. "She is unhappy in herself."

ORGIES

Things were falling apart. Ever since the dark moon party, and even more since Terdsak and his men had arrived on the scene, the 4H Club's surface tranquillity was beginning to crack and craze. Chloe was still hot, but the earlier mood of surrender to a great, humid, all-encompassing whole had fled. She was weighing the relative merits of a dip shower from the big water jar or a nap when Tip reminded her they had to have a talk. In private.

"And it's better if you keep your notebooks outside the dorm," she told Chloe. "Come with me tomorrow and I'll show you a better place. And you can help to give me some information I need."

31 heroes die young

Show me a hero and I will write you a tragedy.

F. Scott Fitzgerald

They passed Freddie's hut on the way, but neither the Organization Man nor Olga were anywhere to be seen. Chloe noticed a new addition to the heap of artist's supplies, a rusted-out exhaust manifold from a motorcycle. She and Tip continued on deeper into the forest, the trees lending a cooling canopy of shade. At one point Chloe was accosted by a thorny climber that wouldn't let go. "That's a wait-a-minute vine," Tip informed her, laughing. "You can't be in a hurry."

Finally they entered the clearing. The glade was drenched with mystery and a sense of the sacred, a sense that something dwelt there. Long abandoned by people but still inhabited by presences, this place was a palimpsest of experiences earthly and otherwise. Chloe could see mounds through the undergrowth. One ran in a straight line like a one-yard-wide wall across a corner of the clearing. Under the biggest of the trees surrounding the glade, a ruined structure like a miniature temple stood half-collapsed, partly overgrown with creepers and shrubs, only a few patches of the original plaster on the crumbling red bricks. Tip stopped and knelt to bring her hands together up to her forehead in a *wai* of respect.

"What is it?" asked Chloe.

"A *chedi*. This one may be very old. I don't know its history. But local people believe it has *phii*. Ghosts. Maybe bad things happened here long ago. Now Thais don't like to come to this place. There was a temple here, once, and this was a shrine. People put sacred things in these places. Sometimes the ashes of a holy monk." This is where Tip kept her notebooks and a camera. Nobody else came here, she said, except Prue and Bibi and, sometimes, Freddie, when they wanted to smoke dope. And Al Dente.

Tip *wai*-ed the ruin again before she knelt to pull aside some of the creepers, revealing a short section of weathered plank. Tip put the plank to one side and reached into a recess to remove a tin box much like the one in which Ruthie hid her own stash. Tip's notebooks, wrapped in plastic bags, were inside, together with an old Nikon FM2 camera and two lenses, also wrapped in plastic. Then something crashed in the trees.

"*Shh*. Quiet." Tip pulled Chloe down beside her and they listened. Silence. Then they heard a rustling or two. Maybe lizards. A shaft of sunlight held three tiny yellow butterflies where, on the edge of the clearing, they fluttered and tumbled above a flowering shrub. A bird flashed electric blue in the leaves across the way. "It's okay," Tip said finally. "I think it was a squirrel." They had to have pretty big squirrels around here, Chloe was thinking, when there was another crash, and Olga appeared.

"Ah, I find you. I take another way. To be sure no one follows. I heard you talking last night. I want to talk, too." Then she told Tip, "And I can give the massage I promised."

"Good idea," Tip said. "But please do not break something, okay?"

An inch or two taller than Chloe, all solid masses and smooth swells, Olga was physically stronger than most men. Tip was much smaller. Slight, with gracile wrists and ankles, all the skeletal struts and wires close to surface, she nevertheless evinced her own subtle strength, a calm determination and certainty of purpose. Her short, even black hair—still barely more than a stubble—further suggested the tough vulnerability of a survivor. At the same time there was something tragic about her, foreshadowings that Chloe decided to put down to the mood of this place with all its vestiges of plans and purposes long past.

Olga's laugh abruptly scattered these dark reflections. Tip had perched on a piece of plastered pediment, the better to enjoy her massage, and her sweet chuckle tinkled counterpoint as the Russian gently manipulated Tip's arms, rubbed her shoulders and back, in preparation for the main event. Then, comfortably settled, Tip asked Chloe to relate her encounter with Terdsak, and she obliged, including the punishment of the godfather's errant bodyguard.

"So the guy pissed himself," Chloe concluded. "Right in front of us. I couldn't believe it." She meant Terdsak's behavior, of course. Zero's was entirely comprehensible. "He made him suck whiskey from the barrel. The pistol was loaded and his finger was on the trigger."

"I also know things about Terdsak," Tip said. "And now I will tell you another story. A sadder one."

About a year and a half before, Terdsak had been entertaining business associates, and a guest told Terdsak that one of the hostesses refused to perform oral sex for him. "In Buddhist society," Tip continued in a matter-of-fact voice, "many people believe that the head, the highest part of the person, is sacred, while the lower parts are dirty. People who believe this sometimes do not believe in oral sex." But Terdsak had little patience with such compunctions, and even less time for staff who would cause him to lose face with a good customer. When the girl expressed distaste, even after being confronted with her boss and the disgruntled guest, Terdsak turned nasty. "'No smoke my friend? Okay. You smoke *this*.'" And he fired a couple of shots past the girl's head and into the wall. He made her smoke the barrel, right there in front of everybody. She had to inhale, and she was smoking and coughing and crying and trying to say she was sorry, on her knees with the gun in her mouth. Terdsak told one of his men to come over and take the gun. "'Pull the trigger,'" he said. "His man knew better than to argue when the boss was in that mood, so he did it. The girl was only sixteen years old. She was from Korat. Terdsak told his customer to choose another girl."

There wasn't much to say. All the life had drained from the sun and the flowers and the birdsong.

"That is one thing I hear again and again," Tip remarked after a moment. "Terdsak does not kill people himself. He has other people do it for him. He is afraid of bad karma."

"That's not true. I know it is not true," said Olga. "He does kill. I know this because he is my husband. I am his wife."

Olga had their undivided attention.

"That's why I hide with Freddie."

She had come to Thailand on a tourist visa to learn traditional Thai massage and practice prostitution. "I need money; this is easiest way." But she wound up married to Terdsak, a businessman who turned out to be what the Thai newspapers called an "influential person," if not indeed a "dark influence." It gave him status to have a Western wife, especially one so big and blonde and buxom. Olga lived with him for four months. During that time, she was forced to admire his gun collection and listen to stories of the men he'd killed. "And he had *mia noi*," Olga told them, as though this might be even worse. "'Minor wives.'" Mistresses.

She had been pressing her thumbs on acupressure points in Tip's shoulders. Suddenly Tip jerked in pain. "Olga," she said. "Please. You are too strong." Then she gasped as Olga pulled her outstretched arms back till they almost met behind her back and held them there.

"And he wanted me to know about these wives. Around the time I left, he was planning to move the newest and youngest one into the house. Can you imagine? He even had something with another Western woman—an American, I think. A few times she came late at night and spent hours with him in his office. The guards would not let me near. He told me it was business. None of my business. Her name was something like J. C. You know: *Jaycee*."

It got worse and worse. In the Thai way, Olga was required to sit for hours and days smiling at hundreds of relatives and neighbors and hangers-on, and she was otherwise abused till she wanted to scream. He had beaten her up, finally. In fact, she was bigger and stronger than he was and probably could have pounded the piss out of him—"*Da*. I can beat him, sure"—but she was afraid of his bodyguards. At the first chance she had split, and ever since she'd been on the run from her husband, who was more concerned with matters of face than any alienated affections. He was a powerful man with connections everywhere, and she was afraid to try to leave the country. She hadn't told anyone about her real background. As far as Gorgi was concerned, she was a tourist. And thank God for that because now, it turned out, Terdsak and Gorgi were some kind of business partners. She hadn't realized that. How lucky she'd been that Gorgi didn't know her. Certainly, she'd never seen him during her four months with Terdsak.

As she talked, Olga stretched and massaged Tip's arms, over and over, and Tip responded like a cat, almost purring with pleasure. "But he kills people. Sure." Her husband had gunned someone down in a karaoke bar because the guy wouldn't relinquish the microphone. First Terdsak had his bodyguards beat him up. Then he borrowed a pistol from one of his men and shot the guy himself. The waiters testified that the other guy had pulled a gun, even though the cops never found it, and the whole thing was self-defense. Terdsak had bragged about it to Olga not long before she left.

"I read about that," Tip said. "About a year ago. I believe there is something wrong with Terdsak's mind. He is becoming more and more unstable. Olga, you are his wife? My information says he was married to a woman named Anna."

"Please. You call me Olga."

Tip had been researching a story on Terdsak for a year and a half already. Now she was investigating his connection with Gorgi and the 4H Club. This much Tip had already learned about Gorgi's background: he got his start partly from recruiting burnt-out cases from the full moon parties. "Gorgi says that drugs are strictly out. But who do you think supplies the full moon parties?"

"Not Gorgi?"

"It is hard to say how far he's involved. It has been hard to learn much about him. But, for the past year or two, Terdsak has had a monopoly on everything from farming magic mushrooms to mixing speed soup to dealing ganja and Ecstasy. Freelance dealers on these islands get just one warning. Don't try it."

Terdsak was long established, mostly in the south, as a gangster of no small means. One early game, Tip told them, involved people in a village near Terdsak's home town. There was a bend at the top of a gentle hill descending into town, and they would put oil on the corner. Thai truck drivers drove too fast, and trucks would lose control and go off the road, whereupon the villagers would scavenge the cargo and sell it to Terdsak. One day, an eighteen-wheeler full of dynamite and detonators got caught in the scam. "I would say this was karma, so many villagers died in that explosion and so many were hurt. It was terrible. But the man behind it all is still alive, so it is hard to see how the karma works in this case."

Terdsak soon moved on to bigger and better things. "A good part of the local forests disappeared into his pockets, and now, I hear, he has bought a logging concession in Cambodia. He pays the military." Trawling fleets were also part of Terdsak's game. "The Thai fishermen, they say they have to use smuggled oil. The fish stocks are so poor, now—illegal fishing is destroying the reefs and fish hatcheries—and the costs are so high, they could not survive if they were paying taxes on fuel. Or that's what they say. Some go to foreign tankers anchored outside the territorial waters. But Terdsak's boats use hijacked diesel fuel that he provides himself."

His empire had gradually grown and diversified. Most recently, he had started to see money and, perhaps, a relative respectability in new lines of business.

Yawn

Chloe told Tip and Olga what Terdsak and Gorgi had said about their plans for commercial adventure travel in inner space. What young tourists wanted was adventure, Tip agreed. Great. But most of the forests were gone. The coral reefs were on their way out. Soon there wouldn't be any more *fish*. Everywhere you went there were all these other travelers looking for something exotic, but nothing was exotic any more. It was all McDonald's. So Terdsak was probably right. This *was* adventure tourism. And, directly or indirectly, he would be tying all that in with his established interests in drugs, smuggling, and sex slavery.

Terdsak's operations also catered for another kind of traveler. Some people paid big money for special culinary experiences. Jungle-food restaurants often served more than simple game. Part of the thrill lay in eating rare animals, or only choice morsels reputed to enhance health, sexual vigor, and longevity. "They have farms where they keep bears and tigers and other animals. Many of them come from Cambodia and Burma. These animals are tortured to death. Sometimes, just before they are butchered, they are tortured with steel rods and then lowered in their cage into boiling water so they are cooked alive. Other times they are slowly strangled with ropes. These ignorant people believe that the pain makes the medicine more powerful and the meat more delicious. Some animals are forced to walk on hot coals till their paws are cooked, and then they amputate them to feed the customers. The animals are kept alive for their other parts, the bears for their bile."

Some of these men also believed that another kind of meat was all the sweeter for having suffered. Two years earlier, four girls died chained to a wall in the back room of one of Terdsak's brothels. There had been a fire and no one thought to get the girls out till it was too late. They had been charred beyond recognition, according to the local papers; but two of them were identified from lockets and an engraved bracelet.

"And you're saying Gorgi is involved in all this?" Chloe found that hard to believe. She found it almost as hard to believe that

Terdsak himself could be into so many unpleasant things at the same time.

"I don't know yet what he is part of. But I am getting the idea there is much more to our friend than you first think."

Terdsak, in any case, was into everything. He had a kind of vision. Not just logging because the forest happened to be there, or heroin because you happened to have the connections. To him, every element was part of a massive empire and he constantly sought new ways to maximize the take. Whatever, Terdsak was only the logical conclusion, almost a parody of what you could see everywhere these days.

"Today it's all take, take, and no give," Tip told them. The old social hierarchy of reciprocal privilege and responsibility was collapsing, and a few rich people were getting ever richer. Too many people were caught up in the feeding frenzy. "Sell off the forests, destroy the coral reefs, pollute the beaches, raise the cost of real estate so the men and women who build the cities can't afford to live in them, sell the sons and daughters of the land as cheap labor or cheap sex. They behave like there is no tomorrow. Everything is measured in terms of money and what money can buy. Power is money and guns. If money won't buy it, then take it. Take and take and take.

"The young people, and many of the old ones too, they see which way things are going and they want to stop it. But maybe they can't. It's hard. My husband was killed by soldiers during demonstrations in Bangkok. We had an illegal government in power, a junta. But these dictators didn't realize that things were changing, and they sent the army to silence us. They did not understand that we would not be silenced. This was not the old days. We were not communists or just a few radical students. My husband was a photographer. They shot him down as though he were nothing, a dog. But those were only young soldiers, ignorant, following the orders of other soldiers, who were obeying men who wanted power, who believed they deserved power, that the country needed them in power, and anything that stood in their way had to be crushed."

Chloe was moved by Tip's apparent serenity in face of the terrible things she was telling them. In fact, Tip was positively luxuriating under Olga's ministrations, which were now concentrating on hands and arms.

"My hands get so tired." Tip laughed. "Writing, writing all the time. I can't write fast enough to get everything down, everything I have to say."

Chloe could evoke echoes of a similar passion from years past. And she had sensed new stirrings, these past days.

Now, as her own contribution to the health of the nation, Tip was trying to build a complete dossier on Terdsak and then publish the story both in Thailand and abroad.

"It must be very dangerous, what you're doing."

"I will accept my fate. It is important to do good work. If you do good, good comes back to you. So my husband always said. He was killed. But sometimes you have to do good so good comes back for everybody. You cannot only think of yourself. You are not so important. It is everything together that we must make better. My husband was a hero. All of us must try to be heroes, or there is no hope."

"Why don't you go to the police with what you have already?" Chloe asked. "You have to report all this."

"That would be suicide," Tip replied. "I have friends in the police force, higher up, but even they have to move carefully. We cannot do anything yet. Terdsak has many connections. Read the newspapers. You see pictures of the *chao por*, the godfathers, being hugged in public and called brother by top officials whenever there's a 'crackdown' on 'influential figures.'" Was this collusion, or only subtle tactics on the part of the authorities? Sometimes it wasn't clear, Tip said. Things in Thailand would change, she said. But it would take time. And now was not the time to go to the police.

"Tip, did you and your husband have children?"

"Yes. I have a daughter. Living with my sister. She is eleven. "Song is a good girl. She is smart and happy. Always laughing. She does well in school; she loves to read. She is very pretty." For a moment, Tip looked unutterably sad. "If something happens to me, I don't know what my little girl will do."

Tip herself had lived in the U.S.A., England, France, and South America while growing up. "My father was a diplomat. Now he is dead." She went to university in California, where she did studies in regional development and journalism. She wanted Song to have similar advantages. "Maybe she can study medicine or biology. Or rural development." But money was hard.

"I may not have much time," said Tip. "I feel I am being watched, now, and I am frightened for myself." Tip said this in the same matter-of-fact way she might have said she had a slight headache. "But I am more frightened for my daughter.

"I need someone I can trust. I see how Sweet Mama likes you. Freddie, too. Same as Sweet Mama, he doesn't trust everybody; only a few. And Prue is a good person; she likes you too. You must help me. I need somebody who can write about what I'm going to tell you. You are also a journalist. These notebooks must go to my newspaper friend in Bangkok," said Tip. "If anything happens to me, somebody must deliver these notes. Can you do that for me? And, maybe, can you publish these things outside Thailand if things go wrong?"

Tip had yet another favor to ask. She told Chloe where her daughter was and asked her to check on her welfare later. "If I give you a message, can you pass it to my daughter and my sister?"

Of course Chloe said she would.

"Do you like being a writer?" Tip asked her.

"Yes, I do." As soon as she said it, however, Chloe realized what she really liked was the idea of being the kind of writer she'd dreamed about when she was a girl. She didn't especially like what she'd been doing these past few years. "Sometimes I like being a writer. Sometimes I have to write things that are pretty silly, though. I don't enjoy that so much."

"Why do you do it, then?"

Tip's naïveté sparked a hot flash of pique. But the irritation quickly shaded into something like shame. Chloe had been going to say she did what she did because she had to make a living. But then she realized that wasn't really true. She didn't have to write about these things. At the beginning, tongue firmly in cheek, she'd enjoyed serving this stuff up to a credulous readership. But the fun was mostly gone, and the assignments she tended to accept made no intellectual or creative demands. She wasn't learning anything new, merely confirming a cynicism that brought her little satisfaction.

"I think journalists are special," said Tip. "They can learn and then share this knowledge. They can say what everybody else only thinks or, sometimes, what they should think. So they have a responsibility to the people." Tip told Chloe how lucky she was, being a journalist and having English as a first language. Her potential audience was so huge. And it was so much easier to make a living, writing in English.

"You are married, aren't you?" asked Tip.

"Yes, I am."

"Why are you traveling alone, without your husband?"

"We decided we needed some time alone, away from each other, and we're taking separate holidays."

Tip looked surprised. "Are you happy?"

Happy? Chloe was at a loss for an answer. She thought about her life back in suburban Vancouver, but—even though she'd only been gone a few weeks—it all seemed so far away. Right now she was sort of happy, she supposed. Interested in life, at least. Excited, even. Looking forward to developments. She hadn't felt that way in some time. But Tip had meant to ask if she were happy with her marriage. The last communication from Waylon had been along the lines of, "How are you? I am fine. It rained yesterday." Chloe had asked Gorgi if she could use his account to send an e-mail message, and her own response hadn't been much better:

Waylon, I can't seem to reset the message machine. It isn't easy for me to send e-mail, so this may be the last communication for a while. I hope you're okay. Look after yourself. I'm staying a little longer. There's something I have to do. I've done a lot of thinking about us, and I look forward to talking to you.
Love, Chloe.

"Your husband. Is he a good man? Does he work hard to make a good life for you?"

"Yes, he does. He's a good man."

"How many children do you have?"

"None."

Tip looked surprised and concerned. "How old are you?" she asked.

"Thirty-four."

"It is not too late."

Olga finished with Tip and then gave Chloe's feet and ankles a quick booster therapy. Chloe was amazed at how the stiffness and tension drained so quickly from her muscles and tendons, leaving her invigorated, refreshed.

Then, somewhere in the trees not far away, a branch snapped. "Sh!" Tip said. There was a sudden thrash of leaves. Olga looked scared. They backed away from the edge of the clearing and in behind the chedi, moving as silently as they could. They waited. Nothing. No more sounds from the undergrowth, beyond the usual faint scrabblings and rustlings. Maybe a squirrel.

Eventually Tip said, "Let's go back now." She led Chloe by another route to the 4H Club, while Olga made her own way to Freddie's camp. Olga said she felt okay there for the time being. But she'd have to figure out some way of getting clear of this whole area, now that Terdsak was around.

32 hot-dogs

*Harmony would lose its attractiveness
if it did not have a background of discord.*

Tehyi Hsieh

Chloe faded in and out from scraps of dreams. Even as she dreamed them, she knew these little anomalies weren't real. The seal, for example, wasn't a seal; it was Pup barking. She fought the drowsiness, willing herself to keep her eyes open. Open, but unfocused. Keep the mind attentive, yet unengaged. She was losing. She could hear herself snoring.

"You are not here to sleep. *Atcha*. Fifty baht."

It was worth the money just to catch a few minutes of shuteye. This getting up at four in the morning was killing her. It was hard to sleep at night, as well; the heat had been unbearable for days. Anyway, now she was awake, and she resumed her breathing exercises. *Rising . . . falling. . . .* But what was the point? *Hearing. . . .* It was everybody's else's breathing she was mindful of. *Hearing. . . .* You had the Rev panting at two beats to one of Bibi's gulps; that was the rhythm section. Then you had the woodwinds—Ruthie's sighs of exasperation and Gorgi's mewls of avarice, each of them improvising on different themes. Olga's grunts and groans as she wrestled with enlightenment would normally have provided the horns, but of course she was still hiding.

Rising . . . falling. . . . Rising. . . .
Remembering.

One of the things that Waylon and Chloe had shared, in the early days, was a love of jazz and good jazz bars. Even there, however, they had started to grow apart. Waylon was still into early Coltrane, and nobody could fault that, but some of the Great Man's later stuff went right over Waylon's head, and he wouldn't listen to Ornette Coleman at all. Coleman was one of Chloe's favorites. When it came right down to it, Waylon was a Bach person. He liked the logic, the order of it all. It had gotten so Chloe thought she'd scream if she had to listen to the *Goldberg Variations* one more time. It hadn't been that bad, actually, but still. There'd be lots of time for order and predictability when they were old crocks and waiting to die.

"Jesus Christ, *eh*?" It was only inside her own head, but she heard herself once again pose the great Canadian query. Suddenly Chloe had an impulse to stand up and shout, "Sorry, eh? Jesus Christ, I'm *sorry*." But it wasn't a very strong impulse and she didn't do it. It was just a side-effect of sitting there dwelling on her own psyche hour after hour. And who could blame her if she did start screaming like a looney?

Some people—the Australian Aborigines, among others—believed that the whole universe was a dream dreamed by the Great Dreamer, and all of us participated in the dreaming. Chloe liked the idea that everything, including the entire history of human striving for sense and happiness, was on some level merely imaginative play. Of course, the way things were going these days, you had to think that the Great Dreamer had treated Herself to limburger and pickles before retiring. And thinking of limburger led Chloe by natural stages to thoughts of cheeseburgers with sautéed onions and green peppers and bacon, and in the process of trying to dream a couple of these items into being, she effectively ruined the rest of the meditation session. She was actually slipping back into a meditative state when the juicy big hot-dog reappeared. Once again, a cruel hallucination, it hung there in mid-air where Bibi's mind usually shimmered.

Chloe finally managed to subdue the hot-dog invasion, only to find her mind turning to thoughts of Waylon putting wire ties from bread bags into their special drawer in the kitchen, along with neatly folded plastic bags from the supermarket. Then, for no reason, she recalled the time she and Waylon went to Montreal and heard that great saxophonist. A great jazz club.

Rising . . . falling. . . . Rising. . . .
Remembering. . . .

Montreal smoked meat sandwiches with big dill pickles. Steamed hot-dogs on the Main. Four in the morning, and the wino on the stool beside them, motionless, slumped face down in the extra-large helping of sauerkraut piled atop his steamie. Chloe and Waylon looking at each other with wild surmise, this guy maybe lying there smothered in his own sauerkraut. Then they noticed these little slurps and snuffles, and watched in horror and fascination as the pile grew smaller. All that seemed so long ago, now. She hadn't had a Montreal steamie in years.

And she was surprised at how acutely she missed Waylon. Maybe she should send him an e-mail asking him where he was, saying they should get back together now. She could leave the 4H Club, and they could get back to having their holiday away together.

She wasn't asleep, yet she wasn't exactly awake. Maybe you could have called it a kind of meditation.

Hearing. . . .

Pup was barking again. And Chloe returned to herself.

Then she returned to her selves. She was invaded by a sudden sense of other times and other places, at once her own and not her own. Bibi would probably say they were emanations from previous lives. So would Ruthie. But maybe they were merely intimations of potential lives. Other people and other scenes lurked on the periphery of consciousness like words on the tip of the tongue, at once absent and somehow there—second-hand memories worn to obscurity by time and distance, feeble and mysterious signals flickering in on an old crystal radio set. Then she was losing it. The perception was slipping away, retreating the way dream fragments evaporate in the morning's rush to waking life. She tried to return to simple mindfulness, tried to let go the urge to recollect and analyze the experience. She tried to hold the window open. There. She almost had it; she was on the verge of . . .

"Ow, ow! Ow, fuck. Oh, shit. They got me. I knew it. They finally got me. Fucking *ow*, man."

Chloe experienced an acute sense of *déjà vu* as a sudden stench of burning invaded the meditation sala. She didn't even try the *smelling . . . smelling . . .* routine. "Damn!" she said, and tried to get up; but her legs had gone to sleep.

33 freddie's rape

*Just because you're paranoid doesn't
mean they aren't out to get you.*

Anon.

"Ow, ow! Fuckin' A, man. *Ow.*" Freddie was wearing a new cape, this one a shimmering film of metallicized plastic, and it was on fire. He was rolling around in the dirt, Pup snapping at his legwarmer. "They got me, man," he was screaming. "Ow. Fuckin' A. Ow, *ow*. Big Oil, man. I knew they'd try something like this. Ow!"

Sweet Mama was hiding under a bench trying to pretend it was none of her responsibility.

"Fast Freddie's kind of stressed out today," said Prue. "Probably needs a holiday."

The heat of the day was rising, and Chloe felt she could have used a vacation herself. The cooking and cleaning were okay—kind of restful, a nice break from having to think about anything. The meditation, on the other hand, was wearing her down. And here was Freddie on fire at the top of his lungs. For a moment she almost sympathized with Ruthie, who was yelling at Freddie and calling him several kinds of moron and pain in the ass.

Freddie's latest organization was ablaze and, to Chloe's eye, out of control. It spun crazily for a moment and then toppled over and crashed in flames, gas spilling from somewhere and running a little river of fire right over to where the dry garbage, neatly tied up in bags, awaited collection. Pretty soon that was burning as well, a merry conflagration on a scale sufficient to make the day seem even hotter than it already was. Freddie got his cape off and appeared not too much the worse for wear, laughing and cavorting and generally carrying on as though this were a cool day in the spring of the Revolution. Ruthie signed off her diatribe with, "How the *fuck* am I supposed to meditate with all this shit going on?" before striding off past the sala towards Gorgi's office. But she stopped dead at the sight of Terdsak.

Terdsak was standing by the door talking to Gorgi. He wasn't happy. "What this?" he asked, and then answered his own question. "Is drugadick person. What drugadick person do here? Not have drugs here. This not—how you say?—the *scene*. Not here."

"He is not a bad person, Khun Terdsak." Gorgi pulled at his beard and smiled uncertainly. "Only eccentric."

This didn't really tell Terdsak anything. "This drugadick person. Not polite. Why he stay here? E-go!" Terdsak addressed his lieutenant. "That man. There. *He go*."

E-go was confused. Chances were he thought *he* was E-go, and now the boss was trying to claim the whacko in the jumpsuit was E-go. "That man. There. *E-go*," he'd said.

Ten looked back and forth between Terdsak and E-go, hoping for enlightenment.

Chloe and Prue were listening to all this with growing horror. Freddie, meanwhile, remained blissfully unaware of developments. Still smarting from his self-immolation, he walked over to the pyramid and climbed in for only a second or two before reappearing. "Turn the steam machine off, man," he said. "It *hurts*. Anyway, you can't keep a joint lit with all that fuckin' herbal shit everywhere."

251

Before he'd gotten three steps away from the steamroom, Ten grabbed him. Freddie started thrashing around and swearing, managing to stamp down hard on One's instep before Zero whapped him across the face with his pistol. Pup gave up chasing a couple of hens across the yard, and, happy to find bigger game, shot off without preamble to latch on to Zero's ankle. The guard shook him off and then place-kicked him about two yards away. Pup crawled off yelping and whining to seek shelter under the tree. Sweet Mama was nowhere to be seen.

"You fuck. . . . You *fuck*. You think I don't know you, man? I fuckin' know you, you fuck, man. Big Oil cocksuckers. Ahh! Ahh! *Shit*." Freddie was indignant.

"Dirty mouth." Terdsak came down into the yard. "Dirty person. Look. We see—how you say?—*pee-nut*. And here *pooying*, women. See everything. Drugadick person same-same animal." Terdsak was pretty indignant himself, and the more indignant he got, the more his English turned to pidgin. "Gorgi! Bring medicine. For drugadick person. *Now*."

"I'll kill you, man. You fuck."

They held Freddie outside Gorgi's house for ten minutes, awaiting Gorgi's return.

"You can't do this," Chloe told Terdsak. "Who do you think you are, anyway? We're calling the police." Prue and the Rev backed her up, making supportive noises and saying "police." Al Dente and Bibi just watched, with Bibi making occasional discreet observations along the lines of, "UNBELIEVABLE. They can't *DO* this." Ruthie was inside with Gorgi. Chloe hadn't seen Tip since breakfast, she suddenly realized.

"No, no." Gorgi smiled in all directions and trying to pretend everything was quite standard. No reason for anybody to get upset. "No problem. Just a little misunderstanding. Yes? We don't need the police. No, no. We are fine."

Ten finally managed to pin Freddie while E-go held Freddie's nose shut with one hand and, with the other, administered the herbal mess through a giant syringe. Maybe Gorgi had the recipe for the Rev's soup, because Freddie puked till he was pale and gasping, tears of rage and exhaustion streaming from his eyes. Then they gave him another dose. And another.

"I know 'fuck,'" said Terdsak. "*Pak maa*. Dirty mouth. After clean inside, wash mouth."

When they were done, Terdsak told his men to search Freddie's quarters. When they discovered he didn't even sleep in the 4H Club, they questioned Gorgi before going into the woods, dragging Freddie along. Pup followed after, yapping at their heels.

Chloe looked at Ruthie and saw something savage there in her face.

Terdsak probed with his gold toothpick and came up with a couple of magnificent sneezes. Wiping primly at his nose and calling for his special drink, he looked at the assembly of outraged seekers after peace and harmony and said, "No problem. I help drugadick person. Same-same monk. Is good. First clean poison. Natural way. Change. Better person. I help. How you say? No pain, no grain, *na*? This is the concept."

Terdsak's men found Freddie's hut and they found his hoard of construction materials. They tore down his shelter and burned it together with his materials, his creative bank consigned to a premature consumption. Later that afternoon they drove away, and Chloe and Prue went looking for Freddie. They were scared—they'd heard a shot, just one, from somewhere back in the woods.

By the time they found him, in the clearing with the chedi, he'd already built himself a camouflaged lean-to in the woods nearby. "This is where I live now," said Freddie. "My safe house, man. You know what I mean?"

The caustic soap had blistered his lips and he spoke with a slur, since he didn't want to touch his tongue to anything, even the inside of his own mouth. Chloe and Prue had brought him a flask of cold soup and some chocolate from Prue's stash to suck on. They also brought him a blanket. And cigarettes. If he wanted to start smoking again, under the circumstances, who could say no? Chloe also attended to his self-inflicted burns, which were minor, and the contusion from the pistol-whipping, which was nasty.

"I'm going to stay under cover for a while, man. Time to go to ground, you know? Live to fight another fuckin' day." There was little doubt he was in the mood to fight, as he spun in the dirt, kicking high in all directions, punching low, gouging and snapping in rage. "Pow!" he said. "Pow, pow, pow!" He stopped to catch his breath, hiked up his parts, and sat down on a log. "The Holistic Herbal Garden and Institute of Holographic Healing, man. Think about it. H-H-H-H: Haitian, hemophiliac, homosexual, *heroin* user. What does it add up to? AIDS, man. There's something going on around here and I don't know what it is. You know what I mean?"

"Get some sleep, Freddie," Chloe suggested. "We'll come back to see you in the morning, okay?"

But Freddie was back on his feet, fueled anew by white-hot indignation. "Auto-mo-*beels*, man. Mo' auto, mo' man. Mo*jo*, man. Big metal cocks." Freddie was spluttering, he was cackling, he was doing the Funky Chicken with his eyes rolled back. Freddie was an outlaw shaman returned with the back-room mysteries, a report from the inner sanctum of Consumerism. "Mine's longer than yours. Faster, too. Goes like a fuckin' mink. I got the car, I got the *power*, okay? No. Wrong, man. You got the car, they got you right where they want you. It's all part of it. Part of the big picture. You are your car. And, if you don't got your car, then you don't got you. And then where are you? Nowhere, man. You got your Cock-of-the-Month Club and this month it's the Almighty Benz, man. Mer-*cedes*-Benz. So we have to do a little Bobbitt job on the Benz." Freddie was tugging so hard at his parts, now, you might have thought he was going to demonstrate what he meant right there.

"Have you seen Pup?" the Rev asked when Chloe and Prue got back to the 4H Club. He had some food for him.

34 call of the wild

It's bad taste to be wise all the time.

D. H. Lawrence

Chloe jumped at the sudden flutter and rattle, and a cloud of little birds shot out from where they'd been picking rice grains from a pile of pots and dishes behind the cookhouse. It was Tip's turn to wash up, but she was nowhere to be seen. She was supposed to have met Chloe at one o'clock. After the episode with Freddie, Tip said she might have to accelerate her report. Terdsak seemed to be approaching some kind of critical mass, totally losing his perspective on things, careless of public opinion or witnesses to his increasingly frequent excesses.

Things were quiet without Freddie. Maybe Sweet Mama missed him, because she'd been whining and groveling in the dust under the sala all morning. And Pup was nowhere to be seen. The Rev was sitting under the tree pretending to meditate, although it was plain to anyone who cared to look he was sound asleep, on the verge of falling off the bench right on his head. Al Dente was practicing sitting meditation in the sala, absolutely immobile, and Bibi was sitting beside him casting hurt looks in Chloe's direction. But maybe that was only her imagination. Chloe had been responsible for lunch that day, serving coleslaw with no mayonnaise and a tossed salad that incorporated a yellow chili pepper so hot it had given Bibi hiccups. "UN-hic-*REAL*. TOTALLY . . . hic . . . TOO hic-MUCH. Oh, hic, *FUCK*."

Prue was strutting across the yard, bobbing up and down like some kind of wading bird. Earlier, Ruthie had asked what Prue thought she was doing and, when Prue explained that this was toe-walking meditation—she was firming up her buttocks at the same time she was meditating—Ruthie only gasped, no doubt rendered speechless with admiration. Or maybe she'd been trying to think of some way this could be construed as a fineable offense. Chloe gave Prue's toe-walking meditation a try, but it was too hard to work out and meditate at the same time. She really felt like a full massage today. When she brought fresh food and drinking water for Freddie, out by the chedi, she would ask Olga if she'd mind.

Then Ruthie came over to her. "I've got to talk to you. I have a confession to make." She spoke in hushed tones, managing to look imperious and abashed at the same time. "It was me who took your notebooks."

This wasn't really news, but Chloe didn't say anything.

"I'm sorry. I was only trying to protect Gorgi. And the Institute. You get reporters, you know, and all they want to do is come up with exposés. They do everything they can to dig up dirt. And if they can't find it, half the time, they make it up. Anyway, I'm sorry."

"Don't worry about it," Chloe assured her. "No harm done. They even gave them back to me."

"There's something else. I told them where Tip's notebooks were hidden. I'm sorry." Ruthie wasn't crying, but she looked as though she wished she could. "I'm scared."

Neither Olga nor Freddie had seen Tip. In fact, Freddie had taken the liberty of checking her stash, and found the tin box gone. "I don't like the look of this, you know?" he said. "Man, oh fuckin'

Call of the Wild

man. It don't look good." It did not look good, thought Chloe. And she should go right back to Vancouver. Let Meredith look after herself. Let Waylon work out whatever it was he had to work out. He was never going to believe what was happening to her—not even the parts she could tell him. Now they had Tip's notebooks and maybe Tip herself. Chloe's own notebooks were with Prue's stash at the moment, thank God. She had left them there after coffee, earlier, too lazy to walk back to the chedi.

Chloe skipped the massage. She had just got back to the dorm when Gorgi came by to ask if he could see her in his office for a moment. Terdsak was there. So were E-go and Ten. The Benz had been parked around the back.

"So. Work for me, *na*?" said Terdsak.

"No. I don't think so."

"Tonight you come eat with me. We talk more."

"Forget it."

"Friend, you. The nun. Want talk. Talk you, *na*?"

Terdsak was a criminal, possibly a nutcase besides. He was part of a culture about which Chloe knew virtually nothing. He was a sleazy egomaniac and a total psychopath, if you could believe everything Tip had told her. And he wanted her to join him for dinner.

"Okay," Chloe said.

Even as she heard herself say this, another part of her was screaming no. Don't be an idiot. Going out with a gangster. A killer. She was married, after all. She had responsibilities. Didn't she? She didn't have any children. So what responsibilities did she really have? Waylon had just gone off into the night and who knew what he was doing? She was really only responsible to herself. Even on those grounds, she was still crazy to go out with Terdsak. But maybe Tip needed her help. And how could Chloe write about this character if she weren't willing to get close to him? Beyond that, she realized upon reflection, some obscure compulsion demanded she answer this call to adventure.

She chose the orange-red sundress she'd bought on the beach in Pattaya and borrowed a brown leather bag from Prue.

35 interesting times

May you live in interesting times.
An ancient Chinese curse

Being in the present is always interesting.

Anon.

The regular procession of singers had started up again, once more dressed in full party regalia. The surface of her drink, Chloe noticed, was vibrating in time to the music. Terdsak, solicitous, was leaning over from his side of the booth and mouthing something at her.

Chloe was drunk, but she was drunk with a preternatural clarity of vision that she could only attribute to the weeks spent in meditation and semi-starvation. She was totally and mindfully drunk. She giggled. Then she giggled again to see Terdsak smile and puff up like a fat toad with pride that his remarks were appreciated by this Western lady, even though she hadn't heard a word he said. You wouldn't have heard a grenade go off in the New Rich Club, what with the fifty-megaton amplifier and speaker system. Terdsak reached up to finger the gold chains at his neck, and the gold Rolex slid down to crash into a starched white cuff secured by a big square gold nugget.

Chloe's universe narrowed and focused on the singer, on her flashing earrings, on the purple five-hundred-baht notes pinned to a sash across her bosom. Going only by her attitude of patent heart-brokenness, since Chloe couldn't understand a word of the lyrics, there was probably some problem with a no-good man who'd done her wrong and gone missing when he said he was only going out for cigarettes. Her bee-kissed mouth drooped, sagged at the corners in sympathy with the tiered ruffles of her green taffeta party dress. Her sad, drooping image was multiplied towards infinity in the mirrored pillars and mirrored booths along the walls. The flash and dazzle of her earrings were linked by the beat to the surface of Chloe's drink; linked to her pulse. To *everybody's* pulse. All things were related, and the throb of the drum machine raised echoes in the most distant corners of the cosmos.

Chloe was giving Terdsak big face, at least till she puked in his boots, an outcome that was maybe quite imminent, now that she thought about it. She tried to indicate that she didn't want any more whiskey, but Terdsak signaled the waiter to pour her another glass anyway. Chivas and Coke. He was taking a vacation from his Special Superman, which didn't have the same cachet when displayed in public.

Chloe knew she should be scared. She had been scared. And she hadn't wanted to drink. But Terdsak had made sure the waiter kept her drink topped up, and by now she hadn't the faintest idea how much she'd put away. She was drunk, but underneath it, when she reflected carefully, she saw that she was still terrified. She had to sober up. She had to find an excuse to leave. Not only was she scared at her vulnerability in this strange place with these unfamiliar people, she was confused and frightened by her own foolhardiness. She should never have agreed to come here with Terdsak in the first place. She had to get out of there. Back to the

4H Club. No, he could find her there. Maybe a hotel somewhere. She needed to sleep. Wake up in the morning and collect her thoughts.

Where were the others? Prue and Ruthie and the Rev, and everybody? They should have been here by now. And she hadn't had a chance to phone them.

Prue had strongly advised against Chloe's having anything to do with the man at all. Finally she insisted Chloe at least take her cellphone. Telephones were one of the things that the 4H Club insisted you check when you arrived, but Prue had this one stashed with her stuff in the woods. She told Chloe she'd stayed in constant contact with her broker and her eighteen-year-old son—to think that this total kid of hers, who couldn't look after himself successfully for a long weekend, was a year older than she was when she gave birth to the jerk. Of course, Prue said, she guessed that in itself showed how lame-brained she had herself been at that age. But the idea was that Chloe was supposed to call the others on Gorgi's mobile, which Ruthie had borrowed, if things went wrong.

"Not worry," Terdsak had told Chloe when he invited her. "Friend you, no problem. Come, eat food. Nun come too. Talk with her. You, *douay*. Both. Maybe work for me."

But Tip wasn't there. "Nun, friend you," Terdsak had said when he picked her up. "Cannot come. Sick. Sick too mutt." He refused to tell her where Tip was or to let Chloe out of the car. "Friend you, have little *guh*. Say give message to little *guh*. Tell me where, *na*? Where little *guh*."

The singer finished her set, curtseyed, *wai*-ed, and tripped down off the stage to join a table where four of her most generous admirers sat drinking from the biggest whiskey bottle Chloe had ever seen. Like Terdsak's Chivas, it was set out on a trolley with ice bucket and mix, with waiters keeping one and all topped up. Meanwhile, another in the endless series of singers had ascended the stage to fill the breach.

"Drink." Terdsak held the glass to her lips.

Chloe made a face at the drink, which was sickly with Coke and dangerous with too much whiskey. What had she gotten herself into?

Earlier, Terdsak had taken the karaoke microphone and performed "The Long and Winding Road," rendering it as "The Wrong and Widey Load." This had been followed by "My Way," "Cunty Load," and "The Yeroe Loase of Teksat." Terdsak was being expansive. He had beamed at everybody and ornamented his delivery with a repertoire of gestures that owed something to both Tony Bennett and Adolf Hitler. Chloe recalled what Olga had told her about the last time somebody had bogarded the mike in one of these joints, and what jolly old Terdsak and his men did to him.

Now Terdsak was testing the prawns. A waiter had wheeled up a trolley bearing a gas ring and a pot of boiling water, and lifted the lid from another big pot to reveal a mess of huge crustaceans. Chloe had to fight an inkling of DTs before she saw the contents of the pot were in fact moving. Terdsak proceeded to pick them over one by one, ensuring that each was alive and well. A few did not meet his exacting standards of liveliness, and he dropped them on the trolley. When he had finished, he held his hands out for the waiter to wipe them off with a clean wet towel.

"You like *goong*?" he asked Chloe. "Is Japanese way. Must be alive."

With evident relish, he instructed the waiter in the method and pace of execution, and watched as two of the unfortunate creatures, one after the other, were slipped into the boiling water. "Must be fresh," he yelled at Chloe, after she twice indicated she couldn't hear. He ripped the legs and carapace off one, dipped it in a bowl of sauce and held it up to Chloe's lips.

She recoiled. "I'm not hungry," she yelled back, twice, but apparently he couldn't hear, or didn't care. Finally she took the prawn in her mouth just to get it out of her face. The sauce was spicy-hot, the meat sweet and tender. Chloe remembered what Tip had said. Some people believed animals were best prepared by beating them to cause maximum pain and then cooking them alive. This provided meat at its tastiest. It had something to do with the chemicals produced by the body when stressed to the limit. Maybe it was the same with prawns.

The waiter slipped another into the water. "Kill no good," Terdsak hollered at Chloe. "Bad karma. Bad to kill. *Khaojai, mai*? Understand? No good. Other person kill; we eat, *na*? Hee, hee."

Chloe wondered what the prawns had ever done to merit this end. But she ate another, thinking it might help to sober her up. And what was this stuff about karma? What about the guys Olga claimed he had killed? Of course no one ever said gangsters had to be self-consistent.

In the meantime, the waiter had disappeared on some errand. "E-go," screamed Terdsak above the music. Having got his chief lieutenant's attention, he waved imperially at the trolley, "E-go. Cook *goong, na*?"

E-go looked perplexed, which was nothing new, and patted his stomach to say he was already full.

"No *eat*. Cook. *Khaojai, mai*? Cook!" Terdsak made dipping-in-boiling-water motions. "*Cook.*"

E-go finally got the message and came over to the trolley. He reached in, took a prawn between thumb and forefinger and promptly dropped it, telegraphing acute surprise and disgust. Peering into the pot, he registered further horror at what he saw there. Terdsak's chief gunman found live prawns icky.

Terdsak brought out his gold cigarette lighter, adopted his best Charles Bronson demeanor, and began running his own hand back and forth several inches above the flame. "You. E-go. You *cook*."

With no discernible enthusiasm, E-go plucked another prawn out, put its head on the edge of the trolley and brought a spoon down hard on it, rendering the creature dead or at least unconscious. Then he flung it into the water with a splash.

Fascinated by E-go's cavalier approach to the preparation of fresh tiger prawns, and losing track of where his hand was in relation to the flame, Terdsak suddenly jerked and swore. He put the Ronson away. Reaching for a soothing ice cube from the bucket, he transfixed E-go with a gaze that said: "Do it right, this time, or it's *you* in hot water." But the waiter had returned by this time, and he took over.

E-go retired from the culinary field of carnage with evident relief, and Terdsak said something to the waiter, who couldn't hear. He leaned over so Terdsak could yell in his ear and then looked scared. He performed deeply apologetic *wai*s to Terdsak and anyone within ten feet of Terdsak, and reached to dip his forefinger into the boiling water. Terdsak grabbed his arm and held it there, just for a few seconds. Tears in his eyes, the waiter *wai*-ed Terdsak again, turned the gas ring up, and introduced a new prawn to its fate.

"Must keep control, *na*?" said Terdsak, using his silk tie to polish the crystal on his watchface. "*I keep control.*" He yelled it again so Chloe could hear. "This is basic."

Back at his own table, E-go had resumed his courtship of a young singer dressed in yellow party togs. This was just one of the perks as Terdsak's security chief. Under the circumstances, the woman probably couldn't tell, or didn't care, that E-go spoke nothing but Russian, and she looked happy.

Ten, being on duty, were sipping Coke and looking glum. The two extra gunmen Terdsak had hired for the occasion, young guys in crewcuts, T-shirts, motorcycle jackets, and jeans, were sipping Coke and trying to look bad. As Terdsak had explained it, if you were anybody at all, these days, you needed at least three bodyguards. And if you were going to patronize a place like the New Rich Club, you really wanted five. One-upping the Joneses or, in this case, the other godfathers, had led to escalating security requirements. It was expensive, sure; but it was an essential part of modern business practice. Here and there throughout the huge nightclub, influential men sat drinking with friends, small armies of helpers parked at neighboring tables and booths. You needed the firepower in the event of controversy, for example over how long one individual or another had hogged the karaoke microphone. More than that, of course, it was a matter of status.

And on this particular occasion, Chloe realized, she herself was part of Terdsak's face. Like Terdsak's gold jewelry, like the gold-plated Mercedes parked outside, like E-go the Western lieutenant, like the extra bodyguards, she was merely an accessory.

Were Chloe to write about the New Rich Club for a West Coast magazine, they wouldn't believe it. They would think she'd made it up just to titillate them. Earlier, the audience had been treated to a mass striptease. Twenty singers had herded on to the stage at three half-hour intervals. Their song-and-dance routines had been choreographed by an MC's carny-barker spiel and punctuated by rim shots from the drum machine and applause from the men. Each time they appeared, the women wore fewer clothes. At the end of each set they swarmed off the stage to stalk through the audience. Every time one of them sat on a man's lap and kissed him, a tuxedoed goon would come over and drape a plastic flower garland around the girl's neck and, in exchange, extract fifty baht from the customer. The prettier girls were soon festooned in tacky plastic. Some of the men looked as though they were still in their teens and, drunk, were probably spending their entire rent on kisses and close encounters with singers. It all culminated in a last mass ascension to the stage. This time the singers appeared in one long chorus line, buck-naked but for their high-heeled pumps.

Chloe really didn't want to look at the stage—to tell the truth, she was kind of outraged—but the alternative was looking at Terdsak, who kept his gaze on Chloe throughout it all.

"*Suay, na?*" he said. "Beautiful, no?"

This time, when they came off the stage, the bidding for their company was more spirited and the plastic garlands cost a hundred baht. Terdsak had one girl come sit on his lap and kiss him. She couldn't have been more than eighteen, and she looked scared. But her goosebumps were probably due in part to the air-conditioning. Terdsak bought five hundred baht worth of kisses and fondled the girl's breasts, lifting and squeezing and twiddling, all the while smiling at Chloe, not even looking at the girl. After he was finished with the singer he moved around to sit beside Chloe on her side of the high-backed booth. "Cannot see," he told her. "Cannot see singer."

Chloe knew she should leave. But she was drunk. She had no idea where this place was or where she should go or how she could get there. And she still didn't have the least idea where Tip was or what had happened to her. She had to leave, yet she couldn't. Where were the others from the 4H Club?

The singers—those who remained—had gone back to singing with their clothes on. And the music had dropped to relatively humane volumes. But now Chloe felt exposed. The cocoon of sound had been breached and grim reality gibbered just beyond. She didn't want to have to talk, to understand what was being said. She had liked it better when she could hide in her little sound-around shell.

The next singer wore dark red lipstick, a vivid slash across her pale face, and the cascade of ruffles stopped halfway down her thighs to reveal lovely legs and fine-boned ankles.

"This *guh*," Terdsak said. "She is beautiful. In Thai way, she is beautiful. Come. Whiskey. Is *good*. You drink, *na*? You see skin? How white? *Suay*. Beautiful." He put a companionable hand on Chloe's thigh, just above the knee and just short of where her dress ended. "Beautiful skin, you have *douay*. But foreigner *guh*, why they sleep in sun? Black skin no good."

Chloe tried gently disengaging her leg from Terdsak's grasp, but his grip tightened. With a desultory attempt at making it seem an accident, she knocked her glass over and the whiskey and Coke ran off the table to soak Terdsak's hand and her leg. And his shoe, where his foot had cosied up to hers.

Chloe was impressed, as Terdsak slid out from behind the table, at how E-go took command of the situation. Although she didn't understand how he did this. Effortlessly and without benefit of spoken language, he deployed the two spare men to guard the flanks, just in case this was all part of a larger plot. In an instant, Ten were at Terdsak's booth, with Zero stationed behind Chloe, close enough she could smell his odor, and One beside her, blocking her exit. A tuxedoed flower goon appeared, solicitous, and knelt with a towel to wipe off Terdsak's trousers and his shoe. Another waiter handed a second towel to Terdsak.

"Excuse me, I'm not used to whiskey. I'm sorry." Chloe pushed One gently aside, and stood up. She could hear herself in her Canadian mode, the apologetic incantation warding off any uncivil proceedings. "Sorry, eh? I'll just go to the washroom and get cleaned up."

Terdsak signaled to Zero, and suddenly Chloe felt very strong hands at her shoulders, holding her there. Terdsak sat down and reached with the towel to mop at her legs. "Have beautiful skin. Must take care." He mopped higher, first the front of her thighs and then the insides. She could feel the Rolex scraping as she squeezed her legs together to deny access. He looked into her eyes, hard, and then withdrew the towel to dab at the front of her dress, moving it gently across her belly. "What matter? Not like me? *Na*? Maybe not like *man*."

Terdsak indicated to his man that Chloe should sit down again, and he sat her down again. Without even being told, Chloe took a big hit of whiskey and Coke.

The swirl of security and support staff quickly died down. E-go returned to his table to comb his quiff and re-establish relations with his singer. The other bodyguards looked back at Terdsak and Chloe, from time to time, still nervous. People at neighboring tables were studiously looking anywhere but towards them. Chloe focused on the singer, desperately trying to shut out everything else while she tried to decide what to do.

"Like *pooying khon farang. Chawp maak.*" Terdsak said this with a shake of his head, as though admitting to something very kinky indeed. "Like strange *guh* too mutt." With this pronouncement, he got up and came around to Chloe's side of the booth again, indicating that she should push over.

"I have to go to the washroom. You can sit on the inside. Okay? Let me out for a minute."

"Not sit with me. Why? Not like me? Or not like man. Maybe not like *Thai* man, *na*?"

Heaven forbid that she should appear illiberal or in any way politically incorrect.

"Pants wet too mutt. You make wet." He took Chloe's hand. "Feel." He was dry, where he put her hand. She tried to pull away, but he put his other hand around her shoulders and held her there.

Chloe was frightened and embarrassed at the same time. Here she sat, grappling with this middle-aged man as though they were teenagers in the back row of a movie theater. But this was a public place, and things were more serious than that.

E-go was standing by their booth again, and Terdsak was giving him instructions. Chloe had got her hand back and she was wondering how she could get out of there. She was starting to feel panicky. It was claustrophobia, in part, trapped there as she was against the mirrored wall, trapped in a bar full of foreign people in a land that was becoming more foreign by the minute. She watched E-go communicate something to a waiter and then go over to consult with his henchmen. Terdsak was trying to get his hand up Chloe's skirt again and, just as she was thinking of screaming, the music swelled to its earlier volume and perhaps even louder. E-go, Ten and the two spare security men, meanwhile, had all come over to stand in front of the booth, backs to Chloe and Terdsak, a wall of gunmen watching the stage when the real action was behind them.

Chloe struggled; but what was the point? She was so amazed at what was happening she could scarcely credit it. She felt removed from proceedings, willing to accept almost anything, just for now. A little holiday from reality. She hoped he wouldn't really hurt her. Surely he wouldn't. Not in public. Then she remembered the man Olga had told her about. Chloe just wanted it all to be over quickly; she even found herself accommodating him, only to have done with it.

The seat really wasn't wide enough, and his experiments with hooking one of her legs up on the table were not a signal success. There were real problems getting her panties off, and both Terdsak and Chloe were covered with whiskey and Coke before that much was even half accomplished. The cascade of ice across Terdsak's back, when the ice bucket got knocked over, did nothing to slow him down. But where it spilled off onto Chloe, it helped to bring her out of her hallucinatory fugue. Terdsak was yelling something in her ear in Thai, she hadn't the faintest idea what. Then he switched to English.

"Give my *special* gold," he told her, panting with the effort. He had his trousers open, and was trying to push up between her legs. Chloe inspected the craters on his cheek, ghastly in the flashing lights reflected from the mirrored wall, and she noted the two long black hairs growing from a mole just under his ear. His dickhead weighed heavy, strangely knobbled, as it slid along her thigh. A miniature version of Terdsak's asteroid head. His panting reeked of rotten tooth.

The last time she could remember puking—they'd called it "barfing," back in those days—was about twelve years before. It was at a frat party in Montreal, and oddly enough, it had saved her from a similarly unpleasant fate then.

"*Ee* hee-*yah*!" said Terdsak. "Ahgg!" In his haste to get clear of the eruption, he kneed her painfully in the leg. The empty ice bucket rolled from the table to bonk off Chloe's head before hitting the floor.

She managed to turn her head and direct most of the vomit under the table. She puked till she was gasping and streaming tears. Finally she sat up. Sticky with Coke from head to foot, she pulled her panties up and rearranged her dress. She still had her amulet, not that it was doing her much good as far as she could see.

The screen of bodyguards was breaking up; no wonder he needed five of them. Two of the waiters were organizing towels and water and fresh whiskey-Cokes, dabbing at Terdsak, who shoved them away, and mopping up the table, generally fussing and carrying on as though things were pretty standard; it was a pity about the spilled drinks. E-go handed Chloe a wad of tissue paper, eyes averted, and indicated she should wipe herself off. At no point during the entire episode had she felt so threatened with a total loss of contact with reality.

"Beautiful *pooying*. You." Terdsak was all tucked away and zipped up, and, never mind he was also both sexually unrequited and soaking wet, he seemed pleased with himself. He rinsed the whiskey-Coke from his Rolex in meltwater from the new ice bucket the waiters had already provided, and stood there polishing the crystal face. "Big," he added. "But also beautiful. Beautiful hair. Body, *na*? *Farang guh* not respect men. In my country, must show respect. Understand? Different place, different custom. But my country. Must respect my custom."

A strobe was complicating the light show on the stage at the same time it complicated Chloe's thought processes. She was discovering new powers, doors of perception opened no doubt by a combination of meditation, fasting, whiskey, and adrenaline. She could suddenly see that the singer, for example, was only a mass of atoms, trillions of them, the spaces between each of them vaster than the distances between stars, even between galaxies. In relative terms, she was mostly space, and it was only a fluke of human consciousness that Chloe could differentiate the girl from the air around her, or from the floor or the electric organ. Her earrings and her person were as one. Local eddies, compactions of the same space-time that was Chloe's drink, her table. Chloe herself. Everyone—the singer, Chloe, Terdsak, Waylon, the missing boyfriend from the song—everybody was one with the singer's earrings and therefore one with each other. Everything was connected, all part of a single thought, and the universe found its focus in those earrings. There was no cause without its universal effects. So how did the flash of those earrings as the singer tossed her head stack up against a supernova, or the collision of a couple of galaxies? Or the public humiliation of someone entirely out of her depth, on the verge of panic?

Terdsak poked the gold toothpick up one nostril and probed till he induced an impressive explosion, and then another one. E-go said what might have been Gesundheit, although maybe it was Russian for something else. Chloe wanted to scream. She wanted to kill Terdsak. What she did is she began to cry, and hated herself for it. Then she excused herself to go to the ladies' room and puke some more.

Terdsak signaled a spare bodyguard to go with her and take up his station outside the toilet.

Chloe tore her dress crawling out through the bathroom window. She made her way down the alley and into the parking lot, where the Mercedes-Benzes and BMWs and Jaguars and Toyota Crowns were stacked three deep. A gang of five or six drivers were standing around smoking. They gave her the eye, and one of them said something to her in Thai. "You! Where you go?" asked another. Then Terdsak appeared, E-go and Ten on his flanks.

Then she started puking again. Amazing, she thought. After all she'd heaved up earlier, this had to be some kind of spontaneous generation of matter. At that point she heard Prue calling her name. And then Prue, Bibi, the Rev, Al Dente, and even Ruthie appeared in a swarm, telling her how they had gone to three different clubs looking for her, and how worried they'd been, and how they had a taxi and she should come with them right now. The doctor had said that her illness was very contagious, at this point, and she should really be quarantined.

Terdsak didn't really understand any of the last part, which had been Prue extemporizing, but he was clearly not in the mood to lolligag with a bunch of New Age whackos, beyond which his dinner companion was a stinking mess, so he told his men to start the car and take him away.

"Let's get back," Chloe told the others, waving away their questions for the time being. "I need a shower. I really need a shower."

Chloe was surprised at how keenly she wanted to see Waylon right then.

36 behind the mask

It is, it is a glorious thing
To be a Pirate King.

W. S. Gilbert, *The Pirates of Penzance*

Trapped. One hundred feet beneath the surface. It was pitch black. No light. Waylon was pinned inside the wreck and panic began to seethe like ants in his brain. The space was so small he could barely move. He had to find the exit before the ants swarmed out in all directions, carrying bits of his mind with them.

He groped in the dark. *Feeling.* . . . He squirmed around to bump something—a large, softly buoyant mass. And then he could see. By the greenish glow from the bioluminescent bacteria he saw the gruesomely swollen features of the person they fed upon. The floater bobbed against him, pinning Waylon to a bulkhead. A sudden shrill whistling ruptured into billions of noxious bubbles that tickled and pressed against his face and his chest. The pressure blew open the compartment that held him, releasing Waylon into sunlit waters even as he awoke.

"Tea's ready, Waylon." Jessica was dressed and the curtains were open to the morning. "We're going to be late."

Waylon hadn't shaved in two weeks, and was sporting something that resembled a beard. It itched like crazy, but he wasn't ready to shave it off. He kind of liked it. It suited the new Waylon that he was afraid of getting used to. Wail-On, you could call him. Wail-On. And here Jessica tells him that she's going on a dive cruise and he says sure thing. Was he nuts? She had just happened to catch Waylon riding this wave of euphoria, and he'd agreed to the dive cruise despite his reservations. Just think, she told him: this was going to be the first time they supervised their own dives. Wasn't that exciting? Waylon found the whole prospect chilling, and was trying not to think about it too much. Originally, of course, he had expected Leary, Oscar, and Eddie would be coming as well. Leary had originally offered to set up the boat, and suggested he go along himself, just to keep on eye on things. As it turned out, however, he had to head back to the States to look after some formalities regarding the sale of a house. "Anyway, don't worry, my boy. You got Jessie to look after you. Ha, ha. Only kidding, darn it."

It was funny. Oscar and Eddie had also said they'd help. But just the other night they'd been badly beaten up by a gang of Thai toughs. Oscar blamed a rival dive shop. But that was ridiculous. Jessica's theory was that Nok's brothers had come down from upcountry to check on their little sister, and Eddie merely got in the way. Anyway, they wouldn't be going on any dive cruises for a while.

Jessica had had trouble finding a boat. "Can't you just get us the same boat we used on our wreck dive course, Leary?" she'd asked before he left.

"'Fraid not, Jessie. That boat was stripped right down, the other night. Whoever did it even took the engine. Then they scuttled it. Funny thing, the only other boat I would've thought to take blew up yesterday. Don't know what happened."

Jessica had gone farther afield in the search for a boat, but everybody seemed to have problems.

"No can do."
"Sorry. Engine needs work."
"Cannot. Fully booked."
"No."

Finally, someone had come to her with a boat called *Sumalee*. Waylon had been nervous. He had wanted to check things out with Leary; but Leary had already left.

"Let's just *go*," said Jessica. Too many people were getting curious already. They had to get moving. "It's no big deal, Waylon. It's easy." And she told him that they were going to find a sunken yacht and then dive on it. "But we can't tell the crew exactly what we're doing, Waylon."

"Why not?"

"We're going after something that's *mine*. And people want to take it away from me."

"Welcome." The skipper, an old guy, was apparently deaf. Cigarette hanging from the corner of his mouth, he'd greeted them as they came aboard. And that was the last English they heard from him. After the initial effusion of good will, he refused to acknowledge their presence other than to ogle Jessica, in a low-key way, whenever he had the chance.

The shorter of the two deckhands wore greasy old running shoes slip-on style, the heels trodden down flat. Mirrored aviator sunglasses back high on his head, he had a flat, distant look that never entirely focused except when he talked to somebody or when he stared at Jessica in her swimsuit. Then he would pull the glasses down and slide them on slow with both hands, fixing the object of his attention with twin reflections of itself. His T-shirt read SNATCHATACK. An ugly scar crept out of his collar, up his neck and on to his jaw, while a blue tattooed snake crawled out of one armhole and down the inside of his arm to his wrist, its head obscured by the loose-fitting expansion bracelet of a cheap watch. His flat-top haircut was shaved close on the sides and his right ear was pierced to accommodate two silver earrings. The fingernail on one pinkie was an inch and a half long, and he inserted it in his ear deep enough for brain surgery, rotated it, and then examined whatever it was he extracted. Sombat—or "Bat" for short, as Jessica had determined—said something to her in Thai.

"He says he likes my skin, Waylon." Jessica came as close to simpering at Bat as she was capable. In fact, she was doing everything she could to encourage the young swain, in various subtle and not-so-subtle ways. Waylon could have wished she were paying more attention to *him*. As it was, the other deckie—Somdit, or "Dit"—was paying him more attention than he would have liked. Dit wore rubber flip-flops, Lycra bicycle shorts with rally stripes, and a net tanktop.

"Look at that," said Jessica.

Going Bat at least one better, the taller and more muscular deckie sported four or five rings in each ear, one in each eyebrow and another through the septum of his nose. As you could see when he stuck out his tongue, which was every time he laughed, which was often, he also had a stud in his tongue. Visible through his tanktop were a big ring in each of his nipples and a smaller one in his bellybutton.

"It makes you think, doesn't it, Waylon?"

"What do you mean?"

"You see all these rings everywhere and you just have to wonder. Where else? I mean."

"Yeah, I guess so." Waylon wished Jessica wouldn't look at Dit's crotch that way. The stretchy pedal-pushers didn't leave a lot to the imagination, and if this guy had rings in his dick you could probably see them if you wanted to look closely enough, which Waylon didn't.

Meanwhile, Dit was looking at Waylon with the same general kind of interest Jessica was showing in Dit, and it made Waylon uncomfortable. Dit batted his eyes at Waylon. He didn't wear sunglasses; what was the point of mascara if you wore shades? "Hello, handsome man," he told Waylon, tittering and pulling his long black ponytail around in front and stroking it. His hair was held in place by a purple plastic comb. He had long fingernails on both pinkies and one thumb.

"Don't get so uptight, Waylon," Jessica told him. "Anyway, Dit might be dangerous." To Waylon, the last two suggestions were mutually incompatible. Jessica went on to tell him about how pickpockets, muggers, and sexual scam artists tended to be transvestites and transsexuals. On a barstrip like South Pattaya, the more exaggeratedly feminine and, at first glance at least, the more beautiful the bargirl seemed, the more careful you wanted to be. "They can have knockout bodies," Jessica said. "Great tits and asses."

Dit didn't have notably feminine tits. In fact, if you overlooked the ornamentation he reminded Waylon of the taller boxer at the Gorgon Bar. "But generally they still have an Adam's apple," continued Jessica, telling Waylon more than he needed to know. "That's one thing to watch for. And look out for the whiskey-voiced babes." One thing you didn't want to do, she added, was start trouble with one of them. Forget any Western preconceptions that gays were wimps. These guys could be deadly.

"How do you know so much about it, Jessie?"

"I keep my eyes open."

Maybe. But he'd heard her talking to Bat. Could be she was better at languages than she was at buddy breathing. Then again, maybe there were some things she wasn't telling him.

"Waylon. Do you know why they put studs in their tongues?"

"Jesus Christ, eh?"

Waylon and Jessica were presented with the stern cabin, which had two bunks, one roughly queen-sized, the other big enough to hold their bags. The vessel was a converted tourboat. What had been the seating for day passengers had been ripped out so most of the boat was now one enormous room. Jessica disappeared into their cabin and re-emerged a couple of minutes later dressed in bikini and a frilly haltertop.

Aside from Dit, Waylon was reassured by developments. This boat was twice as big as the last one and, at least to his uneducated eye, three times as seaworthy. The paint was in good shape and there were lounge chairs on the sundeck. But it was not a fragrant vessel. In fact, as Jessica was quick to point out, it smelled like bad cigars. It also smelled something like evil socks and quite a lot like rotten eggs. The big salon was permeated with all of these smells—even their cabin stank. "This fucking boat stinks," was how she summed it up.

Part of the bouquet, they discovered, was durian. "Is good. You eat." Dit handed Waylon a fist-sized pod of some sticky yellow mess. Waylon found he didn't mind the taste, which he could best appreciate if he held his nose while he ate. It was like a rich custard. Jessica wouldn't even try a piece. "That's durian, Waylon," she told him, as though no more needed to be said about the matter.

Then they discovered another element of the smell. There was another passenger, and he emerged from the forward cabin smoking a big stogie. It was the guy with the mustache from Hot Licks. My Bottle.

"Remember, Waylon? The guy I was imagining things about?" Jessica appeared even less happy than she had with the durian.

Not only that, as Waylon told Jessica, *Sumalee* reminded him of that other boat—the one behind the coastguard vessel that had been watching them on the wreck dive.

"Why didn't you say something before, Waylon?" The way Jessica looked landward, you got the feeling she might have been thinking it was time to turn back. But they were already almost out of sight of Samae San.

"I told you there was something that made me nervous about this boat," Waylon said, all the while smiling at My Bottle as he approached.

My Bottle merely sneered and, by way of welcoming them aboard, blew a stream of smoke straight at Jessica.

"What are you doing on this boat?" Jessica's voice was in no way welcoming.

"Go for ride," My Bottle replied. "Nice boat ride."

My Bottle seemed to spend most of his time in the salon smoking cigars and sipping whiskey. In some way, you could see he was the boss, since the crew deferred to him and his occasional commands. Bat and Dit did odd jobs around the boat, while the captain stayed in the wheelhouse, glued to the wheel and intent on the business of getting the boat to wherever it was going.

Sea conditions were fine, with just enough breeze to take some of the heat off the day. Waylon had brought his search and salvage course notes for review, and he stretched out in the sun to read them, cocooned in the engine noise and heat.

Jessica plugged herself into her Walkman and crashed out beside him in a deck chair. Waylon noticed her slipping something into her mouth.

"Jessie," said Waylon. "Didn't you take some pills before we left?"

"Those were for seasickness, Waylon." She didn't say what the current ones were for.

"Well, darn it, I guess they're working." Waylon caught a tinge of Leary in his voice. "All this environmental engineering. The sea's just about like glass."

"What, Waylon? What did you say?" Jessica had to lift an earphone to hear him, but he didn't repeat it. She just got on with engineering her environment, pouring oil on troubled waters, both internal and external. She had her bottle of vodka wrapped in a towel so it wouldn't get broken. She asked Waylon to apply some suntan lotion to her back and shoulders, and she took yet one more pharmaceutical. "Maxiphed, Waylon. I think I'm getting a cold, and I don't want a pressure block when we dive."

They didn't see that much boat traffic, mostly picturesque wooden fishing trawlers like the one on which they'd done their dive courses. About the middle of the afternoon, one vessel, much like all the others except even more weathered, approached from their bows, and the crew indicated they'd like to talk. In fact, they ran right across *Sumalee*'s bows and, when the captain veered away and slowed the engine, pulled alongside.

"Jessie," said Waylon. "They're wearing masks." And so they were. Woolen balaclava masks. If central casting ever needed pirates, these boys would do nicely.

"Relax, Waylon," Jessica replied, drawing upon her ever-more-surprising fund of local knowledge. "They're just fishermen. Thai fishermen. They don't like to get sun on their faces; it turns their skin black."

That was very reassuring. Waylon was further reassured by their smiles, when they took the masks off. What wasn't so reassuring were the assault rifles they produced. But he could see that Jessica was probably right—they weren't wearing the masks to hide themselves. They obviously didn't care about that, which was also not very reassuring. There were five of them. Three of them with rifles and two with machetes.

"I was wrong, Waylon."

Bat and Dit were on the forward deck with Waylon and Jessica, while My Bottle was on the stern. The captain stood at the door to the wheelhouse, hands on his head, cigarette stuck in the corner of his mouth. One of the rifles held the stern, while the other two covered the bow.

The still tableau held for a long moment. Here was Waylon, back in a grade school pageant and he'd forgotten his lines. What was he supposed to do next? But he was spared further embarrassment. One of the pirates, a stocky dark man with flashing teeth who appeared to be the leader, erupted into a brief spate of Thai, aimed mostly at the captain and the men on the bow. Bat translated: "He wants everything. Money, camera, watch. Everything. Give, he say." The pirate leader fired off more suggestions, and Bat said he wanted Jessica to give him her bathing suit. It was a nice bathing suit. And her bag. First the bag and then the bathing suit. She should take it off. The pirate leader smiled at Jessica in what was obviously his most winning manner.

Jessica delved into The Bag to come up with her Walkman. She held it up like a trophy and then placed it on the deck in front of her. She reached back in and pulled out the vodka, holding it up for all to see, and then unscrewed the cap to take a slug. The pirates laughed, most of them, appreciative of the bravura performance.

The pirate leader slung his rifle over his shoulder and jumped across and on to the deck. For a moment he wrinkled his nose in wonder. Then he stepped forward as Jessica reached into her bag again, this time coming up with a gun—a nice little chrome-plated automatic pistol with which she shot their visitor right in the head.

It wasn't a very big gun, and it didn't make a big noise. But it did a good job of leaving the pirate stone dead.

37 holes in the head

*Life is very singularly made to surprise us
(where it does not utterly appall us).*

Rainer Maria Rilke

The morning took on a surreal brilliance, sharp-edged and color-saturated. The hole in the jolly buccaneer's forehead, for example, was round and clean, black-red, blue around the edge. The spray from the exit wound had left a plume of blood on the front salon window even before the fellow had slumped to his knees. Some of the larger beads of blood began to run down the glass. Then Waylon saw it begin to run from the entry wound. Jessica had got him in the middle of the forehead—almost between the eyes, but not quite. Maybe that was why she was looking so irritated, thought Waylon. Her shooting just wasn't what it used to be.

Waylon burped, and was bemused at the odor of durian, like a stale fart.

"Waylon," she hissed. "Get his rifle! For Christ's sake."

"Oh," Waylon said. He snatched up the weapon as the ex-bad guy toppled to one side, yanking to get the shoulder strap disengaged from the dead man's arm. "Do you realize how *dangerous* it is to shoot a man in the head?" Waylon thought this, but didn't say it. Swelling unreality threatened to spin him out of control. But only for a moment. The blast of a shotgun—once, twice, three times—brought him to his senses. The captain, still standing in the door to the wheelhouse, was dispassionately blowing people to bits. Jessica was lying on the deck going root-de-toot with her gun, while more pistol fire reported from the stern. Then the shooting stopped, and Dit leapt on to the other vessel to finish the surviving machete man with a hatchet. A *hatchet*. Dit had gone berserk.

Waylon stood there with the rifle, wondering if the safety catch were on or off and thinking he should be doing something. He pointed it away from everybody so he wouldn't hurt anyone, and pulled the trigger in a tentative sort of way. He felt the rifle lift as it squandered a burst out to sea. The safety hadn't been on. Anyway, there were no pirates left to shoot, which was okay with him.

"Jesus Christ, Jessie," Waylon said. "Are you crazy?"

Bat and Dit scuttled the other boat and then asked Waylon and Jessica what they would like for dinner. Dit was pissed off because he'd broken a fingernail. And Jessica was reacting with some heat to another suggestion from Waylon that she tended towards recklessness.

"I'm not stupid, okay, Waylon? I knew there was a shotgun in the wheelhouse, and I could see the captain was staying good and close to it. Give me a break. And I'd seen My Bottle with a forty-five automatic this morning."

Waylon was amazed, once more, to discover how well informed Jessica was for a simple traveling girl. And, for a claustrophobic drug addict, how unflappable. She hadn't even spilled her vodka in the course of their nice little massacre.

"We have to go back to Pattaya and report this."

"Waylon! Don't be stupid." Now Jessica was pissed off.

"*Mai pen rai*," Bat told him, smiling at Jessica reassuringly. "These are bad guys. No problem. Forget about it."

"Just don't worry about it, Waylon. They know what they're doing, okay?"

"We radio," Dit agreed. "*Mai pen rai*. Radio my *f'en*. In marine police. No problem; they take care."

But nobody seemed in a hurry to make the call. Everyone was very reassuring and eager that nothing should interfere with this nice dive cruise.

"I guess those guys picked the wrong boat," Waylon said to Jessica, expressing only part of his real feelings about the matter.

"They're not the only ones, Waylon." Jessica was starting to suspect something was wrong, she said. Seriously amiss. For one thing, she'd been surprised from the outset that a scow like this would have such sophisticated electronics, including side-scan sonar. And she didn't like the smooth way in which the crew had responded to the pirates. In fact, she had appreciated it—indeed counted on them to follow her lead—but it suggested they weren't the innocent punters they made out they were. Not only that, of course. My Bottle had worried her from the first time she'd set eyes on him, and it was no coincidence he was on this boat.

Later, Waylon noticed that Dit now had a pair of mirrored sunglasses just like Bat's, although he wasn't wearing them, only keeping them hooked on the neck of his T-shirt. And Bat was limping around breaking in a newish pair of tennis shoes, walking the heels down till they were comfortable. My Bottle, more animated than he'd been the whole trip so far, was on the stern deck stripping an AK-47. He told Dit to issue cold beers to everyone, assuring Waylon and Jessica that these were on the house. "On the boat, yeah?" He laughed too loud and too long at his own joke, which none of the Thais had understood. But everyone was in a fine mood and they laughed anyway. Even Waylon, who heard a hint of hysteria in his own effort. My Bottle went back to sneering, but it was a happy sneer.

Stacked up on deck against the aft wall of the stern cabin were a number of items that looked as though they might have come from Mars. "What the hell are these?" Waylon pointed at a heap of what looked like misshapen green rugby balls bristling with vicious spikes. "Durians," replied Jessica in tones suggesting she'd swap them even-steven for a stack of long-dead rats. The boat was loaded with the things, as it turned out.

That afternoon they discovered yet another element of *Sumalee*'s scent. Sun-dried and deep-fried *pla ling maa*, dog's-tongue fish, were about two inches long and made fine salty beer snacks, or whiskey snacks if you preferred, which My Bottle did. The process of deep frying them produced a smell akin to what you'd get if you stewed the socks of an infantry platoon just off maneuvers. My Bottle appeared addicted to them, while Dit seemed immune to the stench of their preparation. A partnership made in heaven. So My Bottle lit up a big cigar, Dit deep-fried a bunch of dried dogs'-tongue fish to go with the drinks, Bat opened a durian, and Jessica went to the stern to puke. Waylon only felt like it.

Overall, however, he was doing okay. He had been so preoccupied that his lip had never had a chance to start quivering. He stretched out in a deck chair and found himself reviewing recent events. "Better than sex," some girl named Beth from Pasadena had written in Leary's bungee-jump guestbook. Waylon preferred sex, on the whole. There was a moment or two of mad exhilaration once he left the platform, arms spread wide with total abandon to embrace the earth as it rushed to meet him. But when he hit the end of the cord there was no shock, no sense of imminent death, just a long lagging letdown as more than two thousand interwoven elastic bands stretched to absorb the force of his plunge, delicately lowering him, finally, to dip head and upper body in the pond. Dripping, then, he was tugged skyward—up and up till he thought he was going to land back on the jump platform. He was twisting and turning as he soared, but at one point he caught sight of Jessica and Oscar and Eddie. "Is this all there is?" He waved and yelled in their general direction. Then it was merely a series of ever-diminishing rebounds, oscillating away at the end of the cord and feeling silly. "It's like every cell in your body *knows* you're going to die," Oscar had told him. "And then you don't. Man, what a rush."

But Waylon hadn't felt as though he were going to die at all. He'd only felt ridiculous, for the most part. He chewed on his lip, thinking it over. It worried him.

But what really worried him, when he thought about it, was that he was on this dive cruise with a gang of killers—even his dive buddy was a killer—and he wasn't nearly as worried as he should have been. He caught a nap in the sun, and his hangover was a distant memory when he awoke. They ran all day at top speed in a smooth sea, and it was almost dark by the time they dropped the hook on the wreck.

Jessica had a GPS, a hand-held global positioning system, in her bag. Of course she did, thought Waylon. And probably a radar. Maybe even a pool table. Nothing he learned about Jessica or her bag could ever surprise him again. A GPS essentially triangulated off a number of satellites, always in contact with at least four at a time, and could place you on the surface of the earth within a hundred yards or less. Even with a hand-held model. But Jessica hadn't told their friends about this bit of equipment. They took her pistol from her, but, not knowing her as well as Waylon did, they didn't search her bag.

As Jessica explained to Waylon, she didn't want to salvage the stuff until after dark. So she wanted to make sure they arrived on the wreck too late to dive in daylight, but with just enough light, ideally, that they could do a reconnaissance. To this end, she gave the skipper coordinates that took them to a place about a quarter of a mile from where they really wanted to be. Then she had them hunt around with their sonar. Eventually, she steered them right in on it. The wreck they were looking for lay in about eighty feet of water eight hundred yards from a little island distinguished by nothing more than some scrub forest and a few rocky outcrops. A cove just around the headland made an excellent overnight anchorage in this season, Jessica said. Nobody thought to ask her how she knew that.

"It's too late to dive today," she told My Bottle. "It would be dark by the time we got on to the wreck. What we have to do is put a buoy on it now and come back to dive tomorrow. Waylon. You can do a quick dive before dark and tie the buoy on. I'll come with you."

"Why you dive on this boat?" asked My Bottle with a chummy sneer, as if to say they were all friends, after all, and they might as well come clean. "No good. Maybe dangerous. For girl, no good." He looked suddenly thoughtful. "Maybe find treasure, yes?"

"No, no," said Waylon. "We dive on it for fun." But that proposition sounded dubious even to him. The guy was probably thinking you had to have holes in your head.

They buoyed the wreck that afternoon. At the last minute, Jessica decided not to go down. The current was too strong. Anyway, what was Waylon worried about? All he had to do was go straight down the anchor line and secure the line to the buoy. They would be right there above him.

Dit helped Waylon into his gear, hands everywhere, twittering about beautiful skin and beautiful hair and making Waylon's flesh crawl. Waylon told himself to relax, but he was a Canadian and Canadians were inhibited, goddamn it. When Dit grabbed his arms to help him to his feet, he realized Dit had hands like bear traps.

Glad to be off the boat, Waylon hauled himself hand-over-hand down the line, staring into the current, taking care it didn't rip his mask off. The bottom of the boat, rough with barnacles, was facing him. The line led him down to where the anchor had hooked a rail amidships on what had been the lower deck. But now, with the boat lying on its side, it was the highest point on the wreck. Getting a firm hold on the rail, he pulled himself head-first over and down into the lee of the current. He tied the line to the buoy on to the railing, and then, squeezing off the rest of the air in his flotation jacket, he drifted to the bottom. Particles of sediment and plankton spun by; a couple of Moorish idols zagged through the beam of his torch. Debris lay strewn across the sand. Two davits protruded like giant insect legs from what had been the top deck; there was no sign of the tender they'd been used to launch. Aside from that, there wasn't much besides some whip corals and a few fish. The vessel, a motor yacht of some eighty or a hundred feet, probably steel hulled, had slid off a low ridge and come to rest on her side, bow higher than her stern, against a big outcrop covered with coral and algae.

Waylon swam to the stern to find twin propellers and a name. *Dark Moon.* Jessica hadn't even told him that much. Written beneath the name was the word "Panama." The current was running so strong, by the time Waylon made it back up the line, that the buoy had been sucked under the surface. He surfaced with a blinding sinus headache—a pressure block, the penalty for forcing his ears to clear on the way down, something Oscar and Eddie had warned him about.

They anchored in the cove for the night. And as soon as she could get Waylon alone, Jessica pumped him for details of what he'd seen, indifferent to his pain. She couldn't wait. Among other things, she wanted to know which way the wreck was lying and whether the stern doors were clear.

"Did you see anything unusual?" she asked him, finally.

"Jesus Christ, Jessie. Yes. It was *all* unusual. What do you think? I go diving on sunken yachts every day?"

Later, when they went back to the stern deck, they found Dit sitting in the dinghy, which they'd been towing since the afternoon dive.

"Jig, jig, *na*?" he tittered. "*Pla meuk*, they see light and think, 'Big party. Good.' So they come, and now they see bee-*oo*-tee-fool little fish, so pretty."

Dit had taped a dive torch to the ladder on the stern, and was casting and retrieving a squid jig on a hand line through the pool of light, its fleet quicksilver wobble designed to incite your average squid to recklessness. Coy as trout, several squid were hanging back in a gang to consider matters. Then one tentacled torpedo shot into the circle of light to grab at the bait.

"See? Jig, jig. There. Oh!"

Once . . . twice, it was almost hooked. All caution forgotten, then, it came in for a fatal third try, impaling itself on a double row of pins. A number of its pals soon followed, once they saw how easy it was.

The Thai-style squid salad was great, if a little spicy. In fact it was hot enough to give Waylon hiccups, and Dit found this enormously funny.

The captain joined them at the table, but didn't eat. Nor did he talk. He only drank Mekhong and water and smoked cigarettes. Neither did Jessica eat anything, beyond two spoonfuls of rice and the chicken out of Waylon's curry. She washed the sauce off the chicken pieces in her water glass before eating them. "You can't trust this water, Waylon," she told him. She slung the water from his own glass out through the door and on to the deck, then poured herself three fingers of vodka and downed it. She also appropriated half of his grilled prawns. She ripped the shells from them, one by one, swishing the meat around in her water glass before eating it. Staring provocatively at the smokers all the while, she deposited each of the carapaces in the ashtray. Bat's response was to drop the butt of his cigarette into her glass of water. Dit flicked ashes on the floor. My Bottle just sat and sneered and sipped whiskey from his own bottle of Black Label. My Bottle smoked cigars constantly when he was drinking. Bat and Dit both smoked cigarettes; Bat kept a pack tucked up in the sleeve of his T-shirt. And Jessie made exasperated noises louder than Waylon would have liked. "Do you *have* to smoke those fucking things in here?" she asked, at one point.

My Bottle, the captain, Bat, and Dit looked set to drink away the night, entertaining themselves with singing and arguing. Waylon and Jessica retired to the stern deck to discuss matters.

"Waylon."

"Yes, Jessie?"

"We go after it tonight."

"Jessie?"

"Yes, Waylon?"

"Piss off." It felt good to say. But it didn't work.

"We're going to wait till after midnight. The tide will change in a few hours, and by that time My Bottle and his pals will be obliterated." Jessica had added a little something from her pharmaceutical stash to their drinks. "Sometimes I have trouble sleeping," she told him, when he asked what she was doing with a lavish supply of Rohypnol.

Waylon discerned in himself a peculiar sense of inevitability. Life had become a series of exercises in madness, and some force beyond himself kept insisting he submit. He was going to go night-diving for contraband, he didn't even know what. With a lunatic for a buddy. And he was going to do this right under the eyes of a gang of dubious characters who would probably take the goods off them at gunpoint. He felt that his lip should be twitching, but it wasn't. His leg was jumping a bit. But that could have been mere excitement.

"That's frig-all," he told himself. "*That's* frig-all." It still didn't sound quite right. The phrase didn't have the careless confidence that Leary put into it. "*That's frig-all*," he said again. This time it sounded a shade hysterical.

Leary had told Waylon about a report claiming a large proportion of men known to have died while having sex were having sex, at the time, with someone other than their wives. "So tell me, Fosdick. Is this an argument for or against adultery?" Live life to the hilt, or set your course by the actuarial stars?

Waylon figured he was so far out on this existential black ice he was fucked no matter much which way he went.

"Waylon," Jessica told him in her most reasonable voice. "I think I can make it. But, if I can't, you're going to have to do it alone."

38 dark moon

*A hero is no braver than an ordinary man,
but he is brave five minutes longer.*

Ralph Waldo Emerson

Just after midnight, moving as quietly as they could, they loaded their gear into the dinghy and went back out to find the buoy. An unseasonable overcast covered much of the sky. A gibbous moon cast its sheen on the water through occasional holes in the cloud cover.

Everybody had gotten drunk except Waylon, Jessica, and Bat, who had drawn the midnight-to-morning watch. But Jessica had spent some time with him, managing to slip him a mickey finn in the course of events. Waylon was rowing, although they could have probably run the outboard if they'd wanted to. They were at least a hundred yards off the boat, downwind and just out of range of its smell, not to mention the amazing chorus of snores. Other than the faintest thump-thumping of the generator aboard *Sumalee*, the night was still. They proceeded across the glassy swell with little more than the slap of water against the inflatable hull of the dinghy, the dip of Waylon's oars, an occasional comment from some nightbird on the island, and Jessica's quick breathing. As they left the shelter of the cove, a slight chop began to rock the dinghy and, Waylon feared, the current was dragging them off their bearing.

"Start the engine, Waylon."

"It's too soon."

"They're not going to wake up till sometime tomorrow, Waylon. I put enough in their drinks to drop a rhino."

"You could kill them with that stuff, Jessica. After all they had to drink. Jesus Christ, eh?"

"Why are you whispering, Waylon?" whispered Jessica.

Waylon didn't answer. He was trying to see the buoy. The island itself was only a blackness against the stars, low to the water and fast becoming indiscernible, except when the moon peeked out from among the scudding clouds.

"More to the right. No, no. *My* right. Waylon," she said, impatient. They had to shoot a line on the headland and the peak of the highest hill on the island, she'd told him. The buoy should be in a straight line with them. After all, search and recovery and navigation had been her favorite subject. Then they started getting sightings of the buoy where it bobbed in the occasional bit of moonlight. Jessica had been right about the tide—the current had died, and now the white plastic bottle rode on surface.

They tied up to the buoy and prepared to dive. Jessica moved with a kind of anxious languor as they wrestled with weightbelts and tanks, fumbled around with fins. The clumsy intimacy of a dinghy required choreography at the best of times.

"You're on my flipper, Jessie. I can't move."

"Well, why don't you stay on your own side, then? How am I supposed to know where your feet are? I can't see anything." She half stood to move away and swung her tank right into him.

"Ow. For Christ's sake, Jessie."

"Now, Waylon. You just follow me. Once we're on the wreck, I mean." She still refused to tell him either what it was they were looking for or where, exactly, they would find it.

"Jessie," he asked again. "What are we looking for?"

"Only on a need-to-know basis, Waylon. You've come this far. Just *trust* me. Okay?"

"Okay," he replied, in much the same way, when he'd left the bungee tower, he had surrendered himself to the Void. But this was far scarier.

"You go first, Waylon."

He rocked gently on the edge of the inflatable, the weight of his tank hooked over the side behind him. Clasping one hand to his mask, regulator mouthpiece in the other, he consigned himself to the depths, performing a back roll, a fine vertiginous topple backwards into the sea. There was no shock as he hit the water—the air and water temperatures were almost the same. But he briefly lost track, in the dark, of which way was up. He switched on his torch as, buoyed by his jacket, he bobbed back to surface. The line was right ahead of him.

Left hand held high to expel air from his jacket, Waylon slipped beneath the surface. It was the same on every night dive—he didn't have enough hands. He had to keep hold of the anchor line, squeeze the expel button on his flotation jacket, and pinch his nose to equalize the pressure in his ears. All at the same time. This was something he'd never got quite right in the advanced course. It was all the more awkward for having a torch dangling from his wrist. Taking it in his left hand, finally, he shone it towards the bottom. Nothing but bits of drifting silt and plankton. No sharks. Statistically, divers stood a better chance of getting bitten by a dog or struck by lightning. So Leary said, and Waylon believed him. Although the statistical sample weren't necessarily diving on wrecks at night. Somehow the cocoon of light didn't seem so cozy without Leary or Oscar at hand.

Dark Moon began to loom beneath them. Waylon's ears were refusing to clear, and he stopped to squeeze the nosepiece of his mask and blow, waggling his jaws and rotating his head. Jessica, impatient, pushed at him a couple of times, and then went past him down the line.

About the time Waylon's ears cleared, something big bumped him.

No shark, it was Jessica clawing past on her way to surface. In the wild spin of his torch and hers he caught sight of Jessica's face. Her eyes goggled, unseeing, behind her mask; storms of bubbles blasted from her regulator. She was hyperventilating. Waylon grabbed her jacket with one hand, the line in the crook of his elbow. He held his torch steady while jabbing a forefinger at his mask, willing her to look at his eyes. *Settle down.* He let go of her jacket for a moment to thump her hard on the shoulder, losing his grip on the line at the same time. Finally he held her gaze, making gentling motions with one hand, the other firmly attached to her jacket. They were still ascending too fast, dive computers beeping an out-of-synch warning duet.

They broke surface to a sea brilliant with moonlight. They were about twenty yards off the dinghy and had to swim back against a light current. They were lucky, Waylon suggested once they'd clambered aboard, that the moon was out and that the current wasn't stronger.

Jessica had seen a huge moray eel, she said; it had been swimming free beneath them. So what? Waylon said. They had learned that morays weren't going to hurt you unless you drove them to it, and, anyway, he thought it was worms that scared her, not snakes or long fish.

"You hurt me, Waylon. Here. Hold my torch." She was still breathing hard, not listening to him, entirely self-absorbed.

He shielded the light with his body, holding it close on Jessica as she extracted a package from the pocket on her jacket and proceeded to pull plastic bag from within plastic bag. "Oh, *fuck.*" Demonic in the light from the torch, her face registered a confusion of rage and panic. "Oh, no. Look at this. Oh, no; oh, no; oh, no." She had wrapped her stash of Valium in three layers of protection, but seawater had still got in and the inner bag was filled with a murky liquid. When she held it up to Waylon's light, he could see some of the pills still dissolving. "Oh, fuck," she said. "Fuck, fuck, fuck." Then she hoisted the bag in the palm of one hand, held the neck together in the other hand and, making a face, took a swig.

"You'll have to go it alone," she told him. She was hugging herself, rocking back and forth down deep in the dinghy. She took another hit from her bag. "I'll tell you what to do." And she described what he was looking for and gave him detailed directions on how to find the stuff. She also passed him a twelve-inch crescent wrench. "You'll need this," she said.

This time the descent went smoothly. He settled on the bottom and adjusted his buoyancy till he was gently bobbing on the tips of his fins, breathing deeply and slowly, in and out, taking care to expel all the air before taking the next breath in. Don't gulp; don't be greedy. Hanging there in the water, he let his muscles go loose and his mind followed.

Breathe in. Breathe out.

Slower.

Breathe in. . . . Breathe out. . . .

He allowed himself a minute to calm down—a little bottom time in a good cause. He would save on air in the longer run. He checked his gauges: time 1:33 A.M.; air 2,050 psi; depth eighty-two feet. He had already breathed up some of his air. He had a maximum of thirty minutes to get in, find the stuff, get out again, find the buoy line, and then return to surface. He needed at least ten minutes for the ascent—with all the diving he'd done already, he had to plan for a safety decompression stop. He did not want the bends.

He checked his gear. His dive knife—razor-sharp, a saw edge on the top of the blade, the point, upon Leary's advice, ground down to a chisel—was strapped to the inside of his left ankle. He had the wrench secured with a Velcro strap to his jacket. In one jacket pocket he carried a spool of thick twine and a waterproof chemical lightstick. In the other, he had a nylon net catchbag and an underwater penlight torch for emergencies. An orange plastic lift bag was tied to his jacket. He switched off his main torch, and brought out the mini-light to test it. Then he killed that one as well and, just for a few seconds, he let the night take him. Vague features gradually emerged from the void. Ghostly bits of bioluminescence crawled on the deck—crabs, perhaps. Waylon let one arm drift in the current and watched the trail of sparkle when he pulled it back.

With hallucinogenic clarity, he heard Eddie's voice: "The second rule of safe diving is this: *Never* dive alone." Especially at night, Waylon had to think. Even more especially at night on a wreck you've never dived on before. He was breaking all the rules he'd only so recently learned. Again, Waylon told himself that he was crazy even to consider doing this. There were just too many things that could go wrong. He had only made his first dive a month ago. Less. This was a classic case of Leary's Law: "'A confident diver is a good diver. An overconfident diver is a dead diver.' Trouble is, about the time somebody gets to the point he's what you might call an almost competent diver, this goes to his head and he reckons he can break all the gosh-darned rules."

Waylon told himself he'd go step by step, keeping a close eye on air and time. He could abort the operation any time he wanted.

Oscar had appealed to another rule, this one a universal law: "Anything that can go wrong will go wrong." Waylon congratulated himself on having the spare torch in his vest pocket.

His main torch was giving him about twenty feet of visibility, and he could make out the wheelhouse to the left, so he went right, swimming along a couple of feet from bottom. Jessica had told him to go in through the doors to the salon from the galley. He swam around the tender to the stern. There were the glass double doors to the salon, just as she'd described them, except now the whole boat was on her side, so the doors lay horizontal, one above the other. "Go to the aft cabin, Waylon," she'd said. "There's just one big cabin in the stern. Go down the stairwell on the port side. You can't miss it." Waylon smashed the glass in the uppermost door with the crescent wrench, and reached in to undo the catch on the lower one. He fumbled briefly before discovering he had to crank a lever up and over to the right. The door opened when he yanked, and he pulled it down and out of his way. There was still something blocking the entrance. A sofa. It appeared to be in pretty good condition. He reached in through the broken door and shoved. It shifted a foot or two. Something heavy slipped and thudded, and then the sofa gave some more.

The general rule in wreck diving was one third of your air going in, one third coming out, and one third in reserve. Do not cheat on your reserve, Leary had told him. Some corollary to Murphy's Law said that that was exactly when something was going to go wrong. All kinds of things could hang you up inside a shipwreck. Waylon estimated he had twenty-seven minutes of air left. About seven more minutes to find the stuff, if he was going to allow ten minutes to make his way back out, and another ten for the ascent. He would never make it, but he wanted to see just how far he could get. He glided in with gentle kicks of his fins, headfirst and on his side so his tank fit through. A big red fish stared at him a moment, as though in disbelief, and then shot past and away into the night.

Blood, also red in the light of the torch, billowed around his head, obscuring his vision. Waylon was suddenly conscious of a cut on his face, a great stinging gash on his cheek, and another laceration on his hand. He must have sliced himself on glass from the door. The thought of sharks crossed his mind again, but quickly passed in light of more immediate concerns.

The room was a confusion of unfamiliar shapes and shadows. What had been walls were now floor and ceiling. The ceiling had windows. Okay. There it was. Just to the left and against what was now the ceiling but what used to be the port wall. A railed stairwell, with the steps spiraling ahead like a short tunnel and then down to a doorway that dropped into the big aft cabin. When the boat had gone over, all the furniture had jumbled up on the port side. Video cassettes and music CDs were scattered everywhere, and Waylon stood on a wooden combination cabinet and shelves to shine his torch into the stairwell. He checked his gauges and looked at his watch: twenty-six minutes left. He still had time for a quick look in the cabin, at least. Tying one end of his twine on to the upper door handle, he prepared, Hansel and Gretel style, to bring the spool with him into the wreck.

He swam in and around, paying out the line behind him, until he was upside down and there was a door in front of him. The scene stirred childhood dreams, dark subterranean worlds full of mystery, Waylon fearful of their resolution. The door had a regular knob, which he turned and pushed before descending headfirst into a mess of junk. Waylon shuddered. Old bedclothes, clammy and insinuating, clung like ectoplasmic Dits. He performed a careful somersault—utterly disorienting himself for a moment, the bonk of his tank hitting something—to settle fins down and wrapped in his line atop a jumbled pile of duffel bags and other items.

Waylon tottered and banged about the cabin for a few seconds, establishing neutral buoyancy and recovering his balance. Where was the floor? A cupboard lay horizontally on his right. There. Straight ahead. The wall-to-wall carpeting, now floor to ceiling, was already coming away. He grabbed a corner and yanked it halfway down to reveal a steel hatch cover like a wall safe bolted into a three-by-two-foot recess. He had about twenty-four minutes left. This was cutting things too fine. He should go back up now.

Waylon decided he would ignore the bundle of rags and a boating shoe he had seen in a corner. And the human skull. With an extra hole where your third eye was meant to be. No problem, eh? Just some dead guy. *Just some dead guy.* Until very recently, Waylon had seen only a couple of dead people in his life. Part of the bundle of rags in the corner, he noticed, was a ribcage wrapped in a T-shirt.

Waylon abandoned his investigations and turned back to the job at hand. Jessica had told him she'd left a couple of nuts on the hatch cover. Actually there were four. They were stainless steel and came off without a problem. But the heavy plate had been designed to lift straight up, and now it was catching on the bolt threads. Waylon jimmied it along with his dive knife till it dropped, bruising his shin on the way down and coming to rest on one of his fins. The visibility was obscured by sediment, but Waylon poked his torch and his head right into the tank and looked around. Just beyond arm's reach lay two sailcloth bags.

His tank and harness prevented him from going any farther in. There was only one thing to do. They had gone over this general situation in both the advanced open water and the wreck diving courses. It was a simple matter to get out of your jacket and harness, do what had to be done, and then put your gear back on. You could still breathe off the regulator. Waylon had done this any number of times already, in the pool and in thirty feet of open water. In the daytime. With his buddy and his instructors right at hand.

Moving with great deliberation, reminding himself to do everything step by step, Waylon unbuckled his jacket and let it and his air tank slide off, dumping it in the corner away from the bits of dead guy. Taking the pencil light from the pocket, he twisted it on before switching his main torch off and putting it down carefully with the rest of the gear. Next to the skull. *That's frig-all. Just some dead guy.*

The regulator hose wouldn't stretch as high as the hatch. Waylon took a big breath of air and let the regulator fall back on his jacket. Then, sticking the torch in his teeth cigar-style, he squirmed half his body into the tank, stretching to grab first one bag and then the other. He pulled them towards himself, stirring up a cloud of sediment in the process and cutting visibility to a few feet. He squirmed back out to drop the bags, one of which was amazingly heavy. He found his regulator, took a hit of air and then another. He sat back on the junk pile to get his arms through the straps on his harness, shrugging his way back into his gear, securing waist belt and chest straps. Killing the pencil torch, he raised the other one again. Looking up, he was startled by a swarming colony of giant silver amoebas, agglomerations of air bubbles trapped against the back.

Eighty feet wasn't much different from thirty feet. You could just as easily drown in thirty feet. "Hell," Oscar had said, "you could drown in your own bathtub, if you tried hard enough." The thing was to know your limitations at any given depth and be comfortable with them. Ninety percent of diving accidents were attributable to panic. So diving inside *Dark Moon* wasn't any different from being in the swimming pool. Just as long as you kept your head. No problem.

Then Waylon's torch started to flicker and dim. The torch, he suddenly realized, that Dit had used for jigging squid. Jesus Christ. His light was going to burn out.

Stop.

Breathe. . . . Breathe. . . .

Think. Slow and easy. Relax. That was it. Think. Check your gauges. He still had eighteen minutes—eight minutes to get out and ten for the ascent. But he had only 450 psi left. He was down into the red zone. Not as calm as he'd wanted to think, he'd been burning up air.

Jesus, Jesus. *Relax.* Breathe in. Slowly and deeply. Breathe out. Breathe everything out, clear all the carbon dioxide before taking the next lungful. *In.* . . . *Out.* . . . There wasn't all that much more to breathe. He had to get out of there.

Torch dangling from his wrist to cast wild shadows, shedding only intermittent and increasingly dim light on proceedings, he stuffed both bags up through the doorway above him and to the side. His torch had gone a sickly pale yellow. It flickered, and Waylon's fear flashed in disproportionate sympathy.

The backup torch. It wasn't there. He checked both pockets in his jacket, pulled everything out till they were both empty. He went through them again, and again, as though he expected the penlight to appear by magic. He shone the dimming main torch around the cabin quickly, but it didn't have enough juice left to look for anything. He was only wasting time. And air.

The torch died.

Stop.

Crushed by the weight of eighty feet of dark sea, trapped in a black labyrinth, Waylon sucked hard on his regulator, breathing deep. He was suffocating. He fought the urge to gulp more air. Calm. Be calm. His mind battered about his skull, clamoring, urgent.

Surface, get to surface. Get the hell out of here *now.*

No. *Stop.* Breathe. . . . *Think.* Never-act-on-the-edge-of-panic. Neveractontheeeedgeofpanic. Think.

He knew how he had come in, and he was going to go out the same way. No problem. Just follow the cord. But which way was the door? Up. It was in the ceiling. Simple. He gave his jacket a burst of air. And nothing happened. He could feel the flotation jacket swell, but he wasn't rising. Jesus.

Hung up on something. That was all. But he couldn't *see.* He had his dive knife, sharp as a razor, one edge of the blade a saw; Leary had told him he could cut himself free from just about any line or net he'd ever encounter. But he was crammed into this tiny space. He couldn't go forward, and he couldn't retreat more than a couple of inches. He couldn't turn around. So he wasn't able to see what he was caught on, much less cut himself free. Claustrophobia began to ring insistent alarms, threatening to swell out of control. He recoiled from a thought he must not think—a glimmering of how Jessica must feel when she was underwater at night.

Think.

Breathebreathebreathe. . . .

Whoa. Just stop. Don't do anything. Settle down.

Think.

And he thought about dying. He thought of Chloe and thought about how she was alive somewhere, unaware of where he was and what he was doing. And he wondered how she would remember him, if he were to die now. Abruptly he realized he didn't want her to remember him the way he was, the way he had become. What had he become? But this was something that merited consideration in its own good time. Right now there were more pressing matters. All of that went through his head in a moment, and he was breathing slowly and strongly. He was focusing.

At the same time he encountered the cold realization that this was for real. If he got it wrong, if he made the slightest miscalculation now, he was dead. This was dangerous. Really and truly dangerous. These things went through his mind as he sat there in the black, hung up, breathing the last of his air, unable now even to see how much air he had left.

For a moment the panic surged back. *Think.* He could drop his gear again, and the bags, grab a few breaths off the tank and then try to swim out. But if anything held him up, he'd be finished. Even if he got out clear, he would have already burned up a lot of his one last lungful. There wouldn't be enough for a safe ascent. And he had to get to the line. If he didn't, with the current up, he might never find the dinghy again and be left to drift away in the dark all night. And the only person who would even know he was missing was Jessica. His buddy. He had to try to keep his gear.

Originally, he had planned to lift the stuff with the salvage bag. Shoving his regulator under the opening, he would have squeezed the purge valve till the bag lifted, and he would have accompanied it to surface. But you don't squander your last breath of air on lifting two anonymous bags from eighty feet. He would have attached a lightstick to the bag in case it got away from him and they had to retrieve it later with the dinghy.

The lightstick. *He still had the lightstick.* He fumbled it out of the pocket and cracked it, watching it begin to glow its ghostly green. Why hadn't he thought of that before? He had to be narked.

Okay. Unbuckle the waist and chest straps. Loosen the shoulder straps. Slowly, cautiously. No problem. Just keep the breather in your mouth. Breathe slowly and deeply. Exhale every molecule. Then take another lungful. Slip out of the harness. Now turn around and find out where you're snagged. Okay, there it is. The octopus hose is caught in the crack of the cupboard door. Lift it away. There.

Working fast, marveling at his own control, he fastened the lightstick to the valve of his tank. That way, if he came up away from the dinghy, or unconscious, or both, Jessica might spot him. He maneuvered his way back into his gear and proceeded up the stairwell, tank and bags clonking against steps and railing, and emerged from the tunnel into the salon. Even with the greenish glimmer from behind his head, he could see the dimmest wash of moonlight leaking through the doors. He cut himself again going out, shoving the bags through ahead of him. He could feel it, though there wasn't enough light to see how badly he was bleeding.

He was still getting air, but he couldn't have much reserve left. A bag in each hand, and guided mainly by moonlight now, he finned back towards the line, praying the hole in the cloud cover lasted.

He found the line.

In a free ascent, when you're right out of air, you jettison weightbelt and anything else you happen to be carrying, and go straight to surface. A good way to get bent. The option, if circumstances permitted, was to oxygenate with a few lungfuls of air, saving the last one or two for a controled ascent. Leary had told him that you could do a controled ascent from ninety feet on one breath of air. It was all a matter of staying calm and going by the book. In fact, Waylon had practiced the procedure, with Oscar's acquiescence, from thirty and then from sixty feet. You had to take care not to hold your breath as you ascended, or the pressurized air would rupture your lungs. So you should try to ascend at about a foot a second, hoping to avoid the bends, mouth open, meanwhile, to let the pressurized air escape on its own. But not too fast— you needed enough to get to surface.

Waylon was going up with everything—weightbelt, tank, mysterious bags, even the wrench, which, in his methodical manner, he had secured in the Velcro loop. He gave his flotation jacket a couple of short bursts and started up, a bag in each hand. He tried for another breath off the regulator and got a dry rasp. He was sucking on an empty tank. Like trying to breathe with a plastic bag tight over your face. Eighty feet to go on less than a full lungful of air.

He gauged his rate of ascent by the beeps from his dive computer—every time it started up, he stopped finning till the warning stopped. Another thing he remembered: with the diminishing external pressure, the bit of air left in an "empty" tank might expand, at around fifty-five feet, to the point you could get another breath. Cautiously, he inhaled. A gift from the gods—half a lungful of air. But his computer was beeping again and he forced himself to slow. Although he couldn't see his depth gauge, he looked up to fragments of moon dancing on the surface, and they seemed close. Now his lungs were empty, and the urge to fill them almost overwhelmed him. The blackness was gathering when he broke surface. And he did suck air, again and again. Catching a splash of wave, he started to choke.

"Waylon?" A faint voice. At least she was awake.

A sack in each hand, Waylon rolled on to his back and allowed the current to carry him, wallowing with the weight of the heavier bag, towards the dinghy, away from the buoy, which was dragging in the race of the current. Jessica pulled and he pushed to get the bag up and into the little boat.

"You took long enough. Did you get both of them?"

"Yeah. Aren't you going to give me a hand, here? I'm tired."

What the hell was he doing, risking his life for this? He had to be nuts. For a moment, to his amazement, he felt a rush of well-being, an urge to laugh. An echo of a street racer's motorcycle screaming at full throttle. He put it down to euphoria at still being alive. Maybe this was the thrill bungee-jumping had failed to deliver.

"Let's see," said Waylon. But Jessica was utterly intent and he was entirely irrelevant. He felt slighted, considering what he'd just been through and all for her.

"Yeah, yeah. My hero." She didn't want to hear about it. "Just hold the torch steady, okay?"

"There was a man in the cabin, Jessie. A dead man."

"No kidding." Jessica was completely absorbed in opening the bags. She took something out of the heavy bag and put it into the other one.

"You have to go back down, Waylon."

"*What*? Are you crazy?"

"Take my tank. And my torch. I have a new plan. You have to go back down. Just go down fast, drop the bag, and then come back up slow. You'll have lots of time to decompress."

"Piss off, eh? Jesus Christ. *No way.*"

Jessica explained that he should take the heavier bag and put it back on the wreck. Maybe in the salon—somewhere he'd be sure to find it the next day. And, since he was so worried about having had to come up fast on the last dive, he should be grateful for the chance to make it up on this one. Jessica could be a veritable encyclopedia of safe diving wisdom, when it suited her purposes. Never mind she had it all wrong in this case.

"What's in the bag, Jessie?"

"Gold."

"*Gold?*" Jesus Christ. The bag had to weigh thirty pounds. "*Gold?* What the hell's in the *other* bag, then?"

"I'll show you when we get back, Waylon. Now just do it. It's very important." She explained that they couldn't just drop the bag over the side; chances were they'd never find it again. And it was vital that they recovered it the next day. Jessica hadn't been idle while he was on *Dark Moon*. She had it all worked out. They would put full tanks on their harnesses that night, so the others wouldn't know they'd been out. The next morning, Waylon should stay on the wreck as long as possible, so it didn't look too easy. Jessica would simply say she was too sick to go down.

"Jessie, if these guys are the kind of guys you say they are—and I have no reason to think they aren't—they're going to take that gold right off us."

That's right," she replied.

39 a bad case of piracy

She knew treachery,
Rapine, deceit, and lust, and ills enow
To be a woman.

John Donne

There they sat, the size of small piggy banks. Two silly ceramic dogs painted in rosy colors, porcelain tongues hanging out. Squat little Pekinesey things sitting up and begging. Waylon thought of Spunky.

They were back in their cabin on the boat and Jessica was staring at the dogs, entranced, glowing with excitement and self-satisfaction.

"Jessica," said Waylon, believing the gravity of the situation hadn't fully registered on her, "I have just flirted with death salvaging a bag of gold and two stupid ceramic puppies. Now I've put the gold back on the wreck so these guys can steal it later, and you're pleased as punch. What's the story?"

By way of response, Jessica drew her dive knife and brought the hammer handle down sharply on one of the dogs, shattering its head and then its body, which spilled Styrofoam pellets. Inside was a stone image of the Buddha. Gray-brown, probably sandstone. It looked old. Jessica wiggled it out of the ceramic base and placed it back on the bunk, brushing pellets off both the image and the automatic pistol that, well greased and wrapped in plastic, had shared the bag with the puppies.

"So that's it. Smuggled artifacts. How much is it worth, Jessica?"

"Not enough, Waylon. Not nearly enough for what I've had to go through to get it. This was nothing but a decoy, in case it was needed." Then she rapped the head of the other dog, more carefully, until it fractured. She tapped and pulled away bits as though she were peeling a hard-boiled egg. Finally it cracked wide open to reveal a treasure.

"The biggest sapphire ever found, supposedly, was almost ten thousand carats. That was the Lone Star. This one must have been bigger, before it was carved." Jessica finished extricating the figure concealed within the dog, tore open a sheath of clear plastic wrap, and brushed foam pellets from it. It was beautiful. Glowing with a soft inner radiance, it seemed to absorb and amplify the dim light from the lamp. "Can you imagine how much this is worth? It's priceless. It's one of a kind. Look at it. Look at the carving."

Serene, enigmatic in its smile and uncertain antiquity, the figure sat composed, perfectly balanced, its polished lines reflected inside itself in such a way that it came alive with the slightest movement or change of light. Waylon found it incredible that it was really a sapphire. It had to be some sort of soapstone. Maybe jade, though he'd never heard of jade this color. It couldn't possibly be a sapphire. My God. It would be beyond price.

"That's not a sapphire," he said.

"What's the stone in your ring?"

"Onyx." Chloe had given him the ring the first year they were married.

"Okay, Waylon. Try to scratch it."

Waylon hesitated.

"Don't worry. Just do it."

She was right. The figure was harder than onyx.

"Can you imagine?" she said. "The stone it was carved from would've weighed several pounds. And look at the color. It's completely natural. They didn't have heat treatment in those days."

A Buddha image carved from a gigantic blue sapphire. Assigning a value to something like that for insurance purposes would be a nice trick. Any figure you came up with would be essentially arbitrary.

It was impossible to say how old it was, according to Jessica. First reported in AD 787, the Blue Buddha was discovered in Ceylon, buried under a ruined temple that was already ancient. Over the next millennium and a half, it had changed hands numerous times, changed countries, been taken as war booty, enshrined, hidden, and lost to history, on more than one occasion, for hundreds of years.

Jessica wrapped both the Buddha images in towels and stuffed them back in the sailcloth bag. "Waylon. We don't have time right now. You have to help me with this."

"With what?"

"Listen. Do you hear that?"

Waylon listened. The frenetic thumping of the generator almost covered the snores on deck. "I don't hear anything."

"The water. Listen to the water." There was a gentle sloshing from under them, a hollow sound unlike the slap of waves against the hull. "That's a tank, Waylon. It's either for water or for fuel. My guess is, it's water."

They rolled up the floormat and found a bolted steel hatch, much like the one on *Dark Moon*. They still had the wrench and Waylon set about stashing the bag in the water tank. While he got the nuts off, working as quietly as he could, Jessica told him more.

There was little mention of the Blue Buddha in the chronicles. The Emerald Buddha (which was not really emerald but rather some sort of jasper), a priceless image with its own dramatic history, was the most revered and historically significant image in Thailand. Legend had it there was a Blue Buddha companion to the Emerald Buddha. An old friend of Jessica's had taught a student in India, a Russian who was doing a thesis in English on the early dissemination of Buddhism in Asia. While advising him on his research and writing skills in English, her friend became intrigued by the story of the Blue Buddha. According to one ancient Sanskrit manuscript the graduate student had come across, the image was last reported in a temple in the ancient Kingdom of Sukhothai, in what is now Thailand. As far as his researches could determine, it then disappeared again in the course of some invasion and had been missing ever since.

Jessica's friend eventually wound up in Thailand, on Koh Samui, back in the first days of tourism there, growing mushrooms and selling wisdom. Normally the local godfather, a guy named Terdsak, wouldn't have tolerated the competition.

"Waylon." Jessica paused. "What are you doing?"

"I'm putting the bag in the tank."

"And how are we going to get it out again?"

"Oh, yeah."

"I've got some fishing line in my bag."

"I'm not surprised."

"Here. And hurry it up. My Bottle and his boys should be out of it till morning. But you never know.

"Terdsak saw how he could use this guy," Jessica continued. "So instead of having him shot or drowned, he merely recruited him. George was his name." George ran a place called Inner Adventures, a New Age center catering to backpackers. This class of traveler had no money to speak of, but they represented a mass market for various drugs and, sometimes, themselves made useful drug mules or companions for rich men. So Terdsak and George started a bigger and better center on the mainland. Terdsak was already into smuggled artifacts. One night when they were having a chat over a few drinks, George happened to mention the story of the Blue

Buddha, and the godfather said he'd like to hear more. Having heard more, and acting on a hunch—painted plaster images had often concealed invaluable figures beneath their humble surfaces—he directed that every Buddha image fitting the general dimensions within fifty miles of the temple mentioned in the ancient chronicle should be stolen and brought to him. They broke most of them before they finally found it.

"He went to all that trouble on the basis of a rumor?" Having attached the bag to the line, Waylon dropped it into the tank and started bolting the hatch back on.

"Terdsak likes to grandstand. He sees himself larger than life." Anyway, it wasn't the huge gamble it might sound like, since Terdsak knew he could get a good price for the heads and hands off the images anyway. "Just put a couple of the nuts back on, Waylon," Jessica instructed him. "Then put the mat back."

The Buddha had been covered with a crude pottery shell and painted. Terdsak had the image brought to his base, where it was photographed, videotaped, placed in a plastic bag full of foam pellets, and concealed once again, this time in a ceramic shell cut in half with a diamond saw and resealed around the Buddha with ceramic glue.

"So where did the gold come from?" Waylon asked. As impressed as he was with the Blue Buddha, he was even more impressed with Jessica's willingness to bestow a sack of bullion on My Bottle and his friends. Never mind Waylon had risked his life to recover it, as he'd pointed out to Jessica more than once already.

"That's a long story, Waylon. Let's save it for now, okay? All you have to know is that George is my friend. And this Buddha belongs to him. And me. And Terdsak double-crossed us."

Waylon suddenly remembered where he'd heard the name Terdsak before—the time he'd overheard Jessica on her mobile phone, when he surprised her atop Captain Ot's wheelhouse. She'd been talking to a guy named George. "And these men," Waylon asked her. "My Bottle and his crew?"

"They must be working for Terdsak. Which is not good news."

Waylon stood staring at the bathroom mirror. A bearded and sunburned version of himself stared back, eyes smudged with exhaustion, a raw wound running from his left ear down across his cheekbone and into his mustache. Hair uncombed since morning. It was scary. Whoever this was looked more like a pirate than the pirates. Jesus Christ. If his clients could see him now. He rolled that idea around on his mental palate for a moment and found he liked it. And he congratulated himself on having had tetanus boosters before leaving Vancouver. He had explained to Chloe how important these things were, though she'd kept pooh-poohing his concern. Maybe it was the beard. Maybe it was the idea that nobody could see his lip so well, but Waylon couldn't remember having had a quivering-lip episode since the night he lost Chloe and Meredith. He rubbed reflectively at his almost-beard.

"Waylon. How did you get that cut on your face?"

"Weren't you listening to *anything* I told you, Jessica?"

"I had a lot on my mind. Get some sleep, Waylon." Jessica conked out in less than a minute, headphones still in her hand, sleeping mask on the floor beside her bunk. Waylon almost wished he had asked for one of her pills.

Lying there reviewing the day's events, Waylon got to the part where he'd dropped his air and gone into the water tank without the regulator. What if he'd gotten hung up while he was in there, with his air supply in the cabin but out of reach? His blood ran cold, and he understood the cliché in a way he had never had to before. Then he thought about the man in the cabin and his blood ran colder still.

The next day they awoke to hard words in a mixture of Thai and English. My Bottle was chewing out the crew, who looked more than a little groggy. My Bottle didn't look any hell himself. Finally he ran out of steam and just sat there, sneering at the new day and wiping his hair flat against his head. Bat staggered out on deck, stretched, installed his shades high on his head, and lit the first Marlboro of the day, sucking smoke down to somewhere around his toenails. He grinned at Jessica. Then he thought better of it and scowled suspiciously instead. Dit headed down to the galley to prepare breakfast.

Waylon examined the bowl of rice soup, wondering whether the raw eggs Dit had broken into it were safe to eat. He was so hungry he decided he didn't care. He stirred them in till the hot gruel was a rich golden yellow, and relished the savory mix of rice, prawns, sliced spring onion, shredded fresh ginger, garlic, and black pepper.

"How you hurt your face?" My Bottle asked Waylon, looking more suspicious than concerned in any other way.

Waylon grinned conspiratorially and nodded towards Jessica, who was out on deck trying for some fresh air. "Women like that," he said, shaking his head and running his hand over the stubble on his face. "You know."

"I be nice to you," Dit assured Waylon.

Bat just pulled at his crotch and grinned in Jessica's direction.

They moved the boat out and anchored on the wreck again. Jessica told everybody she was sick and Waylon went down alone, Dit helping him with his gear, hands everywhere.

The visibility was excellent. You could see the top of the wreck from surface, if you knew what you were looking for. Going down the anchor line in a light current, *Dark Moon* materializing beneath him in the relative gloom, he had to wonder at all the mystery and drama of the day before. This time it was straightforward. There were fresh batteries in Jessica's torch, but he didn't need it to find the bag of gold sitting there safe where he had left it on the bottom, under the stern. Mindful of his wounds, which stung in the salt water, he made his way into the salon again. He checked his air to see he still had half an hour or more, and decided to have another look around. Maybe there was something he could salvage for himself. Aside from an antique-looking carved wooden panel, which was bolted to the forward wall too securely for him to remove, he didn't see anything. Then he noticed a golden chain trailing out from under a cabinet. Shifting the heavy piece of furniture, he found a pendant, a black and white mandala, *soixante-*

neuf pollywogs representing the complementarity of the yin and the yang. Wondering at the twinge of guilt, he slipped it into his jacket pocket.

He returned to surface and swam to the ladder, where Dit put a gun in his face and indicated he would like to take possession of the bag. Even though he batted his eyes and insisted on helping Waylon on deck, hands everywhere once again, Waylon felt he was basically in hostile territory and he hesitated to shudder, since it was not always wise to show distaste for a person who was holding a gun on you. So Waylon turned his shudder into a stumble, as the boat rocked in a gentle swell that was coming off the sea. If you overlooked the pirate raid yesterday, which had been rather more impersonal, he had never before had a gun pointed at him in earnest.

"No, please!" Jessica said. She was still so drugged up she almost yawned. "Not the gold!"

My Bottle was sneering in a joyous sort of way, even laughing and pouring whiskey for everybody. The captain took his glass up to the wheelhouse. Bat and Dit drank theirs down, hoisted the dinghy back up on deck, weighed anchor, and they got underway. There followed much chatter in Thai; and, after the gold, Waylon and Jessica were the chief topics of conversation. Waylon had no idea what My Bottle and the crew were saying.

"Well, Waylon, it looks like they're going to keep me. At least for now. But I think you may be out of luck."

"What do you mean?" Waylon could hardly credit it. Bat was holding the shotgun in a businesslike manner and the focus of interest had devolved on Waylon himself. "How do you know that, Jessica?"

"I just know, Waylon."

Then Dit intervened, speaking passionately and batting his eyes alternately in the direction of My Bottle and Waylon.

"Wait a minute, Waylon. I think you're okay. I believe you've found a champion. You're lucky Dit likes you."

She had to be joking. She didn't even look especially concerned.

Yawn

After lunch, Waylon lay down in the sun on the bow, and the gentle rolling of the boat and the throb of the engine eventually put him to sleep. Later, at Jessica's insistence, they packed up their dive bags and carried them down to their cabin.

"Go on nice trip, *na*?" Bat found this hilarious, for some reason. So did Dit, who tittered and said, "Put me in bag too, Wail-On. Go witt you, okay?"

"Assholes," said Jessica, after they were safely in their cabin with the door closed.

The gold, as she had said, was another story. It was old, but neither as old as the Blue Buddha nor even nearly so precious. It had come off a Chinese junk that had gone down in the Gulf of Thailand about eight hundred years before. The salvage job had been big news in the papers, for a while, although none of the stories mentioned the gold. *Red Tide*, the salvage vessel, was Australian. Terdsak had put up some of the money and protection, something else never mentioned in the press.

Ostensibly, they were after thousands of pieces of pottery that had been on their way from the kilns at Sawankhalok, north of Bangkok, probably to trading centers farther south. And so it went for a couple of months, a team of professionals from *Red Tide* making several dives a day to vacuum away the accumulated sediments and raise the artifacts.

Unbeknown to them, all the while, Thai coastguard vessels sat just over the horizon monitoring proceedings by radar. After all, went the argument, these were Thai waters and this treasure belonged properly to Thailand. About the time they were almost finished, the coastguard made a big deal out of seizing the cargo, bruiting the story about how they'd only moved in to claim it after cleverly letting the foreigners do all the work and spend all the money. The salvors protested this high-handed behavior, claiming they'd been operating in international waters. But to no avail. The Thai press had a field day with it, and officialdom basked in public admiration of their cunning.

"But *Red Tide* had the last laugh," Jessica told Waylon. "Anybody who knew the operations boss knew he wouldn't have gone to so much trouble over such small potatoes. There had to have been something else on that wreck."

And so there had been—a cache of gold and Sung Dynasty ceramics that would have been priceless even back in those days.

Terdsak, who made a point of knowing all things, had tipped off the Australian boss of the operation that they were under surveillance. So they went ahead with the job, and later they made a great public fuss about what they claimed was the illegal seizure of their goods. "But the Thai pottery was only smoke and mirrors."

"Like with the gold today?"

By the time the coastguard made its move, the real goodies had been spirited away in a dinghy, delivered to a boat called *Darunee*.

"And how is all this connected to the Blue Buddha?"

"The sapphire just happened to be on *Darunee* at the time, together with a bunch of lesser treasures, that sandstone Buddha among them. All of them already prepared for export."

"What happened to the ceramics?"

"I've told you too much already, Waylon. Only on a need-to-know basis, remember? It isn't healthy to know more than you have to."

"Where do you fit into all this? Were you sleeping with this guy George?"

"Why the hell do you want to know that? '*Eh?*' Give me a break, Waylon. What difference does it make to you? George and I were friends, and I was on *Darunee* looking after our interests."

"Okay. But what about the ceramics. How much of it was there?"

"There are three big fuel tanks on *Dark Moon*. One of them is mostly full of water. Under a layer of diesel, there are about a dozen bags. Far too much for us to handle, the way things have gone. So there, Waylon. Now you know. Are you happy? You big fucking baby." There was no tenderness in her voice.

Darunee had been carrying a treasure beyond price, and the gold was the least part of it. Terdsak was to split the proceeds of the gold and ceramics with the Australian interests, and share the take from the Blue Buddha with George. "Not only that," said Jessica, "it wouldn't surprise me if he got a kickback from the coastguard for tipping them off in the first place, though I'm only guessing. Terdsak loves to feel he's holding all the strings. The more tangled the better."

Terdsak hadn't wanted to annoy the Australians because that would have been bad business in many ways, and he wanted to keep George on side, since he was an essential part of other plans he had in mind. At the same time, it would have been bad business to pay either the Australians or George their shares if this weren't necessary. So he got a good idea.

Darunee was attacked by pirates—a boat called *Dark Moon*. The pirates spared Jessica, since she was still young and shapely and spunky enough someone would pay good money to break her. And Terdsak was never one to waste an asset. They killed everybody else except the guy who'd been Terdsak's fifth column on board *Darunee*. He had made it easier for them to dispose of the other hard men who crewed her.

Terdsak's man was only cut up a bit and then left aboard *Darunee*, which was set adrift, dead bodies and blood everywhere, eloquent testimony to pirate attack and Terdsak's innocence in the small matter of the missing treasure. But Jessica had recognized her fellow survivor as one of Terdsak's lieutenants, and quickly twigged to the real game. Jessica figured they had intended to deliver *Dark Moon* and its contents to Terdsak's private island—the same island she figured My Bottle was headed for even as they spoke. From there, the goods would probably have gone to Cambodia before being transferred to Europe.

"Terdsak planned on having the last laugh." Jessica laughed. "He was wrong."

Jessica and the loot were moved to *Dark Moon*. Just to celebrate, the pirates had gotten blind drunk. "They had a party, Waylon. And I was the main party toy. Not very nice, *eh*? Do you know how that feels? Trapped on a boat with half a dozen Dits? Think about it. Oh, my. Didn't we have fun. And I knew I wasn't supposed to survive long enough to talk to anybody that mattered because, for one thing, the leader of this little gang told me all about the Blue Buddha and the stuff in the forward fuel tank, wanting me to see how smart he was.

"When I wasn't otherwise occupied, I was responsible for keeping the drinks topped up." That was a mistake on their part. After a while, as it turned out, there was no one capable of driving the boat. "There was still one guy at the end, a fucking teetotaler or something. He took me down to the stern cabin for more fun and games. He was my 'guard,' he said.

"Some guard. I stashed the gold and the dogs in the water tank. *Dark Moon*'s crew had already hidden the Sung ceramics in the fuel tank. Then I scuttled her." Earlier in the evening, she'd pulled the fuses for the bilge pumps, which were on the electrical panel by the wheelhouse. It had only taken a moment to twist the caps off, pull the fuses, and then replace the caps. This disabled both pumps and the bilge alarm system. All that remained was to plug the siphon breaks, and then open the seacocks on the toilets. Even if someone had seen they were sinking, by the time they'd figured out what was wrong, it would have been too late.

Such a handy girl to have around.

"As it turned out," Jessica said, "there was no hurry. No problem. I wrote down the GPS coordinates and opened the seacocks."

"Christ, Jessie. Why didn't you just throw the bags over the side?"

"Do you know how hard it would be to find these bags in a hundred feet of water, Waylon? Even with a GPS? The boat was like a marker buoy. Something to help me find the stuff again."

Even if she'd been able, she said, she wouldn't have driven *Dark Moon* away. It would have been stupid to risk the curiosity a single foreign woman at the helm would have occasioned. So she had to scuttle the boat. And the treasure had to go down with her. "I didn't know where I was going to get to, Waylon. Or who was going to find me. You think, after all that, I wanted to lose the Buddha to some dingbat?"

She set off in the boat's dinghy, coming ashore in a lifejacket with nothing but a GPS reading and a plan.

"And the guard let you do all this, no problem?"

"The guard was dead, Waylon."

"The guy in the aft cabin."

"Yeah." She said this in a way that suggested Waylon was not scoring big on the IQ test. Waylon didn't want to ask how the man had died. But he did.

"It was an accident, Waylon." She didn't care if he believed her or not.

"An accident?"

"Don't worry about it. You don't need to know. You don't *want* to know, Waylon. Trust me."

Jessica wiped grease off the automatic pistol and two loaded magazines from the doggie bag, finishing the job with a damp washcloth and shampoo. She stripped the pistol and left it on a towel to dry on the bed under the fan.

"What about all the other people on board?"

"They drowned."

"What? 'They drowned.' That's all?"

"Yeah. What else can I tell you? They opened their mouths and breathed water. So they died."

Waylon looked at Jessica—his dive buddy, the person to whom he had entrusted his life—and wondered at the reptilian complacency he saw in her eyes. This was the person with whom he had almost gone diving on *Dark Moon*, suspecting none of this and, perhaps, never meant to know any of it. Waylon experienced the same sensation he'd had just after he made it back to the dinghy, after the night dive on *Dark Moon*, when he found himself reflecting on the true risks to which he'd exposed himself.

"They wanted to rip us off, Waylon. But it didn't work."

Terdsak told George, his partner in the health spa racket, that the Buddha had been lost. *Darunee* had been found adrift, decks liberally stained with blood. Obviously a bad case of piracy. It was Jessica who had later related the true account of matters. So now

George the New Age man was determined to settle accounts with Terdsak at the first opportunity, not to mention retrieve the Blue Buddha. "Of course, I had to talk him into it. Just like the last time, George was just never really comfortable with being a badass. That's why he's never got any further in life, Waylon. He's basically just a loser.

"But now we've got a problem. I thought Terdsak believed I was dead. And I reckoned he had no way of knowing George knew about the double-cross. Now I see Terdsak knows I'm alive. I know it's him. He's been watching us all along, just waiting to move in when we found the Buddha. What I can't understand is why George is still alive. Of course, Terdsak gets off on manipulating people. He likes to play with you, cat-and-mouse style. Maybe he thinks he can trump me the same way he out-foxed the Thai navy and *Red Tide*. And maybe he thinks he can use George even though he must realize George would kill him, given half a chance, now that he knows."

With his knowledge of herbal medicine, George could have killed Terdsak any time he wanted to. "I don't know why he didn't do it a long time ago. I think Terdsak had some kind of hold over him." Now that Waylon had seen her in action, and heard some of her history, Jessica had apparently lost any inhibitions about discussions of murder and suchlike. Indeed, with her calm, matter-of-fact delivery, she made it all sound almost commonplace. Small talk.

"This is a very scary man, Waylon."

Coming from Jessica, Waylon felt, this proposition was indeed a scary one.

Terdsak had long been a godfather of considerable standing. From earliest days he had displayed an absolute disregard for the law. In fact, Jessica said, he showed a contempt for any code of rules whatsoever, other than his own, one chief principle of which was that you never let anybody else's rules interfere with good business. He also liked to feel he was always in control. Where people or circumstances interfered with this belief, he was quick to react, favoring extreme measures. In recent years, however, he'd been exceeding even his own reputation for viciousness. Rumor had it he'd gone totally whacko. His own men, it was said, lived in terror of him.

"But I tell you this," Jessica said. "George wouldn't be alive—neither would you or me—if Terdsak didn't think he was still in control, somehow. But he's wrong, Waylon. I'm going to have the last laugh. And the Buddha."

"What about all the ceramic stuff?"

Jessica looked at him, and he saw the reptilian ancestor flicker behind her big gray eyes. "That too, Waylon. That too."

"How did you meet this guy in the first place, Jessie"

"That's another story. And we don't have time."

They traveled all the rest of the day, that eve of the full moon. Jessica estimated they'd arrive on the island two or three hours after dark. Dit fixed them a nice dinner of fried rice and fried green vegetables, and, afterwards, Jessica mixed My Bottle and the crew some nice drinks and served them dressed only in her bathing suit. After nightfall, My Bottle played solitaire for a while, but he couldn't seem to stay awake. Bat and Dit fell asleep with the radio still playing Thai country music. Jessica was doing a great job of engineering inner space for the entire crew. The skipper just drove, oblivious to all else.

"Waylon. Look over there." A mile or two ahead, to starboard, there was what looked like a small city of lights. Some of it was the flicker of big beach fires. "I know where we are, Waylon. And I know what we have to do." There was another island, past the one with the lights, and that's where *Sumalee* was headed, Jessica said. "But we can't be on the boat when it arrives. Or we're dead." Waylon had noted a flair for melodrama in Jessica, from time to time, but ever since the pirate incident he was inclined to take her more seriously.

"We'll have to swim, Waylon."

"What if there's a current? We could wind up in China."

"You stay if you want to. I'm going now. Yes. You should stay. Dit will look after you."

A Bad Case of Piracy

He felt as though they were children playing games. At the same time, he recognized how dangerous a game this was. They stuffed clothes and bunched-up bedsheets under the covers on their bunks. Jessica even stacked Waylon's running shoes under the blanket, soles out, to make it look as though he were curled up on his side. She handed him the sandstone Buddha in a bag together with all the broken bits of ceramic they'd cleaned up. "Waylon. You drop this after we're in the water. Okay? So there's no splash."

Jessica wrapped The Bag with her vodka and other necessities in three black plastic garbage-bin liners, and told Waylon to look after it. It was heavy. They packed a partially filled lift bag in with her stuff to give it a little buoyancy. Then she told him to wait, as though there was somewhere he might be going. He saw her slip her knife out of its scabbard and, gun in one hand, knife in the other, she went up on deck.

Jessica had been gone a couple of minutes when Dit appeared in the doorway. He was looking pretty unsteady. Given the combination of drinks and sedatives he'd consumed, this wasn't surprising. But passion conquers all. Dit was batting his eyes in a way meant to be provocative, and his smile glinted silver. Waylon glanced over to where the crescent wrench lay on the floor. Dit was dressed in nothing but his shorts, which he proceeded to pull down far enough to reveal the rest of his ring collection. Then his eyes stopped batting and he looked past Waylon to the bunk. He looked at Waylon and then he looked back at the bunk, obviously checking his sums and wondering where the crowd had come from. Then you could see his eyes register the sacks on the floor and the wetsuits laid out. He had just started to pull his shorts up again when Jessica hit him with the pistol, right behind the ear. He dropped to his knees and she hit him again.

She stepped over Dit with little show of interest. "This is it, Waylon. There's no turning back. Do you understand? We're not going to that island with them. And they're not taking the Buddha." She underlined her resolve by running the slide on her pistol. He could see the weapon had been freshly greased. The spare magazine went back into its plastic wrappings and into a jacket pocket. She had already had Waylon get the Buddha back out of the water tank, and now she stuffed the sack with the giant sapphire into her jacket. She passed The Bag to Waylon. "Anyway, we've got to hurry," Jessica continued. "This whole boat is a time bomb. As soon as somebody lights a cigarette it's going to blow up."

"What do you mean?"

"Explode, Waylon. You know—*ka-boom*."

"Jessie. Did *you* do this?"

"Yeah. Of course."

He wouldn't have been surprised if she'd told him she had a couple of pounds of plastic explosive in her bag. But it was nothing so straightforward.

"While you were getting our gear ready, I went down to the galley. I slit the hoses to the propane stoves. Propane is heavier than air, so the bilges are already filling with gas. It's a time bomb, Waylon. It's set to go off whenever somebody tries to start the diesels again. Or when somebody lights a cigarette." Judging by her tone of voice, Jessica was voting for the second eventuality.

"I guess you never thought of consulting me?"

"You would've just made a fuss, Waylon."

"Jesus Christ, Jessie. What about Bat? What about the others?"

"I told you. I don't like Bat." She had already told him it was like French kissing an ashtray. How was it, thought Waylon, that Jessica would never tell him anything important, yet would suddenly tell him way more than he really wanted to know about something really stupid? "I don't like any of them. Wise up, Waylon. They were going to kill you. And they were going to let me live long enough to wind up a toy for some pig."

"Jessie."

"What, Waylon?"

"You told me I should stay on the boat."

"No. I said it was up to you." She took a big hit off her vodka bottle to clear her head.

"You know what they told us in the course, Jessie. Alcohol only makes hypothermia worse."

"This fucking water is about eighty-five degrees Fahrenheit, Waylon. Nobody's going to get hypothermia." Nevertheless, she said, they should wear wetsuits. "They're black, Waylon. Perfect camouflage." They also put on their flotation jackets, blew into them till they were half inflated, and moved like furtive puffer pigeons up on to the stern deck. Jessica had another shot of vodka and told Waylon to stow the bottle in her bag.

The only illumination on deck was two bare hundred-watt bulbs hanging off the mast atop the wheelhouse. Waylon had Jessica's bag in one hand and the sandstone Buddha bag in the other. They swung over the side and down on to the little diving platform, just off the water. The moon lay a shimmering path of silver to port. They sat down, the wake streaming away behind them, and got their fins on. Waylon looked to starboard to see three ghostly torpedoes rocketing in and out of the bioluminescence in their wake.

"Look, Jessica. Dolphins!"

"Shut up, Waylon. Do you think this is a game?"

"But look. They're glowing in the dark. That's unreal."

"Waylon. Be quiet! Listen."

Waylon heard: a boat motor. It was coming towards them.

"Don't say anything," Jessica hissed.

"I'm not."

"*Shhh*."

Waylon stared and stared into the night, but couldn't see a thing. No light. Nothing. Then a silhouette crossed the shimmering path of moonlight leading to their boat. A longtail boat—they could see the driver standing by the big motor at the stern. And a voice, in English. A monologue: "Fuck, man. I bet you're working with Them. That's it, isn't it? You're one of Them. I fuckin' knew it. We're gonna drive around here all fuckin' night. Right?" The voice faded away into the night. "How many islands you got around here, anyway? Shit, man."

"Who was that?" Waylon asked.

40 seeing the light

Sanity is a madness put to good uses;
waking life is a dream controlled.

George Santayana

No big deal. She tried to shrug it off. What the hell. She hadn't really been raped, after all. But whether or not Terdsak had actually entered her wasn't the problem. Rape wasn't sex. It was violence. And Chloe's rape—however unsuccessful, ultimately—had been an effective demonstration of brute power.

She felt humiliated. Degraded. Cheapened. All of it—all the clichés. Ultimately, she felt scared. If all your preferences could be so casually brushed aside, your most private places exposed and so contemptuously desecrated, how could you ever feel truly at home in your world again?

"Come with me to the dorm," suggested Al Dente with great seriousness. "Just for an hour. I can help."

"Sexual healing." Prue snorted. "Right. Be gentle, Al Dental."

Bibi merely looked sad.

Bibi and Prue had told her she had to go to the police. Ruthie advised her to go back to Vancouver as soon as she could. And that's what Chloe intended. She'd had enough. She would ask the U.S. embassy for advice on who to contact, and she'd send reports of everything she knew about Terdsak and about Tip's disappearance to the newspapers here and in the States.

"Half of us have been raped," said Ruthie, ignoring the fact that Chloe had taken pains to say she *hadn't* been raped. "Did you know that? Maybe more." She dipped into a oily newspaper sack of sand-roasted chestnuts she'd bought from a vendor on the road outside. It was her turn to cook, and she was playing one-for-you-and-one-for-me with the salad she was constructing. "In a lot of cases it happens in the family. Fathers rape their own daughters. It happens all the time. They want to show us how defenseless we are, that we exist only to be dominated. And then we repress it all because, you know, it's just too much."

Ruthie had dealt herself in as a rape victim, maybe on the theory that misery loved company. It was helping, in fact, not least simply because these ideas were so diverting.

"Your father raped you?" asked Chloe.

"My father was a fucking alcoholic."

"Oh, *NO*." said Bibi. "Did he beat your MOTHER all the TIME and *EVERYTHING*?"

"No. He drank all the time. He just didn't give a shit. Not about my mother, not about me. We could do anything we wanted, as far as he was concerned. No, but I know all about being raped, don't you worry." Ruthie revealed she had undergone past-life regression, never mind your age regression, in search of incestuous rape scenes. "It's happened to me more than once. People like us are survivors," Ruthie assured Chloe. "We've been wounded, but it makes us stronger." She cracked a chestnut in her teeth and offered Chloe the meat.

"My first husband and I had a game," Prue reported. "To tell the truth, I was the one who enjoyed it—I had to talk him into playing. Left to his own devices, he would've stuck to plain vanilla bonking, letting me get on top when he was tired."

Chloe imagined Waylon playing at rape. It would be nothing but "Aw, c'mon, eh?" and "Sorry, eh?" She chuckled. Then she began shaking. To her embarrassment she started to cry again, and Prue moved to hug her gently. "That sleazy son of a bitch. There was nothing I could do. He could've done anything he wanted to me. Anything. He could have killed me." Even Ruthie put a hand out to touch her shoulder, and Bibi yelled, "EXCELLENT! Just let it all *OUT*."

"It's funny," said Prue. "Husband number three loved to play at rape, though he never really hurt me. Of course he wasn't very strong, and one night when I really wasn't kidding—I didn't want to fuck—I beat him up. I think that was the beginning of the end for our marriage. Not that it was any real loss."

"Now they've got this little HYDRAULIC THINGIE to cure *IMPOTENCE*," said Bibi. "*WAY* OUTRÉ. If *EVERY* MAN had to have one installed BY LAW, then MAYBE we could ALSO use it to cure *POTENCE*." She looked confused for a minute, and then giggled.

"That's right," Prue responded. "Then all we'd need is a remote control for the thing. Every man would get the thingie installed, and every woman would get a universal remote control."

"EXCELLENT," said Bibi. Then she looked at Freddie and shut up.

Chloe got to thinking about fantasy and rape and control and Prue beating her husband up. And then she thought about Freddie. How was what had happened to her different from what Terdsak and his men had done to Freddie? In both cases, Terdsak had made it clear to his victims and to anyone in the vicinity that their bodies and wills were nothing but foils for the exercise of his power. He had a point to make, and they were the audio-visual aids. With Chloe, Terdsak had wanted her to know—had wanted everyone to know—that her destiny was his to dispose of. If he wanted to smear her with his seed, he would. If he wanted to kill her, he could. And he had used Freddie in the same way.

Chloe felt a pang of sorrow. Who had been there to offer Freddie solace? He was a man, and men, traditionally, were the rapists, not the victims. His had been more of a sexual assault than hers, in a way. Terdsak had struck right at Freddie's balls. She felt fear and self-pity give way to sorrow and concern for Freddie, and for Tip, and it felt better. All the hugs and tears had helped as well, even if she was embarrassed for herself.

And she was hungry. She wolfed a huge bowl of Ruthie's five-bean salad with chestnuts and brown rice, while talk mercifully turned to other matters.

"This is *good*," Chloe said.

Ruthie took her glasses off for a moment and tried not to look pleased. Then she slid the spectacles back on and went all stern. "It's full of vitamins," she replied.

After lunch, at Chloe's suggestion, she and Prue went looking for Freddie.

There was no sign of him as they approached the old chedi. "Freddie?" Prue called. Then she yelled: "Freddie? For Christ's sake."

They walked into the clearing, and Chloe felt a gentle tug at her leg. Her first thought was that it was another wait-a-minute thorn. Then she jumped at a sudden crash and tinkle of broken glass. She had tripped a booby trap of sorts—an early warning alarm consisting of a cotton sheet full of old bottles and cans suspended in a tree from a tripwire.

"Shh! Shhh! Shit, man." Freddie materialized beside them. He had black mud on his face and wore an elaborate headdress of vines and grass and a couple of flowers. "Quiet! Is anybody fuckin' following you? Shit, man. Be careful, okay? You never know. Come on, let's *go*."

They took off their flip-flops to follow Freddie through a little stream for about fifty yards before taking a series of paths that eventually took them all the way back to the clearing with the chedi.

"I live here now. My safe house, man. Got ghosts all around. Shit. Nobody's gonna bother me here."

"Freddie." Chloe was afraid of saying too much. "Are you okay?"

"No problem, man. They thought they had me. The Powers That Be. They thought they had old Freddie." He ran in a quick circle, flipping his tattered cape of many tapes up behind him. Then he stopped, reached down to arrange his parts and, untypically, looked directly into Chloe's eyes. "They're going to try again. But Fast Freddie's ready, man. Ready to ride and there's no place to hide. Freddie is going to *have* their fuckin' hides, man." He was jabbing both forefingers in the direction of the 4H Club.

"They shot Pup. Can you fucking believe that? They shot *Pup*, man." His eyes rolled back and he made a strangled sound. Chloe realized he was crying. "And they've got Tip."

"We've got to go to the police."

"No! No, man. Are you, like, *crazy*? Or what? No, no. No fuckin' police. Shit, man. They're part of it."

"So what are we going to do?"

"What are we going to do? We're going to fuck them up, man. What do you think we're going to do?"

The shadow of the papaya tree stretched all the way across the sala floor to where Al Dente sat, and Chloe was shocked to realize how long she'd been meditating. Her mind was quiet, a current of anticipation running beneath the surface. She was breaking new ground. She could feel it. She was at the center of a preternatural calm, aware of herself in sharp focus.

But something was happening way out on the far edges of her field of vision. Light. Eddies of soft light rippled and played. She kept her head tilted forward slightly and her eyes half open, unfocused, directed at a point directly ahead and about four feet in front of her. Checking to see that indeed she wasn't focused, that the image was properly blurred, she was nonplused to find that she couldn't find the image. She noted this strange fact without any real alarm, and then experimented, deliberately trying to focus. Only she couldn't. Light registered in some weird, disorganized way. But she couldn't make sense of it. It was as though everything had been digitally decomposed, the way they sometimes do with faces on TV talk shows. But more so.

Chloe was blind and yet she wasn't. She wasn't as frightened as she should have been. She experimented, waving her hands, which she couldn't see, in front of her face and moving her head around. The abnormal calm and mental acuity were still with her. She should have been in a panic, but here she was experimenting with what might be a brain tumor, for all she knew, and she was still in a state of wonder over the mystery she had just experienced.

She had to find some way to tell Tip, and Prue, and the Rev. She had really felt it: a sense of the sacred, a feeling of oneness with a living, breathing universe. If she could somehow hold on to this knowledge, she thought, her whole life would be transformed. She was as amazed at her own reaction as she was at the experience itself. The great cynic. Blown away by a moment of satori.

She remembered the Rev telling Al Dente something, when he had claimed similar enlightenment: "Congratulations. Hold on to it. Just remember: it's easy enough to find a sense of the sacred here, in this kind of place, when basically all you've got to do is sit around and wait for it. The trick is finding that sense of oneness and peace and clarity when the shit is hitting the fan. Try to remember that after you leave here and go back to living your normal life."

But didn't her current situation qualify as a shit-storm? She'd just been raped. And she'd pretty well decided to pack up and leave just as soon as she could get to an airport.

Except that she'd made promises to Tip. And could she simply leave, not knowing what had happened to her? What she should do is go back to Bangkok as soon as possible and ask the advice of the American and Canadian embassies. Surely they'd know what to do. She could notify the English-language newspapers, as well. Then, after she got back to Vancouver, she'd write a story based on everything she knew. God knows she had enough material in her notebooks already, the ones that were safely stashed away with Prue's stuff.

But right now there was this other matter, this going effectively blind and all. She resumed her breathing exercises, at the same time trying to fix in her memory all the symptoms in case she had to tell a doctor about it. What did a brain tumor feel like? With this thought, a squall of anxiety riffled her equanimity.

Finally, she didn't know how much later, her sight returned. Just like that. And she felt a surge of exhilaration together with a profound sense of *déjà vu*. She was congratulating herself and thinking this must be a sign of real progress. Although surely it was too soon. She had only started meditating a month before, and not very seriously at that. Things couldn't be that easy.

So she thought this and she thought that, and then she had this sudden impression that someone had brought an ax down on top of her skull, cleaving it right through the middle to somewhere just between her eyes. The pain was shocking in its intensity.

Back in the dorm, Chloe was not enjoying all the fuss from Prue and Bibi. This had to be how it feels to have a brain tumor, she thought. It was so bad she felt sick to her stomach.

Prue was reviewing the horrible psychic phenomena that can emerge in the course of meditation practice, and said this was almost certainly a migraine. "I've been getting migraines for years, so I know what it's like. What you've got sounds like the classic syndrome. The hallucinations—the visual auras and so on. In my own experience, the main triggers seem to be chocolate, which I love, and my second husband, a guy I never really cared for. Sometimes my period sets them off. I've heard the moon affects some people. Whatever. Mine come just about every month. My God, they can be awful. The only thing that ever helped, aside from massive doses of painkiller, was yoga. Once, I went for more than a year without a real migraine. But sometimes I think it must've been my yoga instructor, this totally hunky Rumanian, because after he disappeared the headaches came back, no matter how much yoga I did."

"I thought I was making progress."

"You are, Chloe. You are. Yes. This might be a very good sign." Gorgi, making a rare visit to the dorm, was chirping. "That is right. Yes." He went on to explain that her meditation had probably touched upon some deep complication in her psyche, and the problem could be worked out through continued mindful explorations. "So. You are making progress. *Atcha*. That will be fifty baht. Hah! No. Only fooling.

"By the way," Gorgi added, "I checked and I believe you are wrong—my calculations show that you must have been born on the dark moon. Are you sure it was the full moon?"

"I was only joking."

"I see. It is not good to joke about these things. *Atcha*. You are wearing a mistuned amulet." Shaking his head sadly, Gorgi left.

"But this is AMAZING." Bibi offered her enthusiastic endorsement. "It's GREAT. You're so LUCKY. This means something is HAPPENING and you should be so *HAPPY*."

Her very first rape—almost, anyway—and now her first migraine. Oh, boy. Chloe wanted to tell Bibi to take her headlines and get the hell out of there, but she meant well, even if her every word was driving spikes into Chloe's forebrain.

"Take these Panadols," Prue said, "and lie down. Let me close the curtains. The best thing is sleep. I know the pain can be scary. But try to relax. It'll pass. When you wake up you should feel fine." A dissenting note was struck by a rooster who, oblivious to the fact it was late afternoon and not the crack of dawn or an hour before that, started crowing right outside the window behind Chloe. "Oh, *NO*," yelled Bibi in what was probably meant to be soothing tones. "That's AMAZING. And just when you *REALLY* need peace and QUIET."

Now she understood how Meredith must have felt when she experienced one of the migraines Chloe had so often secretly disparaged, figuring they were little more than a bid for attention and sympathy. A pain in the ass. She couldn't believe that Meredith was still in the vipassana center. She really wished she could talk to her. The pain was killing. And to think how she'd responded with little

329

more than contempt to Meredith's suffering. She also thought of Waylon, of how solicitous he'd been of Meredith's episodes.

"I had some really strong headache pills in my stash," said Prue. "But they're gone. Somebody cleaned me out—coffee and everything."

"My notebooks, Prue." Chloe didn't want to hear this. "What about my notebooks?"

"God. I guess they're gone too. I'm sorry."

Finally all Chloe's well-wishers left. She couldn't sleep. She didn't even try meditating, although for once mindfulness was both easy and unwelcome. So she was lying in the dark feeling sorry for herself, sorry for Merry, and even sorry for Waylon and herself, when the door to the dorm opened and she moaned, pulling the pillow over her face.

"Shut the door, for God's sake," she said. "The light's killing me."

She heard footsteps approach her cot, two people, and she was about to open her eyes to see who it was when she was grabbed. Someone wrestled a bag over her head at the same time she felt a needle prick her arm.

41 dreamtime

*The armored cars of dreams,
contrived to let us do
so many a dangerous thing.*

Elizabeth Bishop

"Take your dress off."

"Wait. *Wait.* Can't we. . . ?"

"Take it *off.*" Terdsak grabbed the front of Chloe's cotton sundress and ripped downward. The dress had cost something like ten dollars on the beach and the catches at the back snapped without further ado.

"Please don't. I'm *married.*" Even to Chloe's ears this was a surprising appeal, at this juncture. It had little effect, in any case. Terdsak whacked her across the face in much the way you might smack a balky vending machine. Chloe sickened at the shock of it. He yanked again, hauling the dress to her waist and pulling Chloe forward into the expensive scent of his cologne. A big gold pendant like Roy Schuter's medallion hung from his neck. She tried to push away, but her wrists tangled in the armholes. She was wearing a bra because the guidebooks had told her it was polite to wear a bra in Thailand. This son of a bitch should respect that, she thought. A pathetic plea for mercy.

Terdsak put one hand on her shoulder and plunged the other into her cleavage. He tugged hard. Her breasts came free from the frilly cups that hooked together at the front, one of them stained red with blood from where Terdsak's rings had scratched her. Panting with the fury of his resolve and the effort of undressing a large American woman, he pulled the shoulder straps down. "Whore!" he said.

"Take your dress off." Terdsak, calmer now, was unbuttoning his shirt. "Now! Take *everything* off."

It was hot. Sweat poured down her face, down her breasts and tummy and into her panties. Chloe freed her arms from the dress, thinking about what she'd been taught in the community center self-defense class. She measured the kick to Terdsak's crotch. She also remembered what the instructor had told them about men with guns who'd been kicked in the balls. A team of bodyguards with guns had to make you even more thoughtful. "My God, aren't you hot?" she asked Terdsak. He didn't respond except to look into her face. What he read there as she mulled over the alternatives, evidently, he didn't much care for. He stepped back, rebuttoned his trousers and opened the door to the hallway.

"One!" he called. "Zero! Ten. Come here."

The two bodyguards appeared in the doorway.

"You," he said, meaning Chloe. "You like my friend? One. And Zero? They like you, *na*? Hey, Zero. One. You want some of this?"

Zero was staring at her breasts. He wiped at his mouth with the back of one hand. Intricate blue tattoos ran down both arms and the back of each hand. She could see more at the collar of his T-shirt. The other thug fondled his crotch, tugged at the front of his pants even as he stared at hers. There were gold rings with big stones on four fingers and the thumb. The fingernail on his right pinkie extended a good inch and a half beyond the fingertip. Then she saw that all of his fingernails were long, like talons, and painted red.

"Take your clothes off now. Everything. We want to see."

She didn't want this to be happening. Sick with horror, she willed it not to be happening. With a profound sense of not wanting to be who she was, where she was right then, she stepped out of the dress, a bright crumple of orange and yellow on the floor, and hooked her thumbs in the waistband of her panties. She had bought those panties at the same time as she got the bra, a few days before the trip. She wanted this to be a dream. She thought about screaming, thinking it might wake her up.

"This is my country. These people are my people. Mine, *na*? You are mine. I can do anything with you. Understand? Anything I want. I can fuck you. I can give you to my men. I can have you *killed*. Understand? You are mine and I can do anything I want with you. After, maybe I will sell you." Terdsak then instructed his men to leave the room and, clearly disappointed, they obeyed. Just for a moment, Chloe was surprised at Terdsak's new command of English. And, just for an instant, he reminded her of Roy Schuter. But other matters soon demanded her full attention.

There was no air-conditioning, but the bed was big and comfortable. There wasn't much physical pain. What hurt was the humiliation. And it promised to get worse. A nasty, soul-destroying panic lurked just out of mind, threatening some final negation of her person, a nightmare from which she willed herself to awake. Terdsak reared back so he could see, straight-armed, gold chains clunking at his chest. He sneered, and Chloe's fear turned to rage. She twisted to one side, trying to snap him off at the root. Then she twisted the other way. She pummeled him with her fists, but he only thrust harder. Abruptly, she began to pump back in rhythm, banging him, wanting to smash him, her whole body a weapon, a blunt object with which to batter the bastard to death. Suddenly, then—shockingly—she was coming.

Gradually the confusion of fury and lust subsided and the humiliation returned, compounded with shame and wonder at the self-betrayal. Terdsak lay atop, sweat pooling between them. The sheets were soaked. Chloe brushed sweat from her eyes. And tears. Now she was angry at her tears. Terdsak laughed. "I have a job for you," he said. "You will like this."

Then Chloe woke up. It had been a nightmare. Waylon was laughing softly and wiping at her tears. A warm glow suffused her whole person, washing away the shame and hurt. Roy Schuter was there in the bedroom as well and Waylon didn't seem to mind. Chloe was so relieved. Meredith was there too. She was holding a baby.

Chloe's relief gave way to horror as she awakened again, this time for real, to realize she was trapped in a nightmare after all.

When she had first awakened from the drugs, she found herself in a car. She still had the bag over her head, but she knew from the motion and the engine noise they were also on a boat.

After they arrived, she realised she was on an island—the island where they'd had the dark moon party. The bag was removed and she was given a tour. She recognized the guard tower at one end of the bay. Later, she was taken here and locked in this cell. She was alone, with the dying light of day filtering in through a grate about eight feet from the floor. She thought she could move the bed and stand on it to look outside. The concrete cell had a rusty cot with a thin mattress and a single blanket. There was no electric light. A tin pot stood on the floor under the cot. Other than that, the decor consisted of a cheap throw-rug and a framed print in garish colors of three kittens playing with balls of yarn. Chloe had never before felt this alone.

This was no dream, although she tried, just for a moment, to convince herself it was. This was a nightmare, and it was the worse for her utterly lucid sense that she was participating in it and that no amount of wishing would change that.

After they removed her hood, Terdsak subjected her to an interrogation. "Why you ask question too mutt? Want know about my bisnet. Why?"

Among other things, Chloe had written about the four girls Tip had mentioned, the ones who had died in a fire, chained to a wall in the back room of one of Terdsak's brothels.

"Two year, my manager in court," Terdsak said. "Two *year.* Pay ninety thousand baht each *guh. I* pay. Each *guh* police can see who she is. Two *guh.* Must give family ninety thousand baht. Four thousand dollar. Too mutt, *na*? Usually only ten, fifteen thousand baht. Why for me ninety thousand? Why? Manager no good. Not take care. Should not have fire. After I pay for *guh,* manager finit. You know? *Finit.* This is good bisnet. Cut loss, *na?*"

But no problem, he wanted Chloe to know. The Thai Natural Trends Party Complex, otherwise known as TNT, was constructed of very good materials. They wouldn't burn. And there was a sprinkler system. "Sometime big customer here. Fire no good."

So, Chloe supposed, it was safe to have girls chained in back rooms all you wanted. But she didn't say this.

Terdsak was fed up with nosy reporters, he told her. "Friend you, the nun, *na*? Sell. Get money too mutt. Soldier from Kampuchea. You know Khmer Rouge? He like *pooying* reporter *maak, maak.* Like too mutt, *na?*" Terdsak put his hand on Chloe's shoulder in a companionable manner. They were old pals, after all. Hey, they'd even almost fucked right there in the middle of a nightclub. After all. Chloe shuddered and moved away. Terdsak stepped over to her and grabbed one of her breasts, squeezing till she gasped. "Thai *guh* not have. Have *nit noi.* Small too mutt," he said, letting go of her.

He had also seen the story of his life with Olga in Chloe's confiscated notebooks. Gorgi or someone had read it to him. And Terdsak let Chloe know he knew she knew he had killed men before. He preened himself in the knowledge that she knew it. "I want you know who I am," he said.

Zero had brought the Benz to the door, and they drove the half mile to the other side of the TNT Complex. Terdsak told Chloe about how he had brought his car to this island on his boat, a converted war surplus landing craft, and how it was an important part of his face. He had even had the old track from one side of the island to the other widened and surfaced for his car, the only one on the island. "Is Benz. Now customer know who I am."

First, Terdsak had showed her around the more public side of the Complex.

Behind the main buildings there was something that at first sight looked like a kiddies' zoo, with several deer in a pen, an aviary full of various exotic fowl, a monkey house, again with a number of species in evidence, and a fenced-in pit with three tigers. There were also a couple of sheds. One of them was full of snakes, most of them cobras, some of them three or four yards in length. Another held bears in cages. A third shed concealed a shiny stainless-steel and glass processing operation that could turn a snake, for example, into prepared and packaged venom, bile, blood, meat and skin products within seconds. A bear or a tiger took longer, Terdsak told her, but not much longer. Chloe sickened at the medley of hideous smells and sights. "Good bisnet, *na*?" Terdsak was beaming.

They explored the main buildings, entering a large restaurant through a white-columned portico—the whole installation a total anomaly on this otherwise deserted island. The restaurant itself was empty, with the chairs and a cash register still covered in plastic wrap. There was a fine film of dust on everything. Private rooms with glassed windows looked on to a main dining area, opulent with plaster cupids, plastic plants in big ornate vases, and large framed Chinese landscapes painted on fabric. Terdsak and Ten swept her through this part of the Complex without stopping and without comment. But a hidden door at the back took them into another class of establishment altogether.

One enormous room on three levels—two of them dining areas with tables and chairs—surrounded a pit on three sides, arena style. Everything, even the walls, was upholstered in red, black, and purple velour, and crystal chandeliers dangled from a thirty-foot ceiling with a huge painting of a large-breasted blonde woman doing her rendition of Venus on the half-shell, a tropical sunset for a backdrop. Terdsak had probably been inspired by the Sistine Chapel. Windows looked out the back towards the warehouses and the boat pier on the other side of the island. Two enormous picture windows afforded views of Phra Chan Island and, this evening, dense constellations of lights where scores of boats bobbed at anchor and the bonfires and fireworks on the beach. Somewhere over there, Chloe assumed, the others from the 4H Club were worrying about her.

As Terdsak pointed out, the glass was one way—you got a nice view, but outsiders didn't get to enjoy the show inside. All around the walls, including between the windows, deep niches the height of a person stood empty at the top of wrought-iron ladders.

They drove back to where the darker side of Terdsak's operation lay on a deep cove on the opposite side of Phra Chan Noi. Each of the headlands flanking the cove was equipped with a guard tower. In the center of the cove there was a pier with a small crane and a few buildings, boxy concrete constructions that looked much like warehouses, which is what they were. The fanciest of these was where Chloe's tour had begun.

The TNT Complex was a series of surprises within surprises, a Russian doll of a crime king's hideout. They began with a tour of the front building, a two-story shop. On the top floor, floor-to-ceiling shelves were covered with ceramic figurines—elephants and clowns, dolphins, little castles like the ones you put in fishtanks, and dozens of half-life-size Spunkies, silly little dogs sitting up and begging with their tongues hanging out. Downstairs was a showroom for the sort of herbal products Gorgi and Terdsak had shown her at the 4H Club.

"'McMeditator.' Gorgi like this name. I like *douay*, *na*? Good writer. Too bad not have respect."

Thai Natural Trends Inc. was the working name for Terdsak's umbrella company, Chloe discovered. Affiliated concerns were to include McMeditators, the planned chain of New Age centers, and Herbal Happiness, which would market everything from mixes for colonic irrigation fluids to skin creams, herbal medicines, and electronic amulets.

Of course illicit drugs were anathema to McMeditators. On the other hand, Terdsak had ruthlessly established a monopoly on selling drugs at the full moon parties. "Better only one person sell. Must have control. This is important, *na*? If no control, only con-few-*shon*. Fighting too mutt. Soon have high profile. High profile too mutt. Bad bisnet. Not good for everybody." Sometimes other people saw there was money to be made selling these things, Terdsak told her, but E-go would take a few of his men and show these people how it was better for them to do business some place else. "This is good bisnet," Terdsak said. "But not mix. Not have drugs at Institute. Must always lay your best. Lay off, *na*? How you say? Always put egg in many basket. Ha, ha."

Terdsak was a real businessman, someone who thought in terms of diversification and balance. The 4H Club had to remain drug free, but Terdsak supplied the full moon parties. He dealt in endangered species and in slaves, yet he had an orphanage and made a big deal about contributions to temples.

In back of the shop there was a warehouse, with crates of ceramic figurines, as well as a workshop complete with kilns, power tools, and all the material needed to make or repair pottery. The workers, Terdsak told her, were mostly Burmese. "Cheap," he explained with tangible satisfaction, smiling benignly at his personnel, who ranged in age from about eight years to eighty. A couple of them smiled back—especially one toothless crone who grinned and cackled as though Terdsak were her favorite nephew. The others kept their eyes down, intent on their work.

Terdsak was anxious for Chloe to understand how diverse and how balanced his interests really were. "Make good arrangement. Sell nice ganja to Canada. Then some—how you say?—bear bile come Thailand. You know how much, bear bile one hundred gram? One kilo rhino horn from India, *na*? Pay thirty thousand dollar in Taiwan. More. Soup from tiger *pee-nut*, one bowl, can get four hundred dollar. One bowl, *na*? But most time only man in middle. Understand?

"You, you!" The crone had been following them and was now plucking at Terdsak's belt. He put the guided tour on pause for a moment, while E-go and Ten encouraged the lady to go back to work.

"Good bisnet, *na*? Many egg, many basket. And double up, double up." So Terdsak would have some things to ship. Maybe some diesel fuel at a good price—tax rates were a sin and his customers were very happy if they didn't have to pay them. It was only good business. These vessels looked like old fishing boats, but they were really tankers: "Carry mutt oil. Other thing, too. *Pooying*, sometimes. *Guh*. Ha, ha. Smartass *guh*. And old statue, people pay money too mutt."

It was the same with the jungle food restaurant. After the various bits of bear and tiger and deer meat were consumed, everything from the bones to various internal organs could be dried and ground up and sold to medicine shops around Asia and America.

Terdsak pulled on a white plaster Venus de Milo with smudged breasts, and a storage shelf mounted on a heavy steel door swung away to reveal another room. One side of the floor was stacked with cases of what seemed to be a variety of herbal whiskies. There were also about two dozen big drums marked DANGER: GASOLINE, FLAMMABLE. Probably for the Benz. More interestingly, Chloe saw rank upon rank of Buddha images, broken-off heads and hands. Richly carved stone lintels. Most of the artifacts were stone, though some were wood or earthenware. One shelf held a selection of the ceramic figures from the other room, even sillier here, next to these sacred objects.

"These are all genuine?"

"Real. Old, *douay*. Some from Thailand. Some from Kampuchea. From Laos. Vietnam. Many people pay mutt money. Old pot, old plate. Little statue. Head from statue. Old. People like old thing. But have other bisnet. Hee, hee. Not here. Make stone statue, and wood. Look old same-same. But not." He explained that it was better to sell fakes, since then people didn't always have to pay so much for them. At the same time, the genuine articles could stay in their temples and in their own countries, and there was less temptation to sell off your national heritage. "Better like this, *na*?"

Terdsak had been carrying on like a regular patron of the arts. Now, with great pride, he revealed an even bigger surprise. Another concealed passage led them to the largest depot of all. And it was packed with weapons and ammunition. Terdsak was a true renaissance man. A patron of the arts and a gun-runner too. Chloe was impressed, and Terdsak was pleased that she was impressed. Some of the stuff had U.S. ARMY stenciled on the cases, and looked as though it had been abstracted during the Vietnam War. But there were more modern materials as well: cases upon cases of bullets, anti-personnel and anti-tank mines, grenades, mortar rounds, and rockets. Cases of rifles, machine guns, mortar tubes, rocket launchers, maybe a ton or two of dynamite, and blasting caps. There was even a store of fireworks—roman candles, pinwheels, skyrockets and suchlike, not to mention a whole bunch of firecrackers.

"Many people want gun," Terdsak suggested, with the self-righteous satisfaction of one who proposes to put a chicken in every pot. "Bomb *douay*. Rocket. Many thing. Want for many reason. Some people maybe bad people. But some people good. Who can say who is good and who is bad? Have Cambodia fight Cambodia. Karen fight Burma? Have *douay*. Burma fight Burma. Never stop. Who is good and who is bad? Maybe only gods know. But no bad money. Bisnet is bisnet, *na*? Everybody want gun. I sell. Fight and fight and somebody win. Sometimes. This is karma, *na*? This is basic."

The shed next door held one hundred tons of hijacked fertilizer—Terdsak was quite precise about the quantity, which he thought was impressive—and a bunch of drums of fuel oil. Ammonium nitrate fertilizer and diesel in the right proportions, Chloe remembered reading, also made a powerful explosive. This storage facility was only temporary, of course. Eventually, the arms would be stored in a hardened bunker under construction on another island. "Dangerous too mutt, *na*?"

And Chloe could see what he meant, especially when he introduced her to the last feature of the installation. A staircase led beneath the war weapons to a dingy corridor lined either side with windowless doors. He opened one of them, and Chloe saw an attractive brunette in her early twenties. She was dressed in a loose shift and crouched atop a mean cot on the far side of the tiny cell, pressed up against the wall and plainly terrified. Terdsak closed the door again. These were holding cells for new staff, he explained. "Before many. Now have only one here. No, wait. Forget. Now two." He giggled as they showed Chloe to her own cell.

"And have many other *guh douay,*" Terdsak informed her. "Tonight special party. Many special guest. You come, see how I do bisnet." Terdsak turned back to wish her a good night. At his instruction, One tossed her bag into the room, where it landed on the floor at her feet. "Not smoke in bed, *na?*" Terdsak laughed. "Fire no good."

Contemptuous, wanting her to know he felt in no way threatened, Terdsak had returned her notebooks together with her bag. In the remaining light, she read the last note she'd made in her meditation diary, a mix of things Tip and Gorgi had talked about combined with half-digested ideas recalled from flirtations with philosophy at university.

You Are Your World

This world, the one you think of as being "real," is no more real than, is just as illusory as, your dreamworld. On a deeper level, you have to understand that you are not real, in the sense your ego is anything more than the sum of its fleeting perceptions. Your ego is basically just as ephemeral as those perceptions. The distinction between the self and the world is an illusory one. You are one side of the process by which your world is constructed. You are defined by your world even as you define your world.

And so we are dreamed by a world that comes into being according to how we participate collectively in the dreaming. Chloe had lost herself in the circularity of that line of thought. She remembered the Buddha images, carved as they were in different styles from a variety of materials at different times in history, brought here from different lands. These faces—each of them different, yet each of them serene, supremely composed—appeared to Chloe to be dreaming the same dream together, and it was a true one. The roomful of images, if only for a moment, had spoken collectively to her. They spoke of a peace and clarity transcending the trials of getting from one minute to the next in a world gone mad with threat and anger and confusion. But Chloe hadn't been able to hold the vision.

She tried to take command, to exercise the equivalent of lucid dream control with what was passing for real life. This was stupid, she told herself. Yet it helped. If she had to accept what was happening here as really real, then she was going to start screaming, collapse. But then she'd be little good to herself or to Tip or to anybody.

If we all participate in the Great Dreaming of the universe, Chloe thought, then we should have some control over what we think of as our waking life as well as our dreams. But she had no idea what was coming next, only that it was likely to be unpleasant in the extreme, and she could imagine no means of doing anything about it. She was at the mercy of a monster, a whiskey- and drug-addled gangster who was himself out of control, at the mercy of his own demons. What was happening to her was very like a dream, just as arbitrary and irrational. And her attempts to assume control of things were proving just as futile as her experiments in lucid dream control. She was failing the Rev's can-you-be-cool-in-the-shitstorm test.

Prue and Ruthie understood dream control therapy as a matter of behavioral conditioning, a means of existential engineering, ridding yourself of inconvenient fears and complexes. Tip had shown Chloe other dimensions to the discipline. The process of falling asleep, according to Tip, was the closest thing we knew to dying and then returning to awareness in another realm. Dream control was preparation for taking command of your experiences in an alternative existence. And this, ultimately, was practice for when you finally made the crossing from this life to whatever followed. She thought of Tip's courage and that of Tip's husband. These people were able to stare death down because they believed in something more important, something more permanent, than themselves. But what did Chloe believe in? She was afraid of dying, in no way prepared for her passing. She was scared. Scared in a way she had never before imagined being scared.

She discovered she'd been rubbing Gorgi's electronic amulet between her fingers. Some protection. Chloe wouldn't have believed it possible, under the circumstances, but she had finally dozed off. And she dreamed of rape and babies and things.

Only to reawaken to her nightmare.

42 control

*If women didn't exist, all the money
in the world would have no meaning.*

Aristotle Onassis

Chloe recoiled at the stench of decay and despair. The bear in the cage was mad with pain and frustration and deprival. Insects sipped at its eyes, rheumy red and glaring, and the heavy wire mesh of the cage cut into the bear's haunches. The animal had gigantic claws. It scraped at the bars with the one paw it could move and it cried. It made bleating noises that sounded to Chloe like crying. Did animals despair? What went on in the mind of a creature that, from infancy, had known only the confines of this five-by-three-by-three-foot universe? A plastic tube with a little metal tap led to an ulcerated hole in the bear's belly. "Take bile three, maybe four time one week. This bear old too mutt. Six year. Six year in cage. Never come out. Now we see, good to eat?"

"You are monsters. Fucking monsters."

"This is karma. In other life, maybe do bad thing. Now pay. Next life maybe better." Terdsak's laugh was almost joyous. He picked up a liter bottle. "Special dinner tonight. Start with Superman. Thai whiskey with bone from *thai-guh* and special Chinese medicine. And snake blood. Must come from snake when alive. Make you long and strong, *na*? Hee, hee. After, snake go in soup. Is good. Make more delicious with deer horn and *pling thalay*—how you say, 'cucumber of sea'—and other strong food. But everybody wait for bear paw. Come for this. Delicious, *na*? But better when bear hurt. More tender, better taste. And help bear pay for sin, give good life more soon."

"So everybody's happy," said Chloe. If only she kept talking, if she could keep her voice level and her conversation sensible, this would enforce a kind of normalcy on proceedings, such that she would finally be delivered from this nightmare and get to go back to Vancouver and live happily ever after, please God let it be true.

"Do in special way. Customer eat soup and look. Tie bear to bamboo and tell *pooying*, some *guh*, come play with him. They squeeze—how you say?—the egg. Squeeze egg in wood. This hurt too mutt. Then do other thing and finally bear die. Cut off paw and steam. Eat with three sauce. *Aloi*. Delicious too mutt. Customer say our bear paw number one. Good bisnet. I do it my way. Customer pay ten thousand dollar, one bear. Give Superman and soup free. And entertainment."

"Ten thousand dollars? Who pays ten thousand dollars for this?"

"Many people. From China, Vietnam, Laos. From Thailand. From everywhere. From U.S.A. Good service and top product. This is basic."

Chloe got to see the tiger pit again, where three mangy, dispirited beasts yawned toothless yawns and tried to scratch with no claws. "One thai-guh claw, get money too mutt, *na*?" Terdsak said. And he showed her more. There was a room with bottles and jars with mysterious things in them. Dried tiger penis, giant centipedes a good seven inches long, snakes coiled and pickled in grain spirits.

Other objects and liquids that defied description in Terdsak's English. Some of the fringe-element feminists back home reacted to all things longer than they were wide by condemning them. It seemed a lot of men in Asia responded to the same things by putting them in their soup and waiting for long life and much pussy.

She had her notebook in her bag, but she didn't write in it. Maybe if she didn't write anything Terdsak would think it was okay to let her go, finally. But she was trying to remember everything. It was one way to take her mind off the terror, the sense that she was utterly at the mercy of alien forces that could at any moment turn on her in new and unthinkable ways.

They passed the bear on the way back out. Oddly, at what seemed the most inappropriate moment conceivable, Chloe felt a oneness with the creature, a oneness with all of it. The epiphany lent her an abrupt understanding of how everything, animate and inanimate alike, was an expression of a single stream of being that comprehended lives of despair and lives of privilege, the cage and the bear, Chloe and the dried tiger penises, people like Tip and people like Terdsak, this and that, now and then. Everything and everywhen. Before the bear was born and after it was dead.

Only for a moment, things all seemed whole and sensical, everything as it should be. The perception, a profound sense of the sacred, as quickly passed and once again she sickened with horror. She sickened further when Terdsak ran his hand over her bottom and said, "Next time, *na*? You play with bear. Do good job, maybe can eat."

The restaurant was full of people and noise. Tonight, the TNT Complex were hosting a special gala evening. Terdsak was wearing a red silk tie with gold Mercedes-Benz logos all over it, the knot just so and pulled tight to the collar. He had already explained to Chloe that he was going to show something very, very unusual. He was clearly excited.

In the meantime, everybody was to try the herbal whiskies. As a special treat, Terdsak announced in English—English being the lingua franca in this cosmopolitan establishment—he was going to offer, this time only, samples of his own *special* Superman whiskey. In honor of the occasion, everybody had to try his secret elixir. At each place there was also a basket of creams and pills and a complimentary electronic amulet personalized for each guest. Masseuses stood ready to service the customers. A couple of these individuals were Asian, and might have been Thai, Chloe thought, but most were foreign, including a couple of Westerners, a willowy blonde who revealed a British accent, when at one point she exclaimed "No! Please. *Don't*," and a luscious dark beauty with samba hips, maybe from South America. All of them were naked, though none appeared in the least concerned on that account. In fact, none of them seemed much concerned about anything. Given their dull gazes and lethargic manner, Chloe suspected they were drugged.

Women with bottles of Special Superman and not much else, aside from high-heeled shoes and the occasional ankle bracelet or tattoo, moved from table to table dispensing Terdsak's personal elixir.

"You drink," he told Chloe. It was vile, and she managed to leak most of it back into the glass.

"Not be shy. Hee, hee. Take off dress. Be convenient." Chloe wanted to believe he meant "comfortable." In any case, she left her dress where it was.

Terdsak's own masseuse of choice was sitting on his lap and unbuttoning his shirt. She started to remove his tie, but stopped when he told her no. She flipped the tie up over his shoulder and began to smear herbal oil all over his hairless belly and chest, nuzzling his ear at the same time. "See?" He squeezed the girl's breasts, first one and then the other. "Good *guh*. Have respect."

The dinner was designed to entertain Terdsak's customers. As he explained, these included buyers for both artifacts and arms. But it was also meant to introduce the range of products from Thai Natural Trends to bulk buyers as well as those who merely wanted to enjoy "health foods" and herbal medicines themselves. If they preferred, Terdsak would sell them live animals and women. These could be enjoyed on the premises or they were available as take-away. Terdsak told Chloe he had three live bears, two tigers, and an assortment of lesser creatures including king cobras and monkeys. He even had such exotica as pangolins and flying lemurs, if you were really bored and indifferent to the extinction of entire species.

Terdsak's specialties included both exotic game and exotic woman flesh. Also on the take-away menu were three Thai women, a Japanese, four Chinese, four Russians, a Brit, a Venezuelan, and two Americans. "Chinese *guh*, Thai *guh* cheap. Cheap too mutt." Terdsak pronounced "Thai girls" as *thai guh*, which was confusing, given the disturbing images of tigers fresh in Chloe's mind. "But friend you, not same-same. Can get good price. Know market. And one Chinese *guh*, eleven year old. Virgin. Very clean. Very good for old man."

Terdsak believed in efficiency. Some of the Chinese, Thai, and Cambodian women he ran to Japan, for example, doubled as drug mules, with condoms full of heroin stashed wherever these items would conveniently go. The yakuza would unload the carriers and then employ them as prostitutes for as long as it took to repay the cost of buying them and transporting them to Japan. Given the interest rates on these friendly loans, repayment could take a long time indeed. In fact these ladies would be lucky to live that long. The price of the heroin was not deducted from this sum; after all, it really took very little effort on their part, since they were going to Japan anyway. But you had to be careful. Just the month before, one valuable mule had been overloaded, it seemed, and a condom had burst. She had gone into convulsions and died before anybody could do anything. Not only did Terdsak lose what his customers were going to pay for her, he lost his investment in the cargo she was carrying, since the rubber didn't break till she was at the airport.

"No good, *na*?" he told Chloe. It was the same as if one of his fishing boats were to sink complete with cargo of bootleg diesel and stolen artifacts.

Overall, though, things were going well. "Must always want other people be happy. This is rule for life and rule for bisnet. This is *metta*. Want good things for other people. Everybody want something special. Something different. You know? Japanese and American *guh*? I make good money—in dollar, *douay*. Good bisnet. And Russian, many *guh* big, blonde. Expensive, *douay*. Ha, ha."

So was Chloe one of these hot commodities? She was afraid to ask. She was afraid even to think about it. Terdsak had told her much more than she wanted to know. She didn't want to ask why he wasn't worried about her learning too much.

And what about Waylon? He didn't have any idea where she was. How long would he wait before he went to the police? It hardly mattered, since, even if they were interested, the way things were going she would soon be long beyond help. Anyway, for the meantime Terdsak had seemingly forgotten his suggestion that she should get undressed.

The ambient murmur of appreciation changed tenor, swelled to a hubbub. The place filled with rich aromas as attendants laid out plates of deep-fried meat morsels and bowls of steaming soup. Then a perimeter of soft spotlights came up.

The wall niches Chloe had seen earlier in the day were now occupied by living statuary dressed in diaphanous veils and lit to museum standards. Someone, a European man up on the third level, spoke to one of the roving hostesses, who handed him a red laser pointer. He entertained himself, and confused everybody else, by trying to shine the laser in the eyes of two or three different statues, who kept ducking and covering their faces with their hands. Finally he settled on one tall blonde, checking her off with the red spot, more and more violently, until a member of staff got the idea and went to help her down from the niche and led her to the man's table. For a minute, it looked as though he didn't want to give up the laser gun; he wasn't through having fun. Chloe watched as another girl was led into the room and ascended to the wall niche.

Terdsak had been pointing around the room, boyish in his pride and enthusiasm, explaining who everybody was. The guy with the laser was an art dealer from Germany.

The man at the next table, a Malaysian mining baron, was preparing to smoke a fat twelve-inch cigar. The naked girl seated at his feet was the brunette Chloe had seen in the cell beneath the arms cache. She looked heavily sedated.

"E-go," said Terdsak, pleased that his guests could see this Westerner jump to do his bidding. "Light cigar my f'en."

E-go merely stood there. Chloe could almost hear his language-processing machinery grinding and clanking.

"E-go. Give light. Fire! *Fire.*" Terdsak brought out his gold Ronson and gave it to E-go. "You light. Light! *Fire.*"

Terdsak's young companion, meanwhile, had extricated his penis from his pants and was fondling it, maybe trying to cool the godfather off. No one could see this except for Chloe, E-go, the girl, of course, and the men at the next table if they cared to look. Terdsak's cock was mostly flaccid and—something Chloe had not had the opportunity to notice before—its rim was pierced and set with gold studs, seven of them, twenty-four carat, judging by the garish yellow color.

The whole situation was unreal. Chloe found herself slipping over into panic, something like madness. She looked into her soup and saw tentacles. She had to get a grip on herself. She willed her eyes to go unfocused and began breathing with mindfulness. *Rising . . . falling. . . . Rising, falling. Rising, fallingrisingfalling. . . .* Falling towards madness again. She tried counting, inhaling on the odd numbers and exhaling on the even: *One . . . two. . . . Three . . . four. . . . Five . . . six. . . .*

Her eyes, despite her efforts, focused, and they were focused on Selene. It was the girl from the day-after-the-dark-moon party, the one with the mushrooms. She was dressed the same way she had been on the beach, but now she appeared even more fey. When she moved, she also looked as though she'd been drugged. She stood beside the table of an individual with an ugly scar that gave him both a hare lip and a cleft chin, an otherwise boyish looking Cambodian arms dealer who pulled her down on his lap and whispered in her ear. Her expression, or lack of expression, didn't change. Her only response was to kneel by his chair and then start fumbling in his crotch, face against his thigh. He grinned and said something to his dinner companions, who laughed.

"Many *guh*, get from hospital," said Terdsak. "Tourist sometime take drug too mutt, *na*?" He signaled for another glass of his special medicine, and watched while a new bottle was broached. Zero poured a little into a glass and swirled it, savoring the bouquet. Then he sipped at it, rolling it around his palate before swallowing. He nodded, his eyes red and staring, and poured a larger dose into Terdsak's glass. Chloe wondered how many samples Zero had already tasted. Terdsak indicated Zero should dispense the rest to neighboring tables.

"Other *guh*, some *guh*, they do drug bisnet. On my island. *Mai dee*, *na*? Big mistake. And three Russian *guh*, they come my country be prostitute. Not pay tax. Nothing. Not help Thailand. Work for me better. Many *guh* have no paper, *na*? Nobody know *guh* in Thailand. No problem for me. Another Russian is tourist; but no problem. In hospital for crazy people, take drug too mutt. Big doctor, my friend, say have good *guh* for me, tourist all alone, no friend. She okay now. Quiet. Buyer speak Russian cannot, *na*? So not know if *guh* crazy or only Russian. No problem."

Chloe wasn't sure if it was her, or whether it was everybody else. But things were going a little weird. As though the tape were running at the wrong speed. Maybe a touch fast. And the Indonesian arms dealer had taken to aiming down his cigar at her, grinning and jabbing it in her direction.

"Have many customer, like something different. Something strange make them pum-pum too much, *na*? They like foreign *guh*. Even you. Old, but smart. Writer. My friend, some like that. Some customer, my friend, they like Thai *guh* too. But they like Thai *guh* who is reporter, *douay*. Or environmental person. Make trouble too mutt. And smart. Number one is writer and smartass, also beautiful. More nice teach respect. How to behave."

"My husband knows where I am. Lots of people know where I am. You wouldn't get away with it."

"No problem," said Terdsak. He was thinking of auctioning Chloe, he told her, just the way he'd already done with Tip. Or the Indonesian arms dealer would probably buy her. "Need new *guh* every month. Have—how you say?—special need." Terdsak was also thinking he could rent her to some people to play with "shorttime," and then dispose of her. Terdsak told her all about the full moon parties. "Good bisnet. Sell many thing, make many people happy. And I send men to hunt. Find *guh* for TNT, and sometimes boy. Always give customer what they want. Is good bisnet. And find people carry some thing when they go other country." He pointed out through the front windows, across to Phra Chan Island, where Chloe could see bonfires, an occasional roman candle or flare going up. "Tonight have party. At full moon party, sometime, people take drug too mutt. How you say? OD, *na*? Freak out. Hee, hee. Sometime fisherman, they find dead people in water. Other people go in hospital for crazy people. Take mushroom too mutt, maybe other thing *douay*. Bad for brain. You get the concept? Husband no problem. Police no problem."

He was speaking in such reasonable tones—the model of the prim, self-congratulatory businessman—it was hard to believe he was actually threatening her life. Right there at the table while a naked girl played with his penis.

A flash of acute anxiety, an electric jolt of paranoia penetrated the shocked numbness. She found herself imagining life in Vancouver with Waylon and Meredith and. . . . What? A blank, an existential hole where she ought to be. She tried to imagine life going on without her and she started to feel like crying again. This was ridiculous. She was on a holiday. Where had things started to go wrong? Waylon, that knucklehead, had been full of gloomy prognostications about the trip and she'd been so impatient. She'd really been thinking about divorce. Now it turns out he'd been right. Although that was ridiculous; he shouldn't have been right. People just don't go on a vacation and have this sort of thing happen to them. She wasn't even sure what it was that was happening. Only that it was terrifyingly dangerous.

She could see the myriad lights of boats in the bay on Phra Chan Island. Just a mile or two away, thousands of people were drinking and dancing and screwing in the sand, careless of the morrow. Were the others from the 4H Club there? Surely they were wondering what had happened to her. Would they have notified the police? Would that do any good? Tip, for one, had suggested it would not.

Terdsak was also looking at the lights. He had E-go hand him the cellphone, and he punched a number, listened, and tried again twice more, getting more upset with each try. "E-go," he said. "Boat late. No answer mobile. You check, *na*? Boat must come. Must have Buddha tonight. *Tonight, na*?"

On the drinks trolley beside their table, a rag doll lay atop a tissue box done up as a little quilted silk bed. Terdsak was ripping tissues from the doll's bosom, quick bright eviscerations, to wipe at himself. This was his own special dispenser. The other diners tore spirals of toilet paper from frilly dispensers on the tables. Bones, bits of gristle, greasy little balls of tissue paper littered the tables. The slurpings and smackings were punctuated by an occasional *be-dang* as one of the diners spat a rib or knuckle bone into a brass spittoon.

"*Oishi!*"

"*Aloi!*"

"Delicious!"

Terse testimonials to the quality of the fare in five languages or more issued from lips slick with grease. From outside came the bark and howl of dogs scenting the carnal orgy.

"E-go, check dog," said Terdsak. "What kind of dog? How we know somebody come when dog bark, bark every time? Make quiet."

Chloe was surprised to hear Terdsak give such elaborate instructions to E-go. Maybe the Russian had been doing intensive English studies in the past day or two. But E-go didn't so much as hesitate. "Sip! Come," he said, and he took One and Zero outside. There was a sudden stutter of shots, a yelp, a howl and then another volley. The barking stopped. The diners had stopped too, but only for a moment; then they went back to the feast. E-go and Ten returned.

"E-go, you shoot dog. This is yes?" Terdsak was passing his left hand back and forth over the flame of his lighter and speaking his most careful English.

"*Da, da*. Shoot."

"E-go. You not have the concept. How can dog guard some place when dog is dead?" To Chloe he said: "Now I think I shoot E-go, good idea. But dead security chief cannot guard anything *douay, na*?" Terdsak gave something like a laugh. "They go out and watch." Terdsak indicated that E-go should deploy four of his other men. "E-go. Sip. You stay."

A sudden bustle of activity saw the tables mostly cleared, including Chloe's bowl of biological specimens, and each table was set anew with plates of charred animal bits. Some of these, she learned, were bear paws. She wouldn't have guessed, if Terdsak hadn't told her. He tried a piece, smacking his lips loudly and looking askance at his Venus on the ceiling as though consulting some gastronomical muse. Then he turned to Chloe: "Here. You try."

She tried to keep her lips shut, but he was insistent. To her, it tasted like grilled meat. No more than a vehicle for the sauces. It might just as well have been beef or pork, and they could have spared the creature all the pain.

The Musak abruptly gave way to sweetly discordant Oriental music. The lights dimmed and one of the wall niches lit up to display what was described by a staff member as an eighth-century Khmer *apsara* in sandstone, originally from the Angkor area of Cambodia. The bare-breasted figure almost danced from the stone, such had been the genius of her creator. Spirited bidding quickly pushed the price up to twenty thousand dollars, and an Indian-looking man had the figure brought to his table so he could examine it more closely with magnifying glass and flashlight. He decided against bidding higher, and a Westerner with a German accent soon picked it up for a mere twenty-two thousand.

The lights came up again long enough for everyone to have sherbet and champagne, and then they dimmed again to another change of soundtrack. Some seventies disco music heralded a procession led by a muscular man in shorts and leather vest holding a coiled whip. Following him was another man, similarly dressed, who led a statuesque redhead into the pit at the end of a fine golden chain attached to a neck ring. The woman was attired in a white veil, a gold anklet, and a gorgeous big frangipani blossom behind one ear. Tip had told Chloe that in Thailand the frangipani was known as the flower of sorrow. Somebody started to clap and another followed his lead, but only briefly. One of the audience hawked and spat into a cuspidor. Terdsak barked, and an attendant unveiled the merchandise. The redhead, to everyone's delight, had a generous red bush to match her hair. The auction began at ten thousand dollars American. An Indonesian logging tycoon and a Taiwanese shipping magnate were soon engaged in a bidding war. Chloe couldn't see the Taiwanese too clearly, in the dim light. She could only hear his calm and implacable bids.

"Forty thousand dollars," he said. The bid was repeated, more loudly, by one of Terdsak's staff. The Indonesian looked pissed off in the way you look when you don't want to look pissed off in a way anybody can see it. "Fifty thousand," he responded.

"He's going to pay fifty thousand dollars for what?" Chloe couldn't help herself. "For one *night*?"

"No, no. For one *guh*." For one girl. "Can keep, *na*?"

Ten thousand dollars for a tiger and fifty thousand for a living Barbie doll. Much, much more for a quart of bear's bile.

Terdsak's girl had by this time climbed off his lap and was now under the table performing even more intimate services for the boss.

"Sixty thousand," said the Taiwanese, and Chloe thought she could hear the Indonesian grinding his teeth. He came down to their table and whispered something in Terdsak's ear. Terdsak nodded and, pointing from the Indonesian to the girl and back, said, "E-go, you show."

E-go led the man down into the pit, where the girl, standing very still in the center, smiled desperately at him and then up at Terdsak. The Indonesian began to examine her, squeezing her arms and thighs, looking closely at her skin and teeth. He took a hank of her long red hair and held it to his nose, inhaling deeply. He reached down to spread her lips and bent to see. Looking thoughtful, he turned her around for a look at her bottom, which he slapped playfully, eliciting titters from the gallery, and then returned to his seat. "Sixty-five thousand," he called out.

"Seventy thousand," said the Taiwanese in the same flat tones he had delivered his earlier bids.

Terdsak, looking happier than he had since the auction started, signaled for another glass of his whiskey. But something was missing. "E-go. You find what happen. Where boat? Where Buddha?"

Still, the auction had gone well—even if the Buddha, Lot Number Three, was still missing—and Terdsak had a fresh case of his Special Superman brought out and opened. Drinks were poured all around and he proposed a toast. "To TNT," he said. "Keep us long and strong forever." Chloe managed to spill her drink.

The taped music came to an end. "E-go!" hollered Terdsak. "We sing."

This idea inspired a brief silence in the room while E-go processed the command. Chloe could hear, very faintly, the clicking of gold studs against the girl's teeth. The girl under their table.

Then E-go barked at One, and the gunman barked at a spare hostess, and within a minute Terdsak was presented with a large Beer Singha, a *bia sing*, half in a frosted pint glass and half still in the bottle. Terdsak smiled. He smiled at E-go and he smiled at Ten. He smiled at all his guests who, sensitive to his moods, smiled back and were entirely attentive. Then he smiled at Chloe and said, "I not drink Beer Singha. I not ask for Beer Singha. Not want Beer Singha," just as though it were somehow her fault. He shoved the girl away from his crotch and his voice rose and quickened as he lapsed deeper into pidgin. "*Bia sing* no same-same sing-a-song. We *sing*. Sing-a-*song*. *AI* HEE-*YAH*."

Chloe didn't know what Terdsak was saying, at this point, and neither did E-go, evidently, but everybody understood it was less than complimentary.

"Sing-a-*song*," E-go suggested to Zero in tones that would not be trifled with.

Zero began to quaver uncertainly in Thai, describing objects of great pathos in the air with his hands, and One was joining in when strangled noises started to issue from Terdsak's own throat. "Okay, okay! Stop. No sing. *No sing*. We change." His customers were either smiling uncertainly or else looking thoughtful and pretending nothing was happening. The pudgy individual from Malaysia had also started to sing, but he stopped. Terdsak's security force stood there in an agony of indecision, really wanting to do it right, but they had lost the script altogether.

"*E-go!*" Terdsak mimed somebody threatening himself with an ice-cream cone. "We *sing*. Ka-ra-o-ke. *Na*?"

E-go issued new instructions, and almost immediately a microphone appeared. At the back of the room, One pulled down a big video screen.

Terdsak, always gracious, passed the mike to one of the Indonesians, who started warbling incomprehensibly while nevertheless appearing to attend to the bouncing ball that measured out the English lyrics. On the screen, an ungainly great Western woman with long sandy hair interpreted the singer's hysterical rendering of "Put Your Head on My Shoulder," swirling 'round and 'round in the breeze in what looked to Chloe like a parking lot overlooking the sea. All the men were making appreciative noises, although whether for the woman on the screen or for the avant-garde singing performance, she couldn't guess. Then Terdsak got impatient. Clapping loudly, he indicated to E-go that the guest should be relieved of the microphone. Chloe was pleased, she supposed, to see that E-go didn't misunderstand and take to silencing the Indonesian in the same way he had the dogs.

"'Glean, Glean *Hee*-ohs'," directed Terdsak, and Ten, at E-go's instructions, between them found the required laser disc and inserted it in the machine. Now a new Western bimbo, this one a blonde, pouted mightily and squinted into the sun through heart-shaped sunglasses. At the line "hair of gold," Terdsak's face twisted with manly passion and his sonorous growl rose to recall a bull with testicles caught in a barbed-wire fence, while the bimbo swiped woodenly at her temple hairs. At "lips like cherries," the bull, given the even more enthusiastic bellowing, had suddenly learned to enjoy its pain, and the lady on the screen pursed her lips as though she had just thought of something at once naughty and shrewd.

Chloe was both terrified of bursting into laughter and just plain terrified. She concentrated on watching the screen, and wondering where the makers of the video had found this person and how they had induced her to perform this way for the male population of Asia.

The Indonesian logger had the laser gun now and he was taking quick shots across the room at the Taiwanese shipper, who appeared both annoyed and confused, and at the shipper's redhead, who was oblivious. Between them, Ten were showing four very red eyes, when they were all open, and Zero, at least, kept directing his gaze to the bottle on Terdsak's trolley, staring at it as though in search of an answer to some profound question. The Malaysian miner, also red eyed, was focused on Chloe now, one eye squeezed shut and the other winking like a stop light about to burn out. His attendant, the brunette from the dungeon, was enjoying the attentions of the Japanese manufacturer who shared the table. The latter individual was getting her to lean forward to dip her nipples in the sauce for the bear paws, and then sucking it off. The sauce, as Chloe knew, was quite piquant, and the girl kept trying to interest the Japanese captain of industry in the honey sauce for the shrimp cakes instead.

Terdsak sang "Green, Green Hills of Home" twice, and "My Way," to much applause. Then it was Chloe's turn.

"You. Sing Canada song."

"I can't sing."

"You sing."

Chloe didn't know any Canadian songs, not even the national anthem, and she was willing to bet not one Canadian in ten could sing the goddamned thing either. So she sang "I'm a Lumberjack and I'm Okay," which was strictly speaking British. Her voice shook, but not as much as it should have and, strangely enough, it helped to keep the panic at bay. Nobody seemed too disappointed when she stopped after one and a half verses and said she didn't remember any more.

No matter. The sing-a-song was brought to an abrupt end by the arrival of three men, one of them in T-shirts and jeans, another in tight bicycle shorts and a see-through net tanktop, and the third dressed more smartly. This individual had slicked-back hair and a natty mustache that complemented his sneer.

The three of them staggered in like conquering generals returned from war, shot to shit but brimming with good news. A couple of Terdsak's armed guards followed behind as escort. The senior man among the walking wounded took an obviously heavy bag from one of his associates and, sneering extravagantly, moved forward to present it to Terdsak. Terdsak could hardly contain himself. He indicated a place should be cleared for it on the table. Despite herself Chloe felt the excitement and, curious, leaned over to see as Terdsak opened the bag to look. It was gold. Lots of gold. There was a small fortune in gold bars sitting there on the table.

"What *this*? *What this*?" Terdsak was registering displeasure. "This *gold*!" Terdsak was speaking English. Evidently the visitor was not Thai. The sneering man's two comrades had been standing there yawning and looking as though they hadn't been to bed in a day or two. Now they came more alert. One of them, Chloe could see, had rings just about everywhere it was possible to have rings. He also had a wad of gauze taped behind one ear.

"Where the rest?" Terdsak was ranting. "Where Jess-ee-*ka*? Where man? Where Buddha? *Na*? Where . . . is . . . the . . . *Buddha*?"

The sneer was tending to slide off the senior man's face, although he yawned as he responded.

Yawn

"'Got away?'" This was not the answer Terdsak wanted to hear. "*Got away*?" "You! *Maa nii.*" Terdsak waved the sneering leader's beringed companion closer. "*Nii, nii,*" he said, bringing him near enough he could reach one of his nipple rings. Hooking a finger in the ring, he asked another question in Thai. Whatever the answer was, it displeased the boss and he yanked hard, producing a yelp and a spurt of blood. The guy slapped a hand to his breast and then took it away dripping. He examined his hand with astonishment. For a moment, it looked as though he were going to go for Terdsak. But E-go already had the muzzle of his pistol only inches from his head. Ten, slower off the mark, maybe because they'd been sampling the Special Superman, stepped in to point guns at his other temple, though you could see he'd already changed his mind anyway.

Chloe passed from stunned disbelief to mild nausea, and reached for tissues to wipe flecks of blood from her face and arms. Terdsak also snatched more tissues from the rag doll to wipe at himself. He had dropped the ring among scraps of meat on one of the plates, and impatiently signaled it should be taken away.

Terdsak was behaving more and more strangely, his tantrums blowing like squalls. His men—especially Ten—had also been acting oddly. With a pang of alarm, Chloe wondered if she were the one going weird. Maybe everybody else was behaving perfectly normally—as normally as people were able to behave under the circumstances. Maybe she'd been drugged. Could it be the Special Superman? But she hadn't swallowed more than the tiniest sip.

It isn't easy to sneer and beg for mercy at the same time, but the man with the mustache managed the trick as he was dragged down into the pit.

The whole place smelled like a giant fart. The man with the sneer was lying in the pit, moaning piteously and bleeding from a thousand punctures. His two associates, one of them still bleeding from a nipple, stood by trying to stop yawning and look concerned. Terdsak, a master showman, had tried to get the women to throw durians at the guy, but they weren't able to pick them up without fumbling them and making shrill noises, especially the girl who dropped one on her foot. Then Terdsak had his men place a couple on each table and invited his guests to join in the stoning, but only the Cambodian arms dealer, who used the gauzy wrap from his attendant, and the German buyer of the apsara, who either had calluses like horn or else was a masochist, were able to carry a durian close enough to lob it at the man. Finally Ten, both of them wearing canvas work gloves and assisted by the guy with the torn nipple and his young associate, neither of whom got gloves, had to collect all the durians and hurl them in disgust at the miscreant.

Still alive, although not necessarily thrilled on that account, the man was carried back up and forced to kneel at Terdsak's table. "Sometime people cannot talk," Terdsak explained to the assembly in reasonable tones. "Sometime people *kriengjai* too mutt. Not want bother other people. *Na*? So they keep idea, keep information. Sometime must help people talk.

"Where. Is. *Buddha*?" Terdsak asked again, in a less civil vein.

Receiving no additional news on that front, only more moans and noises of denial, he waved E-go over and took his pistol from him. He took a couple of shots at the ceiling, knocking out a light and putting holes in the blonde Venus. Then he rammed the muzzle in the man's mouth, breaking a couple of teeth in the process. "*Nii, nii.* You. You smoke, *na*?" The guy had no sooner taken a toke when Terdsak, still agitated, yanked the gun out again, chipping some more teeth, and passed it back to E-go.

"You! E-go. Fire!"

E-go looked all around, gun in hand, probably thinking he should light somebody's cigar.

"Fire!" Terdsak reiterated. "*Shoot.*"

Finally getting the picture, E-go signaled to Zero, who in turn delegated the unpleasant chore to one of the junior gunmen who had escorted the men in. With no obvious compunction, the sallow youth walked over, aimed his own pistol six inches from the man's head and pulled the trigger.

Covering his face delicately with one hand, Terdsak probed a nostril with his gold earcleaner and sneezed, once, twice, and three times, eliciting what might have been versions of Geshundheit in a few languages. "No problem. Must always help when other people hurt too mutt," said Terdsak, recovering both his composure and his English. "Help stop hurt. This is *karuna*. 'Compassion,' *na*?" He laughed and some of the others laughed with him, rather nervously for the most part. E-go only looked cautious.

Chloe didn't laugh either. She felt funny. Although she'd never fainted in her life, she felt as though she might faint. She had to think that all this was pretty radical even for someone like Terdsak. You didn't just go shooting people dead right in front of a whole bunch of people you hardly knew. She looked at the ceiling, just so she wouldn't have to look at anything else that was going on. Formerly flat, the ceiling now appeared vaulted, more closely resembling the Sistine Chapel, the blonde Venus distorted across a great dome that disappeared into the dark. It was a toss-up whether she was going to faint or surrender to panic.

E-go supervised disposal of the body and tidying up the mess without once meeting Terdsak's eye. Ten, meanwhile, fussed around like spaced-out mother hens, doing everything they could to make the boss happy.

"Take middle way," said Terdsak. He extended a hand towards the other two bearers of ill tidings as though he expected them to come up and kiss it, and indicated they should be released. "And keep control. This is basic. *Khaojai*, *mai*? Basic." Terdsak surveyed the entire assembly and spoke in a louder voice: "Get the concept?"

The festive spirit gradually returned with the clatter of cutlery, the clanging of spittoons, the tinkle of glass. The smell of durian grew even stronger as plates full of the rich yellow pods were served for dessert.

An American trader had hung his electronic amulet on a naked girl and was smearing her with something from one of the jars in his gift pack, alternately smacking her on the bottom and licking the unguent from her dusky skin. Then a British industrialist threw something he found in a soup bowl at the American, who reacted by soaking a ball of tissues in a water glass and hurling the dripping wad at the Brit. Before the episode could escalate into a full-fledged food fight, several comely attendants converged on the tables to clear away the debris and to distract the combatants with soft words and intimate caresses.

The German art dealer had climbed up into the wall niche opposite to conduct an impassioned, if largely one-sided, conversation with the raven-haired statuary stationed there. Suddenly he performed a wild gesticulation and toppled over backwards into the pit full of durians. His screams annoyed Terdsak to the point he had E-go organize a rescue party. Then one of the ushers who were lifting the German out of the pit stumbled and they dropped the fellow again. This elicited even shriller screams, fanning the embers of Terdsak's annoyance to the extent he ordered E-go to go down and shoot the art dealer, only changing his mind after the assignment proved so hard to communicate he suggested he might have Ten shoot E-go instead. At least that's the way Chloe thought it had gone.

Chloe didn't faint, although she did vomit into the spittoon under the table.

Terdsak laughed. "Drink too mutt, *na*?" he suggested, at the same time ordering an attendant to pour her another glass of the Special Superman.

43 blow-up

A 'strange coincidence,' to use a phrase
By which such things are settled now-a-days.

Lord Byron

"You drink," Terdsak told her. He was holding a glass of the Special Superman in one hand and squeezing Chloe's jaw with the other. "Make you sexy, *na*?" The Malaysian and his friends were laughing. Chloe twisted away. She could feel the panic taking her. She had to escape.

Then, as though this were a dream and she was in control, sort of, there came a flash like lightning followed by a dull thud. The windows facing the other side of Terdsak's island empire rattled in their frames. Then they took on a warm, flickering quality. There were more flashes and more thuds. Letting go of Chloe and putting the bottle down, Terdsak turned to his security chief and said, "Fire! E-go. *Fire.*"

E-go, hitherto mesmerized by the living statue in the niche between the two windows on the full moon party side, pulled out his pistol. Clearly prepared to shoot anything his boss deemed worthy of such treatment, he saw no obvious target. Although chances were the German art dealer should have been nervous.

"E-go! Not shoot. *Fire.* Same-same this, *na*?" Terdsak had his Ronson out, snapping it furiously in the general direction of his ammo dump. E-go was still wondering why Terdsak needed a light, when one of the guests came away from a window yelling "Fire!" Some of the other people started to catch on, and "fire" became such a popular conversational gambit that even E-go was getting the idea. "Fire!" he said to Ten. "Fire!" Zero and One ran to a window for a closer look and then took up the refrain themselves. Rising in sympathy with Terdsak's agitation and the generally alarming turn of events, the babel of voices took on a distinct note of hysteria. Two Japanese gentlemen appeared to be discussing the pros and cons of hiding under a table, while the Cambodian arms dealer was scarfing bits of leftover bear paw from his neighbors' plates.

Terdsak grabbed a walkie-talkie from One and began interrogating it. Then he instructed E-go: "Put Benz on boat. Understand? *Khaojai, mai*? Boat. Benz on boat."

Terdsak was screaming orders left and right. E-go and Ten looked totally confused. Eventually, a number of armed men showed up and Terdsak screamed at them for a while before sending them out into the night. Then a squad of uniformed policemen arrived, causing consternation in some quarters, but Terdsak merely yelled at them in much the same way he had yelled at the others, and, weapons drawn, they also went into the night.

"You!" he said, and he issued orders in Thai to one of the lesser gunmen. Given the fact the whole party was emptying into the night like headbangers fleeing a Barry Manilow concert, Chloe's guard wasn't notably pleased at this latest assignment, but he pointed his gun at her and gave her to understand she should stay. Terdsak, E-go, Ten, and several other henchmen ran into the night leaving Chloe behind.

Her guard stood around looking acutely uncomfortable for about ten seconds, and then he grabbed her arm. "You come," he said, and they also abandoned the place.

YAWN

It was bedlam. Naked women, policemen, businessmen, boatmen, and bodyguards were fleeing every which way. A few isolated shots came from inside the building and just outside, while more explosions erupted in the distance. Meanwhile, the Indonesian logging tycoon was making an orderly departure with his security men and with his rival's recent acquisition, the lovely Lot Number Two from the auction. Not coincidentally, perhaps, Chloe had noticed the Taiwanese shipping magnate lying dead, slumped in a corner of the outer restaurant, two messy bullet holes in his face. She had seen an electronic amulet where his shirt was unbuttoned at the throat. Another case of mistuning. Two other men, husky Chinese, lay beside him in their own pools of blood. There were many places Chloe would rather have been just then, even Vancouver. Still, she had frankly had enough of Terdsak's company, so she was counting her blessings and trying to decide where to go from there, when the Cambodian opportunist appeared.

"I see you with Terdsak," the bear paw aficionado told her, unctuous. "You are his woman?"

Chloe shrugged his moist hand off her shoulder.

"I have boat. You come with me." He turned to Chloe's guard: "You go. I take woman."

A dilemma—this rich man standing right there in front of the gunman, telling him to do one thing; and another rich man, his boss, himself nowhere to be seen, telling him the opposite. Chloe's guard agonized for a second and then ran out into the night.

Chloe wanted to get off this island. She desperately wanted this. She had to find Prue and the others, and then, just as soon as she possibly could, she had to escape to the real world. The Cambodian had a boat, but he also had an agenda, and Chloe was pretty sure she didn't want to pay the fare. But by this time, a few of this guy's own security force had reassembled, and they helped to convince her she had little choice but to accompany him after all.

"You son of a bitch," she said. "Where are we going?"

"Bangkok. We go Bangkok. You come."

At this point three things happened. A naked woman appeared on the path in front of them, an otherworldly apparition in the moonlight and the glow from the fires. "The moon is beautiful," she told them, for it was none other than Selene. At almost the same instant, a tiger stepped out on to the track behind her to swing its massive head quizzically in their direction. And, as if all that weren't enough distraction for one moment, a bizarre figure—an amazing specimen dressed in motley and blackface—stepped out of some bamboo on the other side of the path. "Hey, man," he said. "A tiger. Far fuckin' out."

The tiger turned to investigate this latest arrival as Selene raised a pistol and shot the Cambodian in the chest. This surprised Chloe and it surprised the arms dealer. He sank to his knees, gasping and reaching towards Chloe, who moved away as, gurgling, he toppled over on his side. His men took one look at Selene, who was now sighting in on one of them, another look at the tiger and, without even considering what sort of threat the freak might represent, they sprinted into the undergrowth. Chloe heard one of them tripping and crashing to ground before he'd gotten ten yards, and the tiger moseyed off to check it out.

"Whoa, man," Freddie was saying. "Nice shooting. Shit. Can I have the gun, now?"

"Sure," said Selene. "Here."

"Freddie!" Chloe said. "My God. Hi!"

They could hear thuds and thrashes from the underbrush, groans and curses from the bodyguard, and throaty growls from the tiger, no doubt expressing frustration that it had neither tooth nor claw with which to really show this dude a thing or two.

"I came to see if you were all right, man. Like, not blown up and everything. You okay?"

"How did you get here?"

"I got a boat," Freddie proudly informed her. "Even got a fuckin' driver, man. If we can find him. And I let all the animals go. Except the bears. Nothing to do for those poor suckers. Shit.

Wait here a minute." Freddie ran off behind the Complex, gun in hand. Selene hadn't said anything since she surrendered the gun, only stood there quietly as though she'd just stopped by on a visit from another planet.

Freddie. The last person Chloe would have expected to come riding in like the cavalry. This night was taking on a more and more dreamlike quality. It was like a drug trip, too weird for fiction. Just her luck to be participating in a world dreamed by some lunatic. And, even in the thick of events, Chloe found herself remarking how little effect the latest killing was having on her. How many dead bodies did you have to encounter before it seemed fairly acceptable, for example, to have a naked lady shoot a business person dead in cold blood right in front of you? Even if the guy was a prick. Chloe suddenly remembered something—she'd seen him talking on a cellphone, back in the Complex, and she knelt to rummage through his shoulder bag.

Selene jumped and whimpered as three measured shots came from somewhere inside the Complex, and then Freddie reappeared. "Okay, okay," he said. "Let's go, man. Wait a minute. What's that? Whoa. Not me, man. No fuckin' way. I don't use cellphones. You know what they do to your brains? No way."

"It's okay, Freddie. I'll make the call. Let's get out of here."

"Not the pier, man. Everybody's down there, and half of them have got guns and everybody wants boats. My boat's on the other side."

"God, we can't go to the other pier!"

"No, no, man. Over there, like a little private cove all my own."

"Thank God. We've got to get out of here, Freddie. Terdsak has a bunch of ammunition and explosives stashed in one of those buildings. I don't know what's going to happen when the fire gets to it."

"I do. Listen, I got a question for you, man. A sixty-four-fuckin'-thousand-dollar question. Do you know where he keeps his whiskey? I mean, like, his serious shitload of whiskey by the case?"

"Right next door to the bombs."

"I figured something like that. Fuckin' A, man. I got him. Let's go."

"Freddie. There were a bunch of kids and some old people working over there."

"No problem, man. I seen them headed into the hills already. One old babe looked me over, grinning so hard I think she maybe mistook me for a movie star, the way I'm dressed up, here. Shit."

Chloe marveled at Freddie's command of the situation. He appeared focused in a way she'd never seen him before. Competent, sure of himself. Now that she had a good look at him, she saw that he was also out of uniform. "My God, Freddie," she said in tones of admiration. "Who's your tailor?"

"My old guesthouse has this thing, like, they call it a swap shop," Freddie replied, drawing himself up and tugging at his tie before confiding, "I hate this shit." He was dressed in baggy green- and gray-striped pants, a white shirt, and a black tie decorated with an orange and yellow tropical sunset scene. And he wore lace-up black boots that were pretty clean. They looked like army boots.

"Hey, man. Don't worry." Freddie had picked up on Chloe's amazement at this sartorial splendor. "This isn't me. I'm in disguise. I dressed like one of fuckin' them, you know? So I'd have, like, more freedom of movement. You don't have a joint on you, do you? No, no. Sorry I asked. Shit." Freddie had also tied his hair back in a neat ponytail and covered his face with what looked like grease, or maybe it was black shoe polish.

"Come on, man," he said. He reached down to rearrange his parts, but encountered a fly and zipper, which confused him. Unaccustomed to such niceties, he merely tugged at his crotch, lifting one leg a bit to facilitate proceedings. "Let's get out of the light. Let's get the fuck out of here altogether. Shit."

"Freddie. Wait."

"What's happening, man?"

"I've got to see if Tip is here. And we have to find the other women."

YAWN

"No problem, man. Let's do it."

"No problem? Freddie, Terdsak's out here somewhere. He's out of his mind. And he's got an army with him, half of them just about as crazy as he is."

"Chill, man. Old Shitbag and the Forty Fuckups are gone away. I saw them get on a boat and go. And can you believe it? He's still driving his Benz. He drove his fuckin' Bobbitt-proof Benz right on to his boat and they took off for the full moon party."

"Selene," Chloe asked. "Where do you stay? Where does Terdsak keep the women?"

For reasons of convenience, it turned out, the ones that hadn't been bought out or made their getaways already were locked up in the back of the restaurant building. They found six hostesses still confined to quarters. But no Tip. Only one of the two guards argued with Freddie, and he got shot. "That pisses me off, man. First guy I shot in a long time. A fuckin' moron."

Freddie was carrying a cotton shoulder bag, and he reached in to produce a tin of black shoe polish. "Put this on, man. All of you. Put it on." Fast Freddie's Traveling Minstrel Show. Chloe went ahead and smeared some on. But there was the question of the bare-naked ladies. A couple of them had already blacked their faces before it occurred to everyone there wasn't enough shoe polish to have their whole bodies blend into the night as well, and, on the whole, their bodies were going to be more conspicuous than their faces.

They found Freddie's boat without ado, anchored on the beach in a tiny cove. Hiding in the coconut palms behind the beach was the driver from the dark moon party two weeks previously.

"Buk!" said Chloe. "Hi!"

"Ah," Buk replied. His pupils were so dilated his eyes looked like little eight-balls. "Ah," he kept saying. "Ah." He was totally fried.

"I didn't have any money, okay?" Freddie felt he had to account for his driver's condition. "Spent it all on these threads, man. And I needed a longtail boat. But I had some Superman. Two bottles from the cases I loaded."

"You mean Terdsak's drink?"

"Yeah, yeah. No. Not exactly. I added a few vitamins to Old Shitbag's brew. And now it's really good shit. You know? I can handle it. But our friend Buk, here. . . . Whoa. Where has he been all his life? He wants to check this stuff out first thing, before we do the deal. And, after a while, it's like he sees the world for the first time, man. So he figures he's going to show me the whole place in one night, never mind I told him I was in a fuckin' hurry, because we can't find this island no matter where we go. You'd never think he was born and grew up around here. Shit, man. Never knew there were so many islands. And most of them look just the same to me. To him, too. But like I tell you, I don't pay him a bottle of Super Special Superman just 'cause he likes the water. He's supposed to know his way around. This ain't no *Loveboat* cruise, I keep tellin' him."

"Freddie. What are you talking about?"

"I'll explain it later, man. We got to go."

The girls and Buk were already in the boat. In fact, the girls were all huddled up on the stern of the longtail boat, as far away from Freddie and the tiger as they could get. The boatman was even farther back than the girls, looking as though he wished there were some other part of a boat after the stern. Another tiger had appeared, or maybe it was the same one. It emerged from the trees back of the beach to stand beside Freddie, blinking in the moonlight, surveying the little assembly of refugees. Chloe backed off, thinking she might make a run for a tree. But Freddie was talking to the tiger, a tired, toothless old wreck of a candidate for retirement in front of somebody's fire.

"Hey, man," Freddie told it, elaborately casual, trying to put it at its ease. "You want to come with us? Got lots of room, man. Hop in. There's no fuckin' future for you here."

The tiger livened up a little as it considered this novel prospect. You could see it in its eyes. But you could also see another consideration: "Here we have this foolhardy human who thinks a few sweet words can make up for a lifetime of abuse by his kin." The animal stepped forward and batted Freddie with its paw. It did this in a tentative manner, perhaps still not believing the guy was real. So it didn't kill Freddie, only sent him flying several feet sideways where he landed up against a coconut tree and slumped to the ground.

"Fuck, man!" he said. "I think you broke my fuckin' shoulder. What's the matter with you, anyway? *Shit.*"

"Freddie, are you okay?"

Freddie's shoulder wasn't really broken, but the tiger figured that was enough exertion for now anyway and ambled away into the dark. "No problem, man. I still got the gun. Fuckin' tiger. I was only trying to help. Let's go. Shit. Come on, come on. We got to get out of here. We got to get out on the water, man. I got to see this one. Going to Bobbittize the whole fuckin' show. Oh yes. Burn, baby, burn. And we got front-row seats." Freddie was vibrating in the moonlight, and Buk was muttering something over and over to himself. At first Chloe thought he was singing, but then she realized he was probably praying.

From a few hundred yards out, they got a view of the TNT Complex and some of the fire. Other boats were still leaving the pier at the Complex, Terdsak's guests and much of his army fleeing the scene, many of them headed for Phra Chan Island. And Chloe, Freddie, Buk, and the girls hadn't gotten much farther before they also encountered a sizable armada of longtail boats and other vessels coming the other way, from Haad Hey, trying to get closer to the fireworks, probably thinking the whole thing was just part of the local party scene. All in all, it was a totally surreal replay of the Allied landing on D-Day.

They were about halfway to Phra Chan Island, and Freddie was screaming at the driver, who appeared intent on driving them away from any hint of fires or explosions or tigers and out into open sea no matter where they said they wanted to go. Chloe was up on the bow, away from the engine and the pilot, talking on the phone. Talking to Waylon, as it turned out, who was having a hard time hearing her even before the arms depot blew up.

"Waylon?" Chloe screamed into the phone. "*Waylon?*"

Waylon was telling her all about some massive manhunt underway on Phra Chan, with lunatics interrogating people by the dozen, shooting off guns, and generally scaring the shit out of anybody straight enough to appreciate the gravity of the situation. Strange. Waylon's voice had carried more excitement than outrage or alarm. Maybe it was the bad connection.

But it was impossible to talk any more, what with all the cheering and the sound of explosions coming one on top of the other like the gods of darkness slamming at the heavy bag.

"Wait, Waylon!" Chloe yelled. "I'm coming."

What on earth was Waylon doing on Haad Hey?

44 she was right

*Combinations of wickedness would overwhelm
the world, did not those who have long practised
perfidy grow faithless to each other.*

Samuel Johnson

"**A**nd I thought I could trust you, Waylon."

Waylon had lost Jessica's cellphone. In fact he had lost her entire bag and, the way she was looking at him, he wished he'd lost her pistol as well.

Jessica had wrapped the gun in plastic and stuffed it in her flotation jacket. The Buddha she'd wrapped in a towel and returned to its bag, together with a partially inflated salvage bag and a couple of lightsticks, all of which she had also stuffed inside her jacket. She had strapped her dive knife to her leg. The Bag she entrusted to Waylon. But after he'd been swimming for a while, he realized that he was actually carrying the sack with the sandstone Buddha and the bits of broken ceramic. So a few of her things were missing.

Most of her things, actually. The Bag, including essential pharmaceuticals and her phone, was at the bottom of the sea.

They had watched, bobbing away on the swell, as *Sumalee*'s running lights disappeared away into the dark. A moderate chop encouraged them to keep their masks on and breathe through their snorkels, except when they wanted to talk.

"Check everything, Waylon."

"Jessie?"

"Yes, Waylon?"

"I dropped the wrong bag."

A silence. Then: "Are you sure?"

"I don't have it."

"I'm going to kill you." She sounded as though she meant it.

It took them a couple of hours to swim to the beach. Wearing flotation jackets, it was easiest to lie on their backs and kick with their fins, rolling over now and then to check that they were still headed towards the fires on the beach. Waylon was hardly conscious of the swell, except when he rolled on to his front, and watched the beach fires and lights from the boats appear and disappear as he rose and fell. Through one especially big hole in the cloud cover, Waylon recognized Orion, with his three-starred belt and his sword. And Sirius, the dog star. That was about all Waylon remembered of the constellations. Aside from the Big and Little dippers.

"I hate this, Waylon."

"What?"

"Being out here. In the dark."

"You should be getting used to it. At least you didn't sink the boat this time."

"Last time I took the dinghy. It was better. And I did sink the boat this time. Just wait till somebody lights up. Filthy fuckers. That boat really stank, Waylon."

"Jesus, I don't believe it. It's really going to blow up?"

"You're fucking right it is." Her voice was steel. Then, in a different tone: "I'm scared, Waylon. What if there are sharks?"

"Don't worry, Jessie. There aren't any sharks."

"How do you know that?"

He didn't really. But they were testing the hypothesis even as they spoke, and he wished she'd shut up about it. There was a fair chop and some swell, and they had only intermittent sight of the beach. But it was slack tide. The current had fallen right off, and they were gradually swimming out of it as they were swept towards the beach.

"What if the current had been going the other way?" Waylon asked, not for the first time.

"Don't worry about it, Waylon. It isn't going the other way. Anyhow, like I told you, we couldn't stay on the boat. So shut up about it. If we'd stayed, we would have been dead. You're an insurance man, Waylon. Does that sound like a good bet to you?"

Waylon was pretty confident they were on the right heading, checking from time to time that they were homing in on the bonfires and fireworks. Then there came a series of concussions and a sudden light show way off to the west of the beach.

"What was that?" he said.

"That was goodbye *Sumalee*," Jessica replied, sounding more positive than she had since they left the boat. "That was kiss your ass goodbye, Mr. My Bottle and your filthy fucking cigars and your dog's tongue fish. And your durian." Jessica choked on a mouthful of water. Gasping, getting her breath back, she added, "Yeah. And it's goodbye Bat. I hope they've already got you in hell licking ashtrays. Hey. I guess you're never going to get your chance with Dit now, Waylon. Are you sorry?"

Once they were well into the lee of the island the chop wasn't so bad, making it easier for Jessica to talk. Talking helped to keep her calm, and she told him more about Terdsak and George and the rest of it.

Still, Waylon was confused. There was lots Jessica wasn't telling him. "Don't you think you owe it to me to tell me everything, Jessie?"

"Waylon. Let's just shut up about it, okay? You really don't need to know any of this."

They had staggered ashore towards the darker end of the beach, away from most of the boats and the crowds and the fifty-megaton techno music, to be greeted by several naked people sitting in the sand smoking snorkels.

"Wicked!"

"Wow!"

"Cosmic!"

"The Creatures from the Black Lagoon," observed an aging hippie in beaded gray dreadlocks, somewhat overdressed in a headband and bikini shorts. "Far out."

Snorkels were offered, and Jessica took a couple of big tokes. Waylon declined. She asked if anybody had any other drugs, or maybe a phone, but they said sorry. It was clear they weren't hiding anything on their persons.

Jessica was hurt at Waylon's betrayal. "You jerk. You fucking dingbat. Waylon, do you have any money?"

"Sorry."

She buried the Buddha in the sand, up on the deserted end of the beach, farthest from the action. Then she said, "I need money, Waylon." She had to get re-equipped.

So they headed towards the other end of the beach.

Waylon had never seen anything like this. Thousands of people, many of them naked or almost naked, were partying all the way back up into the coconut trees behind the beach. Thousands of candles burned on mats spread out on the sand, tiny twinkling echoes of the myriad boat lights bobbing on the water just offshore. The noise was unbelievable. Heavy metal and techno music, cranked up to brain-addling levels, assaulted you from every direction.

They were halfway along the beach when they encountered a large knot of people at the water's edge. Waylon and Jessica watched as a strange vessel—it looked like a landing craft—came in right on to the beach in the light of the biggest bonfire of all.

"I don't like this, Waylon." Jessica told him to follow her and, moving as fast as they could in the soft sand, they headed for the dunes at the back of the beach.

Yawn

It looked like a landing craft, and it behaved like a landing craft. The squared-off bow dropped forward on to the tidal flat. But, instead of a tank, a big Mercedes-Benz rolled down the ramp and started towards the beach. It got as far as the sand and promptly sank to its axles. This inspired much cheering and shouting among the rapidly growing crowd of spectators, who enthusiastically greeted the Thai man who emerged from the back seat to stand beside the car screaming at them.

"Get *down*," said Jessica. They sank into the shrubbery. "This is trouble, Waylon. Bad trouble."

From the front seat there appeared two other Thai men, one of them short and stout, the other tall and thin, and a second man, a blond Westerner, emerged as though reluctantly from the back.

"We've got to hide. We've got to do something." There was new urgency in Jessica's voice.

The four men stumbled up the beach. The first, clearly the boss, stopped and appeared to try commanding the cast of thousands to get out of his way, much like Moses parting the Red Sea only less successfully. He spoke to his associates, and the short, fat one and the tall, skinny one started shooting pistols off into the air, a procedure that went largely unremarked, given all the other excitement that was going on. A few bystanders assumed it was merely part of the show and began applauding. A dozen glowing examples of the bodypainters' art gathered around, and the boss retreated to the boat again, while his men simply left the Benz where it sat and started moving out through the crowd in a purposeful kind of way.

The music started to fall off and the sounds of shots came more clearly. The men from the landing craft were shooting boom-boxes.

"Look," said Jessica.

The Western guy with the exuberant blond pompadour, together with the two Thai gunmen, were rounding up all the tourist women they could get their hands on, and were standing them in a line in the light of a massive bonfire. Their only response to the chorus of screams and entreaties was to wave guns at the assembly, shouting at them in Thai and, Waylon thought, Russian. Then two more men emerged from the darkness and into the firelight. Bat and Dit.

They walked down the line of women, staring hard into each of their faces as they progressed. Bat was also staring everywhere else as well, while Dit kept looking over his shoulder as though wishing they were examining the men instead.

"Shit. They're looking for *me*, Waylon."

Then the toughs turned to the men. Dit approached one huge specimen of manhood, a guy in khaki shorts and tattoos who'd been threatening legal action at the top of his lungs. "You wouldn't be so brave without your guns, you drongos," he added. Dit gestured hypnotically with his pistol and then kicked the fellow in the balls, hard. He leaned over to stare into the big Australian's face, where he sat hugging himself in the sand. Waylon knew, somehow, that Dit was batting his eyelashes, although he couldn't actually see it in this light.

"They're looking for me too, Jessie."

"Shhh. Not so loud."

Inspection finished, Dit went back to tweak his Australian friend's cheek and then all the gunmen vanished into the dark. The tourist mob immediately desegregated themselves and took to milling around, excitement and relief vying in their voices.

"Waylon. I need a disguise. I want you to paint me." Jessica had two lightsticks, one green and the other orange. She used her dive knife to slit the green one open and passed it to him. "Put lots on, Waylon." She took off her swimsuit top and stepped out of her bottoms.

Waylon had already put a crescent moon under each breast and stars around the nipples, shooting stars down her thighs, and happy faces on the cheeks of her ass, when Jessica began to get impatient. "Do my face, Waylon. That's important."

"Let me finish your back." He had planned to do BEWARE OF THE DIVER in orange, but there wasn't room. He just wrote BEWARE, so he'd be able to identify her among all the other psychedelic ladies on the beach.

"Wait here, Waylon." Jessica stepped out from cover and down to where a huddle of young travelers were sharing something from a bag. She merged right into this group of similarly naked and body-painted funseekers. It had to be a great party, Waylon was thinking, where the best way to be inconspicuous was to strip off and paint yourself fluorescent green. Then he saw another group, this one all male and all fully clothed and much too businesslike in their approach to striding down a beach. They were looking into the faces of everyone they passed. They stopped, at one point, to flip one young lady over for a better look, and then to punch and kick her boyfriend when he remonstrated. But they walked right by Jessica and her new group of friends, only ogling. You've seen one green and orange glowing chick with no clothes on, you've seen them all. The dangerous men passed on down towards the other end of the beach, and Waylon eased up on his efforts to disappear into the dune.

He could see Jessica engaged in negotiations with the glowing people for a moment or two, a transaction that ended with the other party shaking their heads, Jessica pulling her gun, and, finally, some kind of deal being concluded. She headed straight back to where Waylon waited. "Waylon. Have you got a pocket in your shorts? Are they dry? My bag's wet. Keep this for me." She handed him two small plastic bags.

"What's this?"

"Drugs. Don't lose them. We have to find a phone, Waylon."

The beach restaurant, up in the coconut grove, had one pay phone and ten people were lined up waiting.

"This is no good. I can't stand around in the open. You wait here." Jessie was off again. This time she went straight over to a shapely woman in a bikini, one in a thousand on that beach with a cellphone. She was walking back and forth with it, limping slightly and talking on the mobile. Obviously irritated at Jessica's intrusion, the woman shooed her away with one hand, turning back to her conversation. Jessica put the gun against her head and lifted the phone from suddenly obliging fingers. Pointing her pistol at the lady and her friends, two guys and two other women, Jessica backed away, wagging her weapon back and forth at one of the men, a wiry type with cameras and hair like a tent, who made as though to come after her.

Waylon continued to be amazed at his dive buddy, who seemed intent on mugging the entire full moon party, showing no inhibition whatever about going around taking whatever she needed at gunpoint. He thought about asking her to get some hamburgers, but then told himself this was no laughing matter. People went to jail for armed robbery.

"You don't *have* to steal everything, Jessie," he told his buddy, who was back.

"I'm in a hurry, Waylon. Give me the drugs. Give. Yeah, yeah. And the red ones. The other bag. Fuck. And my vodka's gone. Waylon, you asshole." Jessica palmed a mouthful of blue and red capsules and then moved away with the phone out of earshot into the cover of some pandanus palms.

A couple of minutes later, Waylon noticed a uniformed policeman coming up the sand towards their hideaway. "Thank God," he said. Jessica arrived back just as their visitor started to say howdy. She shot the cop. This time she was throwing high and to the left, assuming it was between the eyes she was trying for.

"He was one of them, Waylon. They're all part of it. Don't trust anybody. Do you understand?" The drugs hadn't taken hold yet, and Jessica was having one of her blinking fits.

Stop, Waylon told himself. Breathe. He breathed deeply and regularly. He expelled all the air from his tubes before inhaling, not too fast, slow and easy.

Stop. Breathe. *Think.*

Once again it was brought home to Waylon just how little he really knew about his dive buddy, and he was starting to think it was time to end this association at an early opportunity.

"Waylon, you wait here. I'm leaving everything except the gun with you, understand? So you wait right here. I won't be long."

She had certainly left everything, including a dead policeman and no handy explanation for this circumstance in case he needed it. The body had rolled down into a depression in the dunes, true. And it was fairly dark. But still. Waylon was thinking he might move on and hide some place else, when the phone rang. He moved to switch it off. Then he changed his mind.

"Hello," he said, guardedly, wondering whether this were Jessica's mysterious correspondent or someone wanting the actual owner of the phone.

"Prue?" A woman's voice. Then, "Sorry. Wrong number."

The person had sounded stressed out and there had been engine noise in the background, but the voice was strangely familiar. The phone rang again.

"Hello?"

"Who is this? Can I speak to Prue, please? What number is this phone. . . ? God. *I* don't know, Freddie. Some dork."

"Chloe? *Chloe?*"

"Who. . . ? My God."

"*Chloe?* Jesus Christ, eh? Is that you?"

"Waylon!"

"What. . . ? Where are you?"

"I'm here. In a boat. I don't understand. Where's Prue?"

"Who's Prue?"

"Waylon. Are you okay? Are you sober?"

"Chloe, this is kind of hard to explain. I'm on this island—there's a big beach party going on, thousands of people. It's nuts. And I'm with somebody, eh?" Waylon decided not to pursue that line for now. His voice dropped. "Chloe, there are men with guns, and they're hunting us." He didn't mention the dead policeman.

"Listen carefully. What's the name of the island you're on?"

"I have no idea. But there's a big party. And there are men with guns interrogating everybody."

"Are you on a beach?"

"Yes."

"Can you see another island? Can you see a big fire?"

"Yes. Over there, a mile or two away."

"I'm coming from there. I'm in a boat. I want to talk to Prue, please."

Waylon explained that he didn't know who Prue was, and it was dangerous for him to move around just then.

"Waylon, I'm coming. We're coming in a boat. Keep the phone with you and I'll call back. Don't use it. Save the batteries. If you see Prue, tell her I'm okay."

"Okay. Where have you been, anyway?"

"Not now. Wait. I'm coming."

She said something more, but a sudden crackling cut them off just before a new series of explosions erupted on the far island.

It was time to make a move. Jessica had the gun, and she was clearly as dangerous as the people from whom they were supposed to be on the run. To hell with her. First, he had to find Chloe. Then he wanted to escape this bizarre B-movie of which he seemed more and more a part.

Waylon moved cautiously, making his way to the closer headland. He went from coconut palm to coconut palm, thanking his stars he had kept his dive booties on, some kind of thorns or thistles all over his legs. Something huge moved in the dark just ahead of him, and he heard grunting and soft, wet flatulence. A sudden flash of light from the direction of the sea illuminated the beast—a water buffalo. The animal was staring at him with dull incuriosity, its placid great face parenthesized by the sweep of enormous horns, when Waylon heard more explosions, more powerful than those of a minute before. Careless of cover, now—everybody on the beach was facing the direction of the other island—Waylon moved down to the dunes and raced for the rocks.

Over the din of four varieties of techno blaring from the beach at once, over the concerted exclamations of awe from the throngs of full moon worshippers, over the pounding of Waylon's own heart, there came to him the rattle of gunfire—a rattle elevated to a wall of sound, a mass fusillade from ten thousand rifles and machine guns. Oddly out of synch with the associated series of flashes, a chain of heavy concussions thudded deep in Waylon's gut. The night sky was blasted open, the stars magnified and multiplied and turned colors and hurled in all directions, flash-frozen smoke clouds metamorphosed with each successive burst. Smoke trails soared in the flash-flash of exploding mortar and artillery rounds. Red tracers were lost in multi-colored sprays of fireworks like giant night-blooming flowers. Braying successions of explosions drowned out the crowd on the beach, who roared with one voice, cheering and applauding each new development in the unholy conflagration. They surged as though they were of half a mind to flee back from the water, and half a mind to get closer to the action. The prevailing mood was that the whole thing had been staged as entertainment. The best full moon party ever. The sea between this beach and the other island was covered with small craft, a vast armada that couldn't make up its mind whether it was advancing or retreating. Somewhere down there on the sea, in that vast flotilla of boats serially frozen like disco dancers in a strobe, Chloe was headed his way.

Incoming craft were wending their way in to anchor just off the beach. Chloe was in one of those boats. Why hadn't he gotten her number? He was assuming she'd called from a cellphone.

The phone rang.

"We're landing on the beach now, Waylon. I'm going to be up on the rocks at the end of the beach farthest from the fireworks. Hurry, okay?"

"God, Waylon."
"Chloe."
"Waylon. What happened to your face?"
"I'm growing a beard. I guess."
"No. You've got a big cut. Here."
"That's a long story. What happened to *your* face?"
"Nothing. What do you mean?"
"It's all black."
"That's shoe polish."

"I've missed you, Chloe." It sounded trite to Waylon's own ears, but he realized it was true. "How's Meredith?" There. He had pulled the pin. Now to see if the grenade was live.

"She's fine, I think. I haven't seen her in a month."

Waylon was about to probe further, when all thoughts of grenades gave way to guns. More specifically, Waylon was interested in the gun that Jessica was pointing at him. At them, really. Jessica wanted them to know they were both included in this thing. She had approached without a sound, coming barefoot over the rocks.

"Who's this, Waylon?" Jessica asked.

Chloe didn't say anything, but you could see the same question was on her mind. Especially given that Jessica was entirely naked, if you overlooked the glowing bodypaint and a new shoulder bag for which she'd undoubtedly mugged someone.

"This is my wife, Jessie. Her name is Chloe. Why are you pointing that gun at us?"

"Hello, there, Chloe. You've got a fucking loser for a husband. He's got guts, I'll give him that. And he's in good in bed. But he's a loser."

Waylon smiled at Chloe in a way that told her he wasn't that much of a loser. And not really that good in bed. Not with this outlaw, anyway. In fact, probably they'd never even slept together and this was a clear case of mistaken identity. That was it.

"Why am I pointing a gun at you? Only two people know where the Buddha is, Waylon. And that's one too many. Sorry."

"Jessie. I haven't the faintest idea how to find that thing. You buried it on the beach somewhere, eh? Jesus Christ. There's about a mile of sand here."

"So what are you doing back at this end of the beach? You saw me bury it, Waylon. I triangulated on the big tree and the rock that looks like a dick." She was telling him more than he wanted to know. Besides which she was crediting him with a flair for navigation and search and salvage he'd never really shown in their courses together. "And you had to know about the other stuff, didn't you? The stuff in the forward tank." Jessica waggled her pistol in the way he had come to recognize meant business. "Give me my phone, Waylon."

"Who is this woman?" Chloe asked. But Waylon just shook his head.

Dialing with the thumb of the hand holding the phone, Jessica kept the gun steady, in an absent-minded sort of way, on Waylon's chest. He didn't try anything.

"George," she said. "George, can you hear me? Good. Listen. I didn't get the Buddha. . . . No. The currents were too strong. We'll have to try again. And Terdsak is after me. He thinks I have the Buddha, George. I have to get away from here. I need money and a passport. Fast. Tonight, George. . . . No. Terdsak's men are all over the place. Half of them are stoned on something. And Terdsak's out of his mind. A mad dog. . . . George, it's your shit he's doing. What are you putting in it, anyway? Just get the money to me. . . . Tomorrow, then. Forget the passport." She hung up.

"Who was that you were talking to?" asked Chloe, strangely, to Waylon's mind. "Jessie. . . . *Jessica*? Who is this 'George?' And what do you know about Terdsak?"

"Is your wife always this nosy, Waylon? She's as bad as you. Why don't we tell her something interesting?" By way of emphasis, Jessica shifted her aim to his face. "Who's a better lay, Waylon? Me or her?"

As Waylon was weighing his response the situation abruptly changed, though not necessarily for the better.

The two newcomers appeared just as barefoot, although more fully dressed, and just as silently as Jessica had. For a moment, you could see that Jessica was going to try shooting her way out. But, what with Bat's automatic pistol pointed at one side of her head and Dit's shotgun pointed at the other, she decided to go for tact instead. "Bat," she said. "Let's go away, you and me. I have money." Bat's response was to slide his shades down, one-handed, so he probably couldn't see a thing in that light, and he extended his arm till the muzzle of his pistol touched her head, so it didn't matter if he could see or not. Jessica dropped her gun and Dit hooked it away with one foot, shotgun now covering Waylon and Chloe.

"Wail-On." Dit batted his eyes and simpered. "Hap-*pee* to see you again." He had a wad of gauze taped behind his ear and another one on his chest.

"Do you *know* this guy, Waylon?" asked Chloe.

Waylon smiled at her again, this smile meaning to convey the inadequacy of words in face of life's complexity. "Jesus Christ, eh?" he added.

It was low tide. Bat and Dit paraded Waylon, Chloe, and Jessica out across the sand, past the full moon partiers, the thousands of candles dimmed to insignificance in the light of the evening's spectacle, and across the tidal flats. Longtail boats lay beached, here and there, and cigarettes glowed where drivers hung around smoking and chatting. To the west, you could still see the glow of fires burning and the occasional flash and sharp report of something exploding.

"Looks like we got a bonus, Waylon."

"What are you talking about?"

"When the boat blew, it took a few other things with it."

The Mercedes-Benz was still there on the beach. It was surrounded by people, some of them glowing green and orange in the dark, and some of them simply ghostly in the moonlight. For a moment, in passing, Waylon had the strangest sense that one group of statuesque lady moon ghosts were headless.

They came to where bigger vessels bobbed at anchor in a gentle swell, including the landing craft-type vessel that had dropped the Mercedes-Benz earlier. One of the guys on the flat beside the boat looked familiar. It was the guy with the extravagant blond pompadour Waylon had seen supervising the mass interrogations on the beach earlier. "Chloe," Ego said, coming over to greet them, pistol hanging from one hand. "*Ciao*, baby."

"Do you *know* this guy, Chloe?" asked Waylon, but Jessica interrupted before Chloe could answer.

"Oh, Christ," said Jessica. "Oh, no."

Waylon looked where she was pointing and saw what she meant. He had smelled her even before he turned to look. *Sumalee* was tied off the stern of the landing craft. She looked pretty solid for a boat that had reportedly just been blown to smithereens.

"How the Christ?" Jessica whispered. "Waylon. We've got to get out of here." So they were buddies again. "That whole fucking boat is a bomb."

Waylon took this information with a grain of salt. This was the same bomb that had already triggered the apocalypse, according to Jessica. How many times was it going to blow up in one night?

"What's she talking about?" Chloe asked. "Waylon?" But a couple of explosive sneezes spared him what, of necessity, would have been a tortuous explanation. A man had appeared on *Sumalee*'s deck, up by the bows. He was wearing a white shirt and a tie, the knot dragged wildly to one side, and he appeared to be shoving something up his nose. "E-go! Bring all. I talk to all."

"Terdsak," Chloe said. "Oh, shit."

"What did you say?" Waylon asked.

"I know this man. His name is Terdsak."

"Get serious, eh?"

"First, bring Jess-ee-*ka*. This shit. Bring *now*." Terdsak was snapping a cigarette lighter like a castanet, stepping from side to side to stay upright as the boat rocked in the swell.

E-go sized up the situation and decided he'd delegate this chore to Bat and Dit.

Jessica was still glowing green and orange and she had some weedy stuff in her hair, all of which made her look like a rock-opera version of Ophelia at her worst. "*Phii*," Terdsak was yelling, loud enough for any rock opera. "Ghost. *Mai pen rai*. Never mind. Die same-same. I *kill*."

Bat and Dit weren't too keen on boarding either, given the mood their boss was in. But they threw Jessica into the longtail boat that served as a bridge to the ladder on *Sumalee*.

Jumping the gun on his interrogation, Terdsak started screaming at Jessica: "*Where Buddha?*"

"Waylon." Jessica was losing it in a way Waylon had never seen before, at least on surface. "Do something. Help me! Bat. We can't go on the boat. It's a *bomb*. You have to believe me!"

"Bring her," Terdsak said. "We *talk*." And he disappeared below deck.

"I am not getting on that boat," was the last coherent thing Waylon ever heard Jessica say. "BEWARE," proclaimed her back.

Bat turned back to E-go. "Cigarette. *Mee, mai?*"

E-go waded out to pass him a whole pack.

By this time Jessica was behaving even more dementedly than Terdsak, shrieking and kicking and generally making life so unpleasant that Bat punched her in the head, twice. Then he and Dit wrestled her up on deck.

Panting and shaking out his long hair, Dit waved down at Waylon. "You wait," he said sweetly. "We come back, get you. And your *f'en*."

"What is going on, Waylon?" asked Chloe. "How do you know these people?"

"Not now," Waylon told her. He looked at E-go, thinking he could try kicking him in the balls and then punch him in the head, although he wasn't very good at that sort of thing. But E-go was holstering his pistol. He looked at Waylon and Chloe, said, "*Ciao*, baby," raised a hand in salute and turned to go.

"Chloe! *Run*." Waylon grabbed her hand and started for the beach.

"Waylon."

"Run, Jesus Christ. *Run*."

This kind of thing can be contagious, because E-go started running as well, and then all three of them were covering ground just as fast as they could negotiate the rocks and dead coral and tidal pools in the near-dark. So they were some distance away, although not what anybody would call a safe distance, when the boat blew up.

Jessica had been right.

45 comrades in arms

A hidden connection is stronger than an obvious one.

Heraclitus

"Far fuckin' out, man. Never saw nothin' like that before, except once in 'Nam. Everything got, like, fucked up big time. Oh, yeah. And one night at a Pink Floyd concert in Jersey. Outta sight, man."

"It's the Apocalypse," suggested the Rev in tones of awe, swigging the remains of his malt whiskey and swabbing at the perspiration that glowed in the light from the flames. He appeared to be at one with the world, the only fly in the ointment being the fact he'd broken his favorite pipe. "'Woe is me for my hurt!'" he told them, even though he sounded chirpier than was his wont. "'My wound is grievous; but I say, truly this is grief, and I must bear it.' Jeremiah, chapter ten, verse nineteen." And, no, Freddie's snorkelbong wouldn't do it for him, he told Freddie, but thanks.

Most of the full-moon revelers on the beach were watching the remains of the light show, many assuming this was something staged for their benefit, maybe by the Tourism Authority of Thailand.

Freddie was telling them about the boat trip from Phra Chan Noi to Koh Phra Chan. "Everybody was there, man. One boat full of people—like, they were stoned—they came because they saw all these lights, and they're going, 'Far out. Where's the party?' I couldn't believe it, man."

"Sounds like I missed the best friggin' part of it," said Leary, who'd arrived on the island only hours before. Leary said he was particularly pleased to meet Freddie, the man who'd rescued Waylon's wife from Phra Chan Noi. "Not to mention the gosh-darned desperado who blew the whole TNT Complex right off the map."

They were getting along famously, swigging out of a bottle of something Leary had brought along, trading friggin' phenomenals for fuckin' fantastics. Leary said how much he liked the tie, and Freddie told him, "You take it, man. I've had enough of it, you know?" Then Freddie kicked off his boots, tore off his shirt and pantaloons, and grabbed himself through the Lycra jumpsuit. "Fuck, man. I don't know how they do it. Wearing that shit day in, day out."

While Leary looked on in more astonishment than you'd expect from a fifty-year-old man of the world, Selene, who was herself bare-arsed, decided to help Freddie off with the rest of his gear as well, leaving him standing there much as God made him. Leary didn't take that long to come to terms with the child-of-nature version of his new friend. Before you knew it, Leary and Freddie were comparing notes on such esoterica as techniques for blowing up armored vehicles, as unlikely a pair of comrades in arms as you could imagine.

"How do you do?" said the Rev, speaking of comrades in arms. He extended a hand to Waylon. "I've heard a lot about you. From both Chloe and Merry."

"Likewise," Waylon replied. "At least from Chloe." Jesus Christ, he thought. But he saw no hint of irony or worse in the fellow's manner.

"Oh, *NO*. Chloe's *HUSBAND*." Bibi was also pleased to meet him. "What's your *SIGN*?"

"Um. Pisces."

"I just *KNEW* it."

"Hey, man. Any friend of Chloe's is a fuckin' friend of mine." Freddie reached to rearrange his parts. "You want to treat her right, she tells everybody she's married and everything, man. Shit. You don't find that kind of thing all the time, these days."

Then there was Leary's posse.

As soon as Leary got back from the States, he'd heard that Waylon and Jessica had chartered *Sumalee*. Knowing what he did about the people who operated her, and talking to Oscar and Eddie and some of the others around town, he soon put two and two together. Asking around the waterfront, he got a line on where *Sumalee* had headed and he took off for Koh Phra Chan. Figuring he might need some help, he press-ganged two fishing-boat captains, one of them Captain Ot, who told Chloe "Never mind, never mind," when they were introduced, holding both her and Waylon's hands and beaming at them as though he had just pronounced them man and wife. Leary had also brought Oscar and Eddie and four good policemen of his acquaintance from Pattaya. Oscar and Eddie claimed they'd found two of the thugs who had assaulted them. Despite the fact Oscar was still moving with some difficulty, it seemed they had evened the score, maybe even coming out a few points ahead.

For their part, Prue and the Rev and the others, over Ruthie's protests, had notified the police and then gone to the full moon party. They figured they wanted to be as close to Chloe, and to Tip, as they could get. Perhaps, they thought, they could help the police to find the kidnappers. The cops *had* shown up, Chloe reported. They'd arrived at the TNT Party Complex and, as far as she could see, immediately been recruited by Terdsak to help in the hunt.

Leary's police, the good cops—together with their colleagues, who saw which way the wind was now blowing—were looking for information, but Leary had strongly recommended that Waylon and Chloe and the others opt for strict anonymity. He had spoken with his friends in the force, and they'd agreed that certain aspects of the case didn't really need further investigation. In fact, Leary said, he had a boat coming, if they wanted to spend just one more night here on Phra Chan, and he could take everybody that wanted to go to Pattaya. He was throwing a big party. Nancy was going to be back from Singapore, for one thing. Everybody was welcome. "But tell Freddie he's got to put some friggin' clothes on, okay?"

Anyway, it was good to keep a low profile for a while. There would be too much that needed explaining, and it was hard to see how what Chloe or Waylon could tell the authorities would help anything. And the less said about what roles Freddie and Ruthie played in events the better.

E-go and Ten were among those still unaccounted for. A bigger question, of course, was Gorgi's current whereabouts.

Freddie's Traveling Minstrels, wrapped in beach sarongs, were turned over to the police, who were told something of their history and who promised the ladies would be treated with every consideration. Chloe had told the girls to forget any part she might have played in the night's adventures. A few of them were still so spaced out that this advice probably hadn't been necessary. And they couldn't have identified their other savior even if they had wanted to. Disguised anew by simple expedient of removing all his swap-shop finery, letting his hair down, and washing the shoe polish from his face, Freddie was by now unrecognizable to anyone who had only met him the night before. Beyond that, Selene, using Prue's lipstick, had described flowers and astrological symbols all over him.

Selene hadn't wanted to go with the cops, had shown real distress at the idea. So she was still with Freddie and they seemed to be getting on famously. They may not have been on exactly the same wavelength, but at least they were on compatible ones.

"The moon is beautiful."

"Fuckin' fantastic, man."

46 freddie's coup

*We have to have in mind not an orthodoxy but a
wide and compassionate recognition of the storm
of ideas in which we are all living and in which we
must make our nests—find spiritual rest—as best we can.*

Gregory Bateson & Mary Catherine Bateson

A child of nature, a shaman cloaked in nothing but lipstick runes, Freddie was building an organization right there on the sand. He had found the bottles, though he didn't have any gasoline. Selene helped him scavenge light bulbs and bits of metal, wood, twine and plastic from the line of flotsam and jetsam back of the beach. Rising like some wild animistic shrine to spirits your average citizen never dreamed of, the structure took on a logic of its own as it grew and complexitized, reeling up towards the moon and the sky, a piece of fishing net draped off one side as though snagged there by some cosmic voyager.

"It's all balance, man. Fuckin' control." Freddie had told Chloe that, if he kept building his organizations, and if they were sufficiently complex and if he got lucky, he would eventually come up with something that was genuinely organic—not exactly alive, but something greater than the sum of its parts, the basis for a novel emergence, and this thing would be his gateway into a radically different world. At least she thought that was the gist of it.

Right now, Freddie was explaining to Prue and Ruthie that, if you understood time was infinite and maybe space too, though this wasn't necessary, then everything that happened *had* to happen, sometime. You got all these bits of the universe doing their things, going this way and that way and mixing up together in every way you could think of. "Sooner or later, everything winds up just the way it is now, you see? Not only that. Not only that, man, but, since we're dealing with infinity, here, then everything *has* to wind up this way—and every other way, too—over and over again. For fuckin' ever, man; just this way, again and again forever and ever. *Pow.* Pow, pow, pow, man."

"My God, how depressing." Prue coughed and took a drag off her cigarette. "Chloe, tell me it can't be true. Like, I'm going to have to live with husbands two and three all over again? Husband number one, maybe. But an infinite number of times? Give me a break. Karma doesn't get that bad. It couldn't. Freddie, you're full of shit."

"Oh, yeah? Oh, yeah, man?" Freddie's eyes rolled back so far they might have been undertaking an inspection of his brain stem. "Well, that's where you're wrong. You know? Because, just like there's all these times the world is exactly the way it is now, there's all these other worlds that are different."

"All this stuff you've been doing, Freddie. Your brain is leaking," said Ruthie. "I can't listen to this anymore."

"You get this infinite number of worlds that are only a little bit different from this one, and then you get a bunch more that are more different and so on until you get worlds so different from this one, shit man, you don't even know they're worlds. You get worlds with no Big Oil and no Coca-Cola. You get worlds where the Screw, Ruthie here, knows her ass from her elbow and everything. Fuckin' A, man. It's amazing." Freddie stood on tiptoe and threw a noose up over the highest member of his organization, ready for a hanging.

"Yeah? Well, what's the good of all these worlds if all we got is the one we're in?" Al Dente asked.

"*YEAH*," said Bibi.

Pretty good, for somebody who was only *al dente*. Chloe was impressed. She was also impressed that Freddie had actually used Ruthie's name. Was he going sweet on her, or what?

Freddie was hanging something in the noose.

"Freddie! *You* took the hood ornament." Prue was delighted.

"What did you fuckin' think, man?" Freddie was surprised she could have believed anything else.

"Yeah, man," he continued. "It's like this. You choose, okay? And every time you choose, you choose a new world. Can you handle it? I mean, like, the responsibility, man. Every time you decide to do something—every time you do this instead of fuckin' that, then you got a new world on your hands. It's only a little bit different. And it's going to happen again and again, just like the old one. And the same for the next one, and the next. But if you keep making the right decisions, then, after a while, you start to get a situation where things are really changing.

"Only most of us just go on making decisions. No, no; that's not right. We don't make decisions. We let the world do that shit for us, and we never really get anywhere. You know what I mean? Most of us never actually *choose* the world we live in."

"That's nothing but karma you're talking about, Freddie," said Ruthie. "Hey, everybody—Freddie's just reinvented the bicycle, here."

But Chloe was impressed. Fast Freddie was laying down a rap amongst raps.

"This dope, man. It's okay. It brings me down, you know? I can think better. Hey, has anybody got any money? I can buy some gas from one of those boatmen down there."

"Chloe." Waylon was back. He lay down beside her. "No problem. Looks like I'm finished with the police. And Leary says I

Freddie's Coup

can start the medic first-aid scuba course day after tomorrow. That's Monday. The following Saturday we're going to have a party. Back in Pattaya. Leary says to invite all your friends. If any of them want to come with us tomorrow, he can put them up, no problem.

"Hey," Waylon asked. "What's that?"

"It's a fuckin' organization, man. Got any money for gas?"

"I can get some. How much do you need?" Waylon went off towards the restaurant to look for Leary.

"I didn't know you'd been in Vietnam, Freddie," said Prue.

"Me? I never been to 'Nam. You crazy?"

"And you've never seen a Pink Floyd concert in Jersey, I suppose?" asked Chloe.

"Never even been to Jersey. Hey, man. Nobody in their right mind ever went to Jersey."

After Freddie went for his gas, Chloe and Waylon lay back and gazed at the sky. Chloe recognized the Big Dipper. She followed the handle to the Little Dipper, and experienced a sudden, comforting sense of continuity with the young girl growing up in the Oregon countryside, the person she used to be, who knew all the constellations in the sky. Other names for these two were Ursa Major and Ursa Minor—the Big Bear and the Little Bear. Chloe felt another glow, however slight, at the thought that Terdsak's bears had won their release. Not just those creatures he had had caged, but all those he would never get to torture in future.

Some diehard remnants of Terdsak's army were still on the island, searching, although most had long since fled the scene.

It had been a night for heroes. Freddie, of course, had distinguished himself. And Leary and his posse had taken a few of the rogue gunmen and scared more into running. Even the 4H Club had gotten involved in a tussle with two hard men who were armed with nothing more than sticks and misplaced confidence. Al Dente had wielded his iron exercise bar with good effect, while the Rev broke the stem on his favorite pipe by dint of thrusting it up hard under the jaw of one of the thugs. Ruthie further pacified the latter individual with a deadfall coconut, and Bibi fetched sturdy rope from the line of flotsam and jetsam at the high-water mark, showing them a few knots she remembered from Habonim, the South African Zionist equivalent of the Girl Guides.

"'Some on this side, and some on that side: they smote them, so that they let none of them remain or escape,'" the Rev pronounced. "Joshua, chapter eight, verse twenty-two."

Olga, according to Ruthie, had offered herself in voluptuous embrace to one young thug and then broken his neck. Knowing Olga, of course, that could have been accidental. The Russian masseuse had disappeared shortly afterwards. No one had seen her since, and everybody was worried. She had more courage than good sense, Chloe had to think, or she would have been long gone and far away by now. What on earth could have induced her to come to Phra Chan Island, knowing that Terdsak and his men might be around?

More police were on the way, Leary said, and they shouldn't worry. In the meantime, the cops wanted them to stay on Phra Chan, kind of under house arrest—at least until they got things more straight in their heads. But they had told Leary that there wasn't any real problem. They knew that the 4H Club members weren't involved. It was more for their own protection than anything.

What the hell, Chloe told Waylon. It looked as though they were going to get their tropical beach vacation together after all.

But for now everyone was exhausted. The best thing was to get some sleep. They would never find bungalows at this point, so, as Leary said, best slop on bug repellent and sack out on the beach.

Freddie's organization, it was generally agreed, was his best yet. Coming alive in the flames, it reeled and gestured, reaching for the sky before, consumed by its own passion, it fell in on itself. Later, after it had burned down to a soft glow behind them, embers popping and cracking, Freddie said, "You awake, man?"

"What is it, Freddie?" asked Chloe.

"I was in 'Nam, I guess. Sure I was. Special Forces. Super Special Fuckin' Forces. A special education. That's why I'm so smart today.

We killed some people, man. Farmers. And their little boys and girls. Even their dogs. Their cats and their pigs and every fuckin' thing. But I didn't mean to. Yeah. And some of my friends never came back neither, you know? So I don't talk about it."

Then he brightened. "Anyway, it's best not to say too much. They start getting information on you, man, you don't know where it's going to fuckin' stop. Next thing, they know what brand of toothpaste you buy and where you bought it and what you do with it, and everything. Then you're fucked. You know what I mean? They can work out every move you make. But you got to keep them guessing. Bob and weave. Now you're here, now you're not. Smoke and mirrors, man. Then you put a monkey wrench in the nice hi-tech World Processor and listen to it grind away. Give the Powers That Be a little indigestion, okay?"

"Sleep," Selene told him.

Waylon and Chloe slept together for the first time in a month. With everybody else sprawled out there beside them all they did was sleep, and talk a bit.

47 space cadets

One should always be a little improbable.

Oscar Wilde

Chloe was awed. An enormous orange disk loomed just off the horizon, close enough to touch. And she wanted to touch it. She felt its pull.

"OH, WOW. LOOK at the MOON." The nearly full moon had inspired veritable tsunamis in Bibi's neural protoplasm. "JUST AWESOME. That's *INCREDIBLE*."

"Cosmic." Al Dente was passing the snorkelbong to Freddie and going, "Like, far out; that's what it's all about," and generally giving the impression he had arranged the whole thing.

Chloe and Waylon had both declined the snorkelbong in favor of more cold beers.

The police had concluded their investigations on Phra Chan for the time being, although they had left a presence on the island just to reassure the tourists. Waylon and Chloe and all the others spent the day swimming and sleeping and getting to know one another. Leary, meanwhile, had invited the whole crowd from the 4H Club to come and stay in Pattaya for a while. He had lots of vacancies, he said, and could put everybody up in his bungalows.

He was especially pleased to have met Waylon's wife, about whom he had heard so much. "We get back to Pattaya," Leary said, "you can meet my wife Nance, just back from Singapore. Gosh. You're going to love my Nance."

Waylon was telling Leary again how he'd dived on the *Dark Moon* three times in one night. "Darn it, said Leary. "The current out there was a friggin' ripper. That's gotta be the biggest tide I seen in ten years. And you say you were inside that wreck at night. Fosdick, my man, better you than me. Gosh."

Chloe looked at Waylon again, and couldn't get over how different he seemed from the man who had traveled here with her just a month before. Prue had already given him her stamp of approval: "He reminds me of my first husband, only Waylon's better. I like him, Chloe."

"Yeah. He's nice," Ruthie agreed. Ruthie had discovered that she, Chloe, and Prue were all menstruating at the same time. Bibi had just finished her period.

The idea of blood brothers was a warlike tradition, Ruthie told them, based in violence. As blood sisters, on the other hand, they represented a nurturing tradition, and were united through a monthly cycle of pain and sacrifice for the good of the species. Synchronized menstruation was a sign that the moon and close association had brought them together in a new communion in harmony with the larger cosmos.

"Jesus Christ, eh?" Waylon sighed in the way he often sighed at Meredith, which told Chloe this was the basis of a sure-fire feature article.

"*COOL*," Bibi demurred, but her enthusiasm flickered and dimmed as she watched Al Dente move off to sit on a beach dune by himself. He had awakened from a drugged sleep after the party to discover mysterious designs all over his body. In her considered opinion, Ruthie had told him, the rusty-red pigment in question was menstrual blood; and Al Dente had run squawking for the water, hands out to either side for fear he'd touch himself. And now just about everybody was a suspect.

"The human body is ninety-eight percent water." Ruthie was spouting figures again. "Saltwater. We're still part of the sea. We evolved from the sea and now we carry it around inside ourselves. So it shouldn't be a big surprise if the tides affect us."

"You think it's the moon, man," Freddie was still bringing himself down from the Super Special Superman with dope and beer. "But it's, like, the *man* in the moon. That's where the real control is. The *man*-i-pew-lay-tors, man. Fuck them. Some of it's the moon. Sure. They'd like us to believe it's all the moon. And the sun, and the stars and all that shit. But you got to break the cycles, get outside of it. Pow! Never be in the same place at the same time. Pow, pow, pow. Bob and weave, dodge and burn, baby, *burn*."

"So we're swimming in our own seas." Chloe liked the idea. "Self-contained marine environments."

"Sure," said the Rev. "Our ancestors emerged from the oceans, and simply took the sea with them when they went up on land."

"The way we wear scuba gear underwater," Waylon suggested.

"Waylon, I want to learn to dive," Chloe told him. "Before we go back home."

"Great. Let's do it." Waylon was just grinning and taking it all in. He liked them all, even Ruthie. And Waylon's friend Leary. What a guy. He had just come back from supervising the salvage of Terdsak's Mercedes-Benz using a team of water buffalo. "Listen to this," said Leary. He had a little AM/FM radio tuned to an English-language Bangkok station. "They've been broadcasting this on the hour."

> Authorities are still trying to piece together what set off the orgy of murder and mayhem on Phra Chan and Phra Chan Noi islands last night, in which at least thirty people died and a hundred more were injured.

Space Cadets

Listeners may recognize Phra Chan as the main venue for the notorious "full moon parties" that have attracted so many young people to Thailand's southern waters and so much media interest from around the world. Last night Phra Chan saw even more action than usual. A mysterious series of fires and explosions demolished extensive facilities on Phra Chan Noi belonging to Thai Natural Trends, Ltd., a leader in the booming trade in herbal and New Age products.

Evidence suggests that events might have been related to a war between powerful foreign criminal elements and a local godfather known only as Terdsak. The trail of death and destruction finally led to Phra Chan itself, where several people, including four unfortunate full moon revelers and a policeman, were murdered. Scores more were beaten or robbed. Two boats were burned and sunk at anchor on Koh Phra Chan, while at least one Mercedes-Benz was beached . . . *um . . . that's what it says here, folks* . . . beached and then vandalized.

Many of the dead and wounded were from tourist boats that got too close to exploding ammunition on Phra Chan Noi, apparently under the misapprehension that the display was part of the full moon festivities.

A gold rush followed the discovery of a large quantity of bullion in the form of one-quarter-kilogram bars aboard one of the burnt-out boats on Koh Phra Chan. Scavengers also found a number of sizable gold nuggets among the charred bodily remains of Terdsak, the local godfather who reportedly died aboard the vessel while in the process of smuggling priceless artifacts out of the country. So-far unsubstantiated reports have it that a foreign woman, long sought after by Interpol for crimes ranging from smuggling to murder, died with Terdsak.

Locals and tourists alike had a field day collecting souvenirs, some of them valuable antique carvings, that had been strewn across the beach when the boats exploded.

Tourism officials, not wishing to go on record at this point, could only say that they were amazed by events, and they wanted the public to know that, in future, the full moon parties would incorporate more traditional entertainments such as classical dance and buffalo fighting.

> In related news, a mainland hospital is treating a number of badly bruised individuals who claim to have been savagely mauled by tigers on Phra Chan Noi.

They loved Chloe's account of the escape from Phra Chan Noi and the tigers. And they admired both Freddie's narrative embellishments and his tiger bruises, which were also lurid. But the full story of how Freddie came to be there in the first place was still something of a mystery for most of them.

"You wouldn't have believed it," Prue was telling them. "Terdsak's Mercedes-Benz is up to its axles in the sand, the tide coming up. The gold hood ornament's gone, the car's covered in fluorescent paint, and there's Freddie and half a dozen naked women in blackface. We come up to the car—the Rev, Bibi, Al Dente, and me—and Freddie's in a complete state. He's dressed up like a lunatic and he's got a *gun* in his hand. 'This is not a drill!' he's saying. He's frantic. 'Repeat, man. This is *not* a fuckin' drill.' A fifty-year-old guy with beaded gray dreadlocks and no clothes is sitting at the wheel, staring through the windshield up at the crowd on the beach. Two other people are fucking in the back seat, their feet sticking out the door, which is open. A couple more are sitting on the roof smoking a snorklebong. 'Hey, man,' goes Freddie. 'Get out of there. There's a bomb in this car. The guy at the wheel doesn't move, he just keeps humming that old Beatles song—'*Baby*, nh-nh, nh-nh, nhhh'—and once in a while he goes, 'Beep-beep 'n' beep-beep, *yeah*.' So Freddie grabs the keys from the ignition, hits the trunk release, and wades around to the back of the Benz to yank the trunk open. It's empty. No booze. No bomb. 'Just what I fuckin' thought, man,' he tells us. 'But you can't be too careful, you know?'"

"That's right," said Freddie. "And then Terdsak's boat blew up right behind me and I didn't know what the fuck was going on. Whoa. The whole night, man—a Fourth of Fuckin' July straight out of hell. It was like the hydrogen bomb. Bigger." Freddie cackled with glee, and so did everybody else. Even the Rev, who was a man of the cloth, sort of, and who shouldn't have been going around celebrating this kind of stuff. "'As wax melteth before the fire,'" he intoned, "'so let the wicked perish at the presence of Freddie.' Psalms. I can't remember which one."

Freddie blushed right through the lipstick daisies on his cheeks.

"AMAZING," remarked Bib. "Like it was GOD'S WRATH. *INCREDIBLE*. DRUGS and BOMBS and *EVERYTHING*."

Freddie had launched a two-pronged attack. His Super Special version of Terdsak's Special Superman was intended to enlighten the man or, failing that, put him on some other planet where maybe he couldn't hurt anyone anymore. At the same time, Freddie had replaced several bottles of Special Superman with gasoline and fused them, intending to blow the car up that night in the garage— hitting Terdsak where it hurt, but injuring nobody else.

"How on earth did you manage to get at the special whiskies?" asked Chloe.

They were kept in the inner sanctum of sanctums and Freddie was *persona non grata* at the 4H Club besides. But politics and war made for unlikely bedfellows, and this bed contained Ruthie, Gorgi, and Freddie—one of the unlikeliest threesomes anyone could imagine. In fact, it was Ruthie who had gone looking for an ally in Freddie. Ruthie adored Gorgi, and she hated to see what Terdsak was doing to him. So she had sought a way to wreak terrible revenge. "Terdsak was getting out of control," Ruthie told them. Her hero was being led astray, while the whole enterprise was being put in jeopardy by Terdsak's erratic behavior. What with one thing and another—Chloe's near rape, Freddie's mistreatment, and Tip's disappearance, among others—Ruthie, for one, was convinced that things had already gone too far. She had an idea that the Special Superman had been messing with Terdsak's head. Even Gorgi had been alarmed. He was scared of what Terdsak might do next, especially now that Terdsak was taking a direct hand in the operation of the Institute. And Gorgi knew how casually Terdsak killed.

"I wanted to hurt that bastard," said Ruthie. "I wanted to pay him back for what he was doing to Gorgi and the Institute, and for what he did to Chloe and Tip. And Freddie. I wanted to hit him where it hurt, and Freddie's idea sounded better than anything I could think of, short of shooting the son of a bitch."

As it happened, Gorgi, supposedly in Bangkok on business and well out of the way, had returned to the 4H Club and come upon Freddie and Ruthie as they were fixing the fuses. Gorgi told Freddie how sorry he was about what had happened to him, but he had to understand that Terdsak was the boss. "The money man," as Gorgi put it. "Yes?" Ruthie explained she was helping Freddie prepare his masterwork, an organization on a new scale, incorporating innovations such as timed detonators. Gorgi said he was pleased. In fact, he had taken a great interest in exactly how the fuses were constructed.

But if Terdsak's car blew up, and Terdsak held Gorgi responsible, then where would Gorgi be? "Dead," he told them. "Ha, ha." If it had been only a matter of blowing up the Benz, Gorgi would have been a fool to risk both his sinecure and his neck for so little return. But he saw a way to turn Freddie's plan to greater effect. If the bomb went off when Terdsak and his main security force were on the boat, this was another matter. This might be a good idea. But Freddie said that was too risky. He didn't want any collateral casualties: "Fuck, man. Nobody goes down to friendly fire, okay?" No, they had to blow the car in the garage.

Gorgi also heard about the plan for the medicine, and he said he could help with that. "Next thing," Freddie told them, "Gorgi and me, we're mixin' up the medicine, and he says, man, I got some mushroom we can add, some magic and everything. And I go, that's okay; but you never know, with this natural shit, about your quality control. 'I am studying herbal medicine for seven years,' Gorgi tells me. '*Atcha*. My mushrooms are reliable.'

"'Okay, my friend,' I say. 'Okay.' But I got to be sure we're in control.' So I add some LSD to make sure this fucker sees the light. Some cosmic vitamins for old Shitbag, you know what I mean? A little shortcut to where it's at and all. Some *Super* Special Superman, man—send him all the way back to fuckin' Krypton. But all I got is Windowpane, and you know how it is when you handle that stuff. You fumble it and you don't know where you're at. You don't even know if you dropped it or not. That's why they call it Windowpane, these tiny little squares, you can see right through the shit. I don't know if it goes in the mixer or not, so I throw in a few more to make sure, man."

"And can you believe it?" asked Ruthie, shooting Freddie a steely-prim look through her glasses. "Then he takes a hit himself."

"Well, yeah," replied Freddie. "You never know. Maybe I got ripped off with this acid, you know? It happens. But no, this is good stuff and chances are it all went in the brew. The mushrooms seemed pretty good too. Anyway, I been around, man—this shit is no problem for me. I been there. But not old Shitbag."

So that was the Super Special Superman. They filled a couple of cases with this stuff, Terdsak's own special reserve, half of it to be shipped to the TNT Complex. Then there was the little matter of the car bomb.

"Where did you learn about bombs, Freddie?" Chloe was still impressed with the idea that she'd been transported to Phra Chan Noi inside a live bomb.

"We did some hunting on the Web," Ruthie explained. "It was easy. Manuals for anarchists and militias, blueprints for revolutionaries—whatever you need, you can find. It's scary."

"The Web, man. And who's the spider? They're hooking the computers up with the TVs and the telephones and the credit cards and the databanks and, pretty soon, your toaster and your shitcan, and they're fuckin' feeding us all to the Great World Wide *World Processor*. You use the phone; you switch on the TV; you order a pizza; you take a look around on the Web—it's like you're a fly. The lines start to quiver away and the Spider says, hmmm, so that's where my little fuckin' fly is right now. I'll mark that down, here, just so I know what I've got and where I've got it when I need it. And the Internet. The *Net*. Like, who's the fuckin' *fisher*, man?"

"Give me a cigarette," he told Prue. "This is a special occasion, okay? Yeah, so we turn this shit against the Powers That Be, man, the people that made it all up. That's the only fuckin' way."

They had browsed the Web, looking for technical help because Freddie wanted to be sure this would go just right. "I didn't want to hurt anybody, okay?" He had been experimenting for a couple of days already before he discovered that one of Terdsak's medicinal barks—a material of uniform thickness and consistency—acted as a reliable timer for the battery acid. It took the acid almost exactly six hours to eat through three thicknesses. And that's how they set the fuse. Freddie had kept some of the details a secret. For example, the powdered substance that he'd prepared—the stuff that reacted with the acid—was a mystery. "I used to know something about this stuff, man. No more. Bygones are bygones, shit under the bridge and all."

Freddie dropped fuses into a few of the bottles and recorked them. Simple. "But then I waited up in that fuckin' tree for hours, man. Watching. And nothing happened. Now I don't know what's going on. Maybe I got the timing wrong, I'm thinking. Or maybe we didn't punch the fuses hard enough. Come morning, I see them drive the Benz on to Shitbag's boat, which is really a landing craft, and I'm thinking this could be a bad scene. The whole boat could go up and good riddance, except I don't even know who's on board. Chances are, whoever they are, they're going to die, and there's been enough killing for one time around. So I see I have to do something. But I can't get on the boat, and by the time I get to the pier they're gone."

In fact, the stuff was loaded on to Terdsak's landing craft and taken to the TNT Complex with Chloe drugged and tied up in the back seat of the Benz. Freddie didn't know that for sure, but he heard right away the next day, after Terdsak had left, that Chloe had disappeared. "And we still don't know where Tip is," Freddie said. "One way or the other, I had to defuse the Benz, man. Even if I had to fire-bomb the sucker."

Freddie's and Chloe's accounts together made it clear what had happened.

The whiskey cases in Terdsak's Benz had been off-loaded on the pier beside the fuel and arms depot. The Special Superman, which

Freddie had transformed into Super Special Superman, was then driven across to the TNT Party Complex. The straight export-quality Superman, which included two cases of what was really gasoline with time fuses, however mistimed they might have been, went into storage right beside a stockpile of fuel and fireworks. All this, in turn, was stashed right next to maybe a couple of tons of dynamite, blasting caps, probably a few thousand mortar shells, at least that many grenades, quite a lot of rifle and machine-gun ammunition, anti-tank and anti-personnel mines, and who knew what else.

The fireworks, Terdsak had explained to Chloe, were for special occasions, and the firecrackers were to scare evil spirits away. After this little display, you had to think, you weren't going to find an evil spirit within a hundred miles of the place.

The bomb had finally gone off, setting fire to the warehouse next to the arms cache first. The fuel and the fireworks had been the first show on the program that night. If only he had survived, Terdsak might have made life painful for the contractors who told him the TNT Party Complex was flameproof. Because it was only a matter of time before the ammo went up as well. In all fairness, of course, the contractor probably hadn't envisioned the extent to which his claim would be tested.

"That first bunch of explosions saved my neck, Freddie," Chloe said. "I was in big trouble, thinking there was no way out—it was horrible—when all of a sudden we get this diversion, a gift from God, and everybody's in a big panic."

"That's good, man. But I was afraid you were going to get blown up with the Benz, man. I knew I had to find that fuckin' car and make sure it didn't go up at the wrong time in, like, the wrong place." So Freddie, ripped as he had been, had managed to find the island and go looking for the Mercedes-Benz. "I thought they had me, one time there. I hear all these dogs barking and I think, 'They got me.' Then I hear shots and no more dogs. I get up a little closer and I see it's the same dudes that killed Pup, and I know I'm going to get these fuckers."

"How did you ever get Buk to take you?" Prue asked. Buk hadn't been too keen on going out to Phra Chan Noi even the first time, before he got beaten up.

"He didn't want to do it. He didn't want to go anywhere, man. Not till he'd had a drink or two. And Gorgi and me, maybe we tried too much of this medicine we're mixin', because everything got all fucked up.

"I've got two bottles of whiskey with me, yeah? One of them is the regular stuff, like, in case I need to negotiate, and one is the Super Special, just for emergencies. Cool. I tear a corner off the label of the straight shit, so I'd know, you know? So I give Buk this bottle and he takes a big hit off it.

"Next thing he's spewing this stuff all over the place. Then I see he's got a gun—a fuckin' pistol, man—and he's waving it at me and speaking Thai. I don't know what the fuck he's talking about, so I say 'Chill, man,' and I take a sniff and I see he's been drinking gasoline, which is not what I thought was in the bottle, man.

"Now I don't know what shit's gone where or how much. I'm worried I'm trying to blow up Shitbag's Benz with Super Special instead of gasoline, but, like who knows, maybe it works after all. And my friend, here, is still waving the gun. So I get out the other bottle, it's his life or mine, and I say, 'Chill—go easy, yeah?' But I guess his mouth tastes like shit because he uses the first couple of hits to rinse out and then he downs a couple more to clear his throat."

"Goddammit, Freddie," said Ruthie. "Will you get to the point?"

"Hey, man. That's what I'm doing. Pretty soon he clears his throat and probably his brain and his aura too, and I'm looking for a chance to get his gun off him because, to tell you the truth, I don't think he's competent. You know?"

Freddie's eyes had disappeared and he was going ack-ack-ack like Spunky OD-ing on peanut butter. Then they could see he was laughing.

"But I figure, so long as he has a co-pilot, yeah? Space cadets, you could call us. Still, he doesn't want to go to this island, man.

Not a chance. So I tell him Phra Chan Island, Full Moon Party City, and step on it, my friend. But it doesn't matter, because he can't find any island even if it's written on the back of his hand. So, like I say, we cruise around a bit, tour a bunch of islands.

"He speaks a little English, I guess, and he's telling me how he hates this boat and hates this sea, and now I *know* he's fucked up because he's a boatman, right? And boatmen don't hate the sea. Doesn't make sense. Anyway, I'm trying to chill when I see all this fire and everything, and I say, 'Look. There's the island; you can see the lights from the party,' and he goes 'Far out,' or something like that in Thai, and we go straight there, almost, and I'm happy because, no matter what shit's going down, it's got to be better than spending the rest of my life with Buk Rogers, here, exploring the universe. Give me a cigarette, man."

"Come on, Freddie. You've quit."

48 new directions

You cannot have both truth and what you call civilisation.

Iris Murdoch

On the boat to Pattaya, everybody had to go through their respective stories all over again. Bit by bit, it was all starting to hang together.

"Can you believe it?" said Prue. "She goes looking for a phone and, out of all those thousands of people, who should she run into but me?"

"It was *FATE*," suggested Bibi, taking a possessive hold on Al Dente's arm. "EVERYTHING IN THE WORLD IS CONNECTED."

"She was going to use that gun," Al Dente told them, his eyes big and blue and amazed.

Prue and Al Dente were particularly interested in hearing all about Jessica, someone they'd been personally acquainted with, however briefly. Chloe, of course, shared their curiosity.

Everybody was impressed with the radio report of Jessica's colorful history and Interpol's interest in her. Although, as Waylon said, it was hard to see how they had a line on her identity; there couldn't have been much left of her after the explosion. He tried to sound matter of fact, but, in truth, he didn't like to think about Jessica coming to such a unpleasant end, no matter how convenient it might have been. He kept trying to answer questions about what kind of person she really was, at the same time trying to fudge the fact they'd been shacked up together the whole of the previous month.

He was also getting to tell the story of why Gorgi wanted Terdsak dead—at least part of it—and of how Jessica turned *Sumalee* into a time bomb.

Although Ruthie was yet to be convinced, it was pretty clear that Jessica's George and the 4H Club's Gorgi were one and the same individual. "He may have had to do some things just to stay alive," Ruthie told them, "but he's one of the finest people I know."

Terdsak realized that Jessica was still alive. And if she were alive, then Gorgi must know about the double-cross. Why hadn't he simply grabbed her and interrogated her? Maybe it was the Special Superman. Or, as Jessica had suggested, maybe he thought he'd play the same game with her he had with the navy. Let her do all the work, salvage the goods for him.

But Jessica had played the same game, only better. Waylon told them part of the salvage story, a wild tale of multiple double-crosses. But some of the most interesting episodes he kept to himself. For instance, how she'd faked out Terdsak's men with the gold. He told them about recovering the gold. He didn't tell anybody about the Blue Buddha or the porcelain.

Even without the best stuff, his story went down at least as well as Chloe's and Freddie's had.

"You wait," Leary said, responding to the second telling of the actual salvage dive. "This man is gonna put Cousteau in the shade before he's through. Even if he does have doggone doo-doo for brains. The chances you took. Gosh, Fosdick. Another thing: I'd say Jessie hadn't counted on you being around to tell us all this."

"What do you mean?"

"I don't believe she would have told you these things if she thought they were going to go any farther. Fosdick my friend, I reckon you weren't supposed to come up off that wreck alive. You count your lucky stars Jessie didn't like to dive at night."

A little later, Waylon and Leary were up on the bow looking at the lights of the town as they approached Pattaya. Waylon was feeling purely good. He was back with Chloe, and they had decided to take another week's vacation and just relax, all the drama behind them.

"I always wondered what happened to *Dark Moon*," Leary was saying. "Darn it. She was the only boat around here that would've made a decent live-aboard, not that live-aboard diving is much of anything around here. But I would've liked to buy her.

"Anyway, now she sounds like one of your best dive sites around. Perfect depth, great location. Although it *is* a good three-day trip, there and back and a day of diving, so I guess we do need live-aboards now."

Waylon decided this was as good a time as any to ask Leary what he thought about the idea of his giving up the insurance game and going into commercial sports diving. "A lot of people are going to say I'm crazy. That this is just some kind of mid-life crisis."

"'Mid-life crisis'? Gosh. Don't get me started. They got to put a label on everything these days. And I'll tell you why. It's so we can turn it into something we can yawn at and say, 'Oh, yeah. My cousin had that last week. A gosh-darned mid-life crisis. No problem. It'll go away. Relax.' Sure. It's just like what McDonald's did to your corner hamburger joints. They're just about extinct. It's because the big chains promise no surprises and everybody wants to be safer than sorry. They never give you nothing really bad to eat. Everything is standardized. Homogenized. Everything's safe and predictable. Even our lives and our friggin' life crisises. You don't get any nasty surprises but, darn it, you don't get any good ones either. And that's what your mid-life crisises and your male menopauses and the rest of that gosh-darned malarkey is all about. 'Relax,' they're telling you. 'Don't worry. Be happy. Have a Valium. You think you're anything special? Friggin' forget it. This is something that comes with the passing of so many years and filing income tax returns once too often. That's all. Forget it. Everybody goes through it. Gosh. Don't do anything rash. Turn on the TV. Have a Big Mac. It'll go away.'

"Start your own dive business? Fosdick, I think it's a great gosh-darned idea. You got a natural talent for diving. You want to start up a dive shop? Do it. Just don't think about it too much, that's all. Gosh. You're the way you are, and that's the way you friggin' are. Stuff happens and you deal with it. You do it good, sometimes, and sometimes you screw up. But you can't be always worried about it. Darn it. There ain't enough time for that. You got to get on with living your life. No matter which way you go, you'll wind up dead one day anyway."

It was premature to talk to Leary about that diveboat, but Waylon was thinking they might be able to come up with something together. Leary had the know-how. And he had connections. He might even know how you went about disposing of priceless artifacts nobody even knew existed. Gorgi knew about the Blue Buddha, of course, but he didn't know it had been salvaged, much less where it was buried.

Nobody could claim you were stealing part of some nation's heritage, since this particular artifact had always been without a country anyway. What the heck, it might not even be there, whenever Waylon managed to get back to look for it. And if it weren't? No big deal. He still wanted to talk live-aboards with Leary. After he got his instructor's training out of the way, of course. And supposing he and Leary were still friends. He reckoned he would mention the Sung ceramics to Leary. It would be better if he got there before anybody else did. But he wasn't ready to talk about the Buddha.

"'I took bearings on the big tree and the rock shaped like a dick.'" That's what Jessica had said. And he vaguely remembered the spot anyway. Waylon felt guilty, of course. Especially as far as Chloe and Leary were concerned. When he examined his own motivations, he decided his secret was a kind of insurance. More than any possible financial windfall, the Blue Buddha was insurance against going stale again, a guarantee of more adventure whenever he needed it.

He'd tell Chloe eventually. After she heard the rest of his story, and after he listened to hers. And after he explained how he intended to go into sports diving full time, just as soon as they could settle their affairs back in Canada. It was hard to say how she was going to react to this news, but, he told himself with some wonderment and much pleasure, that decision was strictly nonnegotiable.

49 route maps

If two lives join, there is oft a scar.
They are one and one, with a shadowy third;
One near one is too far.

Robert Browning

"You look wonderful," Waylon told her.

Chloe felt wonderful. She had a great tan. And the weeks of vegetarianism and near-teetotalism, not to mention all the exercises she'd done with Prue, had honed an already lean body to a ten-years-younger ideal. Waylon also looked different. His body was harder and his skin had gone darker than hers.

"I like your beard," she said, thinking it would have to go. "And your scar." That could stay. "It looks like a dueling scar." She ran a finger along the angry red weal. Chloe sensed more to the changes in Waylon, and she looked forward to acquainting herself with them. But what she said was, "There's so much to tell you." Some of it would have to wait, but she wanted to tell it all, in its own good time.

She found more marks on Waylon—all of them mere scratches and bruises—and he found some of hers, the superficial ones. He found her amulet and asked about it, and she found his mandala. They swapped. "But don't wear it in the shower," she told him. She felt shy. It was as though they were meeting for the first time again, only they were different people now. The same, but different.

"Waylon, let's make love." Chloe wanted to fuck. More than that, she wanted to make love.

"What are you doing, Chloe?"

This question was to some extent rhetorical, since anybody could see Chloe was at that moment rolling a condom down over Waylon's penis.

"*Too MUCH. WHOLLY GIGANTIC.*" Bibi and Al Dente were next door, in the other half of the duplex bungalow, and it appeared Bibi's admiration for Al Dente was being requited. As was Al Dente's own. Love is blind.

Bibi and Al Dente were in what was Jessica's bungalow, only a month ago. Not that that caused Waylon any guilt, since he'd never slept there. Not that Jessica had ever slept there, come to that.

Chloe and Waylon began their own lovemaking, keeping it slow and easy. "Shh," said Waylon.

"To hell with it," replied Chloe. "*Ow.*" Waylon had come across one of her bruises.

Waylon kissed her everywhere he could find a wound, at the same time soothing injuries he couldn't see.

He thought the ugly rash on his hand must be fire coral. Probably also from inside the wreck. Chloe listened to him, to unself-conscious talk of sealife and dire hazard, at once enthusiastic and matter of fact, and she rejoiced. She saw Waylon as a semi-stranger, in a new light. Or, perhaps, in an old one. This was more like the person with whom she had first agreed to share a life. This was her Waylon of old, but, if anything, a new and improved version, tested and tempered in ways she could only guess at so early in their new life together.

Chloe found the cut, still infected, where Waylon had scraped himself on the hatch when he went in after the bags. Waylon traced the raw scratches from where Chloe had slipped and fallen in the longtail boat, setting out from Phra Chan Noi with Freddie's Traveling Minstrels. Chloe asked about the hint of the rash on Waylon's shoulder where Jessica had pissed on him, and he told her some part of it. And so it went, two road maps of adventure and trauma that had led them back together again. Waylon touched the bruise where Terdsak had rammed Chloe's thigh against the edge of the table in the New Rich Club, first with his fingers, ever so gently, and then with his tongue. He went farther, and a letting-go grew in her, the start of a healing. Waylon was closing wounds at the same time he was opening her to the pleasure of this moment, opening her to a whole new horizon of possibility. She opened to her husband, and she came and she came.

She cried when she told him what Terdsak had tried to do to her.

Waylon held her, took her tears on his lips, and she loved him for the questions he didn't ask. Not yet.

"He's dead," she told him.

"Good."

"So how was your vacation, Waylon?"

"Interesting. How about yours?"

"Interesting. It'll take some time to tell you about it."

"Chloe?"

"Yes, Waylon?"

"I want to sell the business. I'm going to open a dive shop."

"Okay. Waylon?"

"Yes?"

"I want a child." She was just about as surprised as he was.

50 insurance

Most of us are still looking for security when we're lying there on our friggin' death beds. But it's a myth. A superstition. There's no such thing, and that's pure and simple fact.

Leary

Much as a fisherman might try this plug or that popper, the lovely Number Seventeen at Van Go-Go's Starry Night had taken to casting winsome bumps and languishing grinds at Leary.

"Are you a fisherman, Fosdick? No? Well, when you're fishing for bass, as soon as you get a bite you yank on the line. Bass don't deliberate. Gosh, no. Neither do pike. They bite or they don't, and when they do, they don't mess around. They swallow the whole darned bait—hook, line, and sinker. Trout, on the other hand, they like to dither; and a good trout fisherman understands that. Trout nibble and nudge and circle around. A good trout fisherman isn't going to yank at the first sign of interest. That's enough to put a trout off the game completely. No, you let the fish think it can dither all it likes. You tease it, whip it up into a gosh-darned frenzy of desire till finally it forgets it's a trout and thinks it might be a bass.

"This girl takes me for a bass," Leary concluded. "Thank gosh, because if she was fishing for friggin' trout I'd probably be a goner."

"Leary. What the hell are you doing? Nancy just got in from Singapore last week."

"Darn it, Fosdick. I'm only having a bit of fun. Nance knows I don't mean no harm. Gosh. That's why we been together so long."

They had left the ladies at Hot Licks. Chloe and Nancy and Prue were old pals already. Between them, they appeared to be outlining a user's manual for the modern male. In fact, it was scary how well all the women were getting along. Ruthie, when Waylon last checked, had been explaining to Big Toy and Dinky Toy just how Leary was exploiting them, never mind they were the majority shareholders in the joint, though Ruthie didn't know that.

"Let's leave the ladies alone, just to get acquainted, like," Leary had suggested. "They can compare notes while we retire to Van Go-Go's for some men talk and friggin' overpriced drinks. Lots of time before the party starts."

They were into their second round of expensive drinks when the door to the street opened, disconcerting Waylon with the sudden anomalous stream of sunlight. It was Eddie, who was looking after the Down Down Diving Center office that afternoon. He headed straight over to where they stood at the bar. Eddie was a bass, no question about it. He handed Waylon the piece of paper without ever taking his eyes off Number Seventeen. "Waylon. Got a message for you."

Urgent. Please call this mobile phone number. We must arrange to meet for possible mutual benefit.

The caller's name was George.

Eddie had gobbled the bait, hook, line, and sinker, and went back to work probably thinking he'd staked a claim on Number Seventeen by buying her a cola before he left. But, given the come-ons she was now casting in his own direction, Waylon was getting the idea that this lady had an entirely non-specific affection for the male gender. Although she *was* looking at him in a pretty special way.

"Gosh, Fosdick. You still with us? What's the message?"

Waylon passed the note over and then told Leary about the "George" Jessica had been talking to on her phone. Leary suggested they run the name and number past the ladies back at Hot Licks and see what they came up with.

"Where did you get that?" said Ruthie. She'd recognized it as Gorgi's cellphone right away.

Waylon called the number and arranged to meet Gorgi, a.k.a. George, at one of Leary's bungalows. The venue was ideal, a duplex with interesting acoustics and a connecting doorway to the adjoining unit. In fact, it was the very place where Waylon and Chloe were staying, and it made for ease of eavesdropping while allowing for rapid access from both front and back if needed. It was also well down a quiet lane and away from curious eyes. Gorgi said Waylon should come alone; the proposition he had in mind should be kept discreet. Leary checked first to see that his policemen friends were available, and then had Waylon tell Gorgi that he'd meet him in one hour. Ruthie insisted on going along, and so did Chloe.

Gorgi looked vaguely Pakistani, in his loose cotton blouse and pantaloons, a little white pillbox hat on his head. Chloe had been right. Waylon could see the black stains on Gorgi's cheeks right through the straggly beard.

"So what's the deal, George?" Waylon asked him.

"Yes. Chloe's husband. So nice to meet you. So sorry to hear about Jessica."

"You knew Jessica?"

"Yes, of course. We were old friends. A remarkable woman, yes?"

"Yes."

"Jessica told me so much about you. Yes. She said you are a *good* man. Brave. Nice." Waylon had the impression Gorgi almost gagged on that last proposition. "A good diver."

"I *have* got my advanced open water." Waylon adopted a modest demeanor. "And my wreck diving specialty and half my medic first-aid."

"Precisely. *Atcha*. I believe you and Jessica went diving on a boat. A wrecked boat. A place one day away from Phra Chan Island. She was going to tell me exactly where that vessel was. Before she had this unfortunate accident. But now you know, so you can tell me."

"Sorry, eh? I don't know."

"Don't know? Ha, ha. How can you not be knowing? You dived on this boat. Yes?" George's head bobbled as though he were signaling "no."

"I wasn't paying any attention. We just went there, and I dived."

Gorgi produced a pistol. Waylon had seen enough action movies to recognize the long metal cylinder on the end of the barrel as a silencer. It was remarkable, he thought, how many weapons had been pointed at him in the past few days. "I am asking you another time," said Gorgi. "Where is the boat? You will answer me or I will shoot you in the foot. Then I am asking you again. If you do not answer? Good. I will shoot you in the other foot. And so on. Until you are answering me. Or you are bleeding to death. You decide. *Atcha*. I am giving you two minutes. You should reflect. Meditate. Ask yourself what you are really wanting in this life."

Waylon had a hard time not looking toward the door to the adjoining unit. Leary had proposed the idea of leaving a gun under the sofa for Waylon, in case of emergency, but Waylon had said he wasn't into gunplay. Now he was having second thoughts. How many holes would Gorgi be able to put in him before Leary and the police intervened? "George," he said. "If I tell you what I know about the wreck, will you tell me what you know about Terdsak's part in all this? And where you fit in with Jessica and Terdsak?"

"These things you are not needing to know. In any case, you are in no position to negotiate. I have the gun. *Atcha*. You will tell me what I want to know." Gorgi looked impatient, never mind the civil tone.

"Okay," said Waylon. And he gave him a GPS position quite similar to the one he'd committed to memory. At Gorgi's insistence, he also drew him a little map, one that put *Dark Moon* no more than three miles from her actual location. The main goodies were gone anyway, although Gorgi didn't know that. And that wasn't all he didn't know. No matter how much of an understanding he and Jessica had had, and no matter what red-hot lovers they'd been, it seemed that Jessica had only told him that she *thought* she could find *Dark Moon* again, neglecting to mention her GPS. And she hadn't told him they had recovered the Buddha. Waylon guessed she decided Gorgi had no need to know.

"*Atcha*," said Gorgi, and he did look pleased. "And now I will tell you what you are wanting to know. Why not? You will never tell anyone else."

"No, no. Never."

"Precisely." Gorgi mewled a little and then laughed. "Ha, ha. Okay, ask me."

"How did you know Jessica?"

"You and Jessica were lovers," Gorgi replied, and, before he could stop himself, Waylon glanced at the wall behind which Chloe and Ruthie and Leary and the cops were listening. "She told me. Good. Never mind. Jessica was also with Terdsak, at one time. Yes. But she was my lover first. And last. She and I had a special understanding, and she was always straight with me."

At this point Gorgi was interrupted by a faint wail from the room next door. "Do you hear that?" He chuckled. "You cannot tell if the woman is having an orgasm or getting beaten. Jessica was like that sometimes. Did she ever ask you for the trick with the basket?"

"No."

"No?" Gorgi looked pleased. "Terdsak and I would joke about Jessica, after he thought she had died on *Darunee*. 'The Black Widow,' we called her. Many men who thought they were her lovers are now dead. But enough of that. Now she is dead and I am alive. And you have been lucky. So far." Gorgi underlined this observation by pointing the gun at Waylon's face again. "I want what is mine. Do you understand?

"Terdsak was a dangerous man. But stupid, yes? All his security measures, and a security chief he couldn't talk to. Just because it looked good, gave him big face. And always getting Ten to taste his Special Superman, in case somebody was putting poison in it. Ha, ha. It was already poison. It was eating his brain. Soon he would have died anyway.

"He was so proud of his Special Superman. He thought it gave him control. It was sending him *out* of control. If the drink did not kill him, his own men might have, they were becoming so afraid."

According to Gorgi, it was difficult to say whether their friend Terdsak was crazier before or after he started taking the Special Superman. He was a man who needed to believe he was in control. And although Gorgi was his herbal physician and business partner, that didn't mean Terdsak trusted him.

"He had a life insurance policy—a standing contract out on my life. If Terdsak died before I did and there were any suspicious circumstance whatsoever, E-go and Ten were to kill me." Inappropriately, to Waylon's mind, Gorgi giggled at this. "Slowly and painfully, they were to kill me. *Atcha.* It was as simple as that. They were beneficiaries of the policy, you see, only so long as they fulfilled that condition. And Terdsak neglected to tell me who was administering the benefits.

"So, the Special Superman was eating at his brain, and I was thinking his men might get so nervous, the way he was going, that they killed *him*, just to be safe. And I am seeing that something else must occur to these men. If they just go ahead and arrange for Terdsak to die—why wait, after all?—then they can be killing me and collecting their money right away.

"You can understand I was already nervous. Yes? But then Terdsak discovered Jessica was alive. If he knew that, then he knew I knew he had double-crossed me. I saw my days were numbered, one way or the other. If Terdsak didn't order me killed himself, his men might well kill him and then be killing me just to collect the insurance.

"Then Freddie came along with his plan and I saw a chance to remove both Terdsak and his life insurance beneficiaries." He saw immediately how foolish it would be to screw around with Terdsak in any way but a terminal one. At the same time, he realized how little modification to Freddie's plans it would take to do a proper job on the boss. All that was required was for the fuses to detonate about six hours later than Freddie had set them for.

"And something that Freddie did not know." Gorgi chortled. "Terdsak's landing craft was also carrying a load of gasoline for the Benz. It was like a big bomb."

Gorgi had tampered with the fuses to delay the explosions. But he had miscalculated, adding another two thicknesses of bark, planning for Terdsak and his main security force to die on the boat, not realizing that the more the acid had to eat through, the slower it moved. "Or maybe someone else had already tampered with them. Yes? Maybe someone who hated or feared Terdsak enough to be also wanting him dead, and not merely annoyed. And there is only one other person who knew about the fuses, aside from Freddie."

In any case, the fuses were still working when the cases were unloaded on Phra Chan Noi.

"No matter. The rest is history, as they say. *Atcha*. Terdsak is dead. So, I hope, are his men. And now, my nice young friend, it is time we are saying goodbye." Gorgi gave the silencer a quick twist to make sure it was secure, and raised the pistol.

"You don't have to do that," said Waylon, surprised at how steady his voice was. "I'm not going to say anything."

"That is true. You are most certainly not going to say anything. And neither are some other people. That terrible woman Ruthie, for one. She is also knowing too many things. Better safe than sorry, no?" Gorgi tittered.

There was a sudden wailing, the unpleasant kind of ululation you associate with banshees. Both Gorgi and Waylon whirled towards the sound as the door burst open. At almost exactly the same instant, the window on the other side of the room shattered. Gorgi was of two minds and possibly more, his gun swinging between the window, the door, and Waylon. He finally settled instead on another option altogether, and aimed at the individual who was hurtling towards him from the doorway. At that moment, Waylon dived for Gorgi, bringing him down before he got the shot off. He wrestled the gun away just as the screeching fury got her claws into Gorgi's face.

"You fucking son of a *bitch*," said Ruthie, along with some other things in a similar vein. But a number of uniformed men managed to pry her off Gorgi while he was still fairly recognizable.

"Took your time, didn't you?" Waylon said to Leary, returning Chloe's big hug even as he spoke. She had moved in just about as fast as Ruthie had.

"Jesus Christ, Fosdick," Chloe told him.

"Hey. That was frig-all." Waylon got the intonation just right, not a hint of self-consciousness. "No problem."

"Fosdick my boy," Leary boomed at him, "that move of yours could've gotten you killed. You're lucky one of my friends, here, didn't shoot you by mistake. In that kind of situation you just sit still and let the friggin' professionals handle things. Gosh." Leary shook his head. "*Darn* it."

When Waylon thought about it he could see what Leary meant. It reminded him of when he went into the water tank on *Dark Moon* with his regulator out of reach. He felt a bit of the cold sweat effect, just for a moment there. But what the hell. Things had worked out. He'd be more careful next time.

Next time?

A little later, Leary took Waylon aside. "Fosdick, my boy. I'm a tad confused. Why didn't you just tell Gorgi you already salvaged the gold? That it was long gone. Then he wouldn't have had to go on about shooting your friggin' knees off, and suchlike."

"Jessie told him we never actually got the stuff. So he wouldn't have believed me anyway."

"Gosh. You're probably right. But I've been thinking. What about the news reports of all the gold they found after the boat blew up? I don't suppose there was something else on *Dark Moon*, then? Something nobody else knows about?"

"Now that you mention it, Leary, there was something." And without further preamble Waylon told him about the loot in the forward fuel tank.

"What are you telling me? Darn it. You mean to say you do know exactly where *Dark Moon* lies, then? But it isn't where you said? And it just happens to be full of gosh-darned priceless ceramics?"

"That's right. So what do you think we should do?"

"Fosdick, my boy. You and I need to have a serious talk. Gosh-darn it, I believe there just might be something to this friggin' mid-life crisis stuff after all."

Just for a moment Waylon also wanted to tell Leary about the Blue Buddha, his little insurance policy against going stale. His proof against mid-life crises and suchlike. But it was better to wait.

51 all's friggin' well

The universe is a hologram. In our little community, we heal each other even as we heal ourselves.

Gorgi

"**W**aylon."

"Meredith."

"My poor Waylon."

"Meredith?"

"I'm in love, Waylon."

And who could doubt it? The way she hung on the Rev's arm causing him to perspire even more than usual.

"Oh, Waylon," she said. "Ernest is so much like you. Dearest Waylon. We're getting married." Evidently the Rev had given up his idea of joining a cloistered order, at least for now and probably forever, if Meredith had her way.

"'Ernest,'" said Chloe. "Your name is Ernest."

Meredith was looking great. A veteran of four sessions end to end at Wat Nai Fun, she was slimmer than she'd ever been. And she exuded a new confidence, a sparkling calm nothing like the tranquilizer-induced balminess of old.

"Are you ordering *another* beer, Ernest?" Meredith gave him a forbearing smile. "Is that a good idea?"

"Perhaps not, Merry," he replied, his own smile verging on a wince.

Still, despite the odd outbreak of temperance it was shaping up to be a hell of a party. "Nance don't drink, as a rule." Leary gazed fondly at Nancy, who was at the bar matching Big Toy tequila for tequila while Dinky Toy tended to a bottle of sparkling wine. "I do enough gosh-darned drinking for the two of us."

A fair number of drinks were doing down on all sides, and more than a little fond gazing as well. Hot Licks was packed out and the night was still young. Not that you needed a reason to have a party, but there were plenty of good reasons for this occasion.

Even though Boom wasn't there, she was real cause for celebration. She'd been lucky. Her eyes were okay and the doctors believed there wouldn't be much scarring. Maybe none. Dinky Toy, already delighted for Boom, had more good news. Nancy had come back from Singapore with a surprise. She and Leary and Big Toy hadn't wanted to say anything earlier, until they knew more, but it seemed a plastic surgeon was applying new techniques he believed would help in Dinky Toy's case. The operations were expensive, but they had found a formula whereby the costs could be covered out of the operation of Hot Licks. And Dinky Toy was welcome to stay with some of Nancy's friends in Singapore, which would significantly reduce the overall damage.

And nobody was above raising a glass to the demise of Terdsak, local godfather recently deceased. No matter how misunderstood and drug-addled he might have been, he made better company dead than alive.

Gorgi was in jail. In fact, the longer he stayed locked up the better, seeing as how E-go and Ten were still at large and no doubt anxious to collect on Terdsak's life insurance policy. The police had determined that Gorgi's real name, or one of them, was George, although sometimes he was George Montrage and other times he was George Ventrage, nationality unknown. He sometimes carried Indian or Trinidadian passports. His specialty was manipulating people, occasionally killing them, with drugs. As if that weren't enough to disillusion her, Ruthie had learned from Selene that Gorgi, a frequent visitor to the TNT Party Complex, hadn't spent nearly as much time in Bangkok as he'd made out.

Still, almost everybody had reason to celebrate. Big Toy told them Boom was back in her home province of Phitsanoluk. Her cousin had sold some land, and they were going partners on a little restaurant. Nok, the Hummingbird, was planning to join them in a month, when things were better set up. Maybe this was why Oscar was looking at Nok as though he were seeing her for the first time.

"Nok, honey," he cooed, in un-Oscar-like tones, "come here." But she was busy with the cash, still vibrating but more focused, somehow happier. Oscar's expression held hints of baby seal, both the pre-bonked and the post-bonked variety.

Eddie was engaged in serious conversation over beer and cola at a table with Oi. Big Toy had already found replacements for both Boom and Nok. Oi and Oo from the Gang of Four had had enough of Bangkok. Oo was at that moment collapsed at Waylon's table, straight off the bus from Bangkok, face down on her arms. At first Waylon had been uncomfortable with Oo and Chloe in the same room, but Oo acted as though they'd never met. Even though she was now sitting at their table, together with the Rev and Meredith. Upon careful reflection Waylon realized he was miffed, just a little.

And there was Meredith, in love with another man. She had sailed right past and Waylon had survived, ungutted by the nine-tenths of the iceberg that never surfaced.

Even as Waylon and Chloe renewed their relationship, their friends, old and new, were coming together like the parts of an intricate puzzle. Getting to know them was also helping him to appreciate new and sometimes surprising facets of Chloe's personality. This woman was not the wife he had come to know over the past years. Not entirely. Waylon almost felt as though he and Chloe were dating again.

"It's amazing, isn't it?" Chloe remarked. "It's only been five or six weeks since we left Vancouver."

A month and a half had passed since he'd bonked Meredith. About the same time since he'd inadvertently left Chloe. Five or six weeks since he'd seen a human head squashed on the pavements of Bangkok. About three weeks since he'd seen his first man shot to death. He himself had had guns pointed at him on a number of occasions. Looking back now, he could see he'd come close to being killed more than once.

He'd pissed on a woman in the shower. He'd slept with his first bargirl. And his second. Maybe his third and fourth, depending on how you looked at it, and depending on what had happened while he'd been drunker than he'd ever been in his life. He was a certified advanced open-water diver. He was a Wreck Diver, a First-Aid Medic, a Totally Wrecked Diver and a High Diver who was looking forward to doing his Rescue Diver, Divemaster and so on right up to Master Scuba Instructor, and then to owning his own shop.

"I'm looking forward to things, Chloe."

"Me too, Waylon."

The Rev had filled his pipe, leveled it off nicely, and was now applying his pipe lighter, running it around and around the bowl at a precise distance from the tobacco, sucking rhythmically all the while. Flames shot up from the bowl like a volcano, and a shower of burning ashes erupted to settle all over the table. As the Rev slapped at his shirt-front, Oo abruptly came to life, making exasperated noises and brushing wildly at her long mane of hair. The Rev waved apologetically from somewhere within the great cloud of aromatic smoke, little remaining of him but a great Cheshire Cat grin of satisfaction and the beard beneath it. This beard proceeded to waggle with much earnestness. "'He who doth not smoke hath either known no great griefs, or refuseth himself the softest consolation, next to that which comes from heaven.'" The Rev discreetly tipped a silver hip-flask into his glass of water. "Some great man said that. I can't remember whom."

Experiencing a moment of wry recognition, Waylon watched the Rev redeploy his smoking and drinking paraphernalia, ordering his universe. Then, as the Rev exchanged fond gazes with Meredith, who had already risen to flee for the bar, Waylon watched as Chloe performed the experiment of switching the Rev's glass and ashtray. A couple of minutes later, with all due gravity, the Rev tapped dottle into his whiskey. Amazing.

Ruthie was at the far end of the bar, breathing through a tissue. Meredith was looking back thoughtfully at her loved one from where she now stood with Dinky Toy, who was pouring her some wine. Selene was there as well, and she looked smashing in a new cotton dress. From what Waylon heard, this was just about the only time anybody had ever seen her clothed. Freddie was back in costume, resplendent in Lycra jumpsuit and cape of many tapes. Worried about Sweet Mama, he was anxious to get back to the 4H Club. In the meantime, he'd begun construction of what looked like a mini-organization right there on the bar, for starters using Kratingdaeng stimulant cocktail bottles and plastic straws. Captain Ot was standing beside Freddie, listing away and beaming like a lighthouse. Though he couldn't hear it, Waylon knew he was saying, "Never mind; never mind." Freddie was sharing a bottle of Mekhong with Captain Ot and Buk Rogers—whom, it seemed, was going to work as Leary's chief driver. They were mixing the stuff with Kratingdaeng. And lime juice. "Otherwise it's just too fuckin' sweet, you know?"

"Freddie, my boy," boomed Leary from across the room, rattling the windows in the process. "You're not planning to burn the friggin' place down, now, are you? Gosh. If it ain't one thing it's another."

Meredith and the Rev wanted to stay in Thailand for the time being. Meredith was thinking of throwing her psychoneuroimmunological skills into the 4H Club pot, while the Rev had said

433

he could provide a more ecumenical, free-style approach to meditation instruction, one that included chairs for anybody who wanted them.

Bibi and Al Dente, who had elected themselves to the board of directors, were happy with that arrangement, and a newly chastened Ruthie said she would go along with it, she guessed. Everybody wanted to make Prue a partner as well, but she'd had a message from her first husband.

"He's opened an office in Singapore and he wants to see me. I'd have to be crazy to go anywhere near him." From her perch atop a barstool, Prue paused her leg-lifts and lit a new cigarette off the stub of the old one. "I don't like to talk about it, but I've actually married that jerk twice. Can you imagine? In a way, he's both Husband Number One and Husband Number Three, though, thank God, he's nothing like the real Number Three."

"So you're not going." Chloe drew the obvious conclusion for Prue.

"I'm leaving on an evening flight tomorrow. I think I've learned all I'm going to from the 4H Club. Anyway, Singapore has fantastic shopping."

"It's so *CLEAN*, there," Bibi added. "And it's got SHOPS and *EVERY*THING."

Olga's appointment to the 4H Club's Chair of Massage Arts would have been unanimous, but she'd been last glimpsed in the company of a young man with an extravagant blond hairdo. That was the night before everyone had left Phra Chan Island to go up to Pattaya. In fact, they'd received a message from her that day, making it official. She was with E-go.

"What the hell," said Ruthie. "We'll need security. And Olga's a genius at massage. Let's take them both in."

Big Toy, who had a large appetite for the finer things, had sent out for durian. Leary was sulking because the whole bar smelled like a busted toilet, as he put it. Waylon remembered Oo's story of her dead boyfriend, and asked Leary what he thought about drinking and eating durian together.

"Gosh. That stuff'll kill you all by itself. Don't need to drink whiskey with it."

Waylon had a piece anyway, and so did Chloe. The taste was growing on him.

Al Dente refused to try it. He said he was planning to do a book on strange foods of Asia. "But I don't have to eat this crap," he told them. "I'm only going to do the pix. Somebody else can do the words. What about it, Chloe—interested?"

Waylon asked Leary how his own book was going, and Leary told him he hadn't started writing, as yet. Not quite. But he had bought a little tape recorder. "Like the ones those reporters use, you know? I'm going to call it *Half Full*. Darn it, I plan to live to be a hundred. And turning friggin' fifty don't mean my life is half empty. No way. I got this funny feeling the adventures are only starting."

And maybe Leary was right, because a few minutes later Waylon was standing in line, waiting to use the toilet, when muffled thuds issued from inside, together with a clatter and something that sounded like an oath or two.

"Gosh-*darn* it, Nance." Leary's voice came through clearly.

Everybody stood back as the door opened to reveal Nancy standing there, remarkably composed except for a false eyelash stuck to her cheek and a broken toilet seat hanging casually from one hand.

"Yes, what is it?" she said. "We'll just be a moment, *la*."

Leary appeared from behind her, clutching at his head. He staggered past his wife and into the room, looking around at the others with a kind of dull challenge, as if to say, "We haven't been in the toilet *that* friggin' long. So what's everybody looking at?" He accepted a whiskey on the rocks from Big Toy and rubbed it back and forth across his brow. "Gosh," he said. "*Darn*."

Waylon had been dying for a piss. He was relieved to see the fish were still okay. As okay as they could be, given their lifestyle. Back at the bar, he asked, "So, Leary. Is this one of those times somebody up there had to take a leak?"

"What?" Leary staggered to one side, clutching at his head, and took a swig of whiskey. Nancy was over at a corner table talking and laughing with Chloe and Prue.

"Remember? The fish. One minute you're smelling of roses and the next minute you're flapping around high and dry?"

"Gosh, no. Nothing like that. Everything's just friggin' fine. Nance is back to stay and that's purely good news. Things were commencing to become a tad boring around here. Not anymore. Gosh. But, like I say, it's just as well Nance don't drink too much as a rule." Leary looked thoughtful. "Anyway, you wouldn't want to understand the critters. It'd take all the gosh-darned magic out of it. I guess."

Everybody was basically happy. And one signal event: Chloe had finished her basic open water scuba training with flying colors. Not only that, their blood tests were in, and there was no problem. This was something that made Chloe even happier than her new certification, and Waylon had to admit he was pleased as well. "We can start working on a kid right now, Waylon," she told him. "As soon as we get back to the room, I mean."

52 mirror souls

The best mirror is an old friend.

German proverb

Chloe stared into the little lotus pond outside the door to their bungalow, reflecting on her mirror soul. When she was a child, she used to look into the mirror and see another world. She would see herself as someone different, not quite herself, and she would imagine that, if only she could follow that mirror self out through that other bathroom door, she would find herself in a different world, a world full of surprise and new opportunity. Some people believed you also had a shadow soul. How many other souls did she have, she wondered, and how were they manifested?

"Stop and look at yourself," Prue had said. "Ask yourself who you are and why you're the way you are. Just don't expect to find the same thing every time you look. But it's important to keep looking and asking."

Tuk-kae. The sound of the lizard intruded on her contemplation. *Tuk-kae.* She found herself counting: "One, two, three. . . . Four, five. . . . Six. . . . *Seven.*"

Tip had told her that she was learning to listen to herself. And Chloe could see that that was right. She could also see that Waylon, in some way, was learning *not* to listen to himself, at least not so much. Chloe liked the new-model Waylon. And she was learning to like the new Chloe. She smiled. She had collected a single frangipani blossom during her stroll with Waylon just after breakfast. Now she dropped it into the water, gorgeous white against the reflected blue of the sky, and she floated her sorrow and her thanks to wherever Tip was now.

Waylon and Chloe were going up to Bangkok to catch their flight back to Vancouver that afternoon.

53 mile-high

They don't want us treating people holistically. If you're going to treat somebody holistically, you got to treat the whole world. That's holistic medicine, man. You get me? But it's more than that. It's the whole universe. The yin and the yang. If that's out of balance, man, then we're all fucked.

Fast Freddie

"Ow," said Waylon. "Holy *shit.*" He hit the ceiling of the toilet so hard he almost sprained his neck. He also whacked his knee on the sink.

"Shh!" Chloe giggled. "Hey, Fosdick. Did the earth move for you too?" She gasped as the plane hit another air pocket, and they held on to one another, weightless for a moment in that tiny enclosed space, giddy with terror and fun. Then some toddler deity grabbed their aircraft, a toy, and for long moments tried to shake all the funny little people out of it. Waylon and Chloe practiced their respective breathing exercises.

Chloe had maneuvered her dress back down and was straightening it, while Waylon was struggling to get his trousers up and she was telling him to wait till she got out of there, when there was a sudden hammering on the door.

"We'll have to ask you to return to your seat and fasten your seat belt, sir." A polite yet strained chirrup. "We're experiencing some turbulence."

"No shit," said Chloe in an undertone. "We'll be right out," she added in a louder voice. "I mean me — I'll be right out. I mean."

Waylon latched the door as soon as Chloe left, and then heard the stewardess rattle at it again. "Is there someone in there?" she called, with a notable lack of discretion.

"Yeah, yeah. I'm coming."

It might have been mere paranoia, but Waylon felt people were looking at him strangely as he made his way back to his seat. It wasn't his imagination that people turned to stare as Chloe stood to let him back in.

"It's okay," she announced to anyone who cared to listen. "My husband is an epileptic."

"Jesus Christ, eh?"

By the time Waylon was buckled in, they were enjoying fairly smooth weather again.

"Usually I hate turbulence," Chloe said. "This time I hardly noticed. Pretty radical therapy, mind you. Welcome to the Mile-High Club, darling."

"I think I've sprained my neck."

The stewardess who had rousted them out of the toilet brought drinks. She smiled at them and made a special fuss. "I hope your husband is okay now, ma'am," she said, giving Chloe a little grin.

"Hey," said Waylon. "I can talk. You can ask me, if you want. I'm okay. I'm fine. Jesus Christ."

"Your husband isn't really an epileptic, is he?" The woman seated behind Chloe leaned forward to address her in conspiratorial tones.

"Not really."

"I knew it. And I just want to say I admire you guys."
"Thanks."
A little later they saw the woman, a petite blonde in a sundress not unlike Chloe's, make her way up to the toilets. Some ten seconds after that they felt someone getting out from the seats behind them, and a balding man in a striped business shirt and tie proceeded up the aisle.
"Bet you dinner he goes to the same toilet," said Chloe.
"You're on."
Chloe won.
Anyway, thought Waylon, it was easy enough for him. The woman was half Chloe's size.
"I'm not going to ask you about Jessica," Chloe told him, just about the time he was drifting off to sleep.
"Good."
"Was she good in bed?"
"No."
"Good. Waylon, I have a confession to make. Something terrible."
"You fucked Roy Schuter?"
"No. *No.* That wasn't what I was going to say. You remember when we were discussing a trip to Thailand, and you didn't want to go?"
"Yeah?"
"I was thinking of asking you for a divorce."
"What? *Why?*"
"God, Waylon. I was bored. And unhappy. I don't know. But it wasn't your fault. I see that now. Not all of it. Anyway, I just wanted to say I'm glad we're married. I want to be married. I'm glad."
"Jesus Christ, Chloe. Why didn't you say anything? We could have talked about it."
"I didn't know what to say."
"Chloe, I want you to know you can always talk to me. Okay? About anything."
"Waylon?"

"Yes?"
"I did fuck Roy Schuter."
"I know. I was pretty sure."
"He was terrible in bed."
"Good."
"He's a total asshole, anyway."
"I know."
"I'm sorry."
"It's okay."
"Really sorry."
"No problem, eh?"
"Merry really seems to be in love, doesn't she?" Chloe looked at him.
"Yeah. The Rev's a great guy."
"Did you know that Merry had a crush on you?"
"What? No."
"For years. I'm surprised you didn't see it. I'm so glad she's finally got a decent man to call her own."
"Me, too."

Waylon was nodding off once more when Chloe spoke again. "I want you to meet Tip," she told him. "When we go back, I mean."

When we go back. Waylon loved the sound of that.

Tip was alive. Chloe had had word from her just before they left Pattaya. Everybody had assumed she'd been taken, but she was okay. She wasn't dead after all. She wasn't even being kept as a plaything by an ex-Khmer Rouge colonel. She had collected her daughter and gone into hiding — just in time, as it turned out. But she hadn't been able to retrieve her camera and notebooks before she left. She had left Chloe a note in her own notebook, Tip said, but Terdsak must have taken it. She had left another one with Gorgi, and that had never been relayed either.

So Chloe had lost a child—for she'd been determined they would adopt Tip's daughter. But she had gained back a friend and a faith that goodness could prevail. "Chalk one up for the good guys," she said. And Waylon agreed they would still adopt a child.

At the same time, he told her, he wanted to try making their own baby. What was the worst that could happen? They would have two kids.

While she was at it, Chloe seemed ready to adopt just about anybody who got in her way. Freddie, for example.

Freddie's story was that he wasn't anybody and he didn't come from any place. As far as the Powers That Be were concerned, he said, he didn't exist. So he was okay. "But you got to keep movin', yeah? Bob and weave; dodge and *burn*." Chloe had again tried to winkle his background out of him, but all she got was something like, "Where am I fuckin' from? You want my social security number? Do you want to know where I'm coming from? Where my head is at and everything? Forget it, man. Fuckin' forget it. I'm here now; you see me. And that's where I'm from for now. You know what I mean? But tomorrow I might not be here. I could be there."

"Okay. But what does your passport say?"

"I don't carry a passport, man."

"C'mon Freddie. You've got to have a passport. You've got to have a visa just to stay in Thailand."

"I don't have a visa. Not anymore. I used to have one, but I overstayed. Two hundred baht a day, okay? And you can't leave till you pay. They got a jail for people like me, if they can find me. I can't leave even if I want to. Cost me about twenty thousand baht, now. That's a fuckin' problem, man. You know?"

So Chloe was going to help Freddie, never mind Freddie was trying to say no, no, he didn't want to bring attention to himself. He wanted to go on living quietly out there at the 4H Club. And the others said he was welcome as long as he wanted to stay. Him and Selene both. But twenty thousand baht was only about five hundred dollars. They could afford that, Waylon had told her. After all, Freddie had probably saved Chloe's life, when it came right down to it. So Waylon also wanted to help pay Freddie's fines.

"We should be hitting the coast soon." Chloe leaned across to look out the window. "Amazing. It seems like we've been away forever. And it's like we just left yesterday. Both."

"I know what you mean."

Tip, as Leary had told them just the day before, was in fact a celebrated journalist, a rare bird in those parts. "Gosh. That's not the first time that little fighter risked her life doing undercover stories. Darn it. This country could use a few friggin' more like her."

Tip's message had said she and her daughter were fine, and sorry for the worry. And there was more:

Please do not think so badly of us Thais. Not everybody is like Terdsak. But he is the logical conclusion of where we are going, if we are not careful. These days it's all money and guns. What people don't do for greed, they do for fear. Maybe that is the way it has always been, but I don't think so. We have to fight. We have to show how this is bad. We have to show that there are other ways. People like Terdsak can't operate without help from public officials. And these people can't help unless the public lets them. So it is our responsibility to do something.

"My God, Waylon. Look at that." They had switched seats so Chloe could see Vancouver Island as they flew over. It was as though the island had mange. Here and there throughout the otherwise lush terrain, big patches of clear-cut forest looked sore to the touch. "Talk about complacency," she said. "Tip tells me about how logging has destroyed almost all of Thailand's rainforest. And there I am, thinking, 'Third World country. Hope they get their act together before it's too late.' Sure. Just look down there at this nice First World country. Big business and government raping the environment. . . ."

Waylon just kept saying, "Yes, Chloe," "That's right, dear," and other supportive noises. It was like being reacquainted with an old friend. He hadn't heard her so enthusiastically outraged about a public issue since their early days together. She was scribbling in her notebook even as she rapped away.

"Chloe," he said. "I'm going to ease my way out of the business over the next year, and I think we should start investigating the real estate market, see what we might get for the house. Next season, I want to go back and do the rescue diver course, and the divemaster. Leary says then I could work off the cost of the instructor's course at Down Down Diving."

"Hell, Fosdick." Chloe put her notebook away. "Why not just do it? Sell the business. Sell the house. Let's just do it now. Hey. I want to do some more dive courses too."

"Okay," Waylon said, and then he was taken aback at such easy acquiescence. "But what about the kids?" It was *kids*, now. Two of them.

"What about them?"

"Okay. You're right." The future was going to take care of itself. Waylon suddenly saw that, really saw it. And he felt wonderful.

Waylon chewed his lip reflectively. And, upon reflection, he realized that his lip wasn't quivering at all. He was only chewing on it out of habit. He looked ahead to the whole new ballgame that yawned before him. And he yawned right back.

A great satisfying roar of a yawn.